FLOORED

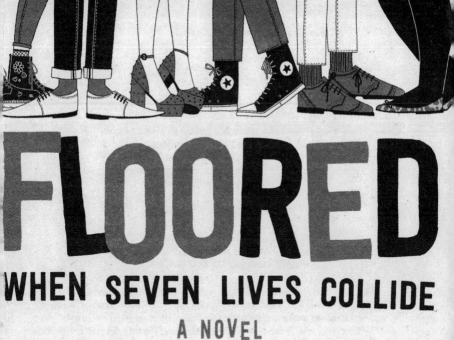

FLOORED

WHEN SEVEN LIVES COLLIDE

A NOVEL

SARA BARNARD | HOLLY BOURNE | TANYA BYRNE | NON PRATT
MELINDA SALISBURY | LISA WILLIAMSON | ELEANOR WOOD

MACMILLAN

First published 2018 by Macmillan Children's Books
an imprint of Pan Macmillan
20 New Wharf Road, London N1 9RR
Associated companies throughout the world
www.panmacmillan.com

ISBN 978-1-5098-6230-6

3 5 7 9 8 6 4

A CIP catalogue record for this book is available from
the British Library.

Printed and bound by CPI Group (UK) Ltd, Croydon CR0 4YY

We dedicate this book to each other.
So glad we got in the lift together.

YEAR ONE

DAWSON

I realize I'm staring at the arse of the guy in front of me roughly seven seconds before he does, but that's all the time I need for several thoughts to run through my mind.

First, I think *nice arse*.

Second, I mentally shout at myself for objectifying this guy based solely on his bum. After everything I've been through, I should know better than to reduce someone to their appearance. I should be more concerned about how intelligent he is, or whether he does stuff for charity, or how he treats animals . . . and all I'm thinking about is how good his jeans look. And they really do—

STOP IT, YOU PERV.

Third, I wonder if I can blame hormones, or would that be a cop out? Is this what happens once you start kissing people? One (slightly – OK, very – drunken) kiss and a bit of a fumble (over trousers) with Olly Pritchard, and the Pandora's Box of Perving is open for business, so now all I can think about is sex. Although Celestia Carey did say boys think about sex once every seven seconds. Wait, that can't be true. Every seven seconds? That's like, five hundred times an hour. No way. No one could think about sex that much. I'll google it later . . .

Fourth – is this really the time to be eyeing someone up? I'm not here to look at bums; I'm here to see my mum.

There. That killed it. The lid is back on the box.

Fifth – what if someone in the cafeteria hears my thoughts and knows I'm the kind of guy who stares at strangers' arses and has to think about his mum to stop himself? What if someone is listening right now?

I look around as surreptitiously as I can to see if anyone is looking at me in disgust. No more than usual, ha ha.

Once again I find myself looking at the arse. I wonder if he's . . .

The seven seconds are up, and all sex thoughts die a million deaths as the owner of the arse turns around and clocks me. He's older than me. Much older – maybe twenty-five. I didn't think he was that old from behind. His arse didn't look like an old arse.

He looks at me, eyebrows raised, and my skin heats. I see the moment he dismisses me, and then I see *it* – the recognition – as if a light has switched on inside his mind, and he does a double take.

Shit.

'Have we met?' he asks. There is a string of spit between his teeth and it makes me feel sick. 'Wait. Are you . . . ?'

I'm gone before I can hear how that question ends, bolting out of the queue and cutting between the tables. I trip over someone's bag, and my shin smashes into a chair, but I don't stop, ignoring the angry voices behind me and slamming through the doors into the corridor.

Outside is buzzing, and I weave through crowds of people – adults in suits, techs in Converse and shorts. Where is the bloody exit? I need to be outside. Weirdly, there's a load of people my age around, all wide-eyed and staring, and I duck my head and try to move past them. Don't look at me. Don't see me.

I turn down the corridor towards the lifts, stopping abruptly

4

when I see how many people are waiting. Someone slams into the back of me, and I grunt.

'Sorry,' a girl says when I turn around.

'No worries,' I say. She has a blue stripe in her hair, like a weird punk skunk. Why just one stripe? It looks ridiculous.

'Are you going to the induction?'

'What?' I can't stop staring at the stripe. It's *really* blue. I wonder if it was a dare. Or an accident.

'The induction. Health and safety. It's on the ninth floor.' Skunk Girl sounds annoyed, so I stop staring at her hair and meet her eyes.

'Erm. No. Sorry.'

'Oh. It's just . . . I thought I recognized you from the briefing earlier.'

'Nope. Not me. I'm not being inducted.' They're interns, I realize. Work-experience kids. One of them will be assigned to Mum, and she'll spend two weeks shouting at them because they'll be on their phones all day and not get her coffee right. It happens every year. Someone gets put on Mum's show, and she'll get angry about it and phone me to rant about how it's because she's a woman, and a mother, and if she was Stewart McConnell she wouldn't have to have an intern, she'd get a proper assistant. And then I'll do my famous Angry Alicia Sharman impression in the *Dedman* green room and everyone will laugh.

Except I won't. Because there isn't a *Dedman* green room this year. Or ever again.

'Dawson Sharman!' the girl says, and I tune back in. 'That's why I recognize you!'

'What?'

'You're Dawson Sharman. From *Dedman High*.'

Shit.

5

'No,' I say, too fast. 'I get that all the time. I mean, I don't see it, personally. But, you know . . .' I smile as though I'm embarrassed. I mean, I *am* embarrassed. But not in the way I want her to think.

'Right. Sorry. I just . . . Yeah. I suppose it would be a bit weird if you were him, just wandering around the UKB randomly.'

'Yeah. Ha,' I say. 'No, I'm here for . . . I work here. As a runner.'

'Oh. Right.' She looks me up and down again. 'Right,' she says again. 'So, do you know where the health and safety induction is?'

'No. Sorry.' I shrug.

The lift pings, and we both turn to it, joining the informal queue to get in as people pour out.

I spot Stewart at the same time he spots me.

Shi-i-i-t.

'Dawson!' he booms down the corridor, causing everyone within a five-mile radius to turn to me.

The girl behind me gasps, and I freeze.

'What are you doing here? Your mum said you were going to a taster day at your new school.'

'Erm . . .'

'Must be weird, eh, at a school for norms after all this time. Still, it'll be good to build some character. Think of it as method acting, that's what I'd do. Just get through the year and maybe you can apply again. Have you thought about one of the Manchester acting schools? Not too far from here, and they might be less picky than a London school.'

'OK, so . . .'

'Anyway, I won't keep you. Your mum was in her office, last I saw. She didn't seem in a great mood though, so have a care.'

'Sure.'

Stewart frowns, as if noticing for the first time that I'm not in a great mood either. 'Your drink is leaking.' He nods at my hand.

I look down and realize I'm still holding the carton of coconut water I was queuing for in the cafeteria. I've stolen it, and while he's been talking, I've been squeezing it, and it's leaking all over the floor. It's not a huge loss, I tell myself. I don't even like coconut water. Celestia says it tastes like spunk, but I wouldn't know. Neither would she, to be honest.

Stewart strides away, and I watch him go, wishing I had the power to kill people with my eyes. I take a small step away from the coconut-water puddle. I should find a bin—

'You lied.'

I spin around, startled; I'd forgotten Skunk Girl was there. It feels like every single person who'd been waiting for the lift has stayed, listening to Stewart, and staring at me. Some of them have their phones out. Probably snapchatting, instagramming. There will be photos all over the Internet of me, people tweeting each other the conversation, looking me up on IMDb and Wikipedia to find out what I'm doing next, a hint of why I'm here. Maybe an audition . . .

Yeah, no.

I, Dawson Sharman – former actor and BAFTA Rising Star-nominated child prodigy – am, at the grand old age of sixteen, a has-been. I am over. All my future holds now is the possibility of an appearance on some telly show where I'm stuck in a jungle, or a house, or on an island with a bunch of other Z-listers, and my only chance of a comeback is if I get off with one of them. My destiny lies in Where Are They Now? listicles. Ones with Before and After pictures. Dawson, aged fourteen, with his amazing bone structure, those piercing green eyes – versus Dawson today, blob fish after a fist fight. What happened to the face that launched a thousand *Dedman* fan edits and head-castings?

Dawson Sharman as Harry Potter. Dawson Sharman as Luvian Fen. Dawson Sharman as Rhys Gold. I used to spend a lot of time online. I know what they said about me.

I know what they say now too. Turns out people don't stop tagging you, even when they're calling you ugly.

I am part of the reason that website created the phrase 'Nevilled Down'.

Ten Actors Who Anti-Longbottomed and Actually Nevilled Down
Number Eight: Dawson Sharman

Former star of *Dedman High*, the most popular children's show to come out of the UK since *Tracy Beaker*, Dawson Sharman was cast aged thirteen as Mason Wright, the bad boy son of the headmaster of a boarding school for troubled teens, who finds out on his thirteenth birthday that he's a vampire. For two years, Sharman dominated online polls for Hottest UK Teen Male, and was the focus of the #PrinceSharming Internet campaign, an online plea for him to attend a young fan's school prom as her date. Earlier this year, however, the show was cancelled at the beginning of its fourth season, with rumours abounding that the reason was a rapidly diminishing fan base due to what insiders termed Sharman's 'unfortunate brush with puberty'.

What they didn't add was that 'Sharman will probably never work again. Unless he can find theatre parts and then spend the rest of his life pretending it's his true calling, because it's more "authentic" and "there's nothing like performing to a live audience, with no second takes", and all the other stuff actors too ugly for television say.'

There was a huge backlash to the article because I was still fifteen when it was published. They took it down in the end. But before they did, I read the comments, and a lot of people said it was 'a shame about me'. And other less polite things.

It was good training for my first day at normal school, let me tell you. And let me also tell you, there is no way I am going back there. I lasted an hour. It was enough. There has to be something else I can do. Somewhere else I can go. I cannot spend the next two years being called 'Count Fagula' by feral kids who think culture is drinking half a litre of cider and then trying to finger someone called Chelsea 'up the park'. I don't even know if 'up the park' is a location, or slang for 'vagina'.

Skunk Girl is still looking at me, and for a moment I want to tell her she looks stupid.

I want *her* to feel ugly too.

'Can you blame me?' I say finally.

She says nothing; in fact, none of them say anything. So I walk past them all and smash my finger into the 'call' button, even though it's already lit. The doors open immediately, and I get into the lift.

KAITLYN

The woman on the reception desk knew. I know she knew. She handed me my lanyard and made me sign a sheet, and then she said the thing that made me sure she knew: 'Would you like someone to walk you to the first induction?'

Subtle, right? Most people wouldn't even read any meaning into it. I wouldn't have once. Not even six weeks ago. But now I notice these things.

I wonder how she knew. It's probably written right there on the list of names. Kaitlyn Thomas, fifteen, work experience – *the blind one*.

Anyway, screw that. I looked right at her – yes I did; I looked *right at her* – and said, 'No, thank you.'

And then I turned and walked away, all confident like, my head ever so slightly tilted, as if it'd help me see around the blurry spot in the centre of my vision. I've done it for years, way before diagnosis, way before the word 'blind', when I thought everyone saw the world like I did, before Stargardt disease and my mother sitting on my bed crying and everything going to shit.

I realize about halfway down the hall that I'm not actually sure where I'm meant to go, but I carry on confidently anyway until I turn a corner and stop. I lean against the wall and open the induction folder I got in the post last week. The induction folder is jazzy, all exclamation marks and laminate shine, like the people who made it couldn't imagine anyone reading it who wasn't SO EXCITED about doing work experience at the UKB. The whole thing screams, YOU'RE SO LUCKY TO BE HERE! CONGRATULATIONS!

Please. Even if I wanted to work in TV or read the news or something, I wouldn't be cartwheeling across the car park to be here. This is work experience for fifteen-year-olds, for God's sake. I'll be making tea for two weeks and sitting in a boring meeting or two and maybe getting to gawk at a celebrity in a lift or something. Lucky, lucky me.

And I *don't* want to be here. I had my work-experience placement all worked out. I was going to help out at my Aunt Nina's hair and beauty salon. She owns the place, so I would have been able to learn stuff about running a business as well as cutting hair. I wanted to be a beautician then. That was my plan. And I was really excited about it all.

But now I'm losing my sight, and that means, apparently, I can't be a hairdresser or a beautician. That means my school cancelled that placement and moved me on to the UKB programme instead, without even asking me first. They acted like it was this great thing they'd done, like I'd be really pleased. Grateful, even. 'How many teens your age get this kind of opportunity, Kaitlyn?' they said.

Like I was too stupid to realize that they'd only done it to tick a box. Sending their only disabled student to a work-experience placement at the UKB is the kind of thing they can dine off for years. Never mind that I've never cared about anything like this, never wanted to be some kind of media high-flyer, that I've been in all the middle sets for years and feeling fine about it. I've never planned to go to university or whatever. I was just plodding along quite happily, practising manicures and learning about eyelash tinting.

Anyway. So here I am. The blind one. The box-ticker. Even though I can see just about fine right now, and I don't need someone's arm or one of those white sticks or anything. Not yet anyway.

Last night, I put a blue stripe in my hair. It looks great. It's like an *electric* blue, and I did it myself, over the bathroom sink, using one of those Schwarzkopf dyes my best friend Avani gave me at Christmas, and it's the best thing I ever did. Mum almost fainted, but there was nothing she could do. It's my head, and my hair, and my life. And now *that's* what people will think of when they think of me; I'm the girl with the blue stripe in her hair.

I flip through my induction folder until I get to the YOUR FIRST DAY! page and scan the timetable. I'm meant to go to the ninth floor for some kind of health and safety induction. *Great.* Inspiring. Health and sodding safety. A horrible thought occurs to me: what if they try to incorporate my sight problems into this induction? What if they tell everyone I'm blind, and so everyone should make sure I don't walk into doors, or something? Oh God. Oh God. Everyone will look at me, like, *That's the girl who's here because she's blind – poor cow.*

Will I have to explain that I'm not blind, actually, and confuse them all? I'll say, 'Well, not yet,' and everything will be awkward because they won't really want to know, and I won't really want to tell them.

People hear 'blind', and they think of darkness. They close their eyes and think that's what it's like. You're meant to say 'visually impaired', really, because it's more accurate, but no one does, and most people don't have a reason to care why the difference matters.

I quite like 'visually impaired'. It's melodic. There's a question mark hanging over it that doesn't exist in the cut-off that is 'blind'.

If I ever have to introduce myself to someone and explain the whole Stargardt thing – and I know I'll have to, one day – I'm going to say that. 'I'm visually impaired,' I'll say. Or, 'I have a visual impairment.' Maybe one day I'll be OK enough with this whole thing to say this without my voice breaking or shaking or doing any one of those things that betray me.

But not today. Please, not today.

I sigh, closing the folder and tucking it under my arm. I hazard a guess as to where the lifts are based on the number of suited men walking confidently in that direction. There's a crowd gathering, waiting in front of three closed lift doors, and out of the side of my eye I'm looking for a space to stand in, and—

Shit! I've walked right into someone. Not even just a little nudge either. I've fully slammed into him.

'Sorry,' I say, oh so casually. Simple mistake. It's not like I'm going blind, ha ha ha.

'No worries,' he says.

He looks familiar. Maybe he's famous. Or a bit famous. He's not good-looking enough to be actually famous. More likely he's on the same placement as me, so I ask if he's going to the induction, but he just looks confused.

'Nope. Not me. I'm not being inducted,' he says, and something about the way he says this drops the penny.

'Dawson Sharman!' I blurt out. He is famous! Sort of. *Was* famous. 'That's why I recognize you!'

Avani and I loved *Dedman High* back in the day. I used to have a poster of Dawson Sharman on my bedroom wall. And now here he is, standing in front of me! He's pudgier than he was back then, of course. Everyone knows the Dawson-got-ugly story. But still. I can feel the old stirrings of fangirl within me.

But then he tells me that he's not Dawson Sharman, that he

just looks like him, that he gets this all the time, and he looks embarrassed and awkward, and I instantly feel really bad. Of course I'm wrong. Imagine me thinking I can recognize someone – me, with my traitorous eyes. This poor guy, being mistaken for the he-got-ugly Dawson Sharman!

'Right,' I say, aiming for breezy. 'Sorry, I just . . .' Make a joke, Kaitlyn! 'Yeah. I suppose it would be a bit weird if you were him, just wandering around the UKB randomly.' Eh, that'll do.

Not-Dawson tells me that he works here as a runner, and he doesn't seem that bothered about the mistaken-identity thing, so I relax. I steal a head-to-foot glance over him – blurred, but good enough – and he really does look like Dawson Sharman. But then what do I know?

A lift pings, and I turn towards the noise, blinking as the people around us surge towards it. Sometimes I get wobbles with my sight; suddenly the whole world blurs. My stomach lurches – *this is what it will be like all the time one day* – and I'm just wondering whether I should go and sit down for a minute when I register that a man with TV-white teeth is coming towards me, beaming. No, not towards me, towards Not-Dawson.

'Dawson!' he booms.

Dawson! Not Not-Dawson. Dawson! I can't help myself – a melodramatic gasp escapes my lips. That sneaky liar!

The man with the teeth is saying words, but I'm too stunned to listen properly. I catch snippets like 'school for norms' (*norms*! Charming!) and 'method acting'. This guy probably loves the sound of his voice as much as he does his shiny white teeth, because he carries on talking even as Dawson just stands there looking mortified. He's trying to cover it with cool, but I can tell. He wants to sink through the floor right now.

No sympathy from me though. When Teeth Man strides

off, I turn to him. 'You lied,' I say.

Dawson looks at me, his expression a little dazed. I can feel from the energy around us that everyone's looking at him, and I hear the telltale click from someone's phone. Twitter is about to light up. *Good*.

'Can you blame me?' he asks.

I try to remind myself that he doesn't know. Why should he? How could he possibly understand that the days when I can recognize someone's face are numbered? That the warmth of recognition, that flash of comfort that comes with your mind going, 'Yes, hello, I know you!' is a gift? A gift he waved in front of me, then threw away.

I don't say anything. I think about my aunt's cosy, cheerful salon and how she'd promised me a box of nail-polish samples. The smell of wet, freshly snipped hair.

Dawson moves past me and presses the button for the lift in front of us. The doors open straight away and he walks in, keeping his back to me. I briefly consider slamming into him again, just because. I feel all ragey – too ragey to go to a health and safety induction and pretend like I give a damn about any of this placement bullshit.

Everything is going blurry again. Oh shit! Am I *crying*? I can't bloody see anything.

'Are you coming in, or what?' Dawson says, but not unkindly.

His voice is like a lifebuoy thrown into the dark, so I grab it. I let it pull me out of the blur and into the lift.

SASHA

I wake up with a jolt when one of the packages slides off the pile on my lap and into the footwell.

'No dozing on the job,' Dad says from the driver's seat, giving me a wry smile.

'Not for you, maybe,' I say. 'I'm just the passenger.'

'Assistant courier,' he corrects, like it actually matters.

Neither of us wants to be doing this, but me and Dad aren't the type of people who get what we want. Dad's the type of person who gets made redundant and can't seem to find another job, and I'm the type whose applications for fancy work placements get as far as someone's inbox and no further.

Still, I'd rather be working with my dad for the week than at the local council, where there's a kind of buy-one-get-ten-free deal on students from my school. One of the ten being Billy Goodart.

I should not have touched his penis.

Another package almost slides off as I wipe the memory off my hands on to my jeans.

'Seriously though, Sash, you need to keep a hold of them,' Dad says.

Dad's been freelancing as a courier driver for a few months now – he says it's better than signing on, that at least he's working for himself and gets to choose the jobs that suit him so he can be around for me . . . not that I need it at fifteen. But Dad's a proud man, and I think it's been good for him to feel like he's working, even if it isn't a job he likes. Or one that pays well.

Three hours in, and I know for sure that this isn't the career for me:

1. *Early mornings*: I've been up since sparrow fart, and (as we've just established) I'm not allowed to nap.
2. *Other couriers*: They'd run you over if they thought it'd get them an extra delivery slot. Seriously. The sub depot this morning was carnage.
3. *Delivering things*: You have to talk to strangers, even if it is just to say 'Name?', 'Sign here,' and 'You have to press hard – the screen's a bit rubbish.' I'd thought Dad would let me off, this being my first morning, but he's all about maximum efficiency and minimum tolerance for my 'confidence issues'.
4. *Magic FM*: It's like being trapped in wedding playlist.

Although I guess that last one isn't compulsory. It's just Dad's terrible taste in music.

Dad said something about a round he's picked up because another driver just had a baby, and I gaze out of the window at a landscape of tiny roundabouts and tall buildings. It's not until Dad pulls up into a parking bay by a curved bank of windows that it clicks.

'Is this MediaCity?' I say.

'Did the giant letters "UKB" give it away?' Dad calls back, already half out the car.

I have to wait for him to come round and take the packages off my knee so I can get out, and I stand while he sorts through the ones in the back of the car, muttering to himself and stacking

17

things on my arms like I'm a human forklift.

I've always been strong – one of the better things about being a big girl. Dad's stature; Mum's colouring. I've seen pictures on Facebook, photos scanned in from when she was my age, me in miniature. A hint of something more permanent than a tan, brown eyes, strong black brows, waves of dark hair. I'd fit right into the Albanian side of the family if I ever met them. Which will never happen. Mum did a bunk when I was little – since then it's phone calls at Christmas and a birthday card that never arrives on time. If I didn't friend her on Facebook I'd know nothing about her life at all.

'You listening?' Dad says.

Obviously not. I'd been on the lookout for famous celebrity types. My friend Michela's always talking about seeing famous people when she goes clubbing with her cousin – claimed she pulled a *UKBabies* presenter once, but everyone ripped it out of her for that, and two weeks later, Michela upgraded to giving someone from *Hollyoaks* a blowjob.

Didn't have the heart to tell her they don't film that in Manchester.

'It would be a lot quicker if you were able to take this lot over to that building there, while I offload the others.' Dad's questions always turn out as statements.

'Do I need the machine thingy?' I say, entirely unprepared for a solo delivery of this magnitude.

'None of the ones I've given you require a signature. You'll be fine.' Dad pats the top of my arm and gives it a bit of a squeeze. 'Get this done quickly and we might get to eat lunch somewhere nice – like Subway.'

Sometimes my dad has a problem detecting irony. Or sarcasm. Or, you know, reality. 'Subway' and 'nice' don't even belong in the same sentence. But he's already over the other

18

side of the courtyard – because why would he wait for a response when he knows I'm going to do whatever he tells me?

It's slow progress round to the back. Any time I try anything more than a cautious shuffle, the pile in my arms starts to slide gently to the side, but eventually I make it through the doors and all the way to the security desk. I have to rotate a bit so I can see the person sitting there.

'Hi!' I say.

The man behind the desk doesn't look up, just carries on playing Candy Crush on his phone. 'Hi.'

'I, er . . .'

In that moment my arm cramps, and the whole pile slides off. The man lifts his phone up a bit as a box falls from the desk on to his lap.

Now he looks up. The git. Or 'Phil' as it says on the lanyard round his neck.

'You need to put those in the pigeonholes.' Phil points just over my shoulder to what looks like an infinite wall of tiny little boxes with writing under each one.

'I . . . What? Really?' Is he winding me up? 'Isn't that *your* job?'

A thin slice of a grin appears on his face as he says, 'Not today.'

I do not like 'Phil'.

Finding the right pigeonholes is a nightmare because the writing's so tiny, and I realize after I've offloaded five packages that I've been putting them in the wrong place because the recipients' names are at the *top* of each slot, not the bottom. Not everything fits properly, and sometimes there's already something in there that I need to take out and re-stack . . .

This is taking forever, and I can feel the minutes racing past, imagining Dad standing by the car and wondering where I've got to.

So much for a Subway lunch.

One package left: 'A. Sharman'.

I hurry back along the pigeonholes, scanning the names: K. R. Shapiro . . . C. Siren (. . . imagine: Sasha *Siren*. So much better than Sasha entirely-forgettable-*Harris*.)

There's no Sharman, A. or otherwise, and I'm starting to get sweaty and panicky, my breath coming in a little faster. Dad made a really big deal about how important speed is, and he's not someone who exaggerates.

'Er, excuse me?' I say, but Phil pretends not to hear me, so I storm back to the stupid desk and thump the parcel down on top of it, hoping that whatever A. Sharman ordered isn't fragile. 'Hey! Hi? Help! I can't find a hole for this.'

You can see a 'witty' retort cross his mind the way a cloud scuds across the moon, but then he thinks better of baiting someone who looks like they might cry.

I have a bit of a thing about letting people down – especially my dad.

'Hang on.' He reads the name off the label and taps in '*Sharman*' one-fingered on to the system like he's still in Candy Crush mode, then. 'Doesn't have a pigeonhole because they don't work in this building.'

I take a moment to breathe. I'm not going to cry; that would be ridiculous. I'll just sweat lots instead. Much better.

'Could you take . . . ?' I start, but Phil's already shaking his head – not unkindly.

'I'm sorry, love – I've got to stay here.'

He tells me to head back to the main entrance and they'll sort me out at reception. As I run back the way I came, I message Dad about the delay.

Be quick!!! comes his reply.

Those three exclamation marks are a bit worrying – Dad thinks anything more extravagant than a full stop is the work of the devil – so I put on a bit of a spurt across to the main reception. There's a glut of people trying to get in, and I hurry on past, yelling, 'Special delivery!' like that's actually a reason people use to jump a queue.

Turns out blind panic can override confidence issues. Who knew?

The girl on the desk doesn't look so impressed, but when I say, 'I need to get this to A. Sharman,' her eyes widen and she does a little gasp.

'Give it to the receptionist on the ninth floor!' The words come out as a panicked squeak as I hurry on past. I'm thinking that whoever this A. Sharman is, I'm glad I don't actually have to hand the package over to them personally. I look down at the label again as I slide carefully around the edge of the crowd of people waiting to get in the lift and I see the words: '*Signature required*'.

Caught in a moment of indecision, I turn back to look at the entrance, wondering whether I should run back and get the machine from Dad and risk taking even longer, or ...

Or what?

Maybe I could just video someone signing for the package and use that as evidence? Is that how this works? Why is this happening to me on my first day as assistant courier during my dad's important new round delivering to someone whose name had the same effect on that receptionist as 'Voldemort' has on Ron Weasley?

Crap. The lift's open and everyone's piling in, and I'm getting jostled out of the way. As I try and squash in, I get a horrible flashback of that time I got stuck halfway down the wiggly slide in the local soft-play centre and loads of smaller kids piled in after me and started crying.

'You're blocking the doors, love!' someone yells, and I give up. Whoever this A. Sharman is, they're not worth triggering my claustrophobia for.

I step away from the doors as another lift *dings* open and people surge around me. Clutching the parcel, I walk into it, quickly followed by a couple of others, and breathe.

HUGO

God, the North is ghastly.

There should be some kind of *law* that prevents anyone from encountering it with a raging hangover. I look out the window of my first-class carriage and can't help but wrinkle my nose as we blast past a giant collection of industrial chimneys. I mean, *chimneys*? Do they still have COAL up here or something? I have no idea how my mother stands to be up here five days a week. Although if it came down to a choice between Manchester and having to share a bed with my father, I can see why she'd choose Manchester.

I rest my head against the cool glass and close my eyes for a second. I only got, like, a MINUTE'S SLEEP last night, and my body is caning me for it. But the moment I drift off, my phone goes.

Saskia: *I had a really good time last night x*

My nose wrinkles again, and I tap out a reply. I'd had higher hopes for this one.

I had a good night too, but that's all it was. Because I don't date girls who have no self-respect.

I smile and screenshot it to send to David. But I don't actually send it to Saskia; I'm not a MONSTER. I'll just not reply. She'll get the hint.

They always do.

David and I share sordid details as the train wobbles its way up towards the shit part of the country. He pulled Octavia last night, lucky bastard. Though according to him, she's got bad breath, so maybe I'm not so jealous after all. Anyway, Saskia was the big win. So of course I got her. God, I hope she's not all CLINGY next week at school. You would think pretty girls wouldn't be. And, at first, they pretend they're not. They know they're hot; they know you have to work for it. So you play the game, and you get there. But then – KABAM! – Psycho Central. Acting like the whole thing meant something.

We're just pulling out of some hellhole called 'Crewe' when my mother calls to check the train is on time.

'Yes, Mother, it's moving on the track and everything. That's what trains do.'

'You really can't be late; it will make me look bad.'

'Calm down, dear. I won't be late.'

'Good. The car will pick you up from the station.'

'See you then.'

She hangs up without saying goodbye, and I sigh and throw my head back. Why does she NEVER trust me to just function? I get that she's pissed off I didn't travel up last night and stay at her flat so we could bond or whatever, but there was no way I was missing David's party. Not when I'm doomed to a week of social oblivion, up here in the middle of nowhere. Oh well, think of the CV . . . think of the CV. Gotta tick the boxes and all that. Life is a game a game a game, and – man – am I good at playing it.

I make the car wait for me while I pick up some coconut water at the station. The driver looks pissed off, but I'm afraid he will have to deal. My head is thumping and, if I'm going to kick ass at the UKB, I need to be fully hydrated and at my charming best. He mumbles something under his breath as I slide into the back of the black Merc.

'What was that, mate?'

He mumbles again. Followed by, 'Nothing.'

'Yeah, it better be fucking nothing.'

Honestly – these people! We roar off through this dingy city, and I don't feel guilty. Not for being late. Not for swearing at the guy. I don't owe my dad a lot, but he did teach me one of the most important lessons in my life: *Some people are better than other people.*

That's not me being a jerk, or him being a Nazi. Nope. Sorry. It's just simple economics. *Law of the vital few.* Eighty per cent of any work done, any money made, anything decent contributed to this world, is done by twenty per cent of people. The rest are just coasters. I am in that twenty per cent, and I'm sick and tired of the other eighty chucking rocks at my family just because they're jealous. Hell, I don't have TIME to throw rocks. I'm too busy CONTRIBUTING.

We ride in awkward silence. Well, awkward on his end. I'm too busy using the mirrored window to sort out my suit. First impressions count, and all. I'm hungover as sin, but I can't look it. I check the collar, and I'm glad I went through the arse of getting it made. I look at least nineteen, I reckon. And even with eye bags the size of a porn star's penis, the fabric makes me look amazing.

We roll up to MediaCity, and I do tip the guy – so he can't get all arsey now, can he? He pulls out my wheelie suitcase, I say thanks, slam the door shut, and make my way up to the main entrance. I notice a few heads turn as I walk up to reception. There are girls my age EVERYWHERE, and I try to return the smiles of the fit ones. I reach the front desk and lean over, waiting for the receptionist. Her attention is taken up by this sweaty wobbling mess of a girl getting in a fluster about some stupid package. The receptionist catches my eye, and I grin conspiratorially. Then the girl waddles off, and I lean over.

'Sorry about that,' the receptionist says. 'Can I help you?'

'I'm Margot Delaney's son,' I tell her. Enjoying the moment her face changes. When the recognition kicks in. 'I'm here to do work experience for a week.'

She sits up in her seat, flicks back her hair, suddenly acting totally competent. 'Yes, of course! Wow, I didn't know she had a son.'

'She does, and it's me.'

The girl laughs too hard, and I immediately don't like her very much. She puts up a finger, asking me to wait, then punches some numbers into her phone. 'Hi, is that Mrs Delaney's office? I've got her son down here . . .' She looks up at me, realizing her mistake.

'Hugo,' I provide.

'Hugo. Yes. Brilliant. OK. Thank you. I'll send him up . . . Right, Hugo. Let's get you signed in, then you can go on up. She's on the top floor. Though of course you know that already.' She laughs like a horse. 'Um, well, anyway. You won't be up there for long. Your mum's assistant said you'll have to do some compulsory health and safety training.'

I raise my eyebrows in disgust.

'Totally non-optional, I'm afraid.' She smiles sympathetically. 'As you can see, it's a busy week for us. Work-experience week. We have students from all around the country. They need to know what to do in a fire.'

There's no way I'm going to health and safety training. I have better things to do with my time than listening to some self-important milk monitor point out bleeding obvious things like, *When there's a fire, leave the building*.' But I take my lanyard from her and pull it over my neck. The colour matches my suit perfectly.

'Where do I go?'

'Oh, the lifts are right over there. Through the lobby.' She points with her biro.

I thank her and can feel her excitement buzzing behind me as I walk away, smirking. I bet that will be her gossip for the day. *'Did you know her SON is here this week? Yes, yes. Hang on, isn't she married to . . . ?'*

There's a cluster of people clogging up the entrance to the lifts, including the sweaty girl with the package, and I try my best to push past them. Ugh, everyone here is just so *predictable*! It's like playing Diversity Bingo, and it's a struggle not to roll my eyes. I'm so sick of everyone telling me how freakin' privileged I am all the time when it's quite obviously the opposite these days. Dad always used to wind Mum up by saying you'd have to be a black one-armed lesbian to get a job in television – and now it's probably even harder than that. Even though I've been editor of my school paper for two years now, even though I'm top in all my classes, even though I've flogged myself half to death, everyone will look at me and go, *'Oh well, he's her son, OF COURSE he got a work placement at the UKB.'* But when the chips are down, when it comes to actually applying for jobs, I bet you I lose out now to some box-ticking gender-fluid Scientologist who has to crawl everywhere on their hands and knees – even if I have better experience. But, nooooooo, *I'm* the privileged one.

Dooph. I smash into some girl who isn't looking where she's going. Oh God, what if she's blind? That would just be the icing on the fucking cake, wouldn't it? But something jogs me out of my bad mood. A flurry of phones being raised above people's heads, the clicking noise of about a dozen cameras going off. I look over the sea of heads to work out what's causing the fuss.

No. Freakin'. Way.

27

This is amazing. This is too good. I whip out my phone and use my height to get a good shot. Then I'm sending it to everyone on my contacts book.

GUESS WHO'S DOING WORK EXPERIENCE WITH HELLFACE???

My phone buzzes instantly.

No way!

Aww bless him. He looks even worse now than he did in that feature last year.

Ask for his autograph!

I laugh and tuck my phone back into my pocket. He looks pissed off by the attention. But I'm sorry, mate, that's just what happens when you go on television. It's not my fault your face did that to you.

It's getting way too busy by the lifts now. What's taking them so long? Some girl is pushed right into me, and it gives me a stirring. Especially as she's forced to stand so close. I give her the once-over. She's a bit sweaty and stressed-looking, but she's a solid eight, even in her obviously cheap-as-shit outfit. She thinks she's a five. A brilliant combination. Much better than girls who think they're an eight but are only a four.

I forgot how horny I get when I'm hungover. Maybe I can work out where this girl goes to lunch? Make some moves? A week would be long enough to lay the appropriate groundwork, I reckon. Maybe health and safety isn't such a bad idea after all. We may have to do partner work . . . role play. And I could pretend to rescue her from a burning photocopier or something . . .

I tell my trousers to calm the hell down, at least until I've figured this girl out. Dawson Sharman pushes past us to jab at the lift button, and as the doors open I follow her in, turning to smile at her as they close.

VELVET

'Velvet?'

'Yeah.'

'That's an . . . interesting name.'

I know exactly what that pause means. I've been on the receiving end of them all morning. All my life, if we're being really accurate.

It means that if I was a posh girl with shiny hair and a double-barrelled surname to go with it, Velvet would be a charming and unusual first name. But I'm not, so I get The Look: almost a sneer, but not quite, because *that* would be rude.

I was named after a girl from this old film, *National Velvet*. In short, it's about a girl called Velvet who wins a horse in a raffle and enters the Grand National – it's terrible. Growing up in the mouldy basement of a condemned old hotel in Bridlington, my mum spent her sad childhood wishing she had a horse. So, she saddled me – so to speak, ha ha – with a stupid name that gets you semi-sneered at when you turn up for work experience and have to get your passport photocopied by some bitch wearing basic black trousers that probably cost more than your entire flat and everything in it. Spoiler alert: my mum never won a horse, or anything else, in a raffle.

I hand my passport over to the receptionist to take a copy, which is the law, apparently. I really, really hope they don't do any further checks and find out about that caution I got last summer. It wasn't my fault; it was my cousin Chelsea who bought the vodka and made me carry it in my bag. It wasn't even that much fun; Chelsea got drunk and puked on my sandals, so I had to wash my feet in the sea. She snogged Jamie King (*after* she'd been sick – it was vile) and she'd gone off with him down behind the arcade when the police turned up, so I was the only one who got in trouble and had to ring my mum to say I had been taken down to the station.

It's funny – when I think of home, I know it doesn't really *sound* that great. If I close my eyes, I can imagine I'm eating chips on the seafront with Chelsea, boys shouting stuff at us, the sound of fruit machines, and that rank smell of rotten seaweed you never quite get used to. Yeah, I know it doesn't really sound that great at all.

But I want to go home. I don't fit in here. This isn't just a 'face your fears and do it anyway', 'challenge yourself and your dreams will eventually come true' stupid, shitty *X Factor* sort of a thing. This is an 'I know I don't belong here and I never, ever will – and I'm not even sure I want to' sort of a thing. This is a total identity crisis.

I look all wrong, for a start. I bought a smart blazer and shiny nude high heels from Primark especially to wear today. Because that's the sort of thing people wear to work, right? I was feeling pretty fierce about my executive costume realness.

Until I got here. All the other girls I've seen so far are wearing normal stuff. A lot of brogues and cute outfits, satchels swinging, eyeliner perfect. They haven't come in fancy dress as a middle-aged receptionist from a Travelodge or something. I look like a total idiot. The irony is, if I'd have come in my normal clothes, that might at least have won me a bit of respect. It would be a bit like the judges calling my play 'gritty' and 'edgy' and being all pleased with themselves for giving me the award, even though it was just about me and my friends doing normal stuff.

The jacket's really sweaty, and the shoes are rubbing my feet. I can't even take the jacket off because all I've got on underneath is a tatty old vest that has a stain under the right boob and shows my bra. I did not think this through. I think I may have only put deodorant on one armpit when I was half asleep this morning, but I can't be totally sure. These people might be looking at me like I'm scum, but I'm not exactly going to start sniffing my own armpit in public.

I can't help thinking: my mum's bloody useless. All these other girls probably have mums who can tell them this sort of stuff, so they know what to do and what they're supposed to wear. I know it's not Mum's fault; she's even more clueless than I am, so I shouldn't blame her.

In fact, I kind of wish she was here right now. She'd make me a cup of tea with three sugars, and tell me to hold my head up and remember I'm from a long line of staunch women. My mum, it is fair to say, has had tougher things to deal with than an office full of swishy-haired private school girls called Sophie and Francesca looking at her a bit funny.

Still, my mum never put herself out there to have to deal with this sort of thing. Easy for her to talk big from the sofa. It's like complaining, 'But I was going to *say* that!' when someone's already told you the right answer – everyone knows it doesn't count.

The thing is, it's struck me today – if I'm going to be somewhere like *this*, it would be easier if I was completely different from my family. If I was the intellectual type who was desperate to get away from my ordinary life in a flat by the seaside. But I'm not. I'm just like them, and mostly I'm glad I am.

I like hanging out with Chelsea and spending hours doing nothing more taxing than painting our nails and bitching about our friends. I like giggling over the *Daily Mail* sidebar of shame with my mum and watching *Love Island*. I genuinely care about the love lives of Z-list celebrities.

I just happen to be really good at writing. I wrote a play that won this award last year. I didn't even want to enter, but my English teacher Ms Parsons took it and ran with it. I think she was trying to *inspire* me or something, which is so deluded it's actually kind of cute. I should probably paint her as some amazing saintly character who came along to my shit school and changed my life, and I suppose she kind of is, but she's also pretty annoying.

Anyway, it was her that got me to apply to do this work-experience thing, and I didn't think I'd even get in, but now it all seems to have spiralled out of control. I mean, I'm *at the UKB*. British broadcasting giant, household name, et cetera. Not only that, but I'm in Manchester by myself. It felt so strange staying in the Premier Inn last night, which Ms Parsons had organized for me through some funding programme thing, and getting the bus in rush hour with the other commuters this morning like a real adult human. It just made me feel like an imposter.

It's like, I know this is a good opportunity. I know I should be grateful. But I kind of hate that.

'Don't go getting all up yourself,' Chelsea's always saying, helpfully. I hate it that she thinks she needs to, that everyone might start thinking I'm different – sometimes I feel like I don't fit in *anywhere*.

I gave in to Ms Parsons' nagging, so I'm here. But there's a big part of me that wishes I was just the beach with my friends like everyone else, helping out in my nan's hotel, and hoping that Griffin Collins might try and snog me again. Just normal stuff.

Instead I'm . . . here.

'Well, *Velvet*, here's your security pass and handbook. Now you need to go to the health and safety induction. Ninth floor.'

'OK. Thanks. Where are the . . . ?'

She's already walked off, so I guess I'll have to figure out where the stairs are for myself. My left shoe is totally crippling me, sweat and possibly blood squishing damply with every step. I should've broken them in at home first.

The reception area is getting busier. It was practically deserted when I got here stupidly early this morning because I was worried about messing up the bus times and being late. No wonder I feel so crap; I'm knackered already.

I catch sight of my own reflection in a glass door and instantly wish I hadn't. I look like I'm in bad fancy dress as a greasy-haired teenage version of Theresa May. Theresa Maybe-not.

Sod this. I can't be the only person here who doesn't have a clue. At least I can be safe in the knowledge that I could probably take any of them in a fight, if it came to it. Hopefully it won't, but it's always good to have a Plan B.

''Scuse me?'

I picked out a girl who looked about my age and equally lost, but I quickly realize this was a mistake.

'Yes?' She looks up twitchily, as though she genuinely believes I'm going to stab her or something.

'Are you going to this induction thing? Do you know which way it is?'

'Yes. I mean . . . Are you? No, I'm not sure . . . Sorry.'

Well, I'll just go die under a sheet of burning plastic then, shall I? I can't figure out if she's just shy or what, but the way she turns her back on me has got to be unnecessary.

Actually, it kind of strengthens my resolve. *I am from a line of staunch women.* I may look crap and feel totally out of place, but I'm here because I deserve to be, and these people are no better than me. For a second, I even kind of half believe it.

I don't bother asking anyone else for advice on where the hell I'm supposed to be going. I just walk like I know. This place is huge, but I'm sure I'll figure it out.

At the end of the corridor, I spot a group of people who look like they know what they're doing, so I kind of casually tag along at the back. I feel shifty, like I'm stalking them or something; they probably think I'm going to try and rob them for their phones.

I follow them to a bank of lifts, keeping my head down. I'm not really a fan of confined spaces – I prefer to be able to run away whenever I need to. Number one rule in life: always have an escape route planned. Still, I guess this is my best option right now.

I simultaneously try to disappear and hope that someone might talk to me, as we all awkwardly stand there. I half smile at the girl next to me, who's clutching a parcel and looking panicked, then remember that my bitchy resting face means my idea of a half-smile is most people's idea of a death stare. Too late.

I swear it's taking the piss, how long it takes the lift to turn up. I could have walked it by now, even in these evil shoes from hell. If I knew where the stairs were.

The longer I stand there, the weirder I start to feel. I'm not sure if it's the shoes, plus the no breakfast and being on the second day of my period (which is always a total horror show), but I start to feel a bit dizzy and sick. I can feel epic levels of sweat trickling down my back, even grossing *me* out – no wonder nobody else wants to talk to me. I wipe my forehead with one hand, and don't even care as I transfer the resulting mess of sweat and foundation on to the side of my skirt.

I'm going to pass out . . .

'Are you all right?'

It's a deep male voice – very posh and weirdly sexy. I try to pull myself together, but all I can see are the buttons of his shirt right up in my face. I think I manage to say I'm fine, just so he'll leave me alone and not look at me, but he's standing so close to me it's suffocating.

Luckily, I don't think he's paying much attention to me. The mass of faces around me are swimming; conversations are buzzing over my head. For a second, I swear I see a kid that looks like Dawson Sharman talking to some girl with a blue stripe in her hair, but I really must be hallucinating. I have got to get out of here.

I hear a *ding*, which brings me back to reality. Instead of running away, I go against every instinct and let the crowd hustle me along with them towards the lift.

Just because I'm getting in, doesn't mean I'm staying, I tell myself. I still feel like doing a runner. As the lift doors close, a weird thought comes into my head out of nowhere: stay or go . . . ? I ask the universe to give me a sign.

JOE

'You all right, Mum?' I ask.

My mum, dressed in her morning uniform of dusky-pink quilted dressing gown and matching slippers, swivels her head in my direction.

'Oh, Joe, I can't get the thingamajig to work,' she says, motioning at the microwave in front of her. She jabs at the buttons as if to demonstrate, her eyes watery with frustration.

'You need to press "power" first, like I showed you the other day,' I say gently. 'Then you just set the time and press "start".'

I show her. As the microwave whirrs into action, she gets me to repeat my instructions, scribbling them down on a Post-it note. She peels it from the block and sticks it to the microwave door.

There are Post-its all over our house, stuck to doors and window frames and electrical appliances, each of them filled with Mum's old-fashioned loopy handwriting.

At fifty-nine, my mum and dad are older than everyone else's parents at school by miles. My big brother, Craig, was twenty-one when I was born and already engaged to Faye. Mum and Dad tried to have another baby for years and had given up hope when they got pregnant with me at forty-three.

'What are you doing up so early?' Mum asks, peering through the glass at her revolving bowl of porridge.

'School trip, remember?' I say, sticking a couple of slices of bread in the toaster. 'The coach leaves at eight.'

Mum looks blank.

'To the UKB,' I prompt.

Her face lights up at the sound of those magical letters.

UKB.

United Kingdom Broadcasting – one of the most respected television broadcasters in the entire world.

'Of course,' she says, consulting the calendar on the fridge. 'How exciting!'

'I know.'

'Do you think you'll see anyone famous?'

'I'm not sure. Maybe.'

To be honest though, it's not the prospect of gawping at celebrities that excites me. My plans are much grander than that.

From the back seat of the bus, Tyler Matheson and his mates are leading everyone in a chant of 'Everywhere We Go!' They're on at least their fifteenth round, their curiously proud yells of coming from 'mighty, mighty Skiddington' showing little sign of dying out any time soon.

If I didn't value my life so highly, I'd ask Tyler to specify exactly what makes Skiddington so 'mighty' in the first place? Skiddington's single claim to fame is as home to Champion Biscuits ('The Nation's Favourite'), its mammoth concrete factory employing over a third of the town's residents. Both my dad and Craig work there on the production line. Mum used to as well until she was made redundant last year. Apart from that though, my hometown is entirely unremarkable in every way.

The singing is getting louder. I've forgotten my headphones, so the best I can do is ball up some tissues and shove them in my ears. I take out my phone and send a text to my best friend, Ivy.

Kill me now.

When St Thomas Moore School went into special measures last year, Ivy's mum pulled her out and started home-schooling her. When I asked Mum if I could be home-schooled too, she looked at me like I'd just grown an extra head.

'Don't be daft,' she said. 'What on earth could I teach you? I didn't even pass my eleven-plus.'

I still see Ivy after school and at weekends, but it's not the same. Without her, the school days feel painfully long, the minutes and seconds stretching out like pizza dough.

Tyler and his idiot mates are still singing when we pull into the UKB car park an hour and a half later.

Shut up and show some respect, I want to hiss at them as I reluctantly remove the tissue paper from my ears. *You're at the UKB, for goodness sake – a national institution, not a football match.* I'd be wasting my breath though. People like Tyler don't listen to people like me, i.e. 'swots'. In Tyler's world 'ambition' is a dirty word.

We pile out of the coach and follow Miss Harley towards the entrance in a messy line. I wish we had a smarter school uniform: a blazer perhaps; a tie at the very least. As it is, in our cheap polyester trousers and navy sweatshirts, the school's emblem emblazoned across our chests like a warning, we're the very opposite of smart. I try to make up for it by wearing nice shoes and carrying my things in a polished vintage leather satchel I got on eBay, but the overall effect is still far from ideal.

In front of me, Tallulah Roberts and Marzina Khan are going on about how excited they are to see the *Strictly Come Dancing* ballroom.

'Wrong television broadcaster,' I say.

They turn around, identical frowns on their faces.

'What did you say?' Tallulah growls.

I clear my throat. 'Wrong broadcaster,' I repeat. 'And anyway, *Strictly* is recorded in London . . .'

'You're joking?' Marzina says.

She looks like she might cry.

'No. Sorry.'

'Then why exactly are we even here?' Tallulah demands. 'I only signed up for this cos I thought I was going to meet Pasha.'

I wince as they spread the word down the line.

When we finally get inside, the foyer is buzzing with people our age. We're the only ones in uniform though. *And* the only ones behaving like a herd of escaped zoo animals. Miss Harley shoos us into a corner and ambitiously tells us to 'wait sensibly'.

'Miss Harley from St Thomas Moore School,' she announces apologetically to the sleek-looking receptionist. 'We're here for a studio tour.'

The receptionist glances over at us with unimpressed eyes and picks up her phone.

I take a large sidestep away from my classmates and allow myself to take in the surroundings. The foyer is bright and airy, full of hope and possibility, sunlight pouring in through the glass. Just the sight of the massive UKB logo above the reception desk sends a shiver of excitement up my spine.

When I was little, I never wanted to be a footballer or astronaut or vet, or any of the other things kids usually come up with when asked what they want to be when they grow up. No, since I was about six years old, I've wanted to work in television. Not as an actor, or a presenter, or anything like that – but behind the scenes, as a producer . . . the one at the very top making everything happen. It sounds a bit dramatic perhaps, but television is probably the only thing in my life (apart from Ivy) that keeps me sane. It's also pretty much the only thing I have in common with the rest of my family. We may have no idea how to talk about emotional stuff, but we can spend hours debating who made the best Doctor (Me: David Tennant; Dad: Jon Pertwee; Mum: Tom Baker), or quoting lines from *Alan Partridge* at each other, or reminiscing about the first series of *Sherlock*. Our family life revolves around the programmes circled with red biro in our weekly copy of the *Radio Times*; television the glue that keeps us together. Which is precisely why I want to be the one who makes it one day.

A man wearing a UKB lanyard and a wide grin strides across the foyer towards us. He introduces himself as Toby, our guide for the day, and distributes ID badges for us all to wear.

'It's not usually this busy,' he explains to Miss Harley as I attach my badge to my trouser pocket. 'But we've got our work-experience programme starting today.'

My head snaps up.

Work experience?

I throw my hand in the air.

'What is it, Joseph?' Miss Harley asks, sighing slightly.

'Yeah, what is it, *Josephine*?' Tyler mimics in a high voice. Cue sniggers from my imbecilic classmates.

'Did you say work experience?' I ask Toby, trying to ignore them.

'That's right,' he says, motioning at the growing crowd behind us. 'Today's their induction. Don't worry though. It won't interfere with the tour; they'll be tucked away on the ninth floor all morning.'

I feel like I've been punched in the stomach.

At the beginning of the year, I asked about the possibility of doing my work-experience week at the UKB, and Mrs Kirk, the careers adviser, pretty much laughed in my face.

'Whatever next?' she'd said, chortling away as she shuffled

bits of paper. 'Work experience at Disneyland?'

I ended up spending my week wearing a hairnet at Champion Biscuits, alongside half my year group.

I should have known not to trust Mrs Kirk. She's the one who ignores me every time I say I want to work in television, banging on about the management training scheme at Champion instead ('Bright boy like you – you could make it all the way to supervisor!').

I look over my shoulder at the work-experience kids. They're all talking and laughing and wearing nice normal clothes – the sort of clothes I wear when I'm not sporting flammable trousers and the sweatshirt of shame. I want to be one of them so badly, my entire body aches.

Tallulah has her hand up.

'Yes?' Toby says.

'Is it true the *Strictly* ballroom is in London?' Tallulah asks, throwing me an accusing look.

'I'm afraid so,' Toby replies, the pained smile on his face suggesting this isn't the first time he's been asked the question. 'We make lots of exciting television programmes here though . . .'

He goes on to name half a dozen amazing shows. Not that this impresses Tallulah.

She doesn't even bother to hide her disgust, folding her arms and screwing up her face like she's just smelt something rotten.

Which is great. Because now Toby will assume we're all complete idiots who know nothing about television and tailor the tour accordingly.

'Any more questions before we kick off?' he asks with over-the-top brightness.

There aren't.

'In that case, if you'd all like to come with me. There's rather a lot of you, so we're going to take the stairs . . .'

He sets off.

I take another glance behind me at the work-experience lot. As far as I can tell, there's no distinction between the ID badges they're wearing and the one I've been given.

Interesting.

My classmates troop off after Toby, hollering and squealing and shoving.

I don't follow them.

The second everyone has disappeared through a set of double doors, I turn in the opposite direction and walk briskly towards the sign marked 'Toilets'.

I duck into the men's and remove my sweatshirt, balling it up and shoving it in my satchel. My white shirt and black trousers look a bit 'waiter', but there's nothing much I can do about that. I fold up the sleeves of my shirt in the effort to look a bit more casual and grip on to the edge of the sink.

'What are you doing, Joe?' I ask my reflection.

I don't have a decent reply. All I know is that I've got to at least try to get myself on this work-experience programme. Even if it means gatecrashing. Even if it means totally embarrassing myself. Even if they suss me out straight away and chuck me out on my ear and Miss Harley goes mad. Even if I have no game plan beyond getting myself to the ninth floor. It's not like I've got anything to lose – quite the opposite, in fact.

Still, my body is trembling all over, and my forehead is shimmering with sweat. I soak up the moisture with a scratchy green paper towel and take a deep breath.

If you're going to be a hotshot producer some day, you're going to need to have proper balls. Might as well grow a pair now.

I exhale, give my reflection a determined nod, and leave the toilets. Without breaking rhythm, I stride towards the lift, where the doors are starting to close. Before I can change my mind, I squeeze through the narrowing gap just in time, smiling what I hope resembles an enigmatic smile at the five other people who are already inside.

You got this, Joe. You got this.

So here we have them: the swot, the fraud, the dutiful daughter, the child star, the fangirl and the asshole. The six of them assembled in an awkward circle, trying not to stand too close to one another in the small lift, and failing. Dawson, in particular, is trying not to stand too close to Kaitlyn in case she takes it as an invitation to ask him what he's been doing since *Dedman High* – but she's still pissed off that he lied to her, so won't even look at him.

Opposite them is Velvet, who is trying to rub away the creamy smudge of foundation from her skirt so she looks less of a disaster, while Joe undoes the top button of his shirt so he looks less like a waiter. Sasha doesn't care what she looks like, but she does care about letting her father down, and she clutches the package so carefully, she may as well be holding a newborn baby. Finally, there's Hugo, back straight, shoulders back, a smug smirk tugging at the corners of his mouth as he sizes up the three girls: the other two aren't bad – solid sevens, even the fat one – but his initial instinct was right. He takes a step closer to Velvet.

They aren't alone for long. The lift stops on the first floor, and a woman with hair the colour of Irn-Bru gets in. She's holding a purple coffee cup, and Velvet can't help but gaze longingly at it. It's been hours since she had breakfast, and it's all she can do not to lean down and lick away the puff of froth that has escaped through the hole in the plastic lid. The woman looks straight at her, as if she knows, and Velvet stiffens.

'Don't judge.' The woman presses the button for the second floor. 'I know it's only one floor, but I can't face the stairs,' she adds with a smile, nodding at Velvet's feet. 'You get it, right? You're in heels as well.' She stops to take a sip of coffee, then licks her lips. 'Are yours new too?'

Velvet nods and the woman chuckles gently.

'Why do we do it to ourselves, eh?'

Dawson hears her laugh and his chest tightens. What did she say? He didn't hear – too concerned with keeping a safe distance from Hugo, who's just taken his phone out of his coat pocket. Dawson's been like that since he got in the lift, his gaze darting furiously from face to face, sure that each of them is staring at him. Was she laughing at him? The woman with the orange hair. Was she laughing at him?

You know who that is, right?

Cue: gushing laughter.

When the lift doors open on the second floor, Dawson can't look at her, terrified that she'll turn back and wink at him. He listens to her heels clack as she strides out into the brightly lit corridor. Glad she's gone.

One less person to worry about.

There's a moment of movement as they shuffle away from each other and back into an awkward circle. It's funny how these things work out, isn't it? There they all were, distracted by their own petty problems, blissfully unaware of what was about to happen. A minute or two either way, and their paths would never have crossed. Later, Joe will ask himself why he did it, why he did something so unlike him, so reckless. If Toby hadn't mentioned the work-experience programme, Joe would have gone on the studio tour and been nowhere near that lift. And if Hugo had not made the cab driver wait outside Salford train station while he got that bottle of coconut water, he would have been on time and in his mother's office by then.

Speaking of coconut water, if Dawson hadn't been caught perving, he probably would have still been in the queue at the canteen, not in the lift. That's something Velvet will wonder about as well – what would have happened if she'd told Ms Parsons to shove it and stayed in Bridlington with Chelsea. Or if Kaitlyn had done her work experience in her Aunt Nina's salon, like she'd wanted to. And what if Sasha's father had delivered that package instead of her? Would he have known what to do?

Probably.

We'll never know, will we? But what we *do* know is this: for whatever reason, the six of them ended up in the same lift at the same time. Call it destiny or fate or good old dumb luck, but there they are.

Just as the doors are about to close on the second floor, a man in a navy blue tracksuit appears, pushing a trolley with a pile of cardboard boxes on it. He must have run for the lift, Dawson thinks, noting his flushed cheeks and the pearls of sweat that have suddenly bubbled up across his forehead. 'Thanks,' he mutters, and sucks in a shallow breath that doesn't seem to help at all as the six of them shuffle apart again to let him in, Velvet and Hugo on one side, and Joe, Dawson, Kaitlyn and Sasha on the other.

Dawson must be staring, because the man turns to look at him, the pale skin between his heavy eyebrows creasing so deeply it sends a bead of sweat rolling between them and down his nose. Dawson is definitely staring now, holding his breath as he watches the glassy drop reach the tip of his nose. It's about to fall when the man catches it, wiping it, and then the rest of his forehead, with his sleeve. He's still panting short, shallow breaths that make his Adam's apple bounce up and down in his throat. He hasn't pressed a floor, Dawson realizes, his own brow pinching. They can't *all* be going to the ninth, surely? His gaze wanders away from the lift buttons and back to the man to find that he's staring at him – staring right at him – and Dawson holds his breath again as he waits for it, for the flicker of recognition.

There it is.

When Dawson summons the courage to look him in the eye, the man looks away, his cheeks even redder. They always do, always try not to stare. Either that or they laugh and whip out their phone to take a photo, like he's a funny piece of graffiti smeared on the side of a bus shelter. He probably thinks he's being polite, but Dawson sees his face soften before he looks away, and that hurts more than the laughter.

The pity.

Kaitlyn pities him. Especially because he lied to her. She's thinking how pathetic it is that he'd rather she thought he was a random runner than who he actually is. But she's not looking at him, rather straight ahead, staring at the charity fundraising poster Velvet and Hugo are standing in front of, hoping that the text will come back into focus. Hugo doesn't give enough of a shit to pity Dawson. He's scrolling through his camera roll from the night before, the corners of his mouth lifting for a moment as he looks at one of Saskia, then deletes it.

When Sasha checks her phone, Dawson thinks that's about him as well, but she's just wondering how Hugo has reception in the lift when she doesn't. Dawson doesn't know that though, or that the only reason Sasha keeps checking her phone is because she's waiting for a *Where are you?!!!!* text from her father, with four exclamation points this time.

Five more floors, thinks Sasha, as she watches the digital panel above the doors change from three to four. If the lift doesn't stop again, she'll be there in less than a minute, maybe back at her father's car in five . . . if A. Sharman doesn't muck her around, that is. Joe, on the other hand, doesn't want the lift to stop. Tyler Matheson and his mates will have done a good job of distracting Miss Harley, but she must have noticed that he's gone by now. She probably did a head count before they went in the studio and has told Toby to sound the alarm. So he wills the lift to slow its ascent, sure that when the doors open on the ninth floor, a red light will be flashing and someone will be calling his name on a tannoy, like he's a lost child in a shopping centre.

Like Sasha, Hugo is desperate to get out of the lift. Actually, he's desperate for the panting, sweaty man with the trolley to get out of the lift. He looks like he's about to chunder, and Hugo is wearing his suede Tom Fords. Sasha isn't concerned about her shoes, but she is concerned that the man with the trolley is ready to keel over.

'You OK?' she asks softly, her gaze falling to his hands.

His knuckles are milk white from holding on so tightly to the trolley that she has to resist the urge to clench her own fists. He tries to smile and fails, but at least manages a nod, clearly incapable of much more. But before Sasha can ask if he's sure, his eyelids stutter shut, and that's it. The trolley slips from his grip and he slumps forward, striking them like a bowling ball that scatters the six of them like pins. There's a series of gasps as cardboard boxes tumble off one by one, landing on the floor in a succession of dull thuds as they each jump back to avoid them.

In the confusion, Hugo drops his phone and Sasha drops the package for A. Sharman, watching in horror as it ends up under the grubby rubber wheels of the trolley. She goes to reach for it, but Joe is in the way as he lunges forward to grab the man's arm. He's too heavy though, bringing Joe down with him as he folds to the floor with a final, desperate gasp.

Then everything is quiet as they each look down at the man, Joe tangled up on top of him, his legs splayed and his arse in the air. Velvet can see the label on the sole of Joe's shoes, can see how he tried to peel it off and couldn't, leaving a scrap of white on the black rubber. Later, she'll wonder why she noticed that and not the man passed out on the floor of the lift . . . but right now, all

48

she can see is that sticker and the outline of Joe's phone in the back pocket of his trousers. The others see the man. He's on his side, his limbs jutting out at odd angles like a marionette that's had its strings cut. That's exactly what it was like, Dawson thinks: one moment the man was standing in the middle of them, holding the trolley; then he was crumpling to the floor, like someone had cut his strings. It's not like it is on television, he thinks: there was no cry; no melodramatic swooning; no out-of-shot mattress to land on. He just fell.

Hugo shouldn't be this rattled, he knows. After all, he sees girls faint all the time (eating disorders and too much champagne aren't the best bedfellows, are they?), but he's never seen a man faint before. Pass out, yes. Plenty of times, in fact – usually in the back of a cab or on one of the sofas at JuJu. But it's usually funny – an excuse to take photos or draw a dick on their cheek.

This isn't funny.

There's a flurry of gasped '*Is he OK?*'s as they each step forward. Except Hugo, who stays where he is, watching as Dawson helps Joe up and picks up the cardboard boxes and puts them back on the trolley to make room. Sasha's first instinct is to dial 999, but when she checks her phone and remembers that she has no signal, her heart begins beating so hard she has to press her lips together, sure that it's about to come up through her throat.

Kaitlyn is the first to speak. 'Everyone get out of the way.' Her voice sounds far steadier than she feels. 'Give him some room.' No one moves though, so she's forced to push Dawson out of the way. 'Press the alarm.' She gestures at Velvet, who just blinks at her.

Sasha reaches forward and presses the button, and as soon as she does, there's a violent screech and she has to reach for the handrail as the lights stutter on and off and the lift shudders to a halt.

'What the fuck?' Hugo grunts, echoing what the rest of them are thinking. 'Why has it stopped?'

'Are we on the ninth floor?' Dawson looks at the doors, waiting for them to open.

When they don't, Hugo straightens and turns to Sasha. 'What did you press?'

Sasha looks at the console, then at Hugo, her heart in her throat. 'The alarm!'

'Why isn't it ringing then?'

'I don't know.'

'Let me see,' Hugo says, striding over to where she's standing and shouldering her out of the way. He presses the alarm and, sure enough, they hear it ringing out in the lift shaft.

He presses it again to prove a point.

'I pressed the alarm,' Sasha insists, looking between Hugo and the other five faces suddenly staring at her. 'I did. I pressed the alarm.'

Dawson licks his lips then points at the control panel. 'You pressed the STOP button.'

'No.' Sasha turns to look at it and, yep, there it is: the STOP button right above the alarm.

'You pressed the fucking STOP button!' Hugo roars, taking a step towards her.

Sasha takes one back. 'No.'

'You fucking idiot!'

'I didn't. I pressed the alarm!' Sasha roars back, the back of her neck burning.

'Stop it!' Joe says. 'Just press it again, and let's get going.'

Sasha looks confused. 'The alarm?'

'No!' Hugo spits. 'The STOP button, you idiot!'

'Stop calling me an idiot!'

'Well, you are an idiot!'

50

'For fuck's sake, you two!' Velvet stands up, her hands clenched into fists at her sides. 'This bloke needs help, and you're bickering over who pressed what. Just press the STOP button again so we can get moving!'

Sasha obliges, but nothing happens.

'Do it again,' Hugo tells her.

She does, but the same thing happens.

Nothing.

'It's not moving,' Joe says, looking between them. 'Why isn't it moving?' Then he looks down at the man in the heap on the floor and all the colour flees from his face. 'Does anyone know first aid?' he asks quietly, but Kaitlyn is already on her knees beside him, carefully rolling the man over so that he's on his back.

'I did a course at the summer camp I was at last year,' she explains, gesturing at Dawson to help her with his legs. He does, straightening them out so the man is laid out in the middle of the lift, his feet pointing towards the doors.

Sasha frowns, her fingers curling tightly around her phone. 'Is he OK?'

'Obviously not.' Hugo sighs wearily, reaching down for his and assessing it for damage.

Sasha crosses her arms and tilts her head at him. 'How is that helping?'

'How is asking inane questions helping?'

'At least I'm trying. What are you doing?'

Hugo holds up his phone. 'I'm calling for help.'

'What? On your magic phone that has reception in this lift when no one else's does?'

Hugo's smirk slips as he realizes she's right, but before he can counter, Velvet stands between them.

'Just shut up, will you?'

Yes, shut up, Kaitlyn almost says. She can't think with them talking, her thoughts jumping back and forth, like a bird hopping between the branches of a tree. The truth is, she didn't do a first-aid course at summer camp last year; she wrote a fic about Jem and Ace from *Dedman High* doing a first-aid course at summer camp last year, but in her panic, she can't remember a flaming thing.

Think, Kaitlyn.

'Dr ABC,' Velvet says, pointing at her. 'We had some bloke from the St John's Ambulance come into school a few years back. Dr ABC. I remember it because Mark Barton kept calling me Dr ASS.'

Hugo sniggers, but they ignore him.

Something in Kaitlyn's brain becomes unstuck. 'Danger. Response. Airway. Breathing. Circulation,' she recites, suddenly a little calmer.

Velvet nods, kneeling down opposite her, the man on his back between them. 'There's no danger. It's not like we're on a main road or something and about to be hit by a bus.'

Kaitlyn nods this time. 'Response.' She takes a deep breath and looks down at the man. 'Hello. My name is Kaitlyn,' she says as loudly and as clearly as her nerves allow. 'Are you OK? Can you hear me?'

Nothing.

'If you can hear me, open your eyes.'

Still nothing.

So she reaches for his hand. It's as clammy as soap. 'If you can hear me, squeeze my hand.'

Nothing.

She looks up at Velvet. 'What's his name?'

There's an ID card hanging from a yellow lanyard around his neck. She turns it over. 'Steven.'

'Steven.' Kaitlyn tries again, shaking his shoulders this time. 'Steven, can you hear me?'

Nothing.

She shakes him a little harder this time. 'Steven, can you hear me?'

Nothing.

Kaitlyn can feel the panic bubbling up inside her and tries to swallow it back. It feels like that time Danny Taylor shook up a can of Coke in the playground and opened it. She was nowhere near him, but she still jumped back as the plume of foam arced out of the red can, much to Danny's delight. That's what the panic feels like right now, like if she opened her mouth it would all rush out of her.

So she closes her eyes and takes another deep breath.

When she opens them again, Velvet is pinching the man's earlobes.

'Why are you rubbing his ears?' Hugo asks before Kaitlyn can.

'I'm checking if he's responsive to pain,' Velvet hisses.

'Is he?'

Velvet looks up at him, her gaze narrowing. 'Does it look like it?'

Now who's asking inane questions? Sasha thinks, arching an eyebrow.

'Airway . . .' Velvet prompts.

Kaitlyn nods and reaches over, pressing her palm to the man's forehead. It's as clammy as his hand. That can't be good, she thinks, putting two fingers under his chin and tilting his head back the way the woman did on that YouTube video she watched when she was researching her summer camp fic. She leans down and waits, trying to hear if he's breathing, but she can't hear a thing.

'Everyone be quiet,' Velvet snaps when she sees that Kaitlyn is struggling.

But no one is making a sound, the four of them huddled around her and Kaitlyn in stunned silence, the man in the middle of them.

'Anything?' Velvet asks.

Kaitlyn shakes her head.

This prompts a flurry of mutters and gasps that make Kaitlyn feel light-headed.

'It's too late,' she says, taking her fingers away from the man's throat.

Velvet stares at her. 'What?'

'He doesn't have a pulse. He's dead.'

'He can't be.' Velvet kneels down next to him again. 'Let me try.'

She presses two fingers to his throat and waits, but there's nothing.

'Try his wrist,' Joe says, then resumes chewing his bottom lip.

She does, but she can't feel anything.

'Maybe we need to do mouth-to-mouth?' Dawson suggests, but Velvet hushes him, her palm splayed on the man's chest and her ear near to his mouth as she checks again to see if she can hear anything.

She obviously can't, and Dawson fidgets with panic. It reminds him of a scene he did for *Dedman High* when the girl he was in love with was in a car crash and he had to bite her, thus saving her life and ending it all at once. At least that's how he saw it, committing her to an eternity of drinking blood and avoiding sunlight. But the viewers loved it, and the scene won him a Teen Choice Award.

'Do you know how to do mouth-to-mouth?' he asks Velvet when she sits up again. She shakes her head, and he turns to Kaitlyn. 'Do you?'

Kaitlyn shakes her head as well. 'He's gone.'

'We have to try.' He looks around the lift. 'Does anyone know how to do mouth-to-mouth?'

'He's *gone*.' Kaitlyn says it more firmly this time.

'Gone where?'

'To Magaluf,' Hugo spits. 'Where the fuck do you think he's gone? He's dead!'

'But he was just here.' Dawson looks down at the man's body. 'He was *just* here.'

They look at one another, all except Hugo, who is staring at Velvet's hand on the man's chest, waiting for it to move. But it doesn't.

And then there were six.

TWO WEEKS LATER

DAWSON

I'm really getting into the swing of my latest, and most challenging, role: Alicia Sharman's Disappointing Son. So far, the cast is just me and Mum – although our first guest star is about to make his debut as the doorman bringing my dinner up to the flat, because I'm not going into the kitchen to make anything while she's in there. Not that there's anything to make; I've eaten everything that we had in while she was at work, and she hasn't bought anything new. I wish I'd ordered before she got home.

I'm watching the pizza tracker on my laptop like a hawk, planning to be in and out of my room before she's even realized what's happened, when she knocks on my bedroom door.

'Dawson? I'm not going to invade your private space, but enough is enough. We are going to have this conversation.'

The tracker stays resolutely on *Quality Control*.

'Dawson, you don't get to be the angry one here. You walked out of school without telling anyone. Again.'

I open a new tab and check my emails. I'm waiting to hear back on two parts I asked Kimba, my agent, to put me forward for. There are twelve new messages, but none I want to read.

'Dawson.'

The doorbell rings, and I check the tracking window. *Out For Delivery* . . . Shit. Seriously?

It is. Of course it is. I hear the front door open, rumbling voices, then the click of it closing.

'Dawson,' Mum calls. 'I've got your food. Nice try. It'll be in the kitchen. With me. And the conversation we're having, whether you like it or not.'

We'll see. I open a new tab. But before I start to type, the screen whites out with a message saying there's no connection. She didn't . . .

'Did you turn the Wi-Fi off?' I shout.

When she doesn't reply, I charge out of my room, down the hall and into the kitchen. She's sitting at the breakfast bar, and my pizza box is open. I watch as she lifts a slice and starts picking the pineapple off. 'Hey!'

She drops a final chunk on to the neat pineapple mountain she's made. Then she looks at me, green eyes meeting mine. It's where I get them from. Green eyes from her, brown skin from my dad. She says I get my love of pineapple on pizza from him too.

'I'm not going back to that school.'

Mum says nothing, pushing the box towards me.

I'm too hungry to refuse.

'Are you all right?' she asks when she's finished her slice.

I shrug, chewing slowly. No, I'm not all right. I haven't been online in four days because I'm sick of photos being sent to me, of me looking gormlessly at a body just out of shot. I'm sick of the 'If only you were a real vampire' jokes that everyone seems to think are so original. I'm sick of my phone ringing with numbers I don't recognize, but I *know* belong to journalists wanting quotes.

'There's nothing you could have done,' Mum says, taking another slice. 'He had a chronic condition.'

'Did you know him?'

She shakes her head. 'No, it was in the papers. I don't think I ever met him face to face. He usually left any post for me with Hanifah.'

That reminds me, I've still got the package for her that I took from that girl . . . but right now I'm more interested in what the reports say.

'Do we have any papers?'

Stupid question. She reads them all. She gestures to a pile, and I bring them back to sit opposite her, leafing through each one until I find the story. I lay them across the table. They're a study in contrasts: all the broadsheets feature Hugo Delaney, and all the tabloids have me. I ditch the tabloids and pull one of the others closer, folding it so I don't have to look at Hugo while I read: *Steven Jeffords, 53* – shit, that's pretty young for your heart to give out. Ten years older than mum – *Chronic undiagnosed condition.*

'Will you go to the funeral?' I ask.

'No. But we're sending flowers from the whole floor.' She wipes her fingers delicately on a tea towel, and I take another slice. 'I have bigger fish to fry. Like what we're going to do with you.'

The pizza turns to sludge in my mouth.

KAITLYN

Are any of the others still thinking about it? They probably aren't. But how could they not?

Two weeks on, and it's still all I can think about. It's not fair. I didn't even want to be there. Not in that building, not on that stupid work experience, and definitely not in that horrible stuffy lift with all those other useless-in-the-face-of-death strangers who just let me try the whole CPR thing, even though I clearly didn't know what I was doing. 'I took a course at summer camp.' Why did I say that?! And now he's dead, and his face keeps swimming around in my mind, both alive and dead, like some gruesome Before-and-After montage. One day, when my sight has got so bad I can't see faces in front of me any more, I'll probably still see his. All dead and clammy. And dead.

The thing is, no one else seems to think it's a big deal. My mother said, 'Not the kind of thing you'd expect from the UKB,' like they'd bloody done it on purpose or something. Like prestige is some kind of force field keeping out ugly things like death. And Hannah, my sister, just wanted to know what Dawson Sharman is like in real life.

'Ugly,' I said, which was mean, and I felt bad straight away, but still I didn't take it back.

'No offence, but I don't trust your opinion on what people look like,' Hannah said, and then cackled like she'd said something funny, so I threw the nearest thing to hand at her face: my phone. But I missed, and so now my phone screen is cracked, and if that doesn't sum up the current state of my stupid little life, I don't know what does.

But at least I still have my stupid little life.

Look, I know it's the biggest, most patronizing cliché in the world to be all 'At least you're alive!' when you've got a disability (or, in my case, one on the way), and I really don't want to be the person who goes, 'I'm seeing things differently now I've seen death!' but . . . well, I think I kind of am. Steven Jeffords is dead. I'm not. That's a thing, and I can't just ignore it.

All of this is why, right now, I'm on a train heading towards a little cemetery near Salford: to say goodbye to a man I never even said hello to. I think it might help. I don't know how, exactly, but everyone says you need closure to move on, right? And what's more 'closure' than a funeral? (Death. No, shut up, Kaitlyn.)

I wanted to buy some white lilies to bring, but they were too expensive, so I got the biggest bunch of flowers I could afford instead. I don't even know what they are, but the colours are nice, all pinks and yellows, and I've decided that that's what matters.

The train slows, and I stand, clutching the stems in my hand as I make my awkward way towards the doors. I know it's a bit weird, going to a stranger's funeral with the wrong flowers and wearing a black dress that's a bit too small because it's actually your sister's, but I tell myself it'll be fine. I'll sit at the back, pay my respects, get my closure, and leave. Tonight, this will all be behind me.

SASHA

Somehow, Michela's work experience at the local paper has turned into a job. It's just tea rounds and picture research, but the way she talks about it you'd think she was the editor.

'Ooh, quick! Grab a copy, will you?'

I don't know why I need to be quick. There's more copies on the table by the door than there are people in the cafe. Michela snatches the paper off me and starts flipping through it as we wait for the elderly lady in front to pay for her pot of tea.

Her hands shake so much that the cup rattles on its saucer as she lifts the tray.

'Would you like any help?' I start to reach out when she freezes me with a look.

'Not from the likes of you,' she says, her mouth pinched in disgust as she turns away muttering. 'Coming over here . . . Think they can do what they like . . .'

Seriously? I am *so* pale that she must have been looking *really* hard for an excuse to air her misplaced xenophobia like that. It's times like these I daydream of being the kind of person who might reply, 'Yes, I came all the way from the Royal Oldham to offer to carry your tea tray. The likes of me are THE WORST.'

Ha! Yeah . . . No.

'Sash?' Michela slaps me with the paper. 'You want anything?'

I want a hot chocolate. I want a Bakewell slice.

'Tap water's fine.' Tap water's free.

At the table, Michela shows me the picture of a man in a UPS shirt sitting on a log and points at the caption, telling me she wrote it: *Courier delivered from death by falling tree.*

'Was it the tree that delivered him from death?' I ask. 'Or was he delivered from death-by-tree?'

'You what?' Michela says round a mouthful of crisps.

'Nothing,' I say, flipping the paper shut and regretting it.

There, on the front page, is a picture of Hugo Delaney, hero of the never-ending hour standing in front of the UKB building. He looks like a newsreader in his suit and tie, top button artfully undone, just to give him an edge.

'I'd bang that so hard, his brains'd fall out,' Michela says, sucking the salt off her fingers as I make an involuntarily gagging noise. 'What? You'd prefer *that*?' She pokes a damp finger on the insert of the boy that was in that nerdy series about vampires.

'I would, actually,' I say. 'At least Dawson Sharman seems nice.'

'And how would you know?' she says, scrumpling up her empty packet.

Because I was there.

But no one knows that. Not even my dad. Who knows what happened to that package I was delivering? Who cares? I watched a man *die*. And then I left before anyone found out. As far as the rest of the world's concerned, there were only five teens trapped in that lift. Not six.

If only that had been true.

My eyes drift to the bottom of the article: *The funeral of Steven Jeffords will take place at 2 p.m., Monday 30 July at Agecroft Cemetery and Crematorium.*

I wonder if Michela wrote that.

HUGO

Here we go a-bloody-gain.

Back up to the stupid North. Past the shitty chimneys.

It starts raining the second we pass them – like the weather just knows where it is on a map. God, the North is so depressing. No wonder that guy just went and bloody died. It was probably out of protest.

I let out a snort. Which isn't attractive, but I'm the only one in first class at this ridiculous time of morning. I can't believe Mum's making me go to the fucking funeral. Like the whole thing wasn't pathetic enough. Now I have to carry a freakin' WREATH around while some news photographer takes some shots for the broadsheets. She was NOT happy with that hell-faced stage-school brat making headlines over me in the news coverage. I mean, *The Times* led on 'Politician's Son Is a Hero', but the tabloids went for the TV star. Mum went so ballistic, you would think someone had DIED . . . Oh yeah, they did. BANTER.

I can't believe I'm being dragged up here again so soon. Work experience was such a waste of time. I didn't pull that girl, I didn't get any bylines, and the stupid editor ignored all my suggestions for stories. What is wrong with people? I swear it was discrimination because I'm southern. Northerners get so het up about the giant North/South divide, like it's an actual thing. Whereas we're all, like, 'Dudes, we don't care. And our house could buy, like, TWELVE castles in your shithole town.'

But at least I don't have to stay the night. I can just rock up to this pathetic photo-shoot funeral, pretend I'm sad that some postie popped his clogs, make my parents happy, and be home in time for David's party tonight. Cassie keeps messaging to check I'll be 'feeling OK to come tonight'. That's the one good thing about this whole dead-guy thing. Girls totally love it. They think I'm all sensitive and damaged now. I've got this great move where, whenever a girl asks about it, I hunch my shoulders and mutter, 'I don't want to talk about it, OK?' Then I apologize for being abrupt and say it's been 'so difficult'. The clincher is when I eventually tell them, 'For some reason, I feel I can talk to *you* about it though.'

Instant score. Back of the net. Double points. It's worked three times already, and will work again tonight with Cassie. Plus, I look so good in this suit Mum ordered specially.

Anyway, it's not like I'm lying. For some annoying reason, I can't get the pathetic dead guy's face out of my head. Maybe it's just a reminder to not end up a sad sack like him . . .

The sun's coming out again, now it's recovered from the horror of being somewhere they put gravy on their chips. That's good. I can wear my new sunglasses so nobody can tell I don't give a flying fuck about this dead guy, and this stupid funeral, and how very traumatic it must've been, and get on with my life.

VELVET

Is it just me, or do all black dresses look a bit slutty? Forget that – I don't even need to ask the question. It's definitely me. Mum says I could make a nun's habit look inappropriate.

The best I've been able to find is a plain dress of Mum's that's a bit too big for me, so at least isn't obscenely tight. It's too short, but there's not much I can do about that except wear flat shoes and hope for the best.

It's not like I've ever been to a funeral before, so I have no idea what is actually expected. And obviously I can't ask anyone, because nobody knows I'm going. They would all think I've gone mad.

Maybe I have gone mad. For some reason, going to this stranger's funeral seems important. It seems like the right thing to do. I know nobody would understand. They're already baffled that I ditched work experience and came home, even though Mum's quite pleased to have me back early.

What else could I do? I asked the universe for a sign, and I got one. I knew I should never have got in that lift. I knew I didn't belong there. I don't need to tell Mum or Chelsea or anyone else the whole story. Ever. A man died, and there was nothing I could do, and life will probably never be quite the same again. They don't need to know that.

I'm home now, and I just want everything to go back to

normal. I can get a job for the summer, help out in the hotel, and hang out with my friends on the beach. Like a normal person. That's all I want. I'm hoping maybe going to the funeral will make me feel normal again, get this out of my system.

'Have you turned into a goth or something?'

I literally jump at the sound of Chelsea's voice, then do an exaggerated eye roll and try to style it out.

'Yeah, right,' I mutter.

'Seriously, babe – you look like you're going to a funeral. What's going on?'

'Nothing!'

FML. Great comeback, Velvet. I'm always being told I'm too smart for my own good, but then, without fail, it deserts me when I need it most – i.e. when Chelsea's being a bitch.

'Well then, get changed and let's go down the seafront. I'm not being seen with you in actual public until you look like a normal person.'

That word again. 'Normal'. It seems to follow me everywhere I go. More to the point – shit – what can I tell Chelsea? She just won't get it. It's not worth the hassle.

Suddenly I have a brainwave – in the form of Hugo Delaney's ridiculously handsome face. I didn't figure out who he was at the time, but he's been smirking at me from every newspaper in the local shop, totally freaking me out.

'I can't,' I tell Chelsea. 'Long story.'

'So tell me the short version.'

'I've got a date. With a posh boy.'

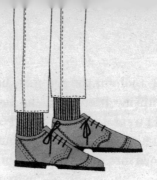

JOE

I'm pulling on my suit jacket when my phone beeps. It's a WhatsApp from Ivy.

What you doing today? Wanna come round mine?

Sorry. Promised I'd do something with my mum. Tomorrow instead?

I press 'send' before the guilt can set in.

Ivy and I have always had this policy: brutal honesty. And, until recently, I've never been tempted to break it. It's just that if I tell her I'm going to the bloke from the lift's funeral, she's bound to want to come with me. And for whatever reason, I feel like this is something I need to do alone. More than that, it's something I *want* to do alone.

Spoiler alert: I didn't end up doing work experience at the UKB. After we'd been rescued from the lift and grilled by three different sets of people, I was returned to Miss Harley, by which point it was time to get back on the bus and return to Skiddington. I think Miss Harley was too embarrassed by the fact she'd completely failed to notice I was missing to punish me. To be honest, getting that close to the inner sanctum of the UKB before being yanked away was punishment enough.

'You look smart,' Mum says when I stick my head round the living-room door to say goodbye.

I glance down at my one and only suit. This will be the third funeral I've worn it to this year. In February, one of my granddads died, followed by my grandma in May. One of the downsides of having older parents: your grandparents are that bit older too. I've only got one grandparent left now – my granddad on my mum's side.

'Where are you off to again?' Mum asks.

'Ivy's,' I lie.

I wait for Mum to ask me why I'm wearing a suit to hang out at Ivy's house, but she doesn't. She just tells me to have a nice day and goes back to frowning at the TV guide spread out on her lap.

I'm waiting at the bus stop, sweating like crazy, when I spot Tyler Matheson and his cronies mucking around on their bikes outside the Tesco Express opposite. I press myself into the corner of the bus shelter, my head down, and will them not to notice me. I spent the final week of term having the piss taken out of me for 'getting lost' on the school trip to the UKB; the last thing I want is to give them further ammunition by letting them see me wearing a black suit on the hottest day of the year so far.

I'm relieved when the bus comes early and I can shove Tyler from my thoughts and focus on the day ahead.

Now, I'm not particularly proud of this, but the thing is, there's more to today's excursion than paying my respects to Steven Jeffords. Call me dim, but it wasn't until I read the article in the newspaper that I realized exactly who I'd been sharing that lift with. While Ivy was busy freaking out over the fact I'd been mere centimetres away from Dawson Sharman (she's a diehard *Dedman High* fan), I was busy freaking out about his mum: basically one of the biggest cheeses at the UKB. Not only that, but the other guy in the lift, this posh guy called Hugo, also has a hotshot producer mum. I have literally no idea how I'm going to turn this to my advantage (neither Dawson or Hugo

71

were exactly friendly while we were waiting to be interviewed), but I can't shift the feeling that the universe put me in that lift for a reason, and now it's up to me to act on it.

That's not all though. There's something else tugging me. Or rather, some*one* else.

Another thing I haven't told Ivy about.

A girl.

A girl called Velvet.

It's the sort of day people wish for at their wedding, not a funeral: sun hanging high and bright in an azure sky. Joe, who is always early for everything, arrives first, his shirt sticking to his back as he walks through the cemetery past the rows of headstones that he tries not to look at for too long.

Or at least he thinks he's first, but Kaitlyn is already there, sheltering from the sun under a tree. Hugo doesn't notice her either, just the flowers she's holding. Cheap, he thinks, as his car pulls up outside the crematorium. 'Wait here,' he tells the driver, reaching for the wreath on the back seat next to him. It feels reassuringly heavy in his hand as he slides out of the car into the sunshine. He was concerned it was too simple, but now he's seen those tragic petrol station carnations, he knows his mother's assistant got it spot on. White calla lilies and eucalyptus. Classic. *Tasteful.*

Plus, they look great with his suit.

Hugo pretends not to notice the photographer as he walks around the back of the car towards the crematorium, but glances over his shoulder as he does to make sure the photographer gets a shot of him in profile, the wreath in his hand. He lingers in the doorway, ready to take off his sunglasses so the photographer can get one of the sombre smiles he's been practising since his mother told him that he had to go to the funeral, but before he can, he hears someone say, 'Oi! This is a funeral. Have some respect!' And there she is, the girl from the lift, in a black dress about an inch short of decent.

The photographer just laughs, then laughs again when Velvet flips him the bird and tells him to put that on the front page,

73

before striding towards the crematorium. She sees Hugo, but pretends not to, her legs a little weaker as she passes, leaving a cloud of scorn and Ted Baker perfume in her wake. Hugo follows her into the crematorium, so focused on her arse that he almost walks straight into her when she stops suddenly. It's empty: just two other people and the coffin, which is sitting on a platform in front of a red velvet curtain. She's never been to a funeral, but she's seen them loads of times on the telly. Isn't there supposed to be a hearse and pall-bearers and sad music?

There aren't even any flowers.

Hugo is thinking the same, because he checks his watch, wondering if he got the time wrong. Sasha has been sitting in the back row of the crematorium for the last half hour, asking herself the same thing. She was about to leave when Dawson walked in, and she knew she was in the right place. He didn't recognize her, dipping his head when he saw the coffin and choosing a seat as far away from it as possible. Now Velvet and Hugo are there, and Sasha can't look at them either, her hands balled into fists as the memory of what happened that day punches her repeatedly in the chest. So she takes a deep breath and stares at the stained-glass window that is sending splinters of coloured light around the room. It's almost too pretty, Joe thinks as he takes a seat – like the persistent peony in his neighbour's overgrown garden that comes back every June despite being almost choked by weeds.

Kaitlyn is the last to summon the courage to walk in. She brought flowers, Dawson notices when she sits two rows ahead of him. Proper flowers, like the ones his aunt wanted at her funeral. No lilies, she'd insisted, and no black. She wanted colour and steelpans and for everyone to get drunk after.

She would have hated this.

An air of uneasiness settles over the crematorium. They all look at the coffin, then at each other, then back at the open doors

74

to the crematorium as they wait, unsure what to do. A bell rings and a priest emerges. He walks slowly to the coffin and stops.

'Please rise,' he says.

They look at one another as it finally dawns on them: this is it.

No one else is coming.

Sasha Harris created group 'Lift People'
Sasha Harris added Joe Lindsay
Sasha Harris added Velvet Brown
Sasha Harris added Kaitlyn Thomas
Sasha Harris added Dawson Sharman
Sasha Harris added Hugo Delaney

Sasha:
Hey guys!!! 😄

Joe:
Hello

Kaitlyn:
Hey everyone

Velvet:
Heyyy

Dawson:
Hi all

Sasha:
WE NEED A NAME

Joe:
Um . . . The Secret Six?
Or is that a bit Enid Blyton?

Kaitlyn:
Just a touch

Velvet:

Googles who's Enid Blyton?!! OH OK I get it

Sasha:

HA! Me too, Velvet!!!

Joe:

You're missing out guys

Dawson:

Not to be the ultimate buzzkill, but the original books are ever so slightly massively racist . . . And sexist. My mum hates them. My nan bought me Folk of the Faraway Tree once, and Mum shredded it up for my hamster. Fun fact, there

Joe:

Noted

Any other, slightly sexier suggestions?

Velvet:

Ummm, the sexy six???

Kaitlyn:

This escalated quickly

Dawson:

That would have been the perfect name if we'd met on an escalator. OK . . . Sexy lift things . . . Going down? Pushing buttons? Something about shafts?

Sasha:

LOL 😂😂😂😂

Hugo:

Oh, hi everyone. Loving how we've made a WhatsApp group born out of a funeral sexy . . . ☺ That's quite impressive.

Joe:

Perhaps using the word 'sexy' was a mistake . . .

Kaitlyn:

Maybe we should stick to The Lift Six for now?

Sasha:

The Lift Lot? (Putting a number on things makes it seem . . . dangerous, like tempting fate??? I mean . . . there were seven. Technically . . . ☹)

Joe:

I'm OK with the Lift Lot

Dawson:

I have it . . . WE SHOULD'VE TAKEN THE STAIRS

Kaitlyn:

Yesssssssssssssss

Hugo:

I honestly don't mind

Sasha:

Velvet? Velvet??? What do you think? It has to be unanimous

Joe:

Like The Beatles. They never did anything without all four of them agreeing. Well, until they all fell out . . .

Velvet:

Should've Taken The Stairs it is! Just like the Beatles. OK, maybe not *just* like the Beatles

Dawson:

The stairs could have been our Abbey Road moment. Instead we have this. What a legacy

YEAR TWO

Hugo:

Hey everyone. I've been thinking really hard about this, and I just feel like we should mark the first anniversary of Stephen's death. I don't know about you, but I think about him a lot. My mum's flat in Manchester is free on the 14th. Anyone fancy coming around for a party? Celebrate our lives and living, etc.?

Anyone? I'm not used to people ignoring my invites to parties. You guys obviously don't know how epic they always are

Velvet:

Sorry for late reply! I think this is a lovely idea, Hugo. I'm in

Joe:

Yeah, sounds good

Dawson:

It's 'Steven'

Hugo:

That's what I meant

Kaitlyn:

Yep, I'm in

Hugo:

Great! The whole gang back together

Sasha:

Um . . . yes. Me too. ☺

DAWSON

I don't realize Kaitlyn has messaged me four times – and actually tried to call – in the last hour, until I get back to my dressing room and check my phone. Josh has messaged too, and my mouth curves into the automatic smile that just seeing Josh's name brings . . . but I reply to Kaitlyn first, saving Josh's message for after, as a reward.

Can't talk now. On set, I reply to Kaitlyn, then instantly regret it. 'On set' implies a kind of coolness, which today's job distinctly lacks. I've barely opened Josh's message when she replies, her response popping up at the top of the screen:

OK. Speak later x

Then a split second later:

Break a leg x

If only she knew how close to the truth she was . . .

Josh's message is to confirm plans for later. I reply to say I'm looking forward to it, and debate whether I should sign off with a kiss. On the one hand, we've been seeing each other for almost two months. I've touched his penis eight times now, and he's touched mine twice, so a kiss isn't out of bounds. But it's very *couply*, and we haven't had 'The Talk' yet. And *he* didn't add a kiss. Is he waiting for me to do it? Should I google 'When to Add a Kiss to a Message'? No, I don't want that in my search history in case I die on the way to the pub, or someone steals my phone. Today is tragic enough.

I'm saved from making a decision when Nita the assistant director appears and tells me I'm wanted, so I send the message without one and hurry after her, back to what they're euphemistically calling the 'set'. The 'set' is, in fact, the hallway of the terraced house owned by the director's mum in Eccles. 'Authentic,' Alun called it.

Cheap, I call it. The whole house smells of cats, and meat.

'Ah, Dawson, you're back,' Alun says when I make my way down the stairs, as if I've been somewhere other than his mum's spare room. 'Don't bother coming all the way down – we're going to do the whole thing one last time. Marty, you get back up behind him.'

Marty, who is by far and away the biggest human I have ever seen, and also who has not said a single word all day, shuffles up the stairs and stands behind me.

'OK, Dawson, from the top. Can you remember what to do?'

It's the eighth time this afternoon that we've done this.

'I sure can, Alun!' I beam at him, and he tips me a wink that makes me feel both pleased with his approval and a little creeped out.

'Ready . . . And . . . action!' Alun says.

I take three steps, then slip my foot over the edge of the carpeted stair. Then Marty grabs my waist, and I let myself fall back, kicking both legs out from under me as if Marty and I are in the world's stupidest ballet. When I'm standing again, Marty releases me, and I make my way to the bottom of the stairs, where I sit and imagine Hugo Delaney watching this advert. I rub my ankle, until Alun yells, 'Cut!'

He smiles at me. 'That was great, Dawson. Best take yet. Your face was a picture. I almost believed you were in real pain.

85

I think that'll do it. All that's left is the stunt double doing the actual fall.'

'Thank you, Alun,' I say, rising to my feet. Nita told me earlier that *Alun* was the stunt double. 'Erm . . . any word on when it'll air?' I ask. 'And where?'

'Sometime in the next couple of weeks, I reckon.' Alun scratches his head as he thinks; I had no idea people actually did that. 'It'll be on the website, for sure. And they're looking into television slots. After *Jeremy Kyle*, and those shows. Get the daytime-telly crowd.'

'Sounds great – I'll have to keep an eye out for it.' I force a smile. 'I'll just get my stuff . . .'

I make my way back to the spare room, slipping past Marty the Human Mountain, who's still on the stairs, and grabbing my phone and jacket. Josh hasn't replied, but he's always a bit slow to, so I'm not worried. Instead I decide to head to the pub early, get a quiet drink, and browse The Stage site.

The pub is empty, as per, with only the one-armed barman working, so I get a vodka and Diet Coke and find a corner near a socket, plugging my phone in. Josh hates it when I order vodka and Coke (he's a pint drinker, but I think it tastes like halitosis), so I'm glad to have some time for a drink I like. Maybe if I drink enough, I won't taste the lager later. My shoes stick to the carpet beneath the table, and I move them, ignoring the sucking sound it makes. I would never have guessed Josh would like this kind of place, but he says it's an undiscovered gem and old-man-pub-chic is very hot right now.

While I wait, I message Kaitlyn back, confirming I'll meet her outside the Slug and Lettuce for a drink before Hugo's party tomorrow. Again she replies so fast, I'm almost impressed:

Can't wait. See you tomorrow xx

My stomach twists then, something like shame niggling at me. I'm not really going. I only said I was to get her to stop messaging me about it. Nothing against her, or any of them, but I don't see the point of it.

I've been thinking really hard about this, and I just feel like we should mark the first anniversary of Stephen's death. I don't know about you, but I think about him a lot . . .

Hugo messaged the group a couple of weeks ago, offering to hold a party at his mum's flat in Manchester. No one had really used the group chat in a while. After the funeral we all did for a bit . . . but life, and stuff, and then Josh happened – at least for me – and it stopped. Sasha still sent animal videos and memes a couple of times a month, but that was it. Until Hugo's message.

You're going, right? Kaitlyn had messaged me. *It might be nice?* A few minutes later, she messaged again. *I'll go if you go. I don't feel comfortable enough with just the others.* As I was wondering why she felt comfortable with me, she messaged AGAIN. *It would be great to catch up properly x*

I know it's a dick move, but I'm going to message her in the morning and say I'm sick. Again, that guilty feeling makes my stomach churn. I down my drink and go back to the bar.

'Can I get—?'

'Two pints of Stella,' a voice says over my shoulder, and I turn to see Josh standing there.

For a minute, I can't quite speak – he always has this effect on me. It's not just that he's gorgeous, but there's something else about him that makes you stop and stare. *Arresting*, that's the word. Josh is arresting. He's way out of my league, like a blond Douglas Booth to my mutant inbred from *The Hills Have Eyes*. I can't actually believe he likes me. I have no idea why he likes me. He says he didn't watch *Dedman High*, so it's not even like it's the novelty value of that.

'Well hello,' I say, leaning forward for a kiss.

'Steady.' He holds up a hand, and I roll my eyes affectionately. He has a weird thing about PDA.

I pay for the drinks and carry them back to the table, taking my phone from Josh when he hands it to me, his own now plugged in to my charger.

'It's almost dead,' he says, then takes a big gulp of his drink. 'Is that glass yours?' He nods at my empty vodka glass.

'No,' I say straight-faced. 'It was here when I got here.' To prove it, I take a huge gulp of my lager and try not to gag.

'So my day was shit,' he says.

'Do you want to talk about it?'

'Nah – it's old news. Just sixth-form crap. I'm over it.' He takes another big swig of his pint. 'You're lucky you don't have to go to school or do an apprenticeship.'

'I'm technically home-schooled,' I remind him.

'Like I said: lucky.'

'I had a shoot,' I offer, when he doesn't say anything else.

'Yeah? For what?' He pulls his phone over and looks at it.

'Just an advert.' I wish I'd kept my mouth shut. It's too tragic to tell him about.

'What kind of advert?'

'Nothing major.'

'Why are you being shy? What kind of advert?'

He leans forward then, blue eyes fixed on mine, and any hope I had of resisting crumbles.

'A legal one. For a law firm.'

'What kind of law firm? Not like a "If you've had an accident in the last fifty years, you could be entitled to a cash payout" one?'

He laughs.

I don't.

'Fucking hell, Dawson. You can't be that desperate!' He laughs again and drains his pint. 'I'll be back in a sec. You all right?' He points at my still-full glass, and I nod.

I can be that desperate, actually. This is the first time I've worked in six months. Two months after the funeral, I did some voiceover stuff on a radio play, and had a small part in a costume drama as a plague victim. Kimba barely responds to my messages any more. So when Alun approached her and requested me for the advert, I couldn't say no.

Josh returns with a new pint and a packet of cheese and onion crisps.

'So what are you doing tomorrow night?' I ask him. If I don't go to Hugo's maybe we can hang out.

'Sixth-form thing,' he says, opening the crisps and cramming them in his mouth.

'What kind of thing?'

'Just a party.' Bits of crisp fly out with his words, peppering the table.

I've never met any of his friends. He says it's too soon, but it's been seven weeks and two days. 'Oh. Well, I'm free if you want some company?'

'It's sixth form. I already know everyone there.'

'I'm just saying I'm free. If you wanted me to come.'

'Nope. You're all right.'

I can't think of a single thing I can say back, so I drink my lager, the whole manky pint of it, and he does the same.

'Your round,' he says when we're done, and because I'm an idiot, I get us fresh drinks.

Two more pints, and his knee is pressed against mine under the table. A third, and his hand drops to my thigh, tracing lazy circles on my leg. A jolt of something like lightning fizzes through my blood. I know what this means. I know what to do. Buzzy and blurry and turned on, I stand, shove my phone in my pocket, and weave towards the door, out into the warm summer air.

A moment later, Josh takes my hand and drags me down the alley behind the pub. He pulls me behind the bins, next to the barrels, which I like to think of as 'our spot'. It's still light outside, the sun turning Josh's hair to gold. I can hear people on the street, laughing and chatting as they walk past. They have no idea we're here. He wants me so badly, I can feel it when he finally kisses me, pushing me against the wall, his lips mashing against mine as he fumbles with my belt. I do the same, reaching for his zip, and wrapping my fingers around him. He moans into my mouth, and I swear to God it's the hottest thing that has ever happened to me in my life. So when he pushes me down to my knees, I don't even mind.

'I suppose you'll be wanting another drink?' he says afterwards, with a smile that's more like a leer. He's so, so pleased with himself, it radiates from him, there in the smirk that won't go away, the swagger of his walk as I follow him back into the pub.

I do want a drink, actually. I feel really weird. After I was done, I tried to kiss him again, and he pushed me away, saying it was 'rank'. He didn't try to touch me.

'I'll get them,' he says, and there's something about it that makes me feel cheap. I don't like it. 'Put this back on charge for me?' he says, handing me his phone before heading to the bar.

Like a robot, I do, having stupidly left my charger in the wall, and as the screen lights up, I see he has a bunch of notifications.

One of which is from 'Sex-face Stacey'.

Come over tonight. My parents are out and you owe me a . . .

Stacey? Who the hell is Stacey? I swipe to try to read the whole message – read *all* of the messages – but don't know his passcode. I'm about to try his birthday, when I see him coming back, so I put it down and reach for the pint he places before me, taking a huge gulp. I watch in silence as he picks up the phone and checks his messages. I watch his smirk broaden into a smile. Then he lifts his pint and pretty much downs it.

'Gotta go,' he says, standing up and pulling his coat on. 'Mum wants me home. I'll message you, yeah?'

Then he leaves. He just leaves. After I . . .

I really am a fucking idiot.

My face burns, and I feel sick, and stupid. And then my phone lights up, and I can't help it; I think he's changed his mind about the party tomorrow, he's—

It's Kaitlyn, wanting to know what sort of thing I'm wearing to Hugo's . . . and for a moment, I'm seriously tempted to tell her to fuck off. I'm seriously tempted to tell *everyone* to fuck off so I can go and die quietly.

Then a weird calmness comes over me.

Probably a tiara and furs, I type. *Something befitting a night at Castle Delaney.*

She replies with the cry-laughing emoji.

Fine, I'll go to Hugo Delaney's party. I'm not sitting at home like a loser. And when Josh asks . . . If Josh asks . . .

Josh won't ask. Who am I kidding?

KAITLYN

My head is having a conversation with itself. An annoying conversation. The kind I'd put my headphones on to avoid if I had the chance.

This is going to be great!

No, it's going to be awful.

It's going to change my life!

No, it'll be terrible. No, worse than terrible. An anticlimax.

I'm standing outside the Slug and Lettuce, as instructed, waiting for Dawson. *Dawson.* A smile spreads over my face, and I clutch my phone a little tighter, looking down at it again to check he hasn't messaged me to tell me he's cancelling. That would be *awful*.

He hasn't. He hasn't messaged me at all, actually, but that's OK. We've made the plan, why would he *need* to message me? I unlock my phone and open WhatsApp, tapping *You on your way? :)* before reconsidering and deleting it. He's obviously on his way, Kaitlyn. Chill out.

I think I'm allowed to be a bit un-chilled about this though. I mean, *Dawson Sharman.* I still can't quite believe that we're friends, let alone the kind who meet up for a drink before going to a cool house party. (I mean, I'm just assuming it's going to be cool, but it has to be, right? Hugo doesn't seem like the kind of guy who does things by halves.)

I thought I wouldn't see anyone from the lift again after the funeral. It was all so depressing, so *sad*, that I thought everyone would just want to forget about the whole thing. But then, somehow, everyone was exchanging numbers, and it would have been rude to be the only one not doing it. And then the group chat was actually quite fun for a while, at least over the summer when I wasn't at school. It was really nice to have people to talk to who didn't know me, didn't know about my sight problems, didn't know me as anything other than Kaitlyn, The Girl from the Lift. It's quietened down a lot since then, but every now and then someone, usually Sasha, checks in every now and then to make sure everyone's doing OK.

But still, Dawson is the only one out of the group that I feel any kind of connection with. I mean, a *real* connection that isn't just we-were-all-in-the-same-lift-when-that-guy-died. I don't know why, really, because it's not like any of the others are awful or anything. There's just something about Dawson and me. We get each other, I think. It's like we have a sense for—

'Kaitlyn?' There's a hand waving in my face. 'Uh, Kait?'

'Hi!' I say, overcompensating by practically yelling in Dawson's face. 'Sorry! Hi!'

His face crinkles into a smile. 'Hi,' he says, like he wants to laugh, and I mentally try to dial it back a notch.

'Where's the tiara and furs?' I ask.

He blinks at me, confused, and I flush. Of course he won't remember some silly jokey text from yesterday. 'Remember, you said you'd wear . . . ? Never mind.'

'No, yeah, the tiara,' he says, nodding. 'I left it at home – damn.'

We stand there nodding at each other.

'Shall we go in?' he suggests.

'Yeah!' I open the door and gesture for him to walk in front of me. 'How are you?'

He shrugs. 'OK. You?'

'I'm good. I mean, just fine. Still getting over exams being finished and me being free, you know?' He's walking straight over to the bar and I follow, wondering as I speak whether I should remind him I'm only sixteen, and it's probably safest if he gets me a Coke. 'I've waited for this moment for so long, and now it's here, it's actually pretty weird. Did you feel like that after exams?' I remember only after I say this that Dawson was home-schooled, so I add, before he can say anything, 'I guess it was different for you anyway. But still, it's a milestone, isn't—?'

Shit.

I've been so busy trying to take in all of his face as we go, I've walked straight into a chair, and oh shit, I'm falling. I'm falling over the chair. This is a disaster. This is a nightmare. This is . . . *Ow.*

'Shit!' I hear Dawson say, and there's a lot going on in that 'shit'. There's, 'What is wrong with this girl?' and, 'I shouldn't have come,' and, 'Who falls over a chair?' and, 'This is so embarrassing. I hope no one's looking at me!' and, finally, a hint of, 'I hope she hasn't hurt herself.'

I tell myself, as I get to my feet and pull the chair up with me, pushing it under the table, that a hint is better than nothing.

'You OK?' Dawson asks in a voice that sounds more wary than actually concerned.

'Yeah,' I say, trying to make my voice light. I want to make a joke, but I can't think of one. I hate how he's looking at me, and I just need to say something, anything, to change that expression, anything but . . . 'I have a sight problem!' I blurt it out. Oh God. God, no, Kaitlyn – why?!

'Oh,' he says. Rabbit in headlights. 'Ah . . . OK.'

It's not even why I walked into the freaking chair! I walked into the chair because I was looking at his stupid face! Why did

94

I mention my sight? Whhhyyyy????

We both stand there in an incredibly awkward silence for a full minute, before he finally says, 'Shall I get the drinks in?'

'Yes, please,' I say.

He gets me a vodka and Coke, and I'm too embarrassed to say anything about being underage, so I just sip it gratefully. I feel like I might cry if I try to talk. Why, after a whole year of avoiding the subject, of trying to decide the best way to tell Dawson without him changing his opinion of me, did I just blurt it out in the middle of a pub? *After tripping over something?* There literally couldn't be a worse way or time to do the big reveal. I'm such a disaster.

'So, uh, Hugo's bash,' Dawson says. He's drained half his drink in one go. 'What do you reckon; cringey posh-boy wankfest, or over-the-top try-hard blowout?'

'Andorboth,' I say, and he laughs, which makes me relax a bit. 'Bet you ten quid it'll be catered or something.'

Dawson's smile tightens. 'I take that bet, but let's not sully the occasion with something as common as *money*,' he says.

'What, then?'

'Honour,' he says. 'Indebted with honour. If it's catered, you win, and I owe you one. If there isn't, I win, and you owe *me* one.'

'That sounds vague,' I say.

He grins. 'Exactly.'

'So basically, whoever wins calls the shots?'

He nods.

'OK, cool,' I say. It's weird, but it has potential, plus having Dawson in my debt means keeping him in my life. And even if I lose, being in his debt doesn't sound all that bad to me.

I sneak a glance at Dawson over his glass and can't help smiling. I know Dawson's got a lot of crap over the last few years

95

for how he went from being super attractive to, well, not-so-super attractive, but since I've got to know him, I've come to really like his face. Plus, if he was still super famous gorgeous Dawson, maybe he'd never have been in the lift, and we'd never have met. And I'm glad that we've met.

'It might be good,' I say. 'We might have fun.'

Dawson twists his mouth in a wry half-smile and shrugs. 'We might,' he says.

We stay at the pub for half an hour before we head to Hugo's place together. It's only a ten-minute walk, but Dawson still suggests we get a cab.

'I'm fine to walk,' I say.

'You sure?'

'Yeah.'

I'm not sure why he seems so uncertain, until he smiles awkwardly and says, 'Do you, um, want my arm or something?'

A smile blooms over my face as I shake my head. 'No, I'm fine. But thanks.' He doesn't look sure, so I add, 'Just let me know if there are any bumps in the pavement, OK?'

We walk slowly, and I tell him a little bit more about Stargardt disease, making sure to keep it light, playing down how completely it has derailed my life. I ask him about his acting, but he shrugs it off, telling me that it's going great, just great, but he doesn't want to jinx anything by talking about it.

When we finally get to Hugo's, we both stop at the end of the drive, looking from the building to each other.

'Look, maybe we should just blow this off,' Dawson says, and then he makes a weird kind of face, like he wants to swallow the words back up again. 'I mean, give it a miss.'

I look at him. 'Is that what you . . . ? Do you want to?' Does he mean he just wants to spend time with me? Alone? Helium right into my heart. 'We can go somewhere else, yeah,' I say. 'We could go back to the pub.'

Dawson looks at me for a moment, but in the growing dark I can't quite make out the expression on his face. 'Er, I guess we should show our faces,' he says. 'Since we're here.'

'Yeah,' I say quickly. 'And we're here for Steven, aren't we?'

'Yeah, for Steven,' he agrees. 'We'll say hi to the crew, toast Steven, and be on our way.'

I smile. 'Are we a crew?'

He laughs, surprisingly self-conscious. 'Nah, I don't know why I said that. Let's just go in, shall we?'

Dawson was right. The party isn't catered.

But there is plenty of wine.

And I am drunk.

The six of us are in Hugo's living room, and it's nothing like as bad as I thought it would be. I'm sitting on the floor by the giant TV, talking to Velvet about my hair. I changed the colour of the stripe from blue to pink after my GCSEs, and it looks awesome, if I do say so myself. Velvet thinks so too, and she keeps reaching out a hand and touching it, saying, 'But it's just so *cool*!' She's a bit drunk as well.

'You should get one!' I say. 'What's your favourite colour?'

'Hey, ladies,' Hugo says, sinking down on to his knees beside us. 'What are we talking about?'

'Kaitlyn's amazing hair,' Velvet says. 'Isn't it great?'

Hugo glances at me, his face making it very obvious that he doesn't think it's great. 'Uh, sure,' he says. 'Kaitlyn, Dawson's looking for you.'

'Is he?' I say, my voice going up a key.

Velvet notices and grins. 'Aw, you and Dawson . . . ?' she asks.

'We—'

'It seemed pretty important,' Hugo interrupts. He leans in and grins at Velvet. *Oh, OK.* 'How are you? Do you need a top up?'

I leave them to it and get up to go and find Dawson. The lights are dimmed low, and Hugo's flat is still completely unfamiliar, so manoeuvring around isn't an easy task. I keep my hand on the wall as I walk along the hall, my vision blurred through the alcohol and, well, being my vision. I make a mental note (that I'll probably forget) to tell Dawson that, in the future, him 'looking for me' should actually involve just that, not the other way around.

'You OK, Kaitlyn?' a boy's voice asks, and I turn hopefully, even though the accent is all wrong, which means the voice belongs to Joe, not Dawson.

'Do you know where Dawson is?' I ask.

'He was out on the balcony of the bedroom,' Joe says. 'Are you OK?' he asks again. 'You're hanging on to the wall a bit.'

'It's a blindness thing,' I say.

'Oh!' he exclaims. 'Are you, um—'

'Just kidding!' I call over my shoulder, spotting the bedroom door. 'I'm fine!'

I walk into the room and head straight for the balcony. I can just make out the outline of Dawson, the sound of him talking. He must be on the phone. 'Josh, please,' he's saying.

I step on to the balcony beside him just as he hangs up with a frustrated growl, shaking his head at nothing, shoving his phone back into his pocket.

'Hi!' I say.

Dawson looks at me, and I try to make out his expression. Confused, a little annoyed, I think.

'Everything OK?' I ask.

'What are you doing out here?' he replies.

'You were looking for me,' I remind him, even though it's a bit weird for him to have been looking for me out here on the balcony, while he was on his phone. But whatever. 'And here I am.'

'Do you want to leave?' Dawson asks.

'No, I like it here,' I say. Through the open balcony door, I hear a shout from inside the house, and then laughter. *My friends*, I think. *My crew*. 'With you.'

'With me?'

Another step closer. 'Yeah.' I lift my face, close my eyes, ready for the first kiss.

There's a pause, and then the worst sound in the world. The sound of Dawson saying, 'Oh no. Oh no, Kaity. It's not like . . . Oh shit.'

I open my eyes, then immediately regret it. I don't want to see the face he's making.

'I'm not . . . It's not you – it's . . . Shit. *Shit*.'

'Never mind!' I say, pushing down the agony and pasting a smile on my face. 'My bad. The wine.' And me. Me being stupid. Me being stupid enough to risk hope. 'Hey, you know what, I think I will leave. So . . .'

He grabs my arm. 'Don't go. I'm sorry. I do like you, I do. I feel like we . . . we can be good mates, can't we?'

Ow. *Ow*. A hundred knives of *ow*.

'Sure,' I say. 'Of course. I'm just gonna go.'

'Kait, no, wait.' He screws up his eyes in frustration, groans and then says, eyes still closed, 'I'm gay.'

Silence. I try to stare at him through the dark. 'You're what?'

'I like men, Kait,' he says. 'I'm gay.'

SASHA

The poshest person I thought I knew was Georgia Darwich, who lives in the loft extension of a big four-bed semi, and has her own forty-three-inch HD telly with Sky, Netflix *and* Amazon Prime.

Obviously I was wrong. Hugo's flat could be the set for *Made in Chelsea: The Manchester Edition*. The floors are wood, the sofas leather, and the pop art on the wall isn't the sort of thing you can buy in IKEA. This place is so posh, there's no knowing what telly they have because it's recessed into the ceiling waiting to be summoned with a clap.

I try another sip of my drink and do my best not to pull a face. Every Christmas – whether it's the whole Harris clan, or just the usual suspects of me, Dad and Nan, who see each other all the time – my nan pops a bottle the second her first guest arrives. Only my drink is always more orange juice than fizz. On its own, champagne tastes disgusting.

Not that any of the others seem to think so – everyone else has necked their first glass in nanoseconds and Hugo's popped at least another bottle since.

'Is there anything to eat?' Velvet says, her skirt riding even further up her legs as she glances round looking for Hugo.

'Let's see.' I put my glass down and hurry across to the kitchen. When I get there, I'm disappointed to find that Velvet hasn't actually come with me. She's wrestling with the massive doors that lead out on to the balcony and yelling at Joe to give her a hand.

'The view will be *lush*!'

We're seventeen floors up, so it will be. I wonder whether anyone else climbed the stairs rather than risk the lift.

One year on, and I still carry the shopping up to our third-floor flat rather than take the Metal Box of My Worst Nightmares. Told Dad it was a fitness thing.

The kitchen's as flashy as the lounge. The stove is one of those flat-glass jobs, so shiny I can see my chins as I frown down at it, wondering how you're supposed to turn it on. The cupboard underneath has exactly one frying pan and one normal pan. Lifting one up, I find a price label on the bottom. Does anyone actually do any *living* here?

'And you're looking for what, exactly?' Hugo's public school drawl startles me, and I smack my knee in my haste to shut the cupboard door.

'Food.'

'Of course.' He's looking at my body when he waves towards the shiny steel fridge. 'Take whatever you want.'

There's a lot of alcohol, even though there's a separate wine fridge next to it. Beyond that, it's a choice of Harrods grapefruit marmalade, smoked salmon mousse and a tub of enormous green olives.

I opt for the olives because I don't want to have to ask Hugo where the bread is.

'It's not for me.' My explanation sounds more like a defence. 'Velvet said she hadn't eaten and—'

'She doesn't need to.' Hugo drains his glass and raises the bottle he's holding. 'Liquid lunch.'

'It's not lunchtime.'

'You're tons of bloody fun, aren't you?' Hugo sneers, topping himself up, then swigging back the dribble that's left in the bottle and beckoning for me to pass him another. 'No, that's cava – no one drinks that shit. The Veuve.'

I don't know which one is the Veuve.

'The one with the orange fucking label.'

I pass him the one with the orange fucking label. He doesn't make any move to open it or offer me any, just points to a cupboard and tells me that's where I'll find the bowls, then leaves.

I hate him. The way he talks, the way he looks through me like my existence barely registers.

Tipping the olives out into a glass dish, I pop one in my mouth, then spit it right back out into my hand. It tastes like it's been marinated in Cif.

I guess that's how the other half live. With a telly you can't see, and food you can't eat.

Back in the lounge, Hugo's taken the bottle out on to the balcony where Velvet and Joe are leaning over the wall ogling the lights of Manchester. There's only Kaitlyn and Dawson in here with their heads close together like they're having the deepest of meaningfuls.

'I found olives,' I say, setting them down in the middle of the glass coffee table.

Kaitlyn looks up with a vague smile, like she isn't even seeing me, but Dawson doesn't so much as register my existence.

'They're disgusting anyway,' I say.

No one cares.

All of a sudden, I want to cry. I hate it here. I don't know these people. Why did I even come? Why are we drinking *champagne* and listening to Kendrick Lamar? Isn't this supposed to be a sombre occasion? Steven Jeffords *died*, for

God's sake, and everyone here seems to be using it as an excuse to party.

I get up so abruptly that even Dawson notices.

'Where're you off to?' he asks as I step quickly across the rug, heading for the hallway.

'The loo.'

The first door I open is a cupboard with hardly any coats in it. The second is a bedroom that looks like no one's ever slept there. This place is more like a show home than a real home, and I wonder how much time it takes to clean. Two Saturdays working for Klean Sweep and that's how I measure houses, now, apparently: in cleaning hours.

'You're tons of bloody fun, aren't you?'

Hugo's voice sends a spike of rage right through me, even though I'm only hearing it in my head. People like him might not need to take a Saturday job on minimum wage, but not all of us have rich, powerful parents. Some of us have a financially questionable parent whose courier career moved seamlessly from temporary to chronic, and another who only exists as Facebook posts that I have to copy and paste into Google Translate to find out she's pregnant. Again. Two half-sisters I've never met. And a half-foetus.

Tomorrow, someone like me will come here and clean up whatever mess we make, but after a shift at Klean Sweep, *I'm* the one who has to clean our house; *I'm* the one who has to make a decision between watering down the bleach to last another fortnight or going without furniture polish. People like Hugo don't spend hours dismantling the vacuum to pick out a rogue hair grip before patching the hose up with gaffer tape – they just order the latest Dyson from John Lewis and charge it to Mummy's credit card.

The last door I try leads to another bedroom so big and

empty that I'm drawn inside, my bare feet sinking into the pile of the same thick rug that's in the lounge. Opposite, there's more expensive art hanging over the enormous bed, and to my right there's a wall of floor-to-ceiling windows leading out on to yet another balcony. Turning to my left, I come face to face with a *bathroom*. Right there, standing on a marble step like the altar of a heathen church, there's a pair of sinks, a freestanding bath, and a frosted screen hiding what I guess must be a shower. Or a toilet? I hope not. That would be gross.

Not believing it will work, I clap my hands . . . and the lights come on!

I hop up to inspect the fancy bottles lined along the two sinks, picking each one up to read the label. Hugo's mum has *eight* different sorts of moisturizer. I use Superdrug's own-brand hand cream.

A mirrored box reveals a cloud of cotton wool nestled inside when I was half expecting a stash of prescription drugs. Nestled on top is a pair of diamond studs.

They might belong to Hugo's mum, but it's my mum they remind me of. Her taking me to Claire's Accessories just after I turned six.

'My little girl.' Mum had cradled my chin and kissed my forehead. I'd long learned not to cry at anything if I wanted to make people happy. 'So grown up. And grown-up girls deserve diamonds.'

She'd reached for a pair of glistening studs just like the ones she always wore. I'd asked if they were real, because I'm an idiot, and Mum had laughed and kissed me again as we walked up to the counter.

'No, Sasha, these are not real.' Then she leaned in to whisper, 'But mine are not either, and no one can tell.'

I pick up one of Hugo's mum's earrings to inspect, twisting it so that it glitters in the light. The ones Mum had bought me were real silver – it said so on the packet – and I'd always felt special about that, but I guess the ones belonging to Hugo's mum are something else. White gold or platinum perhaps.

Weird how people must spend hundreds (thousands?) of pounds on a metal that looks exactly like one you can buy for a fraction of the price.

Cautiously, feeling like I shouldn't, I hold one up in front of my ear.

'Just a little something my boyfriend surprised me with,' I murmur at my reflection and roll my eyes. 'Tiffany's, you know.'

The idea of anyone ever wanting to spend that much money on me is incomprehensible – rich boys can afford to be fussy about who they sleep with. Although let's be real, I'd peel the fingernails from my own fingers before I'd sleep with Hugo. No money doesn't mean no standards.

Replacing the earring on its cotton-wool cushion, I turn to look at the bath. Even empty, it looks so inviting I can't resist clambering in.

Our bathroom at home was designed in Hobbiton, and it's a straight-up choice between knees or boobs whenever I get a chance to bathe, but this tub is so deep I could sit here entirely submerged in hot water and Razzle Dazzle bath oil.

My phone goes off. Although it's muted, the vibration's amplified by the bath, and in this massive empty bedroom it's deafening.

Dad.

I don't want to answer, but he'd take it personally. You can hear it in his voicemails. I get out of the bath and move into the bedroom, where it echoes less.

'Hi, Dad.'

'I thought you were home tonight,' he says.

'Not tonight.' I press my lips together to stop myself from trying to say too much. Elaborate lies are the easiest to spot.

'You could have said.'

I did, over breakfast at the weekend, and in a message this afternoon telling him that I'd taken something out of the freezer for his tea.

'Sorry, Dad. I thought I had. There's Bolognese defrosting by the sink.'

'Where are you?' He's not distracted by my dinner chat. 'Out with Michela again?'

'Uh-huh.' I let Dad's dislike of Michela do the deceiving for me.

'Don't stay out late. Just because you've done your exams, doesn't mean you can party twenty-four seven.'

I close my eyes for a moment. That is so not fair. Like I *ever* party. I mean, I'm at a party *right now* and look at me, stone-cold sober and hiding in the bathroom. If Michela were here, she'd have taken Hugo's bottle of Veuve, poured it down her throat, and turned up the music to grind him like a pepper mill. If not Hugo, then Joe, who might be a try-hard, but is legitimately cute. Not Dawson though, whose features have all grown at a different pace. He has the kind of face my nan would look at, before nodding and saying, 'Give it twenty years . . .' Michela wouldn't give it twenty seconds.

'Sasha? Did you hear me?'

I open my eyes and stare at my reflection. 'Sorry, it went a bit crackly.'

'Nan wants to know which day to expect us over for lunch – is it Saturdays you're working, or Sunday?'

'Saturday.' There's a couple of clients who want their cleaning done then. Klean Sweap were delighted when I asked about working weekends – no one else wants to.

'I'll let her know. Get back to your friends then.' He doesn't sound like he means it, but the call's ended.

My friends. No one in this flat cares who I am. They don't know anything more about me than they do about poor dead Steven Jeffords.

And if I spend the night hiding in the bathroom, they never will.

I need to go back out there and at least *try* to talk to someone. Velvet, maybe. She seems friendly. And normal. I'll talk to her.

There's voices in the corridor, and I clap the lights off, not wanting anyone to know where I am, but the voices get louder . . . *no, no, no* . . .

I look for an escape, but the balcony's too far away, and there's no wardrobes or anything. There's a thump on the door before it bursts open, two people spilling into the darkness inside.

But it's fine, all fine. Hugo's mum's enormous flat has an enormous bedroom with an enormous bath. And I am hiding inside it.

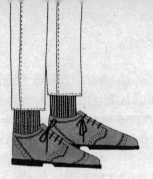

JOE

So, I finally get Velvet to myself out on the balcony, and everything is perfect – the sun is setting a gorgeous pinky orange in front of us, Velvet has laughed at four out of my last five jokes *and* touched my arm twice, and, best of all, Hugo is nowhere to be seen.

My phone vibrates in the back pocket of my jeans. I ignore it. It'll only be Ivy giving me yet more shit about being here tonight. I just don't get what her problem is. The other weekend, she went into Manchester to meet up with a bunch of her home-school friends without me, and I didn't make a fuss about *that*.

'But I thought you said they were knobheads,' she'd pointed out when we met up at the park yesterday and I'd told her about the party.

'They're not *all* knobheads,' I'd replied.

Which is true. The only official knobhead is Hugo, who has been acting like a complete prat since the moment I arrived, uncorking bottles of wine while pretending to be some sort of hip-hop connoisseur. I'm still on the fence about Dawson, figuring if I'd undergone the biggest Reverse Longbottom in history, I might be a bit stand-offish around strangers too. Kaitlyn and Sasha seem nice enough, albeit a bit quiet. To be honest though, I'm a bit too dazzled by Velvet to pay anyone else much attention.

I watch as she takes photos of the view on her phone. She's even lovelier than I remember. The picture on her WhatsApp profile, the one I've been gazing at daily for the past year, doesn't even come close to doing the real-life version justice.

'Here, let me get one with you in it,' she says, turning to face me.

I open my mouth to tell her I look rubbish in photos, but she's already pointing the phone in my direction.

'Smile,' she instructs.

Even though I hate having my picture taken, I do as she tells me, grinning so hard my cheeks hurt. The fact is, I would probably fling myself off the side of this balcony if she asked me to.

I don't ask to see the photo, worrying I might look a bit vain if I do, and Velvet doesn't offer to show me, sliding her phone into the little handbag looped over her shoulder. I don't mind though. There's actually something quite nice and a bit intimate about knowing I'm on her camera roll now, even if the photo itself might be awful. She leans forward and rests her elbows on the railings. I join her, my left shoulder only centimetres from her right one. I can smell her perfume. It's sort of fruity and flowery all at once. I love it.

I dare to edge a tiny bit closer, noticing the blonde hairs on her bare arms are standing on end.

'You're cold,' I say, straightening up and shrugging out of my blazer. 'Here, take this.'

'Don't you want it?'

'Nah, my shirt's plenty warm enough.'

'You sure?'

'Course,' I say, helping her put it on.

'Thanks,' she says, doing up a couple of buttons.

'No problem.'

I love the way it looks on her: the sleeves too long; just her fingertips peeping out. I imagine her wearing other items from my wardrobe – my favourite hoody, my tartan pyjama bottoms, my boxers . . .

Oh God.

She returns to the railings. I glance down to my left at the bright pink cool bag (a fixture at Lindsay family picnics for over four decades) that I've been hauling round with me for the entire party.

It's time.

I take a deep breath, bend down and unzip the cool bag. Nestled on top of the bags of frozen peas and packets of fish fingers (which I shoved in there to keep it chilled) is my golden ticket – a thirty-eight-year-old bottle of champagne.

When my parents got married, back in the very early eighties, they splashed out on a case of champagne to serve at the wedding breakfast. They purposefully kept two bottles aside to pass on to their future children to drink at their own weddings. There's a framed photograph on the mantelpiece at home of my brother Craig popping the cork on his bottle, his wife, Faye, beaming at his side.

My bottle lives in the cupboard under the stairs in a polystyrene-filled cardboard box with 'WEDDING' scrawled on the side in faded black marker pen. At least it did until earlier this evening. Thank God Mum and Dad were still out when I left with it. Even though the champagne is technically mine, they'd lose it if they knew I was planning on drinking it tonight, very much *not* at my wedding. Velvet is worth it though, I'm certain.

I pick up the bottle of champagne, reassuringly heavy in my hands, and contemplate how exactly to play this. I don't want to scare her off with the whole wedding story, but equally I want her to know how special this bottle of champagne is, and how much I want to share it with her. Perhaps I can tell her a half-truth – the bottle *is* left over from my parents' wedding, but it's actually one of several. Yeah, that might work – still romantic, but a bit less full on.

I'm removing the foil with trembling fingers and wishing I'd YouTubed 'how to open a bottle of champagne' when my stomach lets out a massive gurgle.

I freeze, waiting for Velvet to register it and look at me in horror – but luckily she appears to be too engrossed in the view to have heard, gazing out over the water, her expression soft and thoughtful.

I resume my task, discarding the foil and slowly untwisting the wire cage. My stomach gurgles again, only louder and about ten times more insistent.

I put the bottle down on the metal table behind me.

'You OK, Joe?' Velvet asks, glancing over.

'Me? Yeah, fine.'

'You sure? It's just your face has gone a really funny colour.'

Another gurgle – even noisier than the first two put together, and accompanied by some pretty definite movement.

I take a side step away from Velvet and cling on to the railings, silently willing my bowels to let me off the hook and make this a false alarm. I can't leave her now, not when she's wearing my jacket, her hair rippling in the breeze like a goddamn Disney Princess.

But my bowels are clearly not in a cooperative mood, and as horrific as leaving Velvet at this crucial moment is, the possible consequences if I stay are far, far worse. Because, the thing is, and I don't mean to be graphic, but when I need to go, I *really* need to go. And every single second I remain on this balcony is laced with a level of danger I can't even contemplate.

'If you'll excuse m-me for a second,' I stammer. 'I have an, er, important phone call to make.'

Because, even from my very limited experience, no girl ever wants to hear about the massive dump you're about to take.

'OK,' Velvet says, looking slightly confused.

'I'll be right back,' I promise. 'What I mean is, "Don't go anywhere."'

I just about resist sticking a desperate 'please' on the end of my sentence.

I manage to make it through the glass doors and back into the living room like a normal person, before breaking into a panicked run, hurdling over the sofa (my left foot clearing Dawson's head by maybe a centimetre at the most) and skidding down the hallway towards the main bathroom.

Ten minutes later, I flush the toilet for about the twentieth time. And for about the twentieth time, my poo, which I swear is at least a foot long and made of cement, doesn't budge.

I've tried everything – breaking it up with the toilet brush, pouring in hot water from the sink, attempting to hide it with wads of toilet paper, pressing the flush button about a dozen times in quick succession – but *nothing* is working.

Sweaty and exhausted, I sink down on to the floor, my back against the bathtub, and wait for the cistern to fill up again.

When I emerge from the bathroom another ten minutes later, the balcony is empty.

My blazer is draped over the back of one of the metal chairs. The bottle of champagne is gone.

I return to the living room. The only people in here are Dawson and Kaitlyn, huddled at one end of the sofa having what looks like a proper deep and meaningful, their faces only inches apart. I cough loudly. They look up in wary unison.

'You all right, mate?' Dawson asks, clearly annoyed at the interruption.

'Er, have either of you seen Velvet?' I ask, trying my best to sound casual.

'No, sorry,' they say, their voices overlapping.

'OK, thanks . . . Sorry to disturb you.'

I wander into the kitchen, but that's empty too, then stick my head in the bathroom I only recently vacated, relieved to discover it smells OK, before venturing down the corridor towards the bedrooms.

I'm almost level with the door to the master bedroom when Sasha emerges from it, slamming it shut behind her, her face bright red.

When she sees me, she visibly flinches.

'You OK?' I ask.

'Yeah, fine,' she says, unconvincingly, tugging at a clump of her hair as if willing it to grow.

'Look, I don't suppose you've seen Velvet?'

She grimaces. 'Um, you could say that.'

I frown. *What's that supposed to mean?*

'She's in there,' she says, jerking her head at the door behind her.

'Oh, OK,' I say, reaching for the door handle.

'With Hugo,' she adds.

I freeze. 'With Hugo? As in *with* Hugo?'

Sasha nods and pulls another face. 'Gross, right?'

'Right,' I murmur, stumbling back a few steps so I'm leaning against the opposite wall, my hands splayed against the paintwork.

'Wait,' Sasha says, her face crumpling. 'You don't like Velvet . . . do you?'

I hesitate before nodding miserably.

113

'Shit,' she says, covering her mouth with her hand. 'Fuck, I'm so sorry, Joe. I never would have said anything if I knew.'

'No, no, it's fine,' I say. 'I mean, I would have figured it out sooner or later . . .'

She lowers her hand and cocks her head to one side. 'Are you sure you're OK?'

'Positive,' I say, plastering on a smile not dissimilar to the one I did for Velvet when she took my photo.

My phone buzzes – Ivy, I bet. I know she'll say when I tell her all of this: *I told you so.*

'I should probably get that,' I tell Sasha, patting my pocket.

'Oh, OK.'

I turn on my heel and stride back towards the living room and out on to the balcony, where I pull out my phone, expecting to see Ivy's name on the screen. Instead it's filled with missed calls from home.

Frowning, I dial the landline. Dad answers after just one ring.

'Hello, it's me,' I say.

'Joe. Where are you? We've been trying to get hold of you for hours.'

'Sorry,' I say. 'I'm just at Ivy's. My phone was on silent. Is everything OK?'

He sighs.

'What is it, Dad?'

'We went to the hospital today.'

'The hospital? What for?'

'For your mum. The GP referred us.'

'Why didn't you say anything?'

'We didn't want to worry you. Not until we had a diagnosis.'

'A diagnosis? What kind of diagnosis, Dad?'

He chokes out a sob, which, considering the only time I've

ever seen Dad cry was at his mum's funeral earlier this year, is just about the most terrifying sound in the world.

'What kind of diagnosis, Dad?' I repeat, my heart hammering in my chest.

'Al-zheim-er's,' he says in three jerky syllables.

'But that's something old people get,' I say. 'Mum's only sixty.'

'It's early-onset Alzheimer's. People as young as in their forties can get it.'

'But are they sure?'

'They're going to do some more tests, but yes, they're pretty sure.'

I think of the Post-it notes all over the house, the countless forgotten messages and appointments, the lost pairs of glasses and sets of keys, the way Mum gropes for words and gets irritable when we beat her to them.

'Joe? You still there?' Dad says.

'Yeah, I'm here.'

I'm not sure I am though. I feel like I'm floating, but not in a good way.

'Look, we'll talk about it properly tomorrow,' Dad says. 'You, me, Craig and your mum. OK?'

'OK.'

'OK. Have a good night, son. Get home safe.'

There's a pause, then a click as he puts the phone down.

I count to ten, then pick up the pink cool bag and hurl it over the side of the balcony.

HUGO

God, it's been such a night of cock blocks.

I mean, I don't mind. There's nothing I can't hurdle, and it all makes for an even better story to tell the lads later. But still. I'm more pissed off than horny when I finally manage to get Velvet alone on the balcony.

'Well, aren't you just someone who improves a view?' I say, stepping out into the cold air and putting my arm around her like it's a totally normal thing to do. She stiffens initially, surprised by the contact, then softens. Like they always do. I'm handsome and I'm rich; I'm charming and I smell good. It's boring, really, how easy it is. I've rather enjoyed tonight's knobstacle course.

'This flat is amazing,' she gushes, unable to keep a cool edge on things. 'I can't believe you live here.'

I shrug, like it's nothing. To be perfectly honest with you, it *is* nothing. None of us really call this home, it's just Mum's weekly bolthole before she comes back to Putney.

'Hang on,' I say, staring at her intensely. 'You've got an eyelash on your cheek.'

Her hand moves to her face self-consciously.

'It's OK, I've got it.' I reach out gently. 'Close your eyes.'

She obliges, and I lean in and kiss her. Easy as that. Bish, bash, bosh. There's another moment's hesitation before she wraps her arms around the back of my neck and returns my kiss. She tastes of champagne mixed with chewing gum, and I'm instantly horny. This must be one of my longest ever plays. A year – a whole year. But she's just moaned into my mouth, so I reckon the pay-off will be worth it. I pull away, breaking off the kiss, lining up my next move. She looks embarrassed that I've broken it off, her mouth still half open. I smile to reassure her, but only a little. Then reach out and tug on the blazer she's wearing.

'Who gave you this delightful garment?' Though I can hazard a guess: Cock Block Number One.

Velvet giggles and blushes. 'Joe.'

'How very sweet of him.' I raise an eyebrow. 'Should I be jealous?'

I can see her emotional whiplash. The touching, the kissing, the stopping of the kissing, and now acting possessive. She giggles again, and she really does look quite pretty, it has to be said. She's doesn't look like the girls I'm used to – all blow-dries and well-cut tailoring. '*Diamond in the rough*' is what I've been calling her to David and such. I have to win this 'pull a peasant' competition. David will be unbearable otherwise.

'No, there's no need to be jealous.'

She tilts her head up, expecting me to kiss her again, so I don't. I just pull the blazer off and stand behind her, wrapping my arms around her and resting my chin on top of her head. Her shampoo smells of strawberries – slightly cheap and acrid, but not entirely unpleasant. We stay like that, staring out at the skyline for a while, building dramatic tension. I think of all the work I've had to put in to get to this moment. Putting up with the pathetic group WhatsApp filled with stupid videos. Inviting them all up here for the weekend and absorbing their weird jealous hostility that my life is better than theirs.

117

None of them brought anything tonight, can you believe it? The freeloading fuckers! Then there's been the rather complicated process of getting Velvet on her own without her knowing that's what I'm trying to do. This wasn't helped by Puppy Dog Joe mooning over her all evening. Although that's been rather amusing. Do you think he's the one who brought that champagne I see? Watching him twisting himself into knots to impress her, when her eyes have found mine, not his, throughout the night.

My phone buzzes in my pocket.

'Shouldn't you get that?' Velvet looks up, my chin slipping off her head.

I smile like she's more important. 'I'll read it later.'

I know what the message is anyway. It will be from David, asking if I've done it yet. He's been badgering me all night, demanding photographic proof.

She simpers with having my full attention and nudges her arse back into my groin faux-innocently. My whole body stirs. I should move this along now. I really should. She's totally up for it; I'm totally up for it. And yet I find myself looking out at the blinking lights of the city and saying . . .

'Do you ever think of him? Steven, I mean?'

What am I saying? Where did that come from? And yet I find I'm nervous all of a sudden, waiting for her reply.

'Yes,' she answers. 'Every day. I mean, it would be weird if we didn't, wouldn't it? We saw someone die . . .'

'I think about him too,' I find myself admitting. Because I do. His face, and the way it looked, seems to be the favourite feature film my brain plays behind my eyelids. And I think a lot about his funeral, and how nobody fucking came, and how truly pathetic that is. My stomach twists, and I feel my body revolt at this feeling of discomfort. I laugh and say, 'Whoops, sorry –

I'm getting all deep and meaningful.'

Velvet turns around and looks right into my eyes. 'It's OK,' she says softly. 'I don't mind.'

I'm kissing her. I'm kissing her with everything I have, which, let me tell you, is a lot. I'm pushing my crotch into her, grinding my body into hers and plunging my tongue in her champagne-tasting mouth. Then I'm pulling her inside and leading her down the hallway while she giggles and asks where we're going. I reply by kicking the door to the master bedroom open and tugging her towards the bed. I can't wait to touch her. I roughly pull her dress over her head and start kissing her bare shoulders. She lets out a groan, and she may as well have waved a red flag at a bull, because I'm already tugging off my designer jeans with one hand and trying to paw at her knickers with the other. We fall on to each other's bodies and it's all going perfectly to plan when—

A cough.

'What the hell,' I whisper, my head lurching up.

And there, standing in the bath – looking like she's about to shit herself with embarrassment – is Sasha. 'Sorry,' she stammers. Her eyes go to our naked skin, and she frantically tries to look away.

I burst out laughing, because this really is the cock block to end all cock blocks, and she trips as she flees the room. I laugh again into Velvet's mouth as the door slams shut behind me. But she doesn't laugh back.

'Oh God.' Velvet lurches up. 'Do you think we upset her?'

She's covering her eight-out-of-ten body with her hands, and I suppress a groan of exasperation. Will I ever close this? I've been messaged about ten times already this evening, and I can't go back to London without sealing this. I mean, I could always lie. But I'm horny now; I'd rather not have reason to.

119

'She's fine,' I say, and I haven't kept the irritation out of my voice, which is a mistake.

Velvet covers her body further. 'Oh God, I'm so embarrassed!'

My head's racing as I try to work out how to save this. What tactic will work? Charming? Caring? Pushy? Disinterested? I have only a split second to pick one . . . I gently put my arm over her shoulder.

'Hey, don't be embarrassed. She's the one lurking like a creep in a bathtub.'

Velvet laughs and lets me keep my arm there.

'You're so beautiful when you laugh.' I pair the compliment with removing my arm, turning away from her, and starting to put my jeans on. I count in my head . . . One . . . Two . . . Three . . .

'Wait, where are you going?' she asks, as I stand up.

Bingo . . .

I turn to her, feigning surprise. 'Back to the party . . . I thought . . .' I pretend I am embarrassed too. 'I assumed you'd want to go back?'

I watch her weigh up what to say next. She really is a pretty thing. This isn't exactly a bad bet to be following through on. Not like that time Giles made me eat an omelette made of his fried vomit. She reaches out and touches my chest, sending more shocks of lust right to my impatient groin. 'I don't want to go back.'

I smile at her. 'Me neither.'

The mood is dampened though, and it's going to take a while to get her back on course. So I ask her loads of questions about herself and pretend I'm riveted by the answers. Her life sounds fucking ghastly, to be honest. In some rotting seaside town, with only some amoeba called Chelsea to keep her company. She blahs on about liking English at school. I have this weird moment of feeling sorry for her. She's nice. I can tell by the way she talks about books, and I get this twist of something in my gut. I don't like it, so I break off whatever the hell she's saying with a kiss. Velvet responds instantly. And it doesn't take very long to get her dress back off, to have her on the bed, both of us naked. I murmur into her mouth that she's beautiful, and maybe I even mean it. She pauses for a second while I'm putting the condom on.

'What is it?' I ask. Because, yeah I'm shagging the girl for a bet, but only if she actually wants to. I'm not a monster.

'It's nothing. It's just . . .'

'It's your first time?' I'm still being the Caring Guy, though I'm too horny to make this act last must longer.

She nods and blushes. She really is pretty. 'I just . . . thought you should know . . . in case . . . I'm not good or something.'

I silence her worries with a kiss and climb on to her. And I get another twist in my guts, just as I'm about to get there, a feeling that this moment means so much more to her than it ever will to me . . . and then the feeling goes as quickly as it arrives.

VELVET

'Jesus, Velvet – how many times do I have to tell you? Remember the golden rule: legs *or* boobs – never both. Oh well, if you can't be good, be careful . . .'

Those were my mum's final words of wisdom to me when I left the flat earlier. My carrier bag of corner-shop vodka and own-brand Red Bull ready to drink on the train was clanking loudly, and I was wearing the world's tiniest dress, setting off on my way to a strange boy's place – and *that* was the best my mum could do for life advice.

I know she means well. She does her best. And at the time, it seemed funny.

'Thanks, Mum,' I said, grinning as I gave her the middle finger on my way out the door. 'That's massively helpful. In fact, we should probably get a family coat of arms and that could be the motto. We could have it translated into Latin.'

It doesn't seem that funny now. It seems like the reason why I'm the sort of girl who ends up drunk and naked in an unfamiliar bed, feeling a bit sick. The bed seems vast and unfriendly now I'm in it by myself.

It was all good when Hugo was here with me, but the second it was over, he ducked straight into the *very* en-suite shower – semi-visible through the opaque glass in the corner of the bedroom – making me feel a bit grubby and gross. Only a little while ago, I was so happy to have his attention, to be alone with him. But now that happiness feels a bit . . . precarious.

He's been in there ages, giving me more and more time to doubt myself. I'm not sure what I'm meant to do. I can't find my knickers. I don't want to go back out there on my own. Especially after what happened with Sasha.

I thought with these people, I could be someone different. They don't know me as the girl who lives in a dodgy hotel, whose mum always has a new boyfriend she swears is 'different this time'; the girl who everyone knows got fingered by Griffin Collins under the pier. These people seemed to think I was *nice*. Nice and normal, like Sasha, who's so sweet, and Kaitlyn with her cute hair streak. Now Sasha's seen me basically naked, and they'll all think I'm a total slut.

And I'm not, not really. When I told Hugo it was my first time, I wasn't lying. Not quite. Mostly I said it because I was worried he'd think I was crap in bed, but I don't think that time with Griff really counts as actual sex anyway. Under the pier is not the ideal location, and I was drunk, and it just got to the point where I didn't really know how to say no. I couldn't figure out how to make the word come out.

Luckily, the logistics didn't really work – he couldn't get the condom on, and in the end he only had a semi. He sort of tried to stuff it in, and there was a horrible moment when I thought he was trying to stick it up my bum. Then I panicked and said I thought I could hear someone coming and we'd better stop.

Griff was really pissed off. That's probably why he told everyone. And now – ironically – they all say I'm a slut *and* frigid. It's all behind my back, because I'm Chelsea's cousin, and nobody messes with her – but I can hear the whispers, and it's horrible.

I take a deep breath and try to block it out of my head. I was unlucky with Griff, that's all. One drunken mistake. Hugo's not like that. Hugo's a really good person. It's funny, even though we haven't spent much time together, I feel like I really *know* him. I mean, I know his life inside out. I've spent the past year stalking him on social media. Hugo going clubbing with his mates, Hugo with shiny-haired girls who look like racehorses, Hugo on holiday in the Caribbean with no top on . . .

He lives in a totally different world from me, obviously. Which is pretty intoxicating – but it also makes it all the more amazing that we've got this connection. You know, the odds of the two of us meeting like this . . . it's got to *mean* something. I don't want to sound like a total weirdo and say it's *meant to be* – but I kind of can't shake the feeling that it's meant to be.

The sound of running water stops. Hopefully this means Hugo will come out soon, everything will be OK, and he can get the others to leave. My mum won't notice if I come home or not, so I can easily stay the night, just the two of us. Maybe we could spend the rest of the weekend together drinking coffee on the balcony in our dressing gowns, or whatever people with penthouse flats like this do on a Sunday morning. It doesn't matter that I don't even like coffee.

Most importantly, we could finally have the chance to really talk. There's so much to say, and there have been so many obstacles tonight. I know Hugo feels the same – he was looking at me all night like all he wanted was for us to be alone together too. Thank God he's not like Griffin Collins—

Thankfully, my phone beeps and interrupts my thoughts of that creep. I automatically reach for the light in the semi-dark room and see the message flash up on the screen. It takes me a second before it registers.

This is not my phone. Of course it's not. Mine has a cracked screen and a shit cover from Claire's Accessories. This one is newer, shinier, better. Of course it is.

The screen goes dark as I stare at it, but the message is imprinted on my brain. I will never unsee it. I half want to cry and I half want to be sick, but in reality I don't do either. I drop the phone, switch on the bedside light, and go about finding my clothes as quickly as possible. I wrestle myself into my stupid tiny dress – no wonder everyone thinks I'm such a slut – and finally find my knickers over on the other side of the room.

I'm so desperate to escape before Hugo comes out of the shower, I don't bother trying to find my bra. Even though now he'll be able to tell everyone I'm a 32A, and it's mostly padding.

As soon as I leg it out of the bedroom, I run straight into Sasha. Has she been there the entire time?

'Sorry, I was j-just . . . Sorry,' she stammers as I shove my way past her.

Kaitlyn comes out of the kitchen just as I'm by the front door, trying to will myself sober enough to get my sandals on – the multiple little straps are beyond me right now and bending down is not my friend. Taking them off seemed like the polite thing to do when I arrived, what with all the cream carpets in this place, even though Hugo laughed and said I needn't bother. Now I wish I'd trodden dog shit all over the carpet.

If I were braver, I'd do something like that now. Confront him, throw a drink in his face, pour red wine all over the pristine sofa, smash that huge glass vase of lilies on the dining table. But I'm not brave at all. I'm just going to slink away and wait until I'm safely out of sight before I start crying. And then I'll never talk to any of these people again, and nobody ever needs to know this happened. That I was stupid enough to think this time it might be different.

'Velvet, are you OK?' Kaitlyn asks.

I can't even look at her face. It's too kind, confused, and genuinely concerned. I'll start crying, and Hugo will come out and wonder what's going on, and I'll have to tell him what I saw, and that absolutely cannot happen.

'I'm fine. Just getting some air.'

'Hey, then why don't we both go out on the balcony and—'

'Sorry, I've got to go.'

I cut her off mid-sentence and run out of the flat, carrying my shoes in my hands. I feel bad, but I guess it doesn't matter as I'm not going to see any of these people ever again.

'I'll go after her . . .'

Footsteps echo on the stairs behind me. I should probably have taken the lift – but, funnily enough, I'm not that keen on them these days. I run faster and faster, the shiny steps flying underneath my bare feet.

'Velvet – wait!'

I pause for a split second . . . my head spins, and one foot suddenly gives out underneath me. I'm now literally flying down the last set of stairs towards the lobby. I feel my shoulder wrench as I put out an ineffectual hand to try to break my fall, but it's no use and my face meets the marble floor of the grand entrance hall with a brutal smash. I instantly taste blood in the back of my throat.

'Oh my God, Velvet!'

The voice sounds very far away. My shoulder and my knee feel like thunder, my hands come away from my face covered in blood from my nose, and I can feel a shard of tooth rattling around in my mouth, like the wrongest thing in the world.

I look up and I see Joe's face.

'Velvet?' is all he seems able to say.

I want to laugh and tell him he looks worse than I do, like he's just seen a ghost. I want to tell him not to worry about me. But none of that comes out. He looks at me, and I burst into tears. The tears I've been trying so hard to hold in for so long.

Once I start, I can't stop. I cry for everything bad that has ever happened, like I have never done before in my life.

I hide my face in my hands so he can't see me, a mess of tears and snot and blood. I feel him put a hand on my shoulder, very tentatively.

'Don't cry. It's OK. I'm here. Velvet, please don't cry. I . . . I think you're lovely.'

He sounds understandably awkward – after all, he is a boy comforting a weeping, bleeding mess of a girl – but it's weirdly reassuring after Hugo's smooth lines and champagne. Suddenly I'm glad it's Joe here.

Eventually I look up – my face in total horror-movie state – and he is looking at me, and I can see that he was being truthful. He really does think I'm lovely.

His face is so nice, I'm genuinely tempted to fall into his arms and tell him everything, and let him hug me. But I can't. I can't bear to ruin the illusion, the way he's looking at me.

I'm not lovely. I'm gross and common and thick and a slag. I am weird and I don't fit in anywhere.

And Hugo Delaney only shagged me for a bet. His friend David texted him to ask if he'd 'pulled the peasant' yet. I was so fucking stupid, I didn't see it coming. I thought he actually liked me. I thought it meant something – and yes, I know how lame that sounds. I will never make that mistake ever again.

'I'm fine,' I say, pulling myself painfully up off the floor. It hurts, but nothing seems to be broken – not from the fall anyway.

'Velvet, I—'

I can't. I just can't.

'Fuck off,' I snarl, hating myself before the words even leave my mouth.

I limp out of there, still carrying my shoes in my hands. I don't look back.

Joe has never been punched before. Not like a dead-arm punch in the playground, or when Ivy hits him to get his attention if he's distracted by something on his phone – he's had plenty of those – but *properly* punched. That's what it feels like when Velvet says it – *fuck off* – like two swift jabs to his chest.

Then she's gone, and he's left standing there, reeling from the blow. She doesn't even look back, just pushes through the glass doors and heads out into the night, her sandals in her hand. The shock of it winds him, the air rushing out of his lungs with an audible *oof* that makes everything skim out of focus for a second. He can't believe how much it hurts, how much it actually, physically *hurts*. He's hot with it, like a fever that comes from nowhere and devours him whole. He can feel himself swaying, his knees so weak he isn't sure how he's still standing. He tells himself to give into it. It might be nice, he thinks, to lie on the floor for a while, to press his hot cheek to the marble and trace the black feathered veins with the tip of his finger. But the concierge is watching. Joe is aware of him sitting behind the desk in his neat navy suit, and when he lifts his eyelashes to look at him, the concierge turns his face away, and it feels like he's been punched again.

A fresh wave of humiliation burns through him and he's livid with himself because, despite it all – despite the pain in his chest, and his useless, watery legs; despite the fact that Velvet just told him to fuck off – he still wants to go after her and make sure that she's all right. He can't get the image of her splayed across the floor of the lobby out of his head. Even when she was broken, she was beautiful, with her mascara-stained face, rivulets of black leading the way to a bloom of blood the same colour as her lipstick. What was left of it anyway.

All he can think about is how scared she must be, scared and bruised and alone and running, just running. Where's she going? There are no trains this late. How's she going to get back to Bridlington? It's almost midnight. Panic pinches at him as he imagines her sitting at Manchester Piccadilly by herself with her sandals in her hand. But that's Joe, isn't it? Dear, gentle Joe, who's always more worried about everyone else, who feels their pain so much more keenly than his own.

Ivy always tells him that he's too nice.

It doesn't occur to him until that moment that it isn't a compliment.

After the sharp silence of the lobby, upstairs is shockingly loud. Joe can hear them as soon as the lift opens on the top floor, but it isn't like when he first arrived, the sound of a champagne bottle popping and Hugo's booming laugh letting him know which way to go. No, this is different. Hugo's shouting, and not in his usual, obnoxious way. And not to make himself heard over the Rihanna track that's so loud, Joe can feel the buzz of it in the floorboards under his feet. He's *really* shouting. And Kaitlyn is shouting back.

Joe walks a little faster as he heads toward the apartment. Now he can hear Dawson as well, and the sound of his raised voice is enough to make him break into a sprint. He's halfway down the hall when a door swings open and an elderly lady in a pink silk robe appears, a Pomeranian dog under her arm.

'This is a disgrace!' She points in the direction of Hugo's flat. 'That boy is a menace!'

Joe can't disagree with that.

'Always has been,' she goes on, 'even when he was a child, running up and down the hall like a hellion!' She turns her finger on Joe. 'I don't care who his mother is, I'm telling the residents' association.'

'I'm sorry—' Joe starts to say, but the door slams firmly in his face.

He runs the few remaining feet to the apartment. The front door is open, and he follows the sound of voices to find Hugo standing in the middle of the living room wearing nothing but a white towel around his waist. He must have just got out of the shower, Joe deduces from the towel and the fact that he's dripping on to the glossy walnut floor. Hugo doesn't notice Joe standing in the doorway; none of them do, as Kaitlyn, Sasha and Dawson circle him, each of them flushed and furious.

'What's going on, guys?' Joe frowns, but they don't hear him as Hugo tells Kaitlyn to chill.

Hugo says it with such disdain that it provokes the opposite reaction.

'Chill?' she hisses. '*Chill?*'

Kaitlyn's never hit anyone in her life, but it's all she can do not to reach over and slap the smirk clean off Hugo's stupid, smug face. If he pretended to give even half a shit, maybe she wouldn't be so mad, but his nonchalance is making her so angry she can feel her whole body throbbing with it.

'What happened, Hugo? What did you do to her?'

'I told you: I didn't *do* anything.'

'Why was she in such a state then?'

'I don't know.'

'You're lying, Hugo.'

'No, I'm not.'

'You are. You know how I can tell?' Kaitlyn stops to arch an eyebrow at him. 'Your lips are moving.'

'Yeah, good one.' He rolls his eyes. 'Sick burn.'

He laughs – fucking *laughs* – and Kaitlyn finds herself grateful

130

that there's a coffee table between them. He knows that he's crossed a line (she'll give him that, at least. Hugo's an insufferable asshole, but he's not stupid) because he has the sense to take a step back. Sasha is standing behind him though, so he almost walks into her as he does, and spins around to face her, only to find her looking equally angry. Clearly cornered, he hesitates for a moment before turning back to face Kaitlyn.

'What did you *do* to her, Hugo?' she repeats.

He sighs theatrically. 'I told you.' He speaks slowly, like she's a toddler demanding an ice cream at the park, which makes Kaitlyn's cheeks sting. 'When I got out of the shower, she was gone.'

'Why?'

'I don't know. She's just being dramatic.'

'Dramatic about what? You must have done *something* to make her run off like that?'

'The last time I saw her, Velvet was fine.' He licks his lips lasciviously. 'More than fine.'

'Yeah, because it's normal to run off crying after sex.'

Hugo scoffs. 'Like you've had sex!'

Kaitlyn wishes she was holding something so she could throw it at him, but that's what he wants, for her to lose her temper so he can dismiss her as dramatic as well. She tries a different tactic. And it works, because when she takes her phone out of the back pocket of her jeans, Hugo hesitates for the first time.

'Who are you calling?' he asks, his bare chest noticeably pinker.

Kaitlyn ignores him, tapping at her phone then holding it to her ear.

'You're not calling the police, are you?' His chest is red now. 'I told you: Velvet's fine.'

When Kaitlyn doesn't reply, just turns her back so he can't see her smile, he looks concerned.

Dawson hates that he feels a shiver of pleasure as he watches

131

Hugo squirm, but he's never seen Hugo look anything other than completely composed, so it's satisfying to see him sweat. So he can't help but feel disappointed when Kaitlyn stops pacing and says, 'Velvet, it's me. You OK? Call me when you get this.'

Hugo's shoulders fall when he realizes that she's called Velvet, not the police.

Dawson walks over to Kaitlyn and places a reassuring arm across her shoulder. 'Keep trying. I'm sure she'll pick up soon.'

Hugo rolls his eyes. 'I don't understand why you guys are freaking out,' he says, bravado restored. 'I'm the one who should be upset. She got what she wanted and ran off. I feel so used.' With this, he puts a hand to his chest and sighs theatrically, one eye on Dawson.

Dawson knows that he's trying to wind him up, but falls for it anyway, taking a step toward him.

'What did you *do*?' He jabs a finger at Hugo's chest. 'I know you did something!'

'Ow!' he whines, rubbing his chest, then chuckles.

The sound of it makes Dawson's blood pressure spike, but before he can tell himself not to fall for it again, Hugo gestures at the door to the living room, and Dawson turns to see Joe standing there with his hands in his pockets.

'Joseph!' Hugo says. 'Will you tell this lot that Velvet is fine.'

But he doesn't say anything as Dawson wonders how long he's been standing there.

'Is she OK?' Dawson frowns. 'What did she say?'

'Nothing,' Joe finally says.

Dawson's frown deepens. 'Nothing?'

'She just ran off.'

Joe won't look at him, and Dawson knows he's lying, but before he can call him on it, Hugo pipes up, a broad smirk on his face.

'See? I told you – she's just being dramatic.'

Dawson isn't convinced.

Hugo must see that because he adds, 'This is how girls get after sex – all emotional. You'd know that if you'd ever slept with one.'

'You're a pig!' Sasha says suddenly.

It's the first time she's spoken, and they both turn to look at her.

'All men are pigs, Sasha,' Hugo tells her, unfazed at the insult. 'Some of us are *Spam*.' He looks pointedly at Joe and winks. 'And some of us are purebred Ibérico, but we're all pigs, sweetheart.'

'I'm not your sweetheart.'

There's a long moment of silence as Sasha and Hugo stare at each other across the living room. He's waiting for her to look away first, but she won't give him the pleasure and holds her head up defiantly.

Hugo's eyes light up at the challenge. 'I'm not saying nothing happened,' he concedes.

Sasha's gaze narrows, suspicious of his sudden sincerity.

'Something obviously *happened* . . .' He waits another beat. 'But it was all above board. Everyone consented.' He stops and smiles. 'I mean, you were watching, right?'

There's a rush of gasps from the others, and when she hears Dawson say, *What?* her stomach lurches so suddenly, she's sure she's going to puke. Why did she eat those bloody olives?

'I wasn't watching,' she says, her cheeks stinging. 'You walked in on me while I was in the bathroom.'

'Whatever.' He waves his hand dismissively. 'You were there. Velvet was fine, wasn't she?'

Sasha hesitates.

She was fine.

She seemed fine.

Was she fine?

She can feel them all staring as they wait for her to respond, but she can't catch her breath, like she's just run for the bus. A Drake song starts playing, and it's so loud she can feel the bass line vibrating in her teeth.

'Can we turn the music off?' She puts her hands in her hair and pulls. 'I can't hear myself think!'

'Where's my phone?' Hugo looks around the living room, then walks toward the hall.

Kaitlyn steps into his path. 'Where are you going?'

'To get my phone so I can turn the music off. It's in the bedroom.'

'No, you stay here where I can see you.' She nods at Joe. 'You go.'

Joe does as he's told, trying not to look at the tangled sheets as he searches for Hugo's phone. He checks the bedside table, and his heart leaps up on to his tongue when he sees it: Hugo's phone and, right next to it, the bottle of his parents' wedding champagne. He picks it up to find that it's half empty, a smear of red lipstick around the rim. He wants to lob it across the room, but then Hugo's phone lights up, and his gaze is drawn down to the screen. There's a string of messages from someone called David.

Come on, Delaney, admit defeat
I knew you couldn't do it
Dude, don't leave me hanging
You pulled the peasant yet?

Joe almost drops the phone.

'I think I know what happened to Velvet,' Joe announces when he walks back into the living room.

'Enlighten us, young Joseph.'

Hugo's still parading around in a towel like it's perfectly normal, and the muscles in Joe's shoulders tighten at the sight. He wouldn't even do that in front of Ivy.

134

'I reckon she saw this.' Joe holds up the phone. 'That's why she was so upset – why she ran off.'

Hugo clearly has no idea what he's talking about. 'Saw what?'

'The message from your friend David.' Joe reads it aloud: '*You pulled the peasant yet?*'

Hugo's smile slips for the first time. He looks genuinely embarrassed, but recovers quickly.

'What?' He laughs as the others glare at him. 'It's a joke. Lighten up.'

He laughs again, and something in Joe gives way, like a shelf buckling under the weight of too many books. Joe's never punched anyone. He's wanted to, many times, but he's always managed to restrain himself. This time, however, he doesn't even think about it, just swings, but Hugo steps back, and Joe almost face-plants into the sofa. He manages to stop himself before he does, but Sasha has to help him up.

Joe's mortified. He can feel himself blushing from his scalp right down to his toes, and when Hugo laughs and says, 'Careful. Don't hurt yourself, Joseph,' he has to ball his hands into tight fists at his sides to restrain himself.

Hugo doesn't look scared or even annoyed, just faintly amused, and it provokes another heave of fury. But then Dawson is between them, his hands on Joe's shoulders as he tells him to calm down. He almost does, but just as he's about to step back, Hugo smiles at him over Dawson's shoulder, and Joe furiously swings at him again. He has to reach around Dawson to do so, which gives Hugo enough time to step out of the way, and Joe ends up punching the wall instead.

There's a moment of screeching white noise . . . then pain. Pain like he's never felt before . . . and blood.

So much blood.

Hot, bright red blood.

Joe howls, and Kaitlyn is there, at his side, hand cupping his. He can hear Hugo chuckling, and he wishes he was dead, wishes that the fancy Italian sofa would just open up and swallow him whole. The sound of it immediately makes him think of that morning his mother got out of the house while he was in the shower. When he got downstairs to find the front door open, he panicked and ran out into the street to find a group of lads across the road laughing and pointing at his mother who was waiting by the post box in her dressing gown.

'Where's the bus?' she'd asked when he got to her. 'I'm going to be late for work.'

Joe just smiled and took her by the elbow, leading her back towards the house.

'Mad ol' bat,' one of the boys had said as he did, and the look on his mother's face when she realized that he was talking about her made Joe's heart snap clean in two.

'I'm fine. I'm OK,' he tells Kaitlyn, his chin shivering.

But she isn't looking at him, she's looking down at his shoes, and Joe does as well to find his white Converse spotted with blood.

'It's nothing.' He tries to shrug, but even that hurts. 'I just need some ice.'

'I think it's broken,' Kaitlyn says softly.

Of course it is, Joe thinks.

At least he can cross 'Never Punched or Been Punched' off his bucket list.

They all go with Joe to the hospital, with the exception of Hugo, who they leave alone in the flat trying to get the blood out of his mother's Gandia Blasco rug. He's called the cleaner four times, but it's 2 a.m., and she's not answering. So when he hears a knock on the front door, he all but runs, hoping it's her.

But it's not.

It's Velvet.

'Oh,' he says.

That's it – just, *Oh*.

Not, *What are you doing here?*

Not, *Are you OK?*

Not, *I'm sorry.*

Just, *Oh*.

Velvet didn't know a word so small could feel so big.

A couple of hours ago, she would have just barged past him into the flat, but that was before. Before he found the mole on the inside of her thigh with his fingers, before he swept his mouth along her collarbone and said her name like no one else had before, like it was a brand-new word. Now she just wants to run and keep running until she's as far away from Hugo – the memory of him, the smell of his hair, and the weight of him on top of her – as she can be. But to her surprise, she finds herself able to lift her chin and look at him.

'I forgot my phone,' she says, her voice sounding much steadier than she feels.

She waits a beat, for what she doesn't know, there isn't anything he can say, is there? But she still wants him to try and holds her breath while she waits for him to say something – anything – to make her heart stop beating so hard, but he just takes a step back.

'I think I left it in the bedroom,' she says, her voice less steady this time.

He nods.

'Can I go get it?'

He nods again.

Velvet realizes that 'Oh' is all he's going to say, so she mutters a thank you and walks past him into the flat. She holds her breath as she does, half expecting to find the others in the living room, laughing and sipping what's left of the booze – but they're not there, and she feels a stab of something. Shame, maybe? Guilt, definitely. But what was she supposed to say? That she's a gross, common, thick slag who fell for Hugo Delaney's bullshit?

Velvet avoids looking at the bed as she walks into the bedroom. The lights are off, which helps, so there's only the light spilling in from the hall to navigate by. She checks the bedside table, but her phone isn't there, just the bottle of champagne she and Hugo had shared on the balcony. Her stomach knots at the memory of it, the fizz of it on her tongue, how he kissed her and said she tasted like the first time he'd tasted champagne – a bottle of Veuve Clicquot he'd swiped at his cousin's wedding and drunk by himself in the garden.

She walks around the bed and lets go of the breath she's been holding when she finally spots her phone on the other bedside table. Picking it up, she can feel the cracked glass under her fingers as she curls them around it. She heads out into the hall, back the way she came, to find Hugo still standing by the front door.

'Bye, I guess,' she says, because she has to say *something*.

She waits a beat, but Hugo doesn't reply, so she dips her head and walks past him out the open door.

'Don't . . .' he starts to say, then stops to shrug. 'Don't read too much into it. It's not a big deal. It was nothing.' He shrugs again. 'Just a joke.'

You're the fucking joke, she thinks.

The trouble is, he isn't talking about them; he's talking about the bet.

'Shouldve taken the stairs'
Hugo Delaney has left

Kaitlyn:
Shame

Dawson:
Fuckity bye

Joe:
You were right about us not calling ourselves the Lift Six, Sash . . .

Sasha:
☺ Did you get home OK, Velvet?

Velvet:
Yeah. Thanks, guys. I'm fine

Joe:
☺ We're going to keep going with this group though, right?

YEAR THREE

Joe:

Hey guys! I've just worked out it's nearly a year since we last hung out. Wanna try to arrange something? For the anniversary, I mean

Sasha:

Hopefully no risk of bloodshed this time . . .

Joe:

I solemnly promise not to use the fists of fury . . .

Kaitlyn:

What kind of thing were you thinking?

Joe:

I dunno. I just want to see you all really

Sasha:

Awwwww. That would be nice, actually

Dawson:

I'm in

Kaitlyn:

Sure, I'm up for that. Somewhere in Manchester?

Joe:

Works for me. I can get the bus in

Sasha:

Manchester def easiest for me

Dawson:

Well, as a DRIVER, with a CAR OF HIS OWN, may I just say I'm easy with wherever . . .

Joe:

That OK for you, Velvet? We can make it a day thing if that's easier (and if that's OK with the rest of you)?

Velvet:

Sorry, guys! Nice idea, but you'll have to count me out ☹ It's a bit far for me and I can't really afford the train. Have a great time!

Sasha:

☹ x a million

Joe Lindsay created group 'To the rescue!'
Joe Lindsay added Sasha Harris
Joe Lindsay added Kaitlyn Thomas
Joe Lindsay added Dawson Sharman

Joe:
Guys, is there anything we can do?? Club together to pay for Velvet's train fare or something??

Kaitlyn:
I'd love to help, but can we find out how much first?

Sasha:
Um . . . it's £££

Joe:
But it won't be the same without Velvet.

I mean, it wouldn't be the same with any of us missing

Kaitlyn:
cough Hugo *cough*

Joe:
Apart from him

Kaitlyn:
Maybe we could go to Velvet? Where does she live?

Sasha:
Bridlington. It's miles and miles and miles away. Um . . . I can't afford ¼ of the train fare. No way can I get the money for all of it. ☹☹☹

Dawson:

Sounds like you guys need a car. And a licensed driver . . .
If only you knew such a man . . . A cool, funny man, who
recently passed his test and knows his way around a vehicle . . .

Joe:

Do I hear road trip???

Dawson:

All I want, literally ALL I WANT, is for one of you to be impressed
I can now drive. That's all. You don't deserve Tallulah

JOE

I'm brushing my teeth when I get a text from Ivy saying she's outside.

I frown. Even though we finished our exams over six weeks ago, Ivy and I have only hung out a handful of times, and on at least seventy-five per cent of those occasions, she's been grumpy and/or distracted.

'Were you in bed?' she asks when I open the front door in my pyjamas.

She's drunk. Sober Ivy has posture to die for; Drunk Ivy is swaying like a Tokyo skyscraper in an earthquake.

'Nearly,' I say. 'I've got to be up early to go to Bridlington.'

'Oh yeah, to see your new *besties*.' She says 'besties' with air quotes. 'Well, aren't you going to ask me in?'

'Oh, yeah, sure,' I say. 'We'll have to be quiet though – my mum and dad have just gone to bed.'

In the dark living room, Ivy heads straight for the drinks trolley.

'Maybe we should have a sit-down first,' I say, steering her towards the sofa. She must have caught her foot on the corner of the rug or something, because seconds later, she's crashing towards the floor, dragging me down on top of her.

'Shit, Ivy – are you OK?'

She answers me by looping her arms round my neck and

sticking her cider-soaked tongue in my mouth.

I scramble away from her in shock, smacking the back of my head on the fireplace.

'It's because of that Velvet girl, isn't it?' she slurs.

'What? No. I told you, I'm over her.'

I touch the back of my head. It's wet. Shit, am I bleeding?

'Don't lie,' Ivy says.

'I'm not.'

'If you're over her, why are you going to see her?'

'It's not just me. We're all going.'

She snorts.

'Honestly, Ives. We're just mates.'

'The same way *we're* "just mates"?' (The air quotes again.)

'What?'

'Forget it.' She staggers to her feet.

'Where are you going?'

'Where do you think? Home.'

'Can't we talk first?'

'No, Joe, we can't,' she spits. 'Have fun in Bridlington.'

'You've got blood in your hair,' Sasha says.

It's the following morning, and we're standing in a lay-by waiting for Dawson and Kaitlyn to pick us up.

'It's a scab,' I reply, touching it gingerly. 'I hit my head on the fireplace.'

'How'd you manage to do that?'

'Long story.'

'Long stories are my favourite.'

I'm saved by the bell, or more accurately, the car horn.

'What's in the humungous bag?' Dawson asks as Sasha and I pile on to the back seat.

'Just a few snacks,' Sasha says breathlessly, plonking the

bulging plastic bag between us.

'It's only a two-and-a-half-hour drive,' Dawson points out.

'I know,' Sasha says, ripping open a bag of Haribo a bit too enthusiastically, sweets flying everywhere. 'It's just that I've never been on a road trip before. I mean, not with mates anyway.'

Sasha waggles the bag under everyone's nose before picking out a cola bottle for herself. 'I, er, put together a bit of a playlist too,' she continues, her cheeks reddening as she gets her phone out. 'We don't have to listen to it, or anything. I mean, it might be shit . . . in fact, it probably is. So if you don't like it, just say so, and we can put the radio on or something instead, I honestly won't mind . . .'

'Oh, just give me your phone,' Dawson says.

Sasha needn't have worried – her playlist is perfect summer anthem after summer anthem, and as we weave through the city-centre traffic, windows wound down and music blasting, my worry and confusion about the Ivy situation starts to fade.

That's the thing about this lot – we may not have much in common beyond what happened in that lift, but there's something comforting about our limited shared history that lets me take a break from my everyday life for a bit. When I'm messaging them, I'm not Joe Lindsay, Uber Swot; or Joe Lindsay, Disappointing Best Friend; or Joe Lindsay, Dutiful Son. I'm just Joe, and I like that.

'You're a dead good driver, Dawson,' Sasha says as we join the M62. 'Did you pass first time?'

'Yeah.'

'How many lessons?'

'I dunno. Five, maybe.'

'Five! My cousin had forty-two. And he *still* failed.'

'I had to learn for some scenes on *Dedman High*, so I kind of had a head start.'

Sasha and I exchange a split-second glance. It's rare Dawson makes any reference to his TV past, at least not in front of the two of us. I hold my breath, wondering if he'll elaborate, but instead he turns the music up and asks Kaitlyn to unwrap him another Maoam stripe.

At the service station, I blow the last of my pocket money on a dozen Krispy Kremes. I'm waiting for the others near the fruit machines, when I notice Kaitlyn coming towards me. Even though she gave us the heads-up about it on WhatsApp, it's still a bit of a shock to see her using a white cane.

'Those smell amazing,' she says, stopping at my side.

I notice the streak in her hair is now lavender, and I wonder if she did it herself.

'She'll love them,' she adds.

'Who?'

'Velvet.'

'They're for all of us,' I say quickly.

'Yeah, yeah.'

'They *are*,' I say, thrusting the box of doughnuts under Kaitlyn's nose. 'Have one if you don't believe me.'

'Maybe later,' she says, a small smile playing on her lips.

I check my phone. Nothing from Ivy. I can't decide if I'm disappointed or relieved.

'How's your mum doing?' Kaitlyn asks as I slide my phone back in my pocket.

I hesitate. Part of me wants to confide in Kaitlyn. She, of all people, knows what it's like to have your life turned upside down by something you can't control. The other, much bigger part wants to shove all my stress and worry about Mum, along with the weird Ivy mess, in the locked drawer at the very back of my brain, at least until we get back to Manchester.

Even though I know it can't actually be the case, it's like getting the Alzheimer's diagnosis sped up Mum's symptoms. She's gone from having occasional bad days to going weeks without a single good one, asking the same questions over and over, and getting upset when our answers fail to satisfy her, or she can sense us losing our patience. Poor Dad is in bits.

I realize Kaitlyn is waiting for me to respond.

'She's doing OK,' I say eventually. 'You know, up and down.'

Kaitlyn must sense I don't really want to go into it, because she just gives my arm a sort of pat and asks me to earmark an original glazed for her.

The Ambassador Hotel is a bit more rundown than it looks on its website. Tatty net curtains hang at the windows, and the sign above the door proclaiming 'Vacancies' flashes wearily, half the bulbs either dead or on their last legs.

Inside, the lobby is dark and narrow, and smells of cooked breakfasts and furniture polish.

And the perfume Velvet wears.

And just like that, I'm catapulted back in time to Hugo's party, to the last time I saw her, milky mascara tears running down her lovely face like a tragic heroine in a black-and-white film.

And then I clock her, dragging a vacuum cleaner down the hallway towards us, all sun-kissed and freckly and gorgeous and perfect, and my heart is in my mouth, and there's a full-on butterfly farm in my belly, and I know I've spent the last year kidding myself.

Because I, Joe Lindsay, am as mad about Velvet Brown as ever.

Shit.

VELVET

'I don't really see the point in education. What am I going to do with it – get a job? That's for mugs . . .'

I half listen to Griff, distracted from his droning on by my own far-more-pressing concerns. There are so many things for me to be embarrassed about. The fact that Joe, Sasha, Kaitlyn and Dawson Sharman came barrelling into the hotel – all shiny and excited and giggling – while I was pushing Henry Hoover round the brown-patterned carpet and singing along with Heart FM is just one of them. I was really giving it some to 'Total Eclipse of the Heart' as well.

I tried my hardest to hide the utter horror on my face, but I genuinely could not comprehend how they didn't realize 'I can't afford the train ticket' actually translated as 'I don't want to be rude, but I don't fancy it, thanks'. It definitely did not mean 'please turn up at my place unannounced while I'm working'.

I was so shocked to see them, I tripped over and whacked myself in the shin with the vacuum cleaner. Bloody Henry bashed into me with more brute force than I would have thought possible from his smiley cartoon face. Serves me right for refusing to wear the proper chambermaid's uniform – that's what Nan would say. Flip-flops and tiny denim shorts are not appropriate clothes for industrial cleaning. The shorts are way too tight for me at the moment as well: not only are they riding up my bum crack, but the waistband is digging in like a medieval torture device. I'm going to have a bruise, right next to the curly 'G' on my ankle – the tattoo's a couple of months old now, but I didn't follow the aftercare instructions properly, and it's already a bit patchy and sad-looking.

'Surprise!' they all chorused.

'Shit,' was all I could say, while wincing in pain and wishing the nasty threadbare carpet would swallow me whole.

It's like they think I'm Cinderella, and they've come to rescue me or something. The irony is, I was having a pretty good day until they turned up. I actually really like cleaning, and vacuuming's my favourite. Sometimes when I'm pushing Henry around or scrubbing bathrooms, I think: Poor the Queen – she probably never gets to do her own cleaning. She doesn't know what she's missing; how satisfying it can be.

I love mundane work, which is a good thing around here. The repetitive actions are like meditation, or hypnosis, taking me outside my own head for once, making life as small – and safe – as possible.

I had been looking forward to the shower and bacon sandwich I was going to have as soon as I'd finished up, while Griff, no doubt, sat and watched telly in our poky little staff quarters. My days have a pleasing familiarity to them, as they stretch out before me. It's how I like it.

I was not expecting to be disrupted like this. Trekking to the seafront, making conversation, picking at chips and feeling sick at the smell of vinegar. I'm stuck wearing the stupid too-short shorts and my baggy work T-shirt because I didn't have time to get changed before I hustled this lot out of the hotel as quickly as possible. I don't even have any make-up on; I look proper disgusting. If Joe ever thought I was lovely, he definitely won't any more.

Still – somehow – none of this is what I feel the most embarrassed about.

'. . . I mean, education's sort of like voting, isn't it?' Griff goes on. 'Never going to make any difference.'

My hand is sweaty, as he won't let go of it, even while he's busily eating half my chips. I knew he would insist on coming with me and 'my friends' to the beach. I thought about trying to get away with not telling him we were going, but it wouldn't be worth it. Last weekend, he stormed out and left me at Rikki's party by myself because he thought I was looking at Alex White 'in a flirty way'. For the record, I hadn't even realized Alex was standing there.

This may partially explain why I am sitting here in a state of quiet panic, worrying that someone might mention Hugo. I really, really do not want to have to explain to Griff who Hugo is. I don't even want to *think* about Hugo. He is locked inside a box somewhere in my brain labelled Things I Pretend Never Happened.

'Well, I mean . . . obviously everyone's different,' Sasha says kindly, trying to hide the fact that everyone has gone quiet. 'Loads of people do well without going to uni.'

I know I should try to keep the conversation going, as this is all my fault – it's my boyfriend who's shut down their nice conversation about what they're planning to do after their A levels next year. It's not their fault Griff and I aren't doing sixth form. Until now, I hadn't really thought I was missing out – I mostly hated school anyway, and it's been quite cosy, living with Griff in the hotel. It's been a few months now, and it still feels like a sleepover rather than my real, actual life.

'So, what are you planning to do, Velvet?' Joe asks me. 'I remember you saying you were really into creative writing?'

How can he still be so *nice*, after everything? It's all so awkward. This is why I barely contribute to the WhatsApp group, even the new one that doesn't include Hugo. I haven't been able to find the words to talk about what happened last time we saw each other, so I guess I'll always just feel embarrassed and guilty about telling him to fuck off when he did not remotely deserve it.

'Oh, I . . . dunno.' I can't look him in the eye, and I feel myself turning red. 'I mean, I quite like working in the hotel. It's fine for now.'

'For now? Face it, we're not going anywhere!' Griff laughs, even though nobody else does.

I've found myself cringing at everything he says today, and I hate myself for it. I feel like such a traitor; I should be pleased I've finally got a boyfriend who really likes me. I certainly never expected Griffin Collins to want to go out with me – but since we got past what happened between us before, I've realized he can actually be really sweet, when he's not acting like an idiot. It's nice having a boyfriend. I like having someone to look after, someone to have a laugh with; just someone who I know will be there all the time.

It's only now I'm seeing him through other people's eyes that I'm embarrassed. I'm an awful human being. I wish these people had just left me alone to get on with my life; I don't need the disruption.

It's just . . . I hate to admit it, even to myself. Their conversations about uni and personal statements and UCAS points sound quite exciting – they can do anything they want, unlike me. I'm stuck. I never realized it before, but sitting here on the beach with Griff clutching my sweaty hand, it's obvious. Stuck. *Forever*. I mean, for-actual-ever.

Even if I wanted to change my mind, it's too late for me now.

I haven't told anyone yet, but it won't be long before I have to. My shorts aren't just too tight from all those bacon sandwiches in the hotel kitchen.

I'm pregnant.

DAWSON

I never thought I'd meet anyone who was more of a tosser than my ex, Josh, but I'm happy to report that Griffin 'Call me Griff' Collins has, in fact, taken that mantle from him. Mum was right: you do learn something new every day.

Though you *could* argue that Griff is marginally a better person than Josh, because he doesn't actually mind being seen with Velvet. He can't keep his hands off her. It's as if she's made of iron, and his hands are magnets: hand on arse, hand on waist, hand on the back of her neck. He even casually just touched her boob as he pulled her on to his lap. Just popped his hand on it for a second and gave it a light squeeze, like he was checking it was still there. I glance at Kaitlyn, and the outrage on her face tells me she saw it too, and if Griff isn't careful, she'll end up belting him with her stick.

I hope she does. That might make this entire horror show worth it. Even an eight-hour shift at Thunder Burger would have been more fun, and a shitload less awkward. We should have pulled Velvet into the car and kept driving. I could have accidentally reversed over Griff. I doubt anyone except Velvet would miss him.

It was Griff's idea to come to the pub, which was great in theory, as I expect he's significantly more fun to be around if you're drunk. But I'm driving, so I can't drink. Velvet refuses too, and Joe shakes his head after a quick glance at her. Kait doesn't like drinking unless she's somewhere she feels comfortable, and Sasha pats her tummy, saying she's too full.

'I don't bother with all that craft beer stuff,' Griff says, with the air of a man who's seen and done it all. 'Poncey, overpriced southern crap. I like a proper beer. Get us a Carling, love.'

I have to actually bite my tongue so I don't reply, 'Yes, Carling. That most proper of beers. Or lager, as it's often known.'

He sends Velvet off to the bar with a fiver, slapping her on the bum as she stands, and she frowns for a split second, before giggling. The giggle sounds fake. In fact, everything about her today is a bit fake. Fake smile. Fake enthusiasm. It's like she's had some kind of personality transplant. Another glance at Kait watching Griff with narrowed eyes makes me think we're on the same page, and I pull my phone from my pocket to message her, when Griff leans over, all pally like.

'So what about you, Daws?' he says.

'What about me?' I'm ignoring the fact he called me Daws.

Kait gets her phone out. When mine buzzes in my hand, I glance down to see she's messaged me.

Hey, DAWS.

I quickly type back *Piss off*, and put my phone away. I can practically feel her grin.

Griff has continued, oblivious. 'You were a bit quiet on the beach. What are you doing with your life now? You got a job?'

'Yes . . .' I say warily.

'A proper one, or more acting shit?'

Kait sucks in a sharp breath, so I quickly answer. 'I don't act any more, actually. I'm working part time in a burger place in Manchester for now.'

He nods. 'You gonna go full time?'

I suppress a shudder. 'Probably not. It's not a permanent

kind of thing. I was actually thinking about applying to college . . .'

'You should think about going full time,' he says, nodding sagely. 'You could be a manager in five years. My cousin did that, and he's regional manager now at Spoons.' He looks over at the pub door and misses the look of horror on my face. 'So, how long have you two been together then?' he says, still watching for Velvet.

All four of us stare back at him. Does he seriously think Sasha and Joe are together? Joe hasn't stopped making moon eyes at Velvet all day.

'It's funny if you think about it,' he turns back to us. 'A blind girl and the guy who's famous for getting ugly. Ironic.'

I stare at him, a weird kind of buzzing in my ears. Sasha and Joe look between us, both looking as stunned as I feel. Sasha frowns, and Joe opens his mouth, but Kait gets there first.

'Are you fucking kidding me?'

'What? I don't mean it in a bad way.' He holds up his hands. 'No offence, mate. It's just funny, isn't it? And it's not like you're ugly any more. Not that I'm homo, or nothing.'

Kaitlyn rises to her feet. 'Fuck this.'

'What's going on?' Velvet has finally returned, a pint in one hand and a Coke in the other.

'Your boyfriend is a prick, is what's going on. You can't half pick them,' Kaitlyn spits, and then she's off, marching back down the seafront, swinging her cane in front of her viciously, clearly heading towards the car.

'What did you say?' Velvet stares at Griff, spilling the drinks.

'I didn't say anything,' Griff snaps back.

'Well, why is Kaitlyn leaving?' Velvet demands.

'I'm going after Kait,' I lean over and whisper to Joe.

'Do you want us to come?' he asks.

I shake my head. 'Make sure Velvet is all right,' I say, and he nods. 'If we're not by the car, message us.' I give a quick smile to Sasha, and then jog after Kaitlyn.

'Fucking prick,' she says as I draw level with her. 'Fucking, fucking *prick*!' She's shouting now, and an old couple passing give us a scandalized look.

'Hey,' I move in front of her and gently take her by the arms. For a second, I think she's going to wallop me, but she lets me guide her to a bench on the seafront. We sit down, thighs pressed together, and I reach out and take her hand, pulling it into my lap. 'Don't let him get to you. He's a knob. I bet Velvet told him about your eyes, and he was too thick to understand it. He's not worth it.'

'That's not why I'm angry.' She shoots me a furious look. 'I'm angry because that was a shit thing to say about you. Homophobic twat. He just literally "no homo'd" you. And you were *never* ugly.'

I'm a little stunned by that. 'I don't care about that stuff any more,' I manage.

'Well, I do!' Her face is red with fury, and the people over in the shack selling buckets and spades are staring to stare. 'He had no right—'

I quietly sing "Be Cool, Be Calm (And Keep Yourself Together)".

And it does what I hoped it would, and disarms her.

'Idiot,' she says, but it's softer, and she's fighting a smile.

We had a really deep chat last year at Hugo's, about her eyes, and what it meant. What it might stop her from doing. And for some reason, the only blind person that I could think of at the time was Stevie Wonder, and I told her that being blind hadn't stopped him.

160

I thought, for a second, she was going to punch me.

But she didn't. She burst out laughing, and the next thing we were watching videos of him on YouTube, and sharing my earphones, and it was fun.

Until Velvet ran past, crying, and Joe tried to deck Hugo.

I have a lot of regrets about stopping him.

But, something changed after that between me and Kait. At some point, we became actual friends: hanging-out-in-the-week, messaging-all-day-and-all-night friends. I can't remember the last time she wasn't the first person I spoke to in the morning, and the last person at night. They're all my friends – Joe, Sash, Velvet – but Kait is my best friend of them.

Actually, I think Kait is my best friend of anyone.

Huh.

I'd googled everything I could about Stargardt disease when I got home that night. And I listened to a lot more Stevie Wonder. Mum was deeply confused; apparently my nan on my dad's side loved him, he's that ancient. He's pretty classic though, I reckon. And it's cool he didn't let being blind stop him from chasing his dreams.

I squeeze her hand and croon "Don't You Worry 'bout a Thing", wiggling my eyebrows.

She smacks me over the legs with her stick. 'Fuck off,' she mumbles, but I can hear her smile.

My phone buzzes, and I check it, expecting it to be Joe or Sasha, but it's Clive, my boss at Thunder Burger. I scan the message and then tuck my phone back in my pocket.

'Who was it?' Kait asks.

'Clive. Ruby's phoned in sick, so he wants to know if I can cover.'

'Are you going to?'

I shake my head.

She's quiet for a moment. 'Are you really thinking of going to college?'

I sigh. I'm not just thinking about it; I've applied for a year-long course. And I've been accepted. Right now, college is the least humiliating thing I can do, and I feel like shit saying that to her, because however limited I think my options are, they're better than hers. Going blind definitely trumps being famously unattractive in the shitty-life-hand stakes. I want to be an actor – I want my old life back – but it's finally sinking in that it's not going to happen. Agents aren't interested in me. They haven't been for a while, if I'm honest.

And I can't stay at Thunder Burger – or Chunder Burger, as we call it when Clive isn't listening. I don't want to spend the rest of summer wiping down tables after some knob and his mates have just tipped an entire salt cellar on to it, let alone my whole life.

But admitting I'm going to college is admitting my life is going in a new direction. And I don't want to. I like being an actor. I'm good at it.

It's the only thing I'm good at. Being someone else.

'You all right . . . ?' Kait asks.

I realize I haven't answered her last question, and I'm still holding her hand, our fingers laced together. It's nice.

'Is that . . . ?'

She squints into the distance, and I turn to see Joe and Sasha hurrying towards us. I turn my phone off. Sorry, Clive – I understand if you have to fire me.

'I guess that's that then.' I stand, pulling her up with me. 'Come on. Let's go find a sleazy arcade and I'll win you a manky toy before we head back.'

'My hero,' she grins. 'Seriously, what a waste of a day though. I can't believe we came all the way here for this.'

'We came all the way here for Velvet,' I say. 'You can come to mine when we're home, if you like?' I add, finally letting go of her hand. I don't want to be alone. Not now, I feel too weird, and another night going through The Stage might actually finish me off. 'Mum's at some charity function. You could stay over? Pizza and Netflix?'

'Let's ask Joe and Sasha too,' Kait says, and for some reason it annoys me that she wants them there.

But I try to hide it. 'Sounds good.' OK, I could have tried harder.

Kait doesn't seem to have noticed, as she replies 'We might as well try to salvage something from this nightmare,' her slightly unfocused eyes meeting mine. She smiles at me and pulls me into a hug.

And out of nowhere, my stomach does this thing. This weird, driving-over-a-hill-too-fast thing that it does not do for girls. Ever.

Ever.

I pull back.

'What's wrong?' she asks.

'Nothing,' I manage. 'Nothing.'

She shrugs, and looks past me, waving in the direction of Joe and Sasha.

What the actual fuck was that?

KAITLYN

I don't know what the hell is wrong with Velvet, but this is the second year in a row that her choice of shag partner has ruined everyone else's day. I'm trying not to be annoyed with her, because I'm obviously a feminist and stuff, but *seriously*. What the *hell*.

'I should've thumped him,' I say, almost to myself, as Joe and Sasha approach.

'Who?' Dawson asks, already moved on.

'Joe,' I say.

He blinks, and I laugh.

'Obviously Griff.'

'Nah, he's not worth it,' Dawson says. 'Anyone who only sees the stick isn't worth your time.'

I bite my lip to stop myself reminding him that I already know that, and anyway that isn't even the problem. I'm actually pretty OK with people calling me the 'blind one'. It's annoying, but I don't find it offensive, and it says more about the person saying it than it does me. But it *does* bother me that they were all talking happily about all their future plans – university, mostly, and even Dawson's job – and no one asked me. Like, *it didn't even come up*. No one looked at me and said, 'What about you, Kaitlyn?'

I have plans, you know? I have a future too. What do they

think – that I'm just going to sit at home all day with my deteriorating vision doing . . . whatever it is they think people with vision problems do? They probably thought they were being sensitive and kind, not asking. When actually they were being pretty damn *insensitive*.

I would've told them all about my apprenticeship at the florist's. How I only said yes to make my mum happy, because I had literally zero interest in flowers and assumed I'd hate it. And you know what? I *don't* like working with flowers.

I bloody *love* working with flowers.

There's so much I could have said, if they'd asked. The apprenticeship is at a local florist's about ten minutes from my house, and the woman who runs it, Bev, is the coolest person I've ever met. She didn't start her floristry career until she was in her late thirties, and before that she was a prison officer. She is tough as nails, and sometimes, after a shift, she'll teach me a new self-defence move.

And she says I can definitely have a proper job in her shop when I'm qualified. Last week, she showed me the research she's been doing on the kind of accessibility adjustments she can make to the shop floor. She had about two pages of notes.

It's an apprenticeship, so obviously the pay is total crap. But still – at least I *get* paid, and I'll end up with the right qualifications to get paid properly. Most people my age – like my best friend, Avani, for one – are still stuck at school full time. Avani has a part-time job in a *chip shop*, so I'm clearly the lucky one in this scenario.

Anyway. What was I annoyed about?

'Are you OK?' Sasha demands when she and Joe reach us.

Oh yeah. Damn *Griff*. This is all his fault. If he wasn't here, the university/futures talk probably wouldn't even have come up. We could just have all had fun together at the beach, like we planned. Maybe Velvet would even have been happy to see us.

'I'm fine,' I say.

She clearly doesn't believe me.

'Griff is so *awful*,' she says. 'He was so rude!'

I can hear the anxiety in her voice, and it reminds me of something I've thought before, which is that Sasha is the kind of person who feels too much on other people's behalf. Like life isn't hard enough already without overloading on empathy.

'Yeah,' Dawson says, his arm curling around my shoulder. 'Anyway, we're going to go back to mine for a bit. You two should come.'

Sasha smiles, hopeful, and it makes her light up. 'Really? That would be great.' She glances at Joe, who is looking back in the direction they'd come from, clearly hoping to see Velvet following. 'Right, Joe?'

Joe turns back to us. 'Brilliant! We should wait for Velvet though.'

'Should we?' I ask.

'I'll message her,' he says, pulling out his phone.

The thing is, I was really looking forward to seeing Velvet. All of them, in fact; not just Dawson. We have a lot of fun chatting in our little WhatsApp group, and they feel like real friends. That's what I want right now. Real friends.

Avani and I don't talk much any more, that's the thing. Not since we stopped being at school together every day. Though maybe that's not fair – maybe it goes back further than that. To my diagnosis, and her utter horror that made everything worse even though she tried to hide it ('I'd rather go deaf, I think,' she'd said thoughtfully, as if it was an actual choice, and I'd made the wrong one). To my work experience, which she was jealous of ('An actual television studio! It's not fair. Why didn't everyone get that option?'). To the lift, which she didn't understand ('That's so sad. So, did you see anyone famous?'). To Dawson and our unlikely friendship ('Why are you still seeing him? Isn't he, like, a celebrity? Is he researching for a role or something?').

So, yeah. We just don't have much to talk about any more. Plus, she's got a new girlfriend who takes up a lot of her time. I miss her, but I also *don't* miss her. It's weird.

I thought maybe Velvet and I could bond over us both not going on to further education, what with her working at the hotel, and me with my apprenticeship. That could have been our *thing*. But really all she's said to me is, 'I love your hair!' Which is what she always says. Maybe she doesn't really like me all that much. Maybe she thinks my stick is weird.

People do. I wish they didn't, and they pretend they don't, but they do. At the very least, they *stare*. Even Sash and Joe stared when they first saw me with it. Not Dawson though. He never acts like this stuff is even unusual. I'm just Kait to him, which is the best thing.

I've had some deterioration over the last year with my sight – nothing major, but still – and even though I've known since my diagnosis that it would happen, it's a bit scary. I've started bringing the stick around with me so I can get used to it as much as because I actually need it. One day, I won't have a choice – and I want to be ready.

'Can I have a go?' Dawson asked a couple of months ago, when I first brought it with me to hang out with him. He clearly thought it was going to be easy (like everyone does), because he closed his eyes, swished the cane wildly in front of him and walked straight into a bench. 'All right,' he said, when I doubled over because I was laughing so hard. 'Pack it in.'

Everything is just easy with Dawson. And let me just say, thank *God* we never actually kissed or anything. Thank God he's gay. Because now we get to be mates for life (we are definitely going to be mates for life) instead of having a flash-in-the-pan probably-disappointing fling, like what happened with Alfie Mull earlier this year. Talk about anticlimax (*literally*). The whole thing only lasted six weeks, but that was enough, believe me. Imagine if that's all I'd got with Dawson. Washing-machine kisses and some dodgy sex. Ugh, relationships. Totally overrated.

'Velvet says she's on her way!' Joe says, delight in his voice. Joe is such a complete sweetheart. He's the most puppy-like boy I've ever met.

Still, I'm pleased too. If Velvet is coming back, that means there's still time for all of us to salvage this day together. We can have the kind of fun we'd planned, back when Joe had first suggested us all meeting up again on our anniversary. That's what he called it: our anniversary.

'Shotgun the front seat of the car,' I say.

SASHA

Velvet says something about milkshakes, and we all head back the way we came. Like a bunch of insensitive meerkats, we crane our necks to look up in the direction of the pub as we pass.

'He's not coming.' Velvet's voice is strained. Clearing her throat, she adds, 'Griff's always struggled with . . . you know . . .'

'Basic human decency,' Dawson murmurs so that only Kaitlyn next to him, and me, walking close behind, actually hear.

'. . . new people. He gets a bit . . . chippy.'

The prices on the chalkboard are higher than I was expecting – milkshakes are just melted ice creams without cones – but these ones come with organic whipped cream and drizzles of shiny sauce.

Joe nods at the menu and asks what I'm having. My hand closes round my purse. I already spent most of my month's wages on this trip, and there's nothing much left inside. Maybe someone will offer to pay for mine because I bought all the snacks? (They don't need to know they came from the pound shop.)

'I – er – I've not got the cash,' I prompt, like a charity case.

'They take cards,' Kaitlyn says helpfully, waving hers at the machine.

'I don't have a card,' I say. And if I did, it's not like it would have anything on it.

Kaitlyn doesn't hear me though – she's juggling her stick and her purse and the milkshake the person's trying to hand her.

You can tell they're all used to only thinking about themselves, which sounds harsher than I mean it to. Just because that's how they are, doesn't mean they haven't a good reason. Kaitlyn's going blind (I think . . . although she never uses that word), so I guess that's taking up a lot of her brain space. And Dawson's an ex-child star – he's *had* to think of himself on a professional level. Velvet, well, maybe I thought she was less self-involved because she seemed so sweet, but then she was totally oblivious to how weird it was bringing Griff with her before . . .

Joe though – he's not thinking of himself, is he? All he can think about is Velvet. Which I'm guessing is why he holds the door open long enough for Velvet to get through, but not me.

Once on the promenade, they fall into pairs ahead of me: Dawson and Kaitlyn; Joe and Velvet. Rather than try and crash in on anyone's conversation, I get my phone out. There's a new message on the group chat I'm on with Michela and the girls from college, and about fifty unread messages from Billy Goodart. Putting off reading them, I open up Instagram and scroll through my camera reel. The best is the one I took when we were sitting along the harbour wall, which captures everyone's profile: Dawson staring at the horizon, the sun making shadows of his jawline; Kaitlyn, with her long hair blowing forward in the breeze; Joe frowning down at the chips in his lap; and Velvet looking across at me, one freckled shoulder peeping out from her top. And at the end, her bloody boyfriend flipping the bird.

I've chosen the filter and adjusted the contrast by the time I realize I'm not actually in it – now *there's* a metaphor. Only I'm not that emo. Quickly, I find a better one – a group selfie with all of us in it (including Griff) – and post that instead, tagging everyone in it (not including Griff) and adding a hasty caption:

Two years on. I wanted to say something about Steven Jeffords, but it seems wrong to put that on Instagram, somehow.

Another message pops up from Billy. Much as I'd rather throw my phone into the sea than deal with the fallout from a series of increasingly terrible life decisions, it's time I stopped dodging the issue. I read from the top.

Can't we just talk?

I miss you.

We were so good together – you don't want to throw that away.

Sash? Don't ignore me. That's really cruel.

I'm sorry. I shouldn't have said that. You've probably not checked your phone.

How's Bridlington? Was your friend pleased to see you all?

Bring me back a stick of rock or something will you ;)

Please.

This is too tragic. I don't fancy him. I never have. But he's persistent and weirdly loyal. You'd have thought enough time had passed since the disastrous penis-in-the-park incident two years ago to have put him off. Only, he seems to have misinterpreted it as some kind of prophecy that we were destined to do a lot more.

Sorry, I type. *Been too busy to check my phone. Wasn't trying to be cruel.*

(Like I'd ever *try* to be cruel.)

Look. I don't think it's a good idea to keep seeing each other. You know what happens.

(Sex is what happens. Guilt-ridden and disappointing intercourse.)

Billy's online and already typing a reply.

That's what happens when two people who break up still want to be with each other!!!

I feel like shouting, 'TAKE A GODDAMN HINT, GOODART!' at the phone.

Billy, you're a sweetie who can do a lot better than this.

I'm not sure Billy *is* a sweetie, but even a morally mediocre young man deserves to date someone who doesn't brush his arm from round her shoulders. Someone who holds his hand for longer than thirty seconds when he offers it. Someone who doesn't just put up with all his fawning, but actually *likes* it. The way Velvet seemed to like Gropey Griff – even when he beeped her boob. My phone buzzes.

I don't want better – I want YOU.

Hang on. Wait. What? I'm not sure I like the implication of that.

'Guys?' I say. And then louder. 'Guys!'

Kaitlyn turns round fast enough that her stick catches Dawson on the ankle, and even Joe's noticed there's someone other than Velvet talking.

'Yes, Sasha?' Dawson says politely, looking up from where he's bent over, rubbing his ankle. His cat-like green eyes smile up at me through long, dark lashes. If people only ever looked at his eyes, they'd see how gorgeous he still is.

'If you were trying to break up with someone, and they said, "*I don't want better – I want YOU*" –' I hear Kaitlyn hiss through her teeth – 'How would you take that?'

'Badly.'

'Not very well.'

'Are you the one doing the dumping?' Velvet looks impressed. 'By *text*?'

Joe's frowning at the thought of me doing that, and I'm quick to set Velvet straight.

'No! I did it in person. Last night. But he's not taking the hint.'

I hold up my phone to show them the screen – only Kaitlyn reaches between Joe and Velvet to take it from me and have a better look. (See . . . blind? Not blind? Is there something in between I don't fully understand because it's something I've never had to think about? I'd ask her about all this if she wasn't so terrifying.)

'Oh my God, he's digging himself in deeper!' Kaitlyn usually speaks with a slightly husky voice, but it's risen an octave in horror as she reads out, '*I think you're perfect.*'

Kaitlyn looks me right in the eyes. 'Damn bloody straight you are.'

The fierce way she's looking at me makes me blush, wrong-footing me enough that I don't immediately snatch the phone back.

'Oh God, he's sent through another one.' This time her voice drips with pure sarcasm. '*I don't want what everyone else thinks they want* . . . Oh please!'

Everyone starts shouting about how shit poor Billy is, how I'm the one that can do better, and people walking past us along the prom give us dirty looks for being so disruptive. But amidst the noise, Kaitlyn is looking at me again like she knows what I want.

'Do you want me to *end* him, Sasha?'

And I shouldn't. Billy really doesn't deserve the Valkyrie that is Kaitlyn Thomas.

'I mean . . . you don't have to end him, but if you could write a reply that ends the relationship, that would help?' I smile, heart fluttering a bit at sharing so much of myself with everyone.

'You're too nice, Sasha,' mutters Kaitlyn as she drafts a reply on my phone. 'That's your problem.'

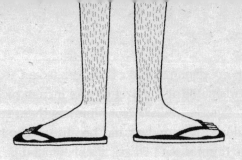

HUGO

Christ, I'm so bloody BORED.

I shouldn't be. I should be BUZZING. I mean, I'm on beer four, there's at least three hot bikinied girls in my line of vision, this playlist David's made is actually pretty sweet (*not that I'll tell him*), and, most importantly, I'm not at home. But – ugh. It's just . . . so . . . so . . .

'Hugo, will you do my back?' Cat saunters over, smiling because she knows I'm going to say yes. You can't really say no, can you? Especially when she smiles like that.

She sits down on the edge of my sunlounger and makes my feet wet as the water drips off her perfect body.

'If I must.'

She hands me the bottle, and I spray her back and rub it in, my hand deliberately slipping under the straps of her bikini.

'Honestly, Hugo,' she pretends to complain.

What does it mean about me as a human that I'm rolling my eyes, but also really want to have sex with her at the same time?

I mean, that's not good, is it?

Summer is too long. Days are too long. Life is so boring. Everything and everyone in my life is exactly the same. The girls are almost impossible to tell apart. They all have the same long hair blow-dried in the same perfect way. They all have the same perfectly sculpted arses shown off in their identikit designer bikinis. Their eyebrows are all perfectly plucked, their voices all have the same plummy nothingness to them, and they're all so pretty in that groomed way. That prettiness you're never sure is real, because anyone can be pretty, really, if they have enough money and a personal trainer and expensive this and that, and . . . God, I am *so* bored. I am so fucking bored, I can't even tell you.

'Done!' I smack my hands on Cat's back to announce my finishing. 'You're all set.'

I'm not sure why, but I find myself pushing her gently off my sunlounger. She giggles and readjusts her bikini strap and pretends not to mind, even though she does.

'I'm getting a beer,' I announce.

I pad my way around the pool into David's kitchen and open his fridge to ferret around for a drink. It's been restocked by the maid in the past hour, and I grab a plate full of fruit too. I should totally eat some vitamin C; I've been caning it so hard since exams finished. David's parents have been gone five days, leaving their country house free, and it's been one non-stop party. The weather is perfect – it's hotter here than where Mum's staying in the South of France. My tan is looking pretty great, hiding the week's worth of excess from showing on my face. It's chill, and everyone's up for it, and I could get Cat tonight at the click of my fingers if I wanted to, and I'm flying out tomorrow to join Mum, and – on paper – everything is pretty damn amazing, isn't it?

But Christ, I'm BORED, and I don't know why.

I find myself pulling up a stool to the breakfast bar, setting my fruit plate down and drinking my beer alone for a moment. The throb of bass music thumps dimly through the triple-glazed patio doors but, other than that, it's quiet. I pick up a piece of freshly cut pineapple and wash it down with a mouthful of beer.

I pull my phone out of the pocket of my swimming trunks and find myself scrolling through everyone's updates. The same basic faces of the same basic people stare back at me. Cat's just posted a photo of her posing next to the pool – her head thrown back, her tits thrust outwards, her toes pointed to make her legs look longer. Hashtag tanning. I roll my eyes again. I mean, I guess I'm still going to have sex with her, but I'm kind of bored by the inevitability of it.

I know I'm going to type her name in before I do it.

There's a moment of kidding myself that I won't, but I've already typed in V and E and L. Her profile comes up quickly, because I've been checking up on her more than I care to admit.

Look, it's not like I care. Last year's pathetic night in Manchester was probably one of the funniest things that's ever happened to me. I managed to get so much material out of it with everyone. *'God, I mean, you think poor people hate us, but they, like, REALLY hate us. I'm surprised I made it out of there alive.'* Those losers being so BRAVE and RIGHTEOUS standing up to me was the most hilarious part . . . I hadn't done anything wrong. Just slept with a girl who was also totally up for it. They think *I'm* the snob, but they were the ones jumping to conclusions. They're the prejudiced ones, not me.

Twats.

And yet, here they are. Staring out of my phone in a cheesy group selfie that Velvet has regrammed.

I knew they'd do something like this today – knew it. So damn predictable. I bet the little saddos have been counting down to it all year. Wanting to inject some drama and meaning into their pathetic lives.

She looks pretty.

But sad . . .

I mean, she's smiling, but I'm around a lot of fake people a lot of the goddamned time, and I know a fake smile when I see one.

I snort at myself. I shake my head and down the rest of my beer. I burp triumphantly, enjoying how it echoes around this stainless-steel-filled kitchen. Then I beat my bare chest and laugh at myself and think, you know what, maybe shagging Cat isn't so boring after all. At least it will keep me busy.

And I need to keep busy at the moment. What with everything.

OK. So here's where we're at. Try to keep up. Kaitlyn used to have a thing for Dawson, but Dawson likes boys, so now they're just mates, which is great, but Dawson thinks that maybe he likes girls as well, which is utterly inconvenient and a massive head fuck for Kaitlyn, who is actually enjoying being friends. Meanwhile, Billy likes Sasha, Ivy likes Joe, but Joe likes Velvet, as does Hugo. Not that he'd admit it, and she'd never say that she likes him either, because she's with Griff – and no one likes Griff.

It's all very complicated.

But that's what happens when you throw a group of teenagers together like that: things tend to get complicated. Don't they have more important things to worry about? After all, Kaitlyn is slowly going blind, Velvet is pregnant, and Joe is losing his mother a tiny piece at a time – each time she forgets how many sugars he takes in his tea, or asks him if his team won their game, even though he hasn't played football since he was ten. Soon she'll forget him altogether, and he'll become that nice boy that opens the curtains in the morning and cuts up her pork chop.

Perhaps that's why. Perhaps all the who-fancies-whom nonsense is a distraction; a way of finding something – or someone – in the miserable mess of their lives to make it feel like they aren't being kicked repeatedly in the heart. Isn't that all any of us want? To find someone who says, 'I get that, and I get you, and everything is going to be OK.' Perhaps the anniversary thing was a distraction as well. After all, it's a strange event to celebrate – a stranger dying in a lift. But it's what brought them together, and marking it somehow kept them together when their lives were pulling them in very different directions.

Not that Velvet had wanted to celebrate it, of course. All she'd been able to think about was the baby and what she was going to do, so she'd completely forgotten about it. She didn't think the others would be bothered, but she'd underestimated how much she meant to them. (Even Hugo, who wasn't there himself, still felt the need to check that she was OK.)

And that's another thing she'd never say out loud: how much she needed to see them. She didn't realize it until they were all there in front of her, each of them genuinely pleased to see her in a way no one ever had been before. She could feel the love burning off them, right through their clothes; could suddenly see the gaping hole they'd left in her life after she'd run off that night at Hugo's party. Since then, she'd filled it with hoovering and bacon sandwiches and Griff – but as soon as she saw them again, she felt that itch, that excruciating, unreachable itch, that made her world extend further than a bag of chips on the beach.

They all felt it, that itch – the realization that there's more to life than this. That you can be with people that you want to be with. Not people that you *have* to be with through *circumstance* or mere geography – family, teachers, colleagues – but people who are willing to make room for you in their lives when they don't have to.

That's not something Hugo had given much thought to, but when your thought process revolves around yourself, it's impossible to consider anyone else. It must be hard to have sympathy for Mr Delaney. He doesn't make it easy, does he? But think of him at that party, by himself in the kitchen, looking at the photo of the others on his phone. It's a terrible thing to be surrounded by people and still feel alone. If you asked him, he'd say that he wasn't unhappy, simply weary of seeing the same people and doing the same things, day in, day out. When you have the space – and the finances – to do whatever you please, it's easy to grow restless, especially when you have no idea what you actually want.

It's not for you or I to say what that is; he has to work it out for himself. In the meantime, there's beer and sunloungers and girls like Cat who touch him in places so many others had before – places that always provoke a reaction, if only for a moment or two, before he goes back to feeling nothing at all. Poor Hugo, with his perfect hair and perfect tan and perfect life. He doesn't have to worry about his clothes fitting or if he can afford a milkshake. His life is just one milkshake after the other. He has it all, and he doesn't know what to do with it.

What he really wants is what Kaitlyn and Dawson have. That bond. To share his life with someone who knows *him* – not someone who knows his mother or his friends or what school he goes to . . . but who *really* knows him. Sasha gets that. Hugo, whose mother is never there, probably thinks he has nothing in common with someone whose father is *always* there, but they both feel distant and disconnected, looking on at the rest of the group, desperate to feel something – anything – that will make them feel like there's someone else on the tiny patch of the planet they all share that they're connected to . . . He'll never admit that though, so instead he complains. Complains that his life is boring, and that he wants something to change.

But he should be careful what he wishes for.

How do you know if you're bi? **Google search**
Am I bi? **Google search**
Can you be gay but like a girl? **Google search**
How can I figure out if I'm bisexual, or if I am just going through a phase? **Google search**
What does bi-curious mean? **Google search**
Dominos Salford closing time **Google search**

Dawson:
> Where are you?

Mum:
Out. Why?

> What time will you be back?

Why? Do you have someone over?
In America they stick a sock on the doorknob.
Do not do that.

> Hilarious. I need to talk to you about something

Dawson, I know you're gay.
It's too late to come out to me now.
So if this is about getting some kind of cake, not happening.
Dawson? You're scaring me. What's wrong?

> What if I'm not gay? What if I'm bi?

I'll be home at seven. Order food.

NOT PIZZA.

Love you xxx

HISTORY

TODAY

Tandoori Palace order online **Google search**

NHS Appointments:

VELVET BROWN – This is a reminder of your appointment at 10:00 tomorrow. Please call the clinic if you can't attend or text CANCEL up to half an hour before your appointment. If you need further support or information, please call our helpline.

YEAR FOUR

Kaitlyn:

So, we're really doing this? We're going on a date?

Dawson:

We're really doing it. In fact, I'm parked three doors down, having a low-key panic attack.

Kaitlyn:

Am I that scary?

Dawson:

Which answer is least likely to get me murdered?

Kaitlyn:

Just come and get me, you loser

Dawson:

OK. OK

One last thing . . . Is it clichéd if I have flowers?

Kaitlyn:

Depends what flowers they are. Obvs

Dawson:

They're pink? Not roses or daffodils.
They're the only flower brands I know

Kaitlyn:

Flower . . . brands?

OMG why aren't you on my doorstep yet?

Dawson:

OK. I'm coming now.
With my pink flowers. BE NICE x

Kaitlyn:

xx

Dawson:

Home safe xx

Was that weird? That was weird. Sorry
Not the message. The other bit

The kiss, I mean.
Sorry

Xx

Kaitlyn:

Maybe a little bit weird?

Dawson:

Oh God. OK. Sorry

Kaitlyn:

Stop saying sorry!

Dawson:

Sorry

Shit

Kaitlyn:

OMG!

Dawson:
I don't want it to be weird
You're my best friend

Kaitlyn:
Not BAD weird . . .
Just . . . weird. The date was great!

Dawson:
But the kiss was weird?

Kaitlyn:
That's not what I meant! First kisses are always weird. This was just extra
For reasons

Dawson:
OK. Hang on.

Kaitlyn:
Why?
For what?

Dawson:
Come outside x

Dawson:

Home again. That definitely wasn't weird. That was definitely good. Wasn't it?

Kaitlyn:

Very good ☺

Dawson:

OK. So. Practice. That's the trick. Lots of practice. Shall we practise tomorrow? I would be up for a practice tomorrow

Kaitlyn:

☺ I think that's a good idea. But I should probably go to sleep now xx

Dawson:

Same. I've got a lecture at nine

Kaitlyn:

Today was really great xx
And tonight ☺ xx

Dawson:

It was
I'm going to need coaching for second base, fyi . . .

Kaitlyn:

I . . . think we already did second base?!

Dawson:

That was 2nd? Damn, I'm smooth. That's not even a base with guys

Kaitlyn:

Or maybe I'm just THAT good at coaching ;)

Dawson:

It's on you when I mess up third then

Wait what is third? Specifically?

Kaitlyn:

☺

Dawson:

I'm googling it

Oh

OK, so maybe not tomorrow

Kaitlyn:

☺

Night xx

Dawson:

Night xxx

Kaitlyn:

What do we do about the others?

Dawson:

I don't want to do any bases with them ☺

Kaitlyn:

:P

Seriously!

Dawson:

Well. . . Maybe let's not say anything until we've figured it out?
Not that I don't want people to know. But . . . it's a lot, you know?

Kaitlyn:

Yeah, ikwym. It can just be ours for now? ☺

Dawson:

Yes. So, tomorrow then? I'll come get you after college?

Kaitlyn:

Can't wait xx

Dawson:

Night xxx

Kaitlyn:

Night xxx

Dawson:

xxxx

PARLIAMENT'S OWN BROKEBACK MOUNTAIN?
Tory and Labour MPs cross-party gay affair revealed

'HE USED ME AS A BEARD' Delaney's 'heartbroken'
wife speaks out against disgraced Tory MP

GAY MP FORCED TO RESIGN Spurned wife leaks
expenses scandal, saying, 'Why should I lie for him
any more?'

Kaitlyn:

http://www.thesun.co.uk/news/politician-cross-party-affair-shock/

Holy crap! Did you all read this? That's Hugo's dad, right?

Joe:

☺☺☺☺☹

Sasha:

Poor Hugo

(Never thought I'd type those words in the same sentence)

Dawson:

Same. He's a dick, but this is shit

Joe:

Just skimmed the full article. It's bad. Really, really bad

Velvet:

Imagine how Hugo must be feeling . . . Nobody deserves that

Sasha:

☹

SASHA

The dress was Mum's. Lots of the best things in my wardrobe were once hers. Unlike my mother, Dad's someone who likes to hang on to the past, and when she went, he shoved everything she left behind into vacuum bags.

If we had any money, I'd go to the Polish tailor on the parade where Dad used to take all his suits when he had a job that required them. As it is, the dress is tight round the boobs and a little short at the hem.

I hope Nan won't mind . . .

Over on the bed, I hear my phone buzz.

What time does the party end again?

I wish Michela wouldn't call it a party.

Starts 3 p.m., not sure when it'll finish. Two hours, maybe? You don't have to come if it's too much hassle, I reply.

You trying to get rid of me? Course I'm coming. You need your friends with you.

There's something about the plural 'friends' that makes me suspicious, but then I hear Dad shout from the kitchen. It's time to get on.

'These arrived—' he starts to say before he sees me. He stops then, stares, reaching up to scratch stubble he shaved off this morning. 'Don't you have anything else you could wear?'

I shake my head. 'Nothing smart enough.'

Dad looks at me again and sighs. 'I'm surprised it fits.' Then he shrugs and waves a hand at some flowers sitting in the sink. 'Those have your name on.'

Hey Sash. These aren't traditional, but it sounds to me like neither was your nan. K xxx

K for Kaitlyn. There's pale yellow roses, some flowers with indigo petals that I don't recognize, and the smiling faces of some deep orange gerberas. I stare at the cheerful colours and hold my breath, suffocating my tears.

'They're from my friend who's a florist,' I say to Dad, emotions back in check.

'What friend?'

'Online friend.'

'One of the ones coming today?' he asks. We had a bit of an argument about that.

'No. One of the others.'

The guys were all super lovely when I messaged them to say that my nan had died. I don't even really know why I did it . . . none of them knew her. It just feels like even though I never see them, Kaitlyn, Joe, Dawson and Velvet are the people I want to talk to the most. I like sending Kaitlyn pictures of flowers and asking her what they are, like a floral Shazam. I ask Velvet about outfits I'm experimenting with, and I'm always bugging Dawson about what programmes to watch out for. Like, I know he's not really doing much acting these days, but he always seems to know what's going to be good on TV before everyone else does.

And Joe? He's been talking to me about his love life. It's nice to have someone actually want my opinion, and coaching someone else through a new relationship is much more fun than bothering to do it yourself. Although if Joe Lindsay was an option, I might reconsider. But he isn't. So that's that.

It was Joe who'd asked if I wanted any of them to come.

Dawson can't. I think he's helping out at his dad's bar – somewhere like Ayia Napa or Ibiza, with sun and sea and lots of drunk people. And Kaitlyn's on holiday, which isn't a huge surprise, it being summer. But Joe and Velvet – they'll be here.

No Hugo. Obviously. He's not someone I ever think of as being part of the group, but when Kaitlyn sent that link . . .

Can you loathe someone and still feel sad for them? Because I kind of do. I composed three different messages to send, and chickened out on all of them. I've never known how to talk to Hugo.

'Sasha?' There's a hand squeezing my shoulder, and I realize I'm still standing at the sink. 'Come on, love. We need to get going.'

The traffic's slow, and Dad switches between radio stations, looking for something that suits the occasion, until he finally settles on silence. It's been like that a lot in the last few weeks. He's not watched anything on telly from start to finish. Not even the weather at the end of the local news, which only lasts three minutes. He used to be obsessive about knowing the forecast.

I scroll listlessly through stuff on my phone, finding the Facebook message my mum sent.

Bubba. I do not have your new number. (I've had the same number since I got my first phone, but sure.) *I am so sorry about your nana. Elaine was a kind woman and I liked her very much. I know it's not like this with you and I, but you can call me. Always. For anything.*

A sign-off to assuage her guilt. When I was little, she would end every conversation this way, but if I called, she wouldn't answer, and I'd get confused by a voicemail in a language she'd never cared to teach me – it wasn't like Albanian was an option in my primary school. If she did pick up, she'd sound annoyed, asking me if it was important. It only made things worse. For me. For Dad. He tries so hard to be everything I need that sometimes he forgets it's impossible for him to be more than one person. That sometimes I crave a conversation with anyone who *isn't* my father.

For so many years, that person was my nan, and now she's gone too.

'My sister's here already then.' Dad swings our ancient Toyota a couple of spaces away from an enormous gleaming Audi.

I don't really know what I'm supposed to say to that. It's not like Auntie Chris isn't going to turn up to her own mother's funeral, is it?

Only then I wonder whether I would turn up to my mother's funeral. Presumably only if someone sent me a Facebook message to tell me it was happening . . . The thought hollows me out so much, I feel sick.

'Tony!' Auntie Chris flings her arms out and pulls Dad in for a hug. Then it's my turn. 'Little Sash – it's been so long . . .'

She goes to hug me, but I'm holding Kaitlyn's flowers, and she ends up going for an arm squeeze. I shake hands with her husband, Mike, and exchange awkward waves with my cousins. Winona – Win, as she's become on all the recent Christmas cards – is fourteen and fashionable. Sean is twenty and halfway through an engineering degree at Oxford. Pembroke College.

Hard to believe someone from my family gets to do something like that.

It's not until we emerge from the path leading towards the front of the building that the place looks familiar. This is where Steven Jeffords was buried.

The place looks totally different for my nan, like it too has dressed for the occasion. Clouds sit low in the sky, a muted, respectful grey over a crowd of people as black and dense as a colony of ants, all murmuring to each other. I hear my name on someone's lips and turn to see Nan's neighbour, who gives me a tucked-in smile of acknowledgement.

Everyone wants to talk to us. Nan lived in the same house all her life, and there's no one here who doesn't remember either Dad or me. I can see Auntie Chris getting a bit frustrated by this, but she left Manchester years ago and only comes back every other Christmas, so I don't know what she expected.

It's all getting a bit much, so quietly, when I think I can get away with it, I slip round the side of the building, flowers and all, and make straight for where I can see two figures, standing some distance away, gazing down at a sad little plaque set into the ground. It's been a year since I've seen them – Instagram doesn't do Velvet justice, and Joe never posts any pictures of himself, so it's with a start that I realize he's grown taller. Broader and stronger.

Better-looking.

Bet Velvet's noticing him now . . .

I'm standing next to them, looking down at the mark Steven Jeffords left on this world, before they realize I'm there.

'Bloody hell, Sasha!' Joe starts. 'Creeping up on people in graveyards is *not* cool.'

'Sorry.' I put the flowers down and wipe my hands on my dress, even though they're not wet. 'Hello. Thanks for coming, guys.'

'Like we wouldn't,' Velvet says, and she steps in to give me the kind of hug I really need. Warm and sweet-smelling. Genuine.

Joe pats me awkwardly on the back.

We break apart, and all three of us look down at Steven's plaque.

'I really hope our friendship isn't going to be like a macabre inversion of *Four Weddings and a Funeral*,' Joe says, and both me and Velvet give him quizzical looks. 'What? Carly really likes romcoms. She's been making me watch one every weekend since we started going out. To educate me.'

Sounds naff, but Velvet laughs. 'Oh my God, Joe, you're so adorable.'

His ears turn pink. Joe might have moved on, but there are some things about a crush that never fade.

There's a shout from over by the chapel. Picking up the flowers, I tug a single gerbera from the bouquet and lay it across Steven's plaque before hurrying back over to my dad, Joe and Velvet trailing in my wake.

I can tell by the way he very deliberately doesn't say anything about it that Dad's annoyed with me for disappearing. Fortunately I've got the flowers as a diversion, and I walk right up to the coffin and place them beside it, trying not to think of what's inside. Wherever my nan is, it's not there. Not really. The bench – *pew?* – at the front has been left free for the family, and I squash in, me and the cousins bookended by Auntie Chris and Dad.

There isn't much I remember about Steven Jeffords' service other than the emptiness of the chapel and the ring of the officiant's words bouncing off the brick walls and wooden benches. I thought that was because I didn't know the deceased, but even here, now, the funeral seems less real than my memories. Making cakes in her kitchen, learning to knead dough, roll out pastry. Flour under my fingernails and smudged across her apron. Helping her in the garden – Nan pointing a finger that never quite made it to straight, asking me to bend over for this, or pass her that – the pair of us picking strawberries from the fruit patch and tomatoes from the greenhouse. Later, when I was that much older, catching the bus back to hers after school because Dad was working late, sitting in her front room gossiping about her neighbours, eating biscuits bought from the shop because baking had become too much of a faff . . .

My lovely nan. My only other family. Gone. I wonder if I'll ever not miss her.

Back out front, the service over and the coffin removed ready for cremation, I'm surrounded by a chorus of sniffing, the susurration of elderly gentlemen digging for handkerchiefs in their suit pockets, and women producing plastic packs of tissues from their bags.

I nod and I smile and I thank people for coming and I say, 'Will I see you at the social club?' so many times that it's like I've forgotten all the other words in the world.

'Sash!' Michela launches herself at me and wraps her arms round my neck so that I can barely draw breath. 'Oh my God, you poor thing. That was hideous.'

Which isn't the word I would have used – I thought it was all perfectly nice. For a funeral.

'That guy who did the reading . . .'

'You mean Albert?'

'You'd have thought he could have kept it together.'

Albert was one of Nan's oldest friends. They'd been to school together. It took him six hours to drive here from Cornwall, and he's nearly eighty. When he heard she'd died, he sent us a letter so sweet and heartfelt that I can't even think about it without wanting to cry.

'Oh, hello. Who's that specimen?' Michela lets me go, smooths her skirt, and subtly flicks open the top button of her blouse.

I don't even need to look to know who it'll be.

'That's Joe. He's got a girlfriend.' I pause a moment. 'And

you have a boyfriend, Mic. Remember?'

And right on cue, there he is. Michela's boyfriend.

He's wearing a suit. Dark grey. Navy shirt. Auburn hair bleaching to ginger at the sideburns, to match his eyebrows.

'Sasha,' he starts to say, but before he can lean in and hug me, before we can find out what I'd do if he did, I step away to pull in the friends that I actually want with me.

'Velvet!' If she's alarmed at how high my voice is, she doesn't show it. I grab Joe too, sandwiching myself between them for safety. 'And Joe. This is my best mate, Michela . . .'

They both wave at Michela, who's giving Velvet a wary glare.

'. . . and this is Bil— I mean Will. This is *Will*.'

Who can say which is weirder, the fact that after ten years of calling him Billy we all now call him Will, or the fact that the guy I lost my virginity to is now dating my best friend?

Tough call. Right?

HUGO

'This is fucking ridiculous.'

Well, that's what I say in my head. It comes out a bit different. Slurry and fluffy and, still, that's beside the point. This little power hungry TWAT won't let me into his pathetic little club, and it is unacceptable.

'Sorry, mate, but you're too drunk,' the twat says, loving every single second. He crosses his arms and smiles and I hate him and I hate his face and I hate how even he probably knows who I am and has probably read about my dad in the news, even though he's an uneducated oxygen-sucking nobody BOUNCER on the shit part of the Ibiza strip and I bet he cannot believe his luck that he's getting to enjoy a moment, just a moment, of feeling bigger than me.

Enjoy while it lasts, arsehole.

Then I call him the c-word. And then I feel my face hurting, and then I'm on the pavement, and I can't see very well because there's blood coming out of my eye for some reason. And, oh, fuck it. I'm being sick. I'm leaning over on the pavement and being sick on to the street.

I chunder it all out, and it hurts, but it's OK and funny and not pathetic if you use the word 'chunder'. David is here and I yell, 'AND THEN I CHUNDERED EVERYWHERE!' But he doesn't seem to get the joke, because he's always had a shit sense of humour.

He's dragging me on to my feet. 'Mate, you need to go back to the hotel and sober up.'

'Since when do we call each other mate?' I laugh, then I feel sick again. But there's nothing else to sick up. David looks somewhat disgusted. He's copying my most common facial expression.

It's so noisy and it's so hot and everywhere I look I can see a sunburned torso hanging out over some nasty shorts. We're causing very little fuss – David and I – sat here next to my puddle of vom right in the middle of Ibiza. At least five drunk idiots have walked through it already in flip-flops, not noticing. It's too busy and everyone's too wasted and the music from all the competing bars is too loud, and I really need to have a line or two, actually, because I do feel quite wankered.

David is saying something. 'Sleep it off . . . Come to the foam party later . . . I can't believe that twat punched you . . . Everyone's in there already . . . Come on . . . take one for the team.'

I stumble to my feet. 'I don't want to sleep it off; I want to get into the foam party.'

'Well, they're not letting you in, mate!' He's talking all common again.

'Stop calling me mate. I'm not your fucking mate.'

I'm not sure why, but I've tried to punch David, and now he's stormed off, calling me pathetic. And I sit back down on the pavement again, stretching my feet out into my vomit.

'Fuck it,' I say, and then I feel dripping and look down and see there's blood all over my shirt. How did that happen? This is my best shirt. My best shirt! Why the hell is there blood on it? Who the fuck BLED on me? What is WRONG with this place?

I lurch up and for some stupid reason my legs aren't working very well and I start walking. I'm not sure where, but I think this is the way back to the hotel. I'll change my shirt and work out who to charge it to and then I'm going to go report that bouncer and tell my father and they won't get away with this . . . they won't . . . I'm so fed up of people thinking this is their moment to pop one at me . . . it isn't . . . My family and I, we're going to come back like a phoenix from the ashes and . . . Where am I? Where the actual hell am I? I need some drugs. I need some drugs to get me sober enough to get back to the hotel.

I push through the throngs of sweaty bodies swirling around, spilling out on to the sandy beach. Everyone's in fancy dress that involves having as little clothes on as possible and neon paint on their faces. Loads of fit but classless girls in hot pants come up to me and try and entice me to go into the bars they're promoting, or to buy a Jägershot off the belt they have hoisted around their tiny, tattooed waists.

I tell them to fuck off, which doesn't go down well, but it makes me laugh.

I manage to find some shitty place that doesn't charge entry. The bar is half empty, with a light-up dance floor. A group of not very pretty girls are dancing on it, and they all stare at me as I push into the bar. I sneer at them and manage to find my way to the toilet.

My reflection is a surprise, I have to admit.

My eye is already almost closed, and there's blood every-where – all down one side of my face – and my shirt is ruined. I try to wash the worst of it off, though there's only one tap working in this disgusting toilet, and the water is only coming out as a trickle.

Maybe I'm a bit drunk, all right?

But I'm in Ibiza! That's the point, right? The big holiday after the A levels that I'm quite sure I've messed up, which really isn't my fault if you take everything into account. A big blowout is what I need. Just to escape my head and my life and try and not be that boy from the news whose dad fucked some twenty-four-year-old Labour MP and it was his own fucking mother who leaked it to the press. There's been photographers everywhere, and Mum trying to get into professional photo shoots about how she's *somehow managed to find the strength to finally leave her psychopath husband*. And Dad ringing me and sobbing down the phone and begging me to beg her to stop, and the whole thing is such a mess, and look at me – I'm a complete mess too . . .

I dry my hands and fumble in my wallet for the drugs. God knows what it is. David got it off *some guy* he knew who *was good for it*. To tell you the truth, I don't even care. I make direct eye contact with myself as I hold a pinch to my nostrils and take a sniff.

It hits instantly, and it was the right thing to do.

I feel clearer and sharper and not as drunk.

I just need to go and change my shirt, find the other lads, sweet-talk my way back into the foam party, and carry on having it large.

It's fine. It's fine. Come on, Hugo, this isn't you. It's all grand. Sort it out . . .

Oww, my head. It's buzzing. It's buzzing with too many things. Why is everything coming at me like I'm in some fucking 4D experience?

Where the hell am I?

I'm trying to find the hotel, but everyone is in my way, and my *heart* – my heart, it's beating too much. Why is it beating so fast? Am I going to die? Oh God, I'm going to die! I'm going to have a heart attack and die. Alone. Even though I'm not alone. I'm pushing through throngs of drunken twats somewhere in Ibiza because I don't know where I am and I can't believe I'm going to die in a shirt that's covered in blood.

The press are going to have a field day.

There.

There's a quiet corner. I need a quiet corner. To die in. To breathe. Why can't I breathe?

WHAT THE HELL IS GOING ON? WHY AM I LIKE THIS? I'M NOT USUALLY LIKE THIS?

Oh God, what if I'm always like this?

What the hell have I taken? What if it makes me like this forever? I'm stuck. I'm stuck in this head and I hate it, and, I'll have you know, I wasn't that happy with my old head, but it was so much better than this new one.

This new one that's going to die.

My lungs.

Ouch.

My heart.

Beating too fast.

I'm crouched in this alleyway and I try to call for help but the music coming out of all the bars is too loud.

I can't . . .

Can't . . .

How did life get like this? What did I fucking do to deserve this?

'Help.' It comes out like a squeak. I can't die. I can't die here in this alleyway. I hold my chest, like the act might make my heart calm down. I force myself up, back into the music and the noise, and I walk and walk through the sand, past the people, towards I don't know where, towards anyone, anyone who might realize I'm dying and try to help me. But nobody is taking any notice.

I'm so alone . . .

So . . . so . . .

alone.

And I've reached the end of the strip because the music has died down and there's fewer drunk people and I collapse into the sand and can't do this any more.

I'm going to die and I'm a horrid person and so is everyone I know.

That's the thought.

The thought I have, so clearly, as my heart speeds faster and faster and my lungs aren't able to take in oxygen and it's all about to go black until . . .

until . . .

'Holy mother of fuck. Is that you, Hugo?'

I look up. I can't believe that he – he of all people – is going to be here when I die.

JOE

'Sasha! Come on!'

Sasha's dad is built like a nightclub bouncer, a 'don't fuck with me' expression on his face to match. As he glares at us, his hand resting on the open passenger door of his navy blue car, it's hard to believe our sweet, gentle Sasha shares half his DNA.

'I'd better get going,' Sasha says, her olive cheeks tinged pink.

'Are you guys all right getting to the club?' she asks me and Velvet. 'It's not far.'

'They can come with us if they want,' Will says. 'I've got my car.'

Michela transfers the dirty look on her face from Velvet over to Will.

'That all right with you, Sash?' he continues, spinning his car keys on his index finger, oblivious (or not) to the venom in his girlfriend's eyes.

'Er, yeah. Course,' Sasha says, licking her lips the way I've noticed she does when she's nervous. 'Thanks.'

Sasha's dad beeps the car horn, making her flinch.

'See you there then, I guess,' she says, hesitating for a moment before scurrying over to the waiting car.

*

'You've got enough space back there, haven't you, mate?' Will asks.

The truthful answer is no (his seat is pushed so far back, my knees are almost level with my chin), but I get the feeling it was more of a rhetorical question.

He revs the engine entirely unnecessarily, drawing disapproving looks from the other mourners returning to their cars.

'Stick Kiss on, will ya, Mic?' he says.

Michela does as she's told, then twists round in her seat to face Velvet and me.

'So, Joel, Velour, you together or what?'

'It's Joe and Velvet, actually,' Velvet says. 'And no, we're not together.'

'Oh,' Michela says, frowning. 'Sash said Joe was seeing someone –' she jerks her head in my direction – 'And I assumed it was you.'

'No,' Velvet says.

'Where's your girlfriend then?' Michela asks, turning her attention to me.

As if on cue, my phone buzzes against my chest.

'She's in Cardiff,' I say.

'How come?'

'That's where she's from. She's a student at Manchester Met.'

'An older woman, eh?' Michela says.

'Only by a year,' I reply, my cheeks getting increasingly hot.

Even though Velvet knows about Carly, I still feel funny talking about my new relationship in front of her. I made that quip about romcoms earlier, but I felt weird doing it, like I was reciting lines in a play, almost.

I met Carly in the spring, volunteering on a student film. I was a runner, and she was heading up the art department. We bonded at the refreshments table over our mutual love of bourbon biscuits (we both like biting the chocolate cream off first). We ended up snogging at the wrap party and have been together ever since.

'How about you guys?' Velvet asks politely. 'How did you meet?'

'Through Sash, I suppose,' Will says, cruising through a zebra crossing despite the fact there's a woman with a pushchair waiting on the edge of the kerb.

As Velvet continues to quiz Michela and Will, I ease my phone from the inside pocket of my suit jacket and open Carly's message. *Blue Steel.*

I press the camera icon and select selfie mode before adopting a pout and snapping five photos in quick succession.

'What are you doing?' Velvet asks.

I drop my phone into my lap.

'Nothing.'

She folds her arms across her chest. 'Were you taking a cheeky selfie, Mr Joseph "I never take selfies" Lindsay?'

'I don't know what you're talking about.'

'Yeah you do! Let me see.'

'No!'

Velvet grabs the phone from where it's slipped off my lap and fallen into the footwell. I try to snatch it from her, but she's too fast.

'What's going on back there?' Michela barks. 'Lovers' tiff?'

'No,' Velvet and I say in unison.

Michela makes a 'pfffft' sound and whacks up the volume on the radio.

My vain hope that the screen on my phone might have locked itself by now is dashed when Velvet bursts out laughing. She turns it towards me. My ridiculous face pouts right back.

I look like a complete and utter twat.

'You practising for *Britain and Ireland's Next Top Model*?' she asks.

I grab the phone and return it to my pocket.

'It's just a game I play with Carly,' I mutter, my face on fire.

'What kind of game?'

'A sex game?' Michela asks over her shoulder.

I hadn't realized she was still listening.

'It's just this thing I do with my girlfriend,' I explain. 'We take it in turns to come up with a look or emotion or something, and then the other one has to capture it in a selfie . . .'

'Sounds thrilling,' Michela says, rolling her eyes before joining in with Will who is rapping in a faux-American-gangster accent along to the radio, complete with hand gestures.

'So what was that supposed to be just now?' Velvet asks.

'Sorry?'

'The look you were doing in your selfie.'

'Oh. Er, Blue Steel.'

'OK, well, that explains it. The duck face, I mean. Good effort.'

I smile weakly.

'Give me one to do,' she says.

I hesitate. The thing is, this is my and Carly's game, and I don't want to confuse things by playing it with Velvet. I feel weird enough just talking to her about it. I'm relieved when Will pulls into a small car park next to a grey concrete building that looks a bit like a scout hut, and announces we've reached our destination.

'Thank fuck for that,' Michela says, getting out of the car. 'I need a drink ASAP. That service was a proper downer.'

'Do you reckon they've got a tab set up?' Will asks.

'Doubt it. Sash's dad is a right stingy bastard. Only one way to find out though,' Michela says, cementing my suspicions that she is nowhere near good enough to occupy the status of Sasha's best friend.

'That's my girl,' Will says, slapping Michela on the bum.

'What a delightful couple,' Velvet remarks as we watch them saunter towards the entrance, Will's hand still splayed across Michela's right arse cheek.

'Some might even say enchanting,' I add.

There's a beat before we crack up laughing and, just like magic, everything feels OK between us again.

'You know who he is, don't you?' Velvet asks once we've stopped giggling.

'Will?'

'Yeah.'

'Who?'

'Billy.'

I frown. 'Wait, as in Sasha's ex, Billy? What makes you think that?'

'The key ring on his car keys,' she says. 'It's got "Billy" on it . . . Plus, Sash totally fluffed his name when she introduced him.'

Did she? I was too busy being pissed off at Michela for the way she was looking at Velvet to pay much attention.

'Wow,' I say.

'I know.'

'Why didn't Sasha say anything, do you reckon?'

'I dunno. Embarrassed, maybe?'

Confused, I follow Velvet through the double doors. I just don't get it. Sasha is probably one of the nicest people I've ever met. So why does she surround herself with so many idiots? I know she doesn't really have much choice when it comes to her dad, but you actually get to pick your mates and your boyfriends. At least in theory.

Inside, there's a brightly lit bar and a cold buffet set out on a couple of trestle tables down the centre of the room. At the far end, there's a small stage with a tatty-looking glitter curtain, barely audible Motown music coming out of the massive speakers on either side. Lots of people from the service are already here, picking at sandwiches and sausage rolls and wedges of soggy-looking quiche. It's a familiar scene. I lost my last living grandparent in December – Mum's dad and my granddad. The funeral was awful. Mum got really confused and kept asking what we were doing there, and then got angry and upset every time we tried to explain.

'Speaking of weird, awkward stuff, what's happening with you and Ivy these days?' Velvet asks as we join the queue at the bar. 'You guys OK?'

I ended up telling the others about the whole Ivy sticking her tongue down my throat thing, and they were pretty great about it. I hadn't realized how isolating having just one close friend to talk to could be until she became the one person I *couldn't* talk to. Suddenly having four (very) different perspectives was kind of awesome – from Sasha's softly, softly approach, to Kaitlyn's no-nonsense one, to Dawson's slightly more irreverent take on the whole thing, I felt about ten times better having spoken to them about it. In the end though, I didn't get the chance to put any of their advice into action. A few days after the Bridlington trip, Ivy messaged to say she'd been totally hammered and hadn't meant what she'd said and to just forget about the whole thing.

So I have.

Sort of.

'We're cool, I think,' I say. 'She's seeing someone, actually. This guy she met through the home-schooling network she's part of.'

We even went on a double date a few weeks ago – me and Carly, Ivy and Ross – sitting in a booth at Nando's, making polite conversation over our chicken and chips. It was OK. I mean, we got through it, but I felt weird all night. Watching Ivy giggle and let Ross feed her frozen yogurt, like she was the only contestant in an 'I'm more loved up than you' competition, felt more like looking at a stranger than my best friend.

'People move on,' Carly had said afterwards when I tried to explain why I'd been so quiet.

I think she might be right.

'How about you?' I ask Velvet. 'Any romance on the horizon?'

'*Any romance on the horizon*?' Velvet repeats, laughing. 'You sound like my gran. You'll be asking me if I'm "courting" next.'

'Sorry,' I say, my face flushing.

'Don't be sorry. It's cute. And the answer is no. No romance on the horizon or anywhere else.'

She doesn't seem bummed out about it though. The opposite, in fact – relaxed and carefree and, I don't know, just really happy. A million miles away from the Velvet who let Griff grab her tits in front of us all last summer. *Light years* away from the Velvet who fled crying from Hugo's party that time.

I'm not going to lie, I couldn't help but smile when I saw the story about Hugo's dad splashed over every paper in the newsagents. I've never believed in karma particularly, and I'm not usually into revenge, but as I read the article and realized the full extent of Hugo's dad's spectacular fall from grace, I was temporarily converted.

We order drinks (including a massive glass of wine for Sasha) and scan the room, eventually locating her in the corner, chatting to a couple of old people who I guess must be friends of her nan's. Poor Sasha. Her face is all blotchy from crying, and she looks like she hasn't slept properly in days.

'We'll leave you young people to it,' one of the women volunteers, once Sasha has introduced us.

'You really don't have to,' Velvet says.

But they're insistent, patting Sasha on the hand before shuffling away.

'For you,' Velvet says, pushing the glass of wine into Sasha's hand.

'Thanks, but I'd better not,' Sasha murmurs, putting it down on the table behind her. 'My dad might see.'

'But you're eighteen,' Velvet points out. 'And your nan just died.'

'I know. He's just a bit funny about things like that sometimes.'

'Your nan sounds like she was a proper legend,' I say. 'I loved the story the officiant told about her false teeth; that was well funny.'

'Yeah, she was the best,' Sasha says, tears glistening in her eyes. Her gaze drifts over my right shoulder. 'Oh God. Not now.'

'What's wrong?' I turn round.

Michela and Will are swaggering towards us carrying two drinks each, Michela shimmying along to Aretha Franklin's "Respect".

'Come on,' Velvet says, reinserting Sasha's glass of wine into her hand and pulling her towards the fire exit.

'Joe, bring crisps,' she instructs over her shoulder.

I do as I'm told, grabbing three bags from the buffet table and hurrying after them.

Out the back of the club, there's a scrubby little play area with a couple of broken swings, a slide with dog poo smeared on it, and a plastic playhouse. It's drizzling a bit, so we crawl inside the playhouse where we sit cross-legged in a little circle on the patchy grass, our knees touching. The girls can just about sit up straight, but I'm too tall and have to hunch over my shoulders to avoid hitting my head on the ceiling.

My phone buzzes. I check it quickly. Carly again.

Blue Steel?!?

I shove it back in my pocket. I swear I told her what I was doing today. She must have forgotten. She can be a bit scatty sometimes.

'To Elaine,' Velvet says, raising her glass.

'To Elaine,' I echo.

'To Nan,' Sasha murmurs softly.

Sasha downs her wine in one big gulp. The second she's finished, she holds out the empty glass in front of her, blinking at it in surprise almost.

I want to say something to make her feel better, but I've been to enough of these things to know it doesn't work like that – that there are no magic words to make the hurt go away. Instead I open all three bags of crisps and put them in the centre of the circle.

'Do you believe in heaven?' Sasha asks, looking up from her glass.

'Depends what you mean by heaven,' Velvet says, pushing a pickled onion Monster Munch on to her finger like a wedding ring. 'Are we talking fluffy clouds and pearly gates?'

'I suppose so,' Sasha says. 'Although I'm not sure Nan would be up for that, thinking about it. She always hated flying, said it freaked her out when she looked out the window and saw nothing but clouds.'

'Well, maybe,' Velvet says slowly, 'you get to pick what your version of heaven looks like. Like, your nan loved gardening, right?'

Sasha nods.

'So maybe her heaven is full of flowers and plants, and she just gets to potter about all day in the sunshine.'

A big fat tear rolls down Sasha's face and plops into her wine glass.

'Shit, sorry – I didn't mean to make you cry,' Velvet says, whipping a tissue out of her handbag.

'No, no, don't apologize. What you said, it was spot on. I mean, what you described, she'd love that.'

God, Velvet is good at this stuff.

My phone buzzes again. And again a few seconds later.

'You should see who it is, Joe,' Sasha says, dabbing at her face with the tissue. 'It might be important. Your mum or something.'

'OK. Thanks,' I say, getting my phone out.

Both messages are from Carly.

BLUE STEEL???????

Are you ignoring me?

I know I should just reply and remind her where I am, or send one of the stupid photos I took earlier, but for some reason I switch off the vibrate function and return the phone to my pocket instead. I don't know why. But then I don't know why I do a lot of stuff these days.

'Everything OK?' Velvet asks.

'Yeah, fine,' I say, patting my pocket. 'All good.'

DAWSON

Hugo Delaney. In Ibiza. God hates me.

I should have kept running. The plan was to have a run, shower, and enjoy my last night in Ibiza. I'm not proud of it, but for a moment I seriously considered pretending I hadn't seen him and just legging it. If our situations were reversed, he'd do exactly that.

Actually, if our situation was reversed, he'd be live-streaming it.

I've seen a lot of people off their boxes on drugs in the last three weeks, but I think Hugo might be in the worst state of any of them. His pupils are huge, and he's covered in sweat – not clean, exercise sweat, but rancid club sweat; I can smell him from two feet away. He stinks of sweat and dried booze, the front of his shirt a homage to Jackson Pollock, made from vomit, blood and sand. His hair is plastered to his head, and someone's taken a swing at him, one eye swollen shut, a cut near his eyebrow. I almost didn't recognize him. If it hadn't been for the press coverage because of his dad, I probably wouldn't have.

I realize I'm feeling something that's way too close to pity, and remind myself that he's a git. Not that I need to, because he looks up at me, and for a second he looks like himself, his lips curving into a sneer, his gaze sharpening in his one good eye, and I brace myself for whatever horrible thing he's going to say.

Hugo starts to cry.

'Shit,' I say aloud. Now I can't leave him.

I look at him and sigh. Then, holding my breath, I try to lift him.

'Get the fuck off me,' he spits between sobs, trying to push me away. 'I don't need your fucking help.'

'You were literally just whimpering "Help", Hugo,' I sigh, hauling him up and waiting to see if he can stand on his own.

'I didn't mean you,' he mutters.

'What have you taken?'

He shrugs, and then staggers. I put my hands on his shoulders, steadying him again.

'Drink this.' I hand him my water bottle and he looks at it, then at me. 'It's water, Hugo. Drink it.' I unclip my phone from my armband and stare at it. Should I call Dad? Kait? An ambulance – no, they'll involve the police, and the cops here are not friendly to drugged-up tourists.

He flips the lid and takes a sip, then a gulp, and then he's glugging it down like he's dying of thirst.

'Steady.' I try to take it from him, but he upends it over his head, and then, to my absolute horror, he howls like a wolf, hauls his arm back, and throws my water bottle maybe thirty feet up the beach. A hen party sat at the bar cheers.

'Hugo, what the hell?' I stare at him.

'Oh relax, I'll buy you a new one,' he says.

'What are you even doing here?' I ask.

'Boys' holiday.' His voice is sharp and slurred all at once.

'Where are the boys?'

'Fucking wankers. WANKERS,' he bellows.

Someone shouts it back.

'Do you know where you're staying?'

He ignores me, gazing off into the distance, tilting his head from left to right.

'Hugo? Do you know where you're staying? Where's your phone?'

He stares at me for a solid ten seconds, then pats his pockets and shakes his head, before throwing his arms wide in the universal sign for *I don't know*.

Shit. Shit. Shit.

Now what?

'Stay there,' I tell him, walking a few paces away and pulling up Kait's number. So much for our secret getaway . . .

'Hey!' She sounds bright when she answers. 'Are you almost back?'

'Listen, we've got a problem.'

'What is it? Are you all right?'

'I'm fine. But . . . Hugo's here, and he's *not* fine. In fact, he's off his tits on something . . . Kait?' I say when she doesn't reply.

'Hugo? As in Hugo Delaney? Hugo is here? In Ibiza?'

I can picture her face as she says it, and it makes me smile. 'The one and only. I was on the way back, and there he was, collapsed on the beach by Savannah. He's a mess, Kait. Doesn't have his phone, doesn't know where his mates are . . .'

'No. I know what you're going to say, and no. Don't do it.'

'Kait . . .'

Again she falls silent.

'It's our last night, Dawson.'

'I know. But . . .' I turn around and look at Hugo, still standing exactly where I left him, staring at the ocean, fingers of his left hand pressed to his wrist. Taking his pulse, I realize. Behind us, the strip is lit up, people shouting and screeching, music pumping. As I watch, a guy runs down the strip, stops, pulls down his shorts and moons at a group of women sitting under white shades. Somewhere else I hear glass smash, and more whoops. It's chaos. Bad enough trying to navigate it sober, but on drugs . . .

Something really bad might happen to him, and it'd be on me.

'I'm going to call Trish and ask her to pick us up,' I say. 'I can't leave him, Kait. We'll just put him to bed and pretend he's not there.'

'If it was the other way around, he wouldn't be a hero for you.'

'I know. But it isn't. See you soon.'

I hang up, and then send a kiss, counting the seconds until she sends one back. Eleven. Moderately pissed off, but still willing to salvage the night. Good times.

Then I call my stepmum, giving her the basics, and ask her to pick us up from the bottom of Carrer de Lepant. It's a two-minute walk – even Hugo should be able to manage that. She doesn't ask questions, just says she'll be there in ten minutes. I like Trish; she's great, really easy-going. Although it does make me wonder what on earth Dad saw in my mum. She and Trish are polar opposites.

When I look back again at Hugo, he's gone.

I see him weaving his way along the strip and sprint after him.

'Let's go and sit down, shall we?' I say, steering him back around.

'I'm not a fucking child,' he says, somewhat losing the high ground as he trips over his feet and lands face first on the floor.

As he sits up, I realize we're being watched. Not in a look-at-those-classic-British-lads-on-holiday way. But properly watched. Two girls, maybe my age, maybe a bit older. Watching me.

As soon as I make eye contact, they grin and come over.

'Are you Dawson Sharman?' the taller one asks in a broad Scottish accent, smiling at me.

'You've got to be fucking kidding me,' Hugo says, leaning forward and burying his head in his hands.

I ignore him. 'I am, yeah.'

'Oh my God, we used to love *Dedman High*!' The second girl's face lights up. 'You were my first crush! Are you still acting?'

'No, I'm not. I've just finished a year at college, actually.'

'Really?' the Scottish girl peers at me. 'What were you studying?'

'Creative writing. Screenwriting,' I tell her. I couldn't quite quit showbiz. It's what I know.

'Like, for films? Are you going to write your own stuff then?' the other girl asks, as she curls a lock of brown hair around her finger.

'That's the plan,' I say breezily. Actually, I've got an interview with Jasper Montagu-Khan when I get home. By some miracle, my lecturer is his godfather, and he put my name forward for a job as his assistant. The pay is essentially peanuts, but I'd get to work directly with Jasper. Me and Kait are obsessed with his last Netflix series. We binged the whole thing in a day, and I've watched all of them at least three times since. He's a genius, and he's only four years older than me.

'Can we get a selfie?' the Scottish girl asks, and I say yes, offering to take it because my arms are the longest. We all squash in, and I take a few shots.

'Is that your boyfriend?' the brown-haired girl asks, looking curiously at Hugo, who is taking his pulse again, right wrist, then left, then back to right.

'God, no. Just a . . . Someone I know. My dad lives here. He runs Beer and Loathing over on Calo Gracia beach. I'm visiting him.'

The tall girl is peering at Hugo. 'Was he in *Dedman* too? I know him from somewhere . . .'

Hugo looks at them then, and even in his messed-up state, he manages to do a quick appraising sweep, and settles on the brunette as the prettiest one. I can tell from the way he leers at her.

She recoils, thank God.

'We'd better be off,' she says warily, eyeing Hugo with disgust. 'Where did you say your dad's bar was?'

'Beach front. Calo Gracia – it's a great place.'

'Maybe we'll see you there?'

I nod non-committally and wave them off, before turning back to Hugo.

'Come on.' I hold out a hand to help him up. To my surprise, he takes it.

He follows me in silence down Carrer de Lepant, saying nothing until we've both sat down on a shaded wall.

'So your dad lives here?' he asks.

'Yeah. He moved here when I was three, with Trish. They got married out here, and opened a bar together. Trish is coming to pick us up.'

He's silent for a moment. 'Was the divorce bad? Between your parents?'

'They weren't married,' I say. I have a sneaking suspicion I know where this is going, and he proves me right a split second later.

'You'll know all about my dad fucking that Labour bastard, I suppose.'

I can't imagine anyone doesn't know. It was the number one trending topic on Twitter for three days running.

I've been there. Not as bad as this; not even close. But I know what it's like to see your face everywhere, and have strangers calling you, asking for quotes, or probing for info. To have people follow you down the street, into shops, into toilets. I know what it's like to be dehumanized and dissected. But you deserve it when you put yourself out there, right? That's the theory. You're asking for it.

'Yeah, I know,' I reply.

'So embarrassing. I just mean, God . . . of all the fucking clichés in the world. And my own mother . . . I cannot believe those people are responsible for my genes. I'm shagged, basically.'

He's starting to sound like himself again, and a little flare of hope bursts inside me. Maybe he'll be sober enough to remember where his mates are, and I can get back to Kait. Because as much as I feel sorry for him, this is not how I wanted to spend tonight. Or any night.

At that moment, my phone buzzes, and I see a text from her.

I've blown up the air mattress. He can piss off if he thinks he's getting our bed x

'Kait? As in Kaitlyn – Kaitlyn from the lift?' Hugo says, and I realize he read my message. 'Is she here? Why is she . . . ? Wait, *our bed*? Are you two . . . ? Oh my, wow. Are you two . . . ? But I thought you were gay.'

And there it is. You know what, Hugo? I thought I was gay too. In fact, I was convinced of it, what with my one hundred per cent only-fancying-men record prior to this. Believe me, pal, no one was more surprised than I was to find out I was attracted to a girl. Not least because, as well as having to figure out how to have a relationship with a girl, it meant having to re-explain my sexuality to pretty much everyone I've ever met. Not my idea of a great time.

'Yeah, yeah – my girlfriend. I know, right. I thought I was gay too, but actually I'm bi . . . No, it wasn't a phase . . . No, I don't think this is a phase either . . . I don't know if my next partner will be a man. All I know is I'm happy in the relationship I'm in now . . . I don't know if it bothers her that I've slept with guys before – I haven't asked . . . Good talk.'

You'd think it'd be easier to be bi than gay. Like my dad said when I told him: 'Sounds like the best of both worlds.' But it's not. I don't belong anywhere – there's no social coding for bisexuality, and neither side is happy you exist. At best, while I'm with Kait I'm invisible because no one cares about a boy and a girl being together. At worst, I'm an indecisive sex maniac who will sleep with literally anyone. And at absolute rock bottom is the fear I'm a fake bisexual, because Kait is the only girl I've ever fancied. What if I'm not bi, but Kait-sexual? How do you know? When do you know?

Hugo is staring at me, and I sigh. 'Yeah. We're together. Turns out I'm bi. It's not . . . It's pretty new for me. I mean, for both of us. We've only been properly together for three months. And Kait has her own stuff going on, so we're keeping it on the down low for now, while we figure it out.'

I realize then that I've told Hugo Delaney about me and Kait before Sasha, Joe and Velvet. How bizarre.

He's silent for a really long time, and then he looks at the ground. 'Do you think that's what my father is? Bisexual?'

I nearly fall off the wall.

'I mean, he must have fancied my mother at one point, surely? Although he did go to Winchester . . . College,' he adds, when I look at him blankly. 'All boys boarder?' He sighs, and I can hear the eye-roll in it.

'He might be,' I say finally. 'It is a spectrum, after all.'

'What is?'

'Sexuality.'

'Oh do fuck off,' he says. 'You sound like the bloody Internet.' He kicks his heels against the wall like a kid.

'How are you feeling?' I ask.

'I don't need counselling, Dawson.'

'I meant because of the drugs. What did you take?'

'Oh. Better, I think. And I don't know. I thought it was coke, but it must have been cut with something else. I'm normally fine on coke.' He shrugs.

Trish's car pulls up then, and she beeps the horn. I hop down off the wall, but Hugo hesitates.

'Well, this has been such great fun,' he says, not looking at me. 'But I think I'll be all right to head back now.'

'You don't have to.'

Hugo looks at me.

'It's late, and you look like shit. You stink. Come back with us, have a shower, get some food and sleep, and we'll drop you back in town in the morning on our way to the airport. We're leaving tomorrow, so you don't have to worry about bumping into us again.'

Hugo looks at the car, down at his shirt, then at me. 'What about Kaitlyn? I'm pretty sure she doesn't want me there.'

'She really doesn't,' I say cheerily. 'And she'll probably make you suffer for it. But, she gets it. You know? She gets being—'

'I need you to not finish that sentence,' Hugo warns me. He takes a deep breath. 'Fine. But only because the key card to my room was in my wallet, which I seem to have lost, and I can't be bothered to deal with the hotel right now.'

He crosses to the car and opens the passenger door.

'I don't think so, my love,' Trish's Black Country tones assault him. 'Not looking like that. You can get in the back, thank you.'

I bite back a smirk. Trish and Dad have two massive Alsatians called Reeves and Mortimer, and the backseat is their domain when they're in the car. Thank God his clothes are already ruined.

Hugo casts me a dark look, closes the door, and walks towards the back.

'Sharman . . .' He pauses. 'This doesn't mean we're friends.'

'Thank Christ for that,' I say, smiling as I get into the car.

When I look at him in the rear-view mirror, I swear he's almost smiling too.

KAITLYN

Maybe this isn't very nice of me, but my first thought when I heard about Hugo's current state – and again when I saw him, pupils saucer-wide, shirt ripped and stained with blood – was the very selfish *Did it have to be* Hugo?

I mean, of all the people to find out about us first. It's not like Dawson and I have many mutuals – which is partly why we've been able to keep our relationship a cosy secret from them – but of all the ones we do have, Hugo is the very last I'd choose. It should've been Sasha, or Velvet, or even Joe.

When he and Dawson arrive at the flat, he tries his usual suggestive smirk, but because he's clearly tripping, it comes out a bit wonky. 'Kaitlyn! What an unexpected pleasure.' He looms towards me, stumbling slightly. 'Can you see me? Should I get closer?'

'Who . . . who is that?' I ask weakly, flailing my arms out, tapping his face all over. 'Hugo? Hugo, is that you?' I enjoy just a second of him looking absolutely horrified, then give his face a light yet definitive slap. 'Yes, I can see you, Hugo, you arse.'

Dawson steps around Hugo, laughing, and bends to kiss me. 'Sorry,' he whispers.

Hugo bends his head down between us, ruining the moment. 'I need the bathroom,' he announces.

Dawson gestures, and Hugo stumbles off down the hall, hand to his mouth. In his sudden absence, I look at Dawson.

'I couldn't leave him,' he says.

I sigh. 'I know.' I smile at him, feeling it spread into my cheeks, crinkling my nose. Smiling never felt like this before Dawson. 'You softie.'

The sound of Hugo's elaborate retching ruins the moment somewhat, but Dawson still touches his fingers to my cheek and smiles back.

How unlikely this all is, I can't help thinking. Not just Hugo vomming into the toilet on what was meant to be mine and Dawson's lovely secret holiday fun-time, but the fact that Dawson and I are here at all. Here in Ibiza, here in his father's flat, here as a couple. 'You were just a poster on my bedroom wall,' I'd said to him the first time we had sex. (After, that is. *After* the first time we had sex.) I realized what an odd thing it was to say as soon as the words had fallen out of my mouth, but Dawson understood, because he chuckled softly in the dark and squeezed my hand.

The thing I didn't tell him is that I still have that poster. Folded carefully and stored in my memory box. Is that weird? Probably. But I could never get rid of it now.

It's not just the fact that he's famous though, or even that he was in a show I loved and that I fancied him once. It's that we were mates, just mates. Long after he was Famous Guy Dawson he was My Mate Dawson . . . My Gay Mate Dawson.

'We're still mates,' Dawson said when I said this to him, wanting to know if he felt the unlikeliness of it like I did.

'Bedmates,' I said.

He grinned. 'Mates who mate.'

'Oh my God,' I said, laughing so hard my chest ached. 'The word "mate" has lost all meaning.'

We haven't said *I love you* yet, Dawson and me. But I do. I love him.

'Christ.' Hugo's voice sounds down the hall, and we both turn in time to see his head appear around the bathroom door, his hands clutching the doorframe. 'I feel like absolute shit.'

'Yeah, you look it too,' Dawson says.

Hugo claws his way out of the bathroom and shuffles a few metres down the hall towards us, leaning against the wall as he goes. All of his usual Hugo bravado is gone. He looks wrecked, actually. Wrecked and strangely young. It's been a long time since I last saw him in person – though I've seen him in the papers since that whole political-scandal thing with his dad, when they kept using that family picture from his birthday – and I realize that I'd been thinking of him as older than he is. But he's the same age as me, however rich he is, and I still feel like a kid most days.

'What did you take?' I ask.

He shrugs. 'I don't know.'

His face wobbles a little, and I take a panicked step back, almost crashing into Dawson. He's not going to cry, is he? I can deal with a lot of things – the gradual loss of my sight, and falling in love with my gay friend, and that customer at the florist's who complained about 'politically correct hiring' to the local paper after I got her order wrong – but I will not be able to handle a crying Hugo.

'Do you want, um . . .' I glance at Dawson, then helplessly down the corridor. What are you meant to give people who are off their face and don't want to be? 'Tea?'

Dawson snorts a laugh, and I glare at him.

'Kaitlyn,' Hugo says suddenly, loudly. I turn back to him reluctantly. 'Your hair is majestic.'

'Wow, Hugo,' I say. 'You really are off your face. Come on.

I'll get you some water as well.'

I dyed the stripe in my hair gold, specially for Ibiza. And I got my tongue pierced, pretty much on a whim, the day before I flew out here. ('Oh, Kaity,' Mum said. 'Not another one.')

'I'll get it,' Dawson says, touching his hand to the small of my back. 'Why don't you go sit on the sofa, Hugo?'

He's speaking to him like a child, but it works. If anything, Hugo seems to like being told what to do. He swings around and begins clawing his way back along the hall, towards the living room.

Lowering my voice, I look at my boyfriend. 'I can do it,' I say, trying not to frown.

'I know,' he says. 'I didn't mean you couldn't. I just don't want to have to sit on my own with Hugo, that's all.'

He laughs a little and grins, but I don't smile back. Does he not trust me to make tea?

Yesterday, I smashed a mug in the kitchen, but it was an accident, and it could have happened to anyone. It was that stupid dog – Reeves, the really annoying one – getting in my way; it was nothing to do with my eyes. But maybe Dawson . . . ?

No, I'm just being paranoid, not to mention unfair. Dawson, maybe more than anyone else in my life, has always been great about my progressive sight loss. He's never patronized me or done anything stupid like talk extra loud or offer to cut up my food for me. He downloaded a bunch of accessibility apps to his own phone just so he'd have a better idea of what my life is like. He offers me his arm whenever we walk anywhere, and never looks offended if I don't take it. It was Dawson who I talked to about maybe getting a guide dog one day. Dawson who created a YouTube playlist of guide dog videos for me. Dawson who I was sitting with when I applied. Dawson who I called when I was officially put on the waiting list.

'OK,' I say, feeling a smile on my face. 'Thanks.'

I make my way across the hall, letting my fingertips graze the wall as I go. Even though I've only been here for a short time, I know the layout of the flat so well I don't need to worry about navigating my way around, because Dawson and I did a special tour of it when I first arrived. And I'm thinking about this, how it's nice to feel like I can walk around as confidently as I do in my own house, when I trip over the sandals that Hugo has carelessly flung off his feet in the middle of the doorway, and I go crashing – *really* crashing – to the floor.

I land heavily, and it hurts. It fucking hurts. Fucking sandals. Fucking eyes. Fucking Hugo.

I've barely had a chance to sit up when Dawson comes running into the room, his voice panicked. 'Kait? Kait?'

I look up in time to see Hugo's head appear above the arm of the sofa like a startled bird. He looks like he's been asleep, even though he's barely been in the room for two minutes. 'What was that?' he asks.

I throw one of his sandals at him. 'You're such an insensitive dick, Hugo!'

This is completely unfair, and I know it is, because there are a lot of reasons to call Hugo a dick, but him taking off his sandals while high as a kite after the year he's had is hardly one of them. But still. It's yell at him, or cry.

God, Dawson and I could have been shagging on the balcony right now.

'Are you OK?' Dawson places his hand on my arm.

Hugo's eyes are childishly wide with confusion and worry. Why can't he be the Hugo I remember, with all that rich-boy swagger, and say something snide in that posh voice of his so I can say something back, and we can properly go at it? That would be so satisfying. I don't want him worrying about me.

'I'm bloody fine,' I snap, jerking my arm away from Dawson and pushing myself to my feet. I kick the remaining sandal into the corner of the room and throw myself on to the sofa.

'Did you hurt your—?'

'Just get the tea, Dawson.'

Dawson looks at me for a moment, more confused than anything, but eventually he shrugs and leaves the room.

'Sorry,' Hugo says.

What a weird word to hear come out of his mouth.

'Yeah,' I say. 'Whatever.'

We both sit there in silence for a while. I can hear Dawson in the kitchen, the soft *thunk* of the bin lid opening and closing. I should probably say something, but I have no idea what. It's not like Hugo and I were ever anything resembling friends, even before the whole Velvet thing.

Thinking of Velvet makes me think about her and Sasha and Joe at the funeral, and I feel a soft twinge of guilt that I'm not there too. But only a tiny one, because I thought they – or Sasha at least – might ask me a little bit more about the 'holiday' I'd said I'd be on, and then maybe I would've told them about Dawson and me. They didn't though. They never do.

'Hey,' I start to say, turning to Hugo, about to ask him if he's been in contact with any of the others since the whole national-scandal thing. But I have to stop, because Hugo is crying. Actually crying. 'Oh shit,' I say.

Hugo is just sitting there – the single sandal I'd thrown at him cradled in his hands – weeping. Fat tears are rolling down his face. His lips and chin are quivering.

Oh God. Is this a drugs thing? Is this just what happens during a comedown? Is this even a comedown? Dawson would know. Actually, where the hell is Dawson? How long does it take to make three cups of tea?

'Don't cry,' I say. My hand reaches out of its own accord and smacks at his shoulder, probably too hard, but he lets out a loud, grateful-sounding sniff, so I do it again.

And then Hugo Delaney tips over and falls on to me. His head is in my lap, his arms are hugging my knees, and he is sobbing.

'Oh my Christ,' I say.

'I'm sorry,' he's saying, over and over, and something else that I can't decipher through the tears.

I try, 'Why?' and then, 'It's OK, Hugo,' but he doesn't seem to notice. The poor guy is going to pieces on my lap, and it's actually kind of heartbreaking.

I finally manage to make out what he's saying, which turns out to be, 'I made you fall over,' and I'm so surprised, I laugh a little. 'Hugo, that's OK,' I say. 'Really, I'm fine.' I feel a tiny bit bad then that I threw his sandal at him. Yeah, tripping over hurt a bit, and it was annoying, but it's not worth him having some kind of breakdown over.

'I'm a terrible human being,' he sobs. 'I hate myself, do you know that? Nobody likes me. Why would they? I don't even like me.'

This is the moment Dawson walks into the room. He freezes in the doorway, three mugs balanced in his hands, eyes widening at the tableau in front of him.

I smile helplessly, still patting Hugo's shoulder.

'Oh, mate,' Dawson says.

Hugo sits up abruptly, dashing the tears from his eyes with a still-bloodstained wrist. He sniffs a few times, coughs, then looks away from us both.

'Hey, don't stop on my account,' Dawson says. He sets the mugs down on the coffee table and kneels on to the carpet. 'No shame in crying, you know. And you've had a fucker of a year.'

I nod. 'Plus all the drugs.'

'And the fact you're stuck here with us,' Dawson adds. He grins at me, and I laugh.

To my surprise, Hugo lets out a hoarse little chuckle. 'Yeah, it's not what I had planned, that's for sure.'

Dawson holds out a mug to him and he takes it.

'Cheers.'

'What actually happened tonight, Hugo?' I ask.

He shrugs. 'I don't even know. I just wanted to forget for a while – this *fucker of a year*. But I lost my friends, and whatever I took messed with my head, and someone punched me . . . I don't know. And then there was Dawson.'

'An unlikely saviour,' Dawson says.

'All right, don't get carried away,' Hugo says, and this time all three of us laugh. 'Look,' he says, 'I'm sorry to ruin your night. I should just get back to . . . wherever the hell I'm meant to be.'

'Nah, you're staying here tonight,' Dawson says, casually but firmly.

'On the sofa,' I add, just to be clear.

Hugo rubs the back of his neck, frowning. 'Are you sure?'

'Course,' I say. 'Sleep it off at least. But maybe you should call one of your friends so they know you're, you know, safe. Not arrested or dead.'

His shoulders lift. 'Oh, no one's worrying about me.' He says this quietly, softly. The way people say true things.

'Then you need better friends,' I say. And then I hear the unlikeliest words come out of my mouth, maybe because he looks so sad and pathetic, or maybe I'm just getting soft. 'You should try hanging out with the group again.'

'From the lift?' Hugo asks uncertainly. 'Don't they all hate me? After, you know . . . Velvet?'

'Maybe,' I say. 'But you could always try apologizing for that and just seeing what happens. Sorry can go a long way, sometimes.'

I see something cloud his eyes, and I guess he's thinking about his dad, but he doesn't say so.

'Maybe I . . .' He hesitates, glancing at me, and then away again. 'I wouldn't know how to start.'

I pull out my phone. 'No time like the present.' I open our WhatsApp group and wave the screen at him.

'Wait a sec,' he begins, looking alarmed. 'What are you doing?'

'Starting,' I say. 'On your behalf.' I click on the camera icon and hold my phone out in front of us. 'Give me your best "surprise-Hugo-in-Ibiza" face.'

For a moment, I think Hugo is going to yell at me and flounce off, but instead his face crumples into a defeated laugh.

'You are nothing like I thought you were, Kaitlyn.'

'Well, same to you,' I say. It's not quite true, but saying anything else would be mean. 'Dawson, get up here. You should take this picture, what with you being able to see properly, and everything.'

Dawson climbs up between us, shaking his head and laughing. 'Are we really doing this?' he asks as he takes the phone from me, positioning it in selfie-mode in front of our faces.

'We really are,' I say. 'Ready? Say . . . *Ibiza!*'

VELVET

Sasha's dad is watching me like I'm a potential criminal while I wait at the bar. It's unsettling. Particularly with cheesy retro pop music playing in the background and drunk old people shuffling around – today's been a bit surreal.

All day, I've seen how Sasha can't get away with doing anything without her dad noticing – and, by extension, neither can her friends. It makes me wonder what it must be like to have a parent like that, who tells you what to do and cares about what you're up to. I honestly can't decide if I'm madly envious, or relieved that's not me. I don't even see much of my mum these days, since she got together with her latest boyfriend. I don't really see much of anyone.

Anyway, right now I'm just glad when some ranty old bloke accosts her dad at the bar, so I can grab my bottle of wine and sneak back outside, where Joe and Sasha are still huddled in the comically small playhouse. I am full of fondness for them both as I climb back into our secret den.

'You're a star,' Sasha says as I fill up her glass. 'You both are.' She smiles at Joe. 'I really needed this.'

'I'm really glad we could come,' I say.

'Me too,' Joe adds. 'I mean, imagine if you only had Michela and Billy – sorry, I mean *Will* – for support. What a shame they had to leave in such a hurry . . .'

The three of us giggle guiltily. I have to admit, I felt a very mean sense of satisfaction when Will got so drunk as soon as we got to the social club that Michela – with a face like pure thunder – had to take him home early. She tried to get Sasha to help out, but Joe stepped in and told her that, today of all days, Michela could deal with the mess herself – literally – when Will puked on his own shoes and a little bit on hers. Joe just calmly left them to it, taking Sasha with him. He handled the whole situation beautifully, I've got to say.

The thing is, even though I've been joining in Joe's good-natured eye-rolling behind their backs, Michela and Will today reminded me a bit too much of my past self. Of me and Griff last summer. Of everything I used to be. Thinking about it makes me cringe. I feel like a completely different person now.

'Couldn't have happened to a nicer couple.' Joe chuckles.

His knee accidentally nudges against my thigh as he shifts to try and get comfortable in the cramped space. I wonder how 'Old Me' would have felt about being in such close proximity to 'New Joe'. It's not hard to guess. I mean, obviously I've noticed that Joe has suddenly grown more handsome. It's hard to put my finger on how – whether it's his haircut, or because he's been going to the gym or something. It's mostly a new sort of confidence. He's become more solid. I suppose he's grown up.

And so have I. That's why Joe suddenly becoming all sexy and getting a girlfriend doesn't have much of an effect on me. I can be genuinely happy for him, as a friend. As a good human being. Because I don't measure my own worth by trying to get boys to fancy me any more. I've realized there are more important things to think about.

'I'm so embarrassed!' Sasha wails. 'I can't believe I ever went there. You know, with Billy. And Michela's not much better these days. You must think I'm such a loser. I mean, Michela's meant to be my best mate. It's all so pathetic.'

'Don't think about it like that,' I say. 'We know you, Sasha, and we love you. You're not defined by other people, especially not *them*. We'd never judge you like that. If anything, it's all because you're *too* nice. You just need to think of yourself and what *you* need sometimes, that's all.'

This all comes out sounding much more serious and intense than I intended it to, and it's only as I say it that I realize I could just as easily be talking about myself. From the way they're both looking at me, Sasha and Joe are obviously thinking the same.

'What happened, Velvet?' Sasha asks gently. 'I mean, after last summer with Griff and everything . . . ?'

Disappearing from the WhatsApp group was the least of my concerns at the time. It was all such a blur, I'm momentarily surprised that she even noticed. I managed to style it out, hide what was happening from pretty much everyone, forget the whole thing. I just went dark for a while. Yet from the looks on their faces now, it was these unlikely distant friends who noticed, who worried about me.

I'm about to laugh it off and make a joke of it, like I always do. Say that today's grim enough without them hearing about my sad life. I don't want them to think I'm a total disaster, these people who have already seen me at my worst. Sasha's even seen me naked, that terrible time in Hugo's flat. Between Sasha and Joe, the two of them know a lot of things about me that I would rather forget.

But they're both looking at me like they actually care, and I realize that these are the people I want to talk to. Finally.

When I try to speak, my throat closes up. It's like I don't even have the language for this; I don't know how or where to start. I haven't said any of it out loud before. Not to my mum or Chelsea – not to anyone. I've been on my own with it for nearly a year, hoping that if I can forget about it, then it never really happened.

I've been trying to focus on the future, and I've been doing pretty well, but sometimes it's so hard to move forward when you've got this big secret that nobody knows about.

'When I saw you all last summer,' I begin, 'well . . . it made me realize a lot of things. I know I went quiet for a bit, so you don't really know the full story. I mean, obviously you know I'm not with Griff any more. But I broke up with him that day, straight after I watched you all drive off.'

'Good riddance,' Joe mutters.

'Yeah, I know. Best decision I ever made. Except it wasn't that easy . . .' I literally take a deep breath, just like people do in films when they have to say something big. I realize now, that's quite realistic. 'I was pregnant.'

Even saying it feels weird. Like it happened to someone else. I'm unbelievably grateful that both of my friends try their best not to look shocked by this news.

'It was super early. I hadn't told anyone. I even considered not telling Griff at all, just getting rid of it without him ever knowing, but I didn't think I could live with myself.' I force a sort-of laugh. 'So, as you can imagine, *that* was a great conversation. It all came out in one go, the poor bloke. I'm dumping you, I'm pregnant, and I'm having an abortion.'

'Bloody hell, Velvet,' Joe says quietly, while Sasha is clearly incapable of forming words right now, let alone sentences.

'I knew having an abortion was the only option. I couldn't stay with Griff; I couldn't have a baby. It would have ruined my life. Actually, worse – it would have stopped my life from ever starting. Griff tried to stop me. He threatened to tell everyone that I wanted to leave him and kill his baby, heartless bitch that I am. That didn't bother me half as much as he thought it would.

I'm not ashamed; I don't care what other people think. But in the end, he said he'd leave me alone as long as I never told anyone and we could forget any of it ever happened. That seemed easier, so I agreed. He's got a new girlfriend now, and he cuts me dead whenever I see them around town. Which is fine by me, really. But it means nobody knows. I've never told anyone any of this. Anyway, I went by myself and I did it. Had an abortion.'

'Was it horrible?' Sasha manages to ask.

I have to think about this. I can't remember much about the day. I had to get the train to Leeds. Two hours each way. I wore my smartest outfit, so they wouldn't think I was some kind of chavvy teenager you read about in the *Daily Mail*. I put on a lot of make-up that morning, trying to look older. But now I think I was just trying to not look like myself. So I could pretend it was happening to someone else. Not me. This could never happen to me.

Everyone at the clinic was actually really kind to me, even though I sort of didn't want them to be, because I was worried their kindness might make me cry. I just remember a lot of hanging around and not making eye contact with any of the other girls in the waiting room. I was the only one on my own. That's what I remember: feeling alone. It was the loneliest day of my life.

The actual procedure – they always said 'procedure'; nobody ever said the word 'abortion' – didn't take long. They gave me a cup of tea and a KitKat after, asked if I had someone to take me home. I lied so I could get out of there.

It was rush hour in central Leeds; I had to stand up on the train. I was so tired. That was what made me cry in the end, the only time. All the respectable commuters pretended not to notice me. Just a girl weeping on the train, too young to feel this old. A little bit pale, trying her hardest not to faint. All alone.

'Yeah,' I say. 'It was. It was horrible. But I knew it was the right thing to do. And then I just had to get on with it, you know?'

I felt like dying when I had to drag myself out of bed at crack of dawn the next morning to go to work at the hotel. But I had to. I couldn't tell anyone what had happened. And from that day on, I've felt stronger. If I could get through that, I can do anything. Well, maybe not *anything*. Let's not get carried away. But *something*.

'I can't believe you had to go through that all by yourself, Velvet,' Joe says.

'I'm glad you told us,' Sasha says, reaching for my hand.

'I mean, don't go feeling sorry for me or anything. I wish none of it had happened, but it's OK. I'm OK. Griff was a shit boyfriend, and I wasn't ready to have a baby. Life is getting better now. I'm starting a part-time college course, English Literature. I don't know exactly how, but I'm going to get out of there. I've got to.'

It's true – the world seems bigger to me now than it ever did before. That's the good side of everything that's happened. I might feel older and sadder than I used to, but for the first time I'm also starting to feel a lot more like myself. I guess, like Joe, I've become more solid. Like Sasha too, who's just lost her nan and is *still* thinking of other people and always trying her best to do the right thing.

'Thank you,' I say, meaning it. 'I know that was pretty heavy, but I'm really glad I could tell you two.'

I'm still holding Sasha's hand, and Joe puts his arm around me. The three of us sit in silence for a moment, and it doesn't even feel weird. I've been feeling so isolated from all my family and friends this past year, so different. All I've been able to think about is how I'm going to change my life, how I'm going to move on; trying to make myself stronger, working hard. This is the first time I've felt contented just in the moment for a long time. It feels like a sign that things are going to be OK.

The silence is only broken when someone's phone dings. Joe automatically reaches into his pocket.

'Is it Carly?' I ask, patting his knee fondly. 'Is she after more of that Joe Lindsay Blue Steel?'

'Nah, it's not Carly.'

His brow furrows slightly as he scrolls through his messages.

'It's Kaitlyn, on the group chat. Let's see what she – Oh my God, what the actual . . . ?'

'Take that dress off. You look ridiculous.'

It's the first thing Sasha's father has said to her since they left the social club. Even then, he didn't say much. By the time she, Joe and Velvet had emerged from the playhouse, warm and giggly from the red wine, the buffet had been picked clean, and aside from a few stragglers lingering by the bar, almost everyone had gone home.

Velvet had suggested they grab something to eat, but when Sasha saw her father sitting alone with a half-empty pint of beer, she told them that she'd better go. Before they could protest, her father rose and snatched his suit jacket from the back of the chair he'd been sitting on. 'Let's go,' he said without looking at her. She turned to Velvet and Joe.

'Bye,' she said brightly. 'Thanks for coming. I really appreciate it.'

They didn't say anything, just hugged her: Joe first; then Velvet, who held her so tight it squeezed fresh tears from the corners of her eyes.

'Text me tonight,' Velvet said when she let go, then hugged her again.

'Me too,' Joe said softly, the skin between his eyebrows creasing as he squeezed the top of her arm.

Sasha just nodded, scared that if she did anything else it would all spill out of her. Not just the tears, but everything else. How miserable she was, how she didn't want to get in the car with him or go home with him, back to their cold, dark house with the empty fridge and the sullen silence that would suffocate her if she let it. She wanted to go to her nan's, eat biscuits and drink milky, sweet tea while she filled her in on the gossip from bingo. But she couldn't. It wasn't her nan's house any more, was it? It was just a house, each room cluttered with cardboard boxes, the walls bare except for the clean white rectangles from where the photo frames had been. Her grandparents' wedding day. Her parents' wedding day. Her Aunt Chris's graduation photo. That picture of Sasha on Blackpool beach when she was three in her yellow bathing suit. Christenings, birthdays, holidays. Their whole lives playing out across the walls of her nan's neat little terrace. Now it was all gone – the photos, the heavy crystal vase that used to sit on the windowsill in the living room – her whole life packed up into boxes.

So Sasha went home, because where else was she going to go?

In the sanctuary of her bedroom, she opens her wardrobe and looks at herself in the full-length mirror. She thinks he said it because he was pissed off with her for wearing her mother's dress. And maybe he was right – maybe she does look ridiculous. It's too tight and too short – far too tight and short for a funeral. She peels it off and kicks it into the corner of the room by the laundry hamper and grabs a pair of sweat pants and a jumper from the chest of drawers.

The flat is always cold. Always. Michela doesn't like coming over any more – she says that it 'smells funny'. It does smell funny. There are damp patches in every room. Sasha has to be careful that she doesn't brush past the one in her bedroom, otherwise she gets black stuff on her clothes. In the summer, it's a relief, but in winter, it's unbearable. She has to sleep in sweat pants, a jumper, a dressing gown and two pairs of socks . . . and even then, her nose is cold. When she wakes up in the mornings, the inside of her windows glisten with frost. She used to draw things in it when she was a kid, hearts and stars and flowers, but now she doesn't bother opening the curtains.

Still, she loves her bedroom: loves the white fairy lights she got from Poundworld in the Arndale that she's wound around her wicker headboard; loves her narrow single bed and her pillows that she can't sleep without, even at her nan's; loves her noticeboard of things that she's ripped out of magazines she's picked up in cafes and waiting rooms, pictures of beaches and mountains and big blue skies that make her feet – and heart – itch. It's not much, but it's *hers*. And right now, it's exactly what she needs.

Sasha grabs the pack of wipes from the top of the chest of drawers and begins taking off her make-up. The red wine they'd drunk in the playhouse had stained her mouth the colour of an old bruise, so she'd borrowed Velvet's lipstick to cover it up in case her father noticed. She doesn't know what brand it is, but it's holding like a grudge. It takes two wipes, but eventually she gets it off and sits on the bed with a weary sigh. She can hear her father moving around downstairs; hear him switching the channels on the television – the news, the weather, what sounds like a football game, that ad for car insurance with the pirate – before he turns the television off altogether.

She hates this, the silence. She wishes he'd just say something, yell at her, call her a terrible daughter – and granddaughter – for blowing out the wake to go and get drunk in a playhouse with her mates. She thinks it would make him feel better, even if that isn't what he's really upset about. At least then it would be out in the open.

She can hear him in the kitchen now, opening and closing the cupboard doors, then the fridge. There's nothing in there, she knows, so she isn't surprised when he swiftly closes it again. She's hungry as well. All she's eaten is the crisps she had with Joe and Velvet. The wine hasn't helped: she feels numb and heavy-headed, her stomach aching.

She suddenly remembers the bag of Haribo Starmix that Velvet gave her. She leans over to grab her clutch from the end of the bed, and a choir of angels bursts into song as she opens it to find the bag of sweets. Of all the things to give her – not a bunch of supermarket lilies or a 'With Sympathy' card with a soothing quote from the Bible, but a bag of Haribo Starmix.

It was exactly what she needed.

Sasha rips into the bag, grabs a cola bottle and bites the top off, then pretends to drink it before popping the rest of it into her mouth. She hears her phone buzz on her bedside table and winces as she grabs it. She'd promised to text Velvet and Joe that evening, but she hadn't.

Sure enough, there's a string of messages from them. Joe had even created a WhatsApp group just for the three of them, which Sasha is grateful for, because she doesn't want the others to have to put up with a string of messages about her nan's funeral. Not that they'd even notice. They have enough to deal with, it seems.

Joe Lindsay created group 'Hey!'
Joe Lindsay added Velvet Brown
Joe Lindsay added Sasha Harris

Joe:
Everything all right, Sash?

Velvet:
Yeah. Let us know!
That lipstick really suited you, BTW! You can keep it ☺

Sasha:

Sorry! Yeah, I'm home and eating Starmix in bed

Velvet:

Nice!

Joe:

I'm jealous. I'm eating an egg and cress sandwich on the train. It is not good

Sasha can see Velvet is typing something and holds her breath.

Velvet:

You really OK, Sash?

Sasha:

Yeah. Fine

Joe:

You sure?

Sasha:

Yeah. I mean, today wasn't fun, but you guys being there really helped

Velvet:

How's your dad? He seemed super stressed

Sasha:

He'd just buried his mother

She regrets it immediately.

Sasha:

Sorry

Velvet:

It's OK. It was a stupid question

Sasha can feel her cheeks burning. It's not worry, she realizes; it's shame. She's ashamed. Ashamed that they've been talking about her, about her father. So she decides to deflect before they can push further.

Sasha:

I'm more worried about you, Velvet

Velvet:

Me?

Sasha:

Yeah

Velvet:

Why?

Sasha:

About Hugo . . .

Velvet:

Oh, him

Sasha:

Are you sure you're OK with him being on the scene again?

Velvet:
It's fine

Joe:
If it makes you feel uncomfortable, we can tell him to do one

Velvet:
Seriously, guys, it's fine. All of that feels like forever ago. I'm over it

Sasha:
You sure?

Velvet:
Deffo. Plus, did you see the state of him? Karma kicked his arse

This makes Sasha laugh so hard, she has to cover her mouth with her hand in case her father hears.

Velvet:
Forget Hugo. WHAT ABOUT DAWSON AND KAITLYN?

Joe:
I KNOW!

He never uses all caps, but if there was ever a time to use all caps, this is it.

Sasha:
I had no idea, did you?

Velvet:
NO!

Joe:
No way. Not at all

Sasha:
I thought he was gay

Joe:
Me too

Velvet:
Maybe he's bi?

Joe:
He must be well confused ☺

Velvet:
How long do you think it's been going on?

Joe:
No idea

Sasha:
Why didn't they tell us?

Joe:
I kind of feel bad. Did they think we'd be weird about it?

> I was thinking that too. I'd never judge them.
> I'm honestly happy for them

> Don't read too much into it. They're probably still getting their
> heads around it themselves. I'm sure they would have told us
> when they were ready, but Hugo scuppered that plan

Say what you like about Hugo Delaney, but his timing was impeccable.

It's been a long, weird day. Sasha's whole body is aching with exhaustion, but she can't sleep. Maybe it was the Starmix, or maybe it was two hours of furious texting with Velvet and Joe about whatever the hell was going on in Ibiza, but Sasha's brain is more awake than it's ever been. She can't help but think of Joe.

He doesn't talk about it, but she's seen the change in him in the last three years. That day in the lift, he was all soft lines and pink cheeks, and now there's a hardness to him. A quiet strength she doesn't see in other boys. Billy may now call himself Will, but he's just as childish with his *that's what she said* jokes and his penchant for shoplifting supermarket beer. She doesn't feel comfortable around him like she does with Joe. Joe has grown up, she supposes. Quicker than he would have liked perhaps, but he has. And as she thinks of him, she feels a tug on the invisible string that connects them, because she gets it.

Gets what it's like to have a mother who's there, but isn't.

Sasha remembers looking over her shoulder, scanning the crowd for him before the service started, but there were so many people there she couldn't find him. The crematorium was full, a solemn hum settling over the pews as they waited for the service to begin. It was interrupted every now and then by the rustle of cellophane as people clutching bouquets of flowers shuffled along to make room for the latecomers. That's when she saw Joe and Velvet. They were standing at the back near the doors, and she recalls feeling a nip of panic as she wondered if they were going to leave. But then Joe stepped forward to help a woman with a walking frame towards one of the pews, and Sasha realized that they were standing so that her nan's friends could sit.

Michela would never have done that, and the thought of it – the thought of Joe and Velvet and their huge, tender hearts – made her own heart strain in her chest. When she looked back at the coffin, she felt it again when she saw Kaitlyn's flowers, remembering what Dawson had told her about his aunt's funeral, about the steelpans, and how everyone got drunk after. Everyone else had brought white lilies, so Kaitlyn's bright flowers stood out like a parakeet on a washing line. Her nan would have loved those flowers. She would've put them on the windowsill in her living room in the heavy crystal vase.

What will happen to that vase now?

Then Sasha remembers the gerbera, the orange one she'd put on Steven Jeffords' plaque, and the guilt is dizzying. His funeral was so different. Empty. Quiet. She still doesn't understand why no one was there. How do you go your whole life without leaving your mark on anyone? The thought terrifies her. It terrifies them all, she knows. That's probably why they kept in touch. Why they're so unwilling to let go of one another. And with that, Sasha feels the question she asks herself every time she thinks about Steven Jeffords bob up. It was bound to happen today. How could it not? She was in the same crematorium, looking at the same velvet curtain, the same splinters of light from the stained-glass window scattered across the white walls like jewels. She tries to swallow it back but here it is again.

Was it my fault?

Sasha has played and replayed the scene in the lift over and over for the last three years, and each time she asks herself whether Steven Jeffords might have survived if she hadn't pressed the STOP button. She's wanted to ask the others so many times, but can't. They may have progressed from sending each other funny animal videos and complaining about their day, but they never talk about what happened that day.

Never.

It was a mistake. Sasha knows it was a mistake. She was scared and panicked and pressed the wrong button. Besides, Steven Jeffords had a massive heart attack, that's what it said in the *Manchester Evening News* the next day. Sick with guilt, she'd read every article she could find about him. One said that it was his third heart attack; another, his fourth. One said that he'd felt chest pains that morning.

Why didn't he go to the hospital?

Sasha had even called 111 a few days later, weak with worry that it was her fault, that if she'd pressed the right button, those few minutes would have been enough to get Steven Jeffords to hospital and he might not have died. That's not what 111 was for, she knew, but she had to know, so she'd lied, told the operator that she'd read about Steven Jeffords in the paper and was worried that the same thing would happen to her father, and that she wouldn't know what to do if it did. The woman must have thought she was a right weirdo, but was very sweet anyway, telling her not to worry, that Steven Jeffords was probably dead before he hit the lift floor, and it made Sasha feel better for a while.

But what if he wasn't? What if those few minutes they'd lost because she pressed the STOP button would have made a difference?

What if?

What if?
What if?

The funny thing is, they'd each asked themselves the same question at some point: Was there was something I could have done?

Dawson often wonders why he didn't ask Steven if he needed help. He saw how flushed his cheeks were when he got into the lift, saw the pearls of sweat on his forehead. If he'd suggested that he sit down and drink some water, would Steven have done it? What if he'd got out at the next floor, where someone might have been able to help him? And why did Kaitlyn say that she'd done a first-aid course when she hadn't? If she'd known what she was doing, could she have saved him?

Was there a phone in the lift? Why did no one think to check the control panel?

Why did no one try to force the doors open when the lift stopped?

Why did they just stand there, waiting for someone to rescue them?

All these questions they'd never have answers for.

Eventually, once the shock had passed and the guilt had become easier to ignore, Kaitlyn sent a message to the WhatsApp group. She didn't say anything, just sent a quote she'd found on Tumblr:

Do the best you can until you know better. Then when you know better, do better.

– Maya Angelou

'Shouldve taken the stairs'
Sasha Harris added Hugo Delaney

Hugo:
Guess who's back? ☺

YEAR FIVE

kaitythom

Manchester Training Centre

Liked by dawsonsharman, sashaharris and 29 others

kaitythom After months of waiting . . . say hello to Remy the guide dog! I met him for the first time today. He's two years old and incredible. I think we're going to be friends . . . ❤❤❤

www.petsandmore.com

Shopping Cart

1 x Standard Food Dog Bowl (medium) *Personalized 'REMY' £6.99

1 x Standard Water Dog Bowl (medium) *Personalized 'REMY' £6.99

1 x R&B Tartan Dog Bed (medium) £34.99

1 x Original Kong (red) £8.00

1 x Original Kong (black) £8.00

2 x Pompidou Complete Dry Dog Food (Chicken) 5kg £20.00

Basket total £84.97

Proceed to Checkout

Continue Shopping

Sasha:

MY BODY IS READY FOR DOUGH BALLS!!! 😊

Joe:

Dough balls, dough balls, dough balls

No lie, I dreamed about them last night. Only they were like ten times the size. And they had to serve the garlic butter in a dish the size of a bathtub. Make what you will of that, Dr Freud

Velvet:

Giant dough balls? Best dream ever!!!

I can't wait to eat ALL THE FOOD . . . and see you guys!!!

Dawson:

Imagine if they don't have any dough balls. Imagine it . . .

Hugo:

What the fucking fuck is a 'dough ball'? Is this a sex thing I don't know about? I find that hard to believe . . .

Sasha:

OH MY GOD, HUGO DELANEY YOU HAVE NEVER KNOWN TRUE PLEASURE. YOU DEPRIVED HUMAN

Hugo:

A ball made out of dough is 'true pleasure'? My, oh my . . . Hang on. Trying to override my urge to be a dick about this . . .

Joe:

Once you go dough ball, you never go back!

Does that make ANY sense??

Sasha:

It does to those of us who've experienced food heaven. (Hugo, you will understand after tonight.)

WHY ISN'T TONIGHT *NOW*????????????????????????

Dawson:

Just look at this as extra time to plan what you'll have if they don't have dough balls, Sash ☺

Joe:

Which branch are we going to again?

Velvet:

Thank God for you, Joe. I guess there is more than one Pizza Express in Manchester??!

Joe:

checking OK, we booked the massive one near the uni!

Velvet:

Space for your giant dough balls

Joe:

Oh yeah!

K, you there? Or are you a poor sheltered dough-ball virgin too???

Not to worry, Sasha will convert you with pure enthusiasm alone. Right, Sash?

Velvet:

Pizza Express should def pay you some kind of commission, Sash

HUGO

'Hugo, you really do look ridiculous in those rosary beads. Promise me you're not going to actually wear them out.'

My fingers go to my necklace protectively, and I feel anger snake up in my stomach. A cutting retort sour on my tongue. But no. Not now. Not any more. I'm not 'That Hugo'. So instead I take a deep breath, down into my ribcage, and imagine blue energy pouring through my body, calming me down.

'So, what you up to tonight, Mum?' I expertly change the subject. 'I told you I was going out, didn't I?'

She shakes her head slightly, a smile playing on her lips. 'Yes, you did. You never used to let me know where the hell you were.' She picks up her tiny cup of espresso. 'India's had quite the impact on you, hasn't it?'

I nod and take a sip of my jasmine tea. I've got really into it since India. Before I went, I would've totally been the sort of person who thought jasmine tea was drunk by massive twats, but now I realize *I* was the massive twat.

Ganesh, I was SUCH a twat.

But not now, not any more. I have grown and changed and matured and progressed, and there's nothing I can do about the past, or the future, all I have is the Now. All any of us have is the Now.

'Well, let's see how long it lasts. I can't imagine you'll fit in

267

very well at Bristol wearing that necklace. I've actually got a phone call with the lawyers tonight,' she says. 'Your father is still trying to ruin us.'

Deep breaths into your ribcage, Hugo. Let it all wash over you. Focus on how your feet are connected to this ground, this solid ground, notice how it feels, concentrate on that.

'The stupid man still thinks he's in love. It's ridiculous; he needs to grow up.'

She carries on with her favourite topic – telling me what a dreadful, cowardly, deceitful arsehole my father is. It's been well over a year and still she is not tired of it. I'm not sure what she expected to happen – after she publically outed him and dragged his name through the mud for months. I mean, Dad is an arsehole. And what he did was a really arsehole thing to do, and I really don't understand why Mum's now so confused about him moving in with this stupid intern and asking for a divorce but ... oh God ... the stress ... No, deep breaths, Hugo. Let it wash over you.

I give her a smile and a hug to interrupt her. She looks surprised and pats my back awkwardly before pushing me away, clopping out of the kitchen in her high heels.

'I meant what I said about those rosary beads,' she calls behind her. 'Really, Hugo, it's a tad embarrassing. You can't wear them to your politics lectures when university starts.'

I sigh a deep and healthy sigh and take myself to the bathroom to check out my reflection. I probably need to wash a little before I meet the others for dinner. Mum greeted me with the words, 'Hugo, you stink,' instead of, 'Hello.' She's been so UNSUPPORTIVE of all the changes I've been through in India. In fact, everyone has. I mean, I know it's cliché for a rich white boy like me to spend their gap yah in IndYA, and come back all chanty and bollocks, but, like, it is ACTUALLY different in my case. I'm not like the others. I went to a proper ashram and everything. I mean they made me scrub the floor! EVERY DAY! David and I'd flown over to Goa and started as we meant to go on – getting wrecked and meeting other travellers who wanted to get as wrecked as we did. But things have been weird between us for years now, and I just wasn't feeling it, really, and then . . .

Then I met Gretel.

I can feel my body melting as I remember Gretel. I've never fallen for anyone like I fell for her. Not that she let me in her pants, mind. That's probably why I fell for her. I laugh and watch myself laugh in the bathroom mirror. She taught me so much about myself. She yanked me away from David and the drugs. She didn't care about how much money I had or who my parents were or which college I was going to in Cambridge. None of my lines worked on her, or my smiles, or my negging, or, when all else failed, my all-out begging.

'You're hot, Hugo,' she'd told me, wrapping a finger around her blonde dreadlock. 'But your soul is ugly as fuck.'

I followed her to the bloody ashram in what I thought was going to be the biggest knobstacle course of my entire life. I'd never CHANTED my way into a girl's pants before. But that girl – I'm telling you, *that* girl – I'd have done anything for. And yet, within days of arriving, pulling Gretel fell away. All of me fell away. This, like, really amazing guru taught me how to meditate, and I had to sleep in this dorm full of normal people, and get up at five and do chores, and at first I thought it was the biggest pisstake of my life. I'd try not to laugh through all the chanting, and I'd swear under my breath while scrubbing the stupid floor, but then look up and smile and pretend I loved it whenever Gretel walked past.

But then, one morning, not very far into the whole shit show, I was up at 5 a.m., doing the freakin' Guru Gita again and . . . well, there's no easy way to admit this, but I'm done hiding from it . . . it all came back. That day in the lift, all of it came back. The look on Steven Jeffords' face as he died, the panic of us accidentally hitting the alarm button, being locked in that space with some dead guy and a bunch of other teenagers I'd never talk to normally. I started shaking and crying and got up and ran out, and Gretel came running out after me, and I found myself howling into her lap, telling her all about it. About how I'm scared to die. About how I'm scared I'm a terrible person. About how I'm so scared about what people think of me, but the opinions I care most about are from people I don't even like. I've done shitty things and treated people like a joke and I thought it was making me happy, but, actually, I'm not even sure what happiness even is.

I never did get to shag Gretel.

She left the ashram, but I stayed.

'You coming?' she'd asked, booking her flight to Cambodia at the crappy Internet cafe we had to ride a bus to get to. 'The killing fields are, like, supposed to totally blow your mind. It really makes you cherish what's important, you know?' She smiled at me like maybe I had a chance. I'm good with girls and knowing when I'm in with a chance. I'd somehow, through weeks of contorting myself into yoga poses, chanting like a mofo, and eating vegan food, managed to eke my way into her affections. I could sense that she genuinely wanted me to go with her. Maybe, after a day looking at the skulls of loads of murdered people, we'd go back to a hostel and talk about how sad it was, and then I'd get laid. And Past Hugo would've been totally up for that morally ambiguous situation, but there was a New Hugo growing at this ashram. A Hugo that had been sprouting since that weird, terrible day in the lift, and I felt I owed it to myself to finally give that Hugo a shot.

'I'm staying here,' I told her. 'I think I need to.'

She raised both eyebrows, all *suit yourself*. 'If you think you need to, then you do.'

So I stayed. Alone. Sleeping in a cruddy dorm, making friends with loads of women in their forties who kept banging on about some book called *Eat, Pray, Love*. I got up at 4 a.m. and I chanted, then I scrubbed the floor for hours, then I meditated, then I meditated some more, and ate some vegan food. I felt several layers of skin shed off me. I began to realize that my problems aren't so very terrible compared to everything else that's going on in the world. And, look – I know. I get it. I AM a cliché. But, you know what? I'd rather be cliché and a better fucking person than the jerk I used to be.

So now, here in Manchester, I'm looking at myself in the mirror, and I like what I see. Not just my looks, but my insides too. I'm about to go to Pizza Express of all places! We're going there because Kaitlyn found a COUPON online!? Three courses for £12.95. Old Hugo would've actually, literally, shuddered. But New Hugo couldn't be more relieved that he's leaving this miserable flat for the evening to hang out with some genuinely decent humans. Humans I was lucky to get another chance with.

I wash my hands and use the water to style my hair a little. I turn my face this way and that, a tiny part of me worried that Mum is right about the rosary beads. I spot the bath behind me, reflected in the mirror. The one Sasha hid in that night I spent with Velvet. Man, I am worried about seeing her again. I still feel like a prize prick about all that, even though the past is the past is the past.

'Bye, Mum,' I call, collecting my keys and phone off the countertop. 'Good luck with the lawyers.'

She doesn't reply.

I've had a missed call since I was in the bathroom, but I swipe it away. It's been over a year since the scandal, but there's still the odd journalist sniffing around wanting to do a 'colour piece' about it being one year on, or something. There's some messages on the group chat though.

Sasha:

MY BODY IS READY FOR DOUGH BALLS!!! 😊

What the hell is a 'dough ball'? I guess New Hugo is about to find out.

JOE

'Is it OK if I have a bit of time to think about it?' I ask.

I'm sitting on my bed wearing underpants, a T-shirt and one sock. I was halfway through getting dressed when Catrina from the HR department at Champion Biscuits called.

'Of course,' she says. 'Close of play tomorrow suit you? It's just that we're going to want to get going with contracts.'

'Oh, right, course. Er, yeah, tomorrow's fine. Thank you.'

'Excellent. I'll look forward to hearing from you then, Joe.'

I hang up and try to work out how I feel – if hearing from Catrina has tipped things in one direction or the other. If anything though, it's made me even more confused.

I finish getting dressed and venture out on to the landing.

Mum is still in the bathroom.

'Are you OK?' I call.

No reply. All I can hear is running water.

Shit.

'Mum, I'm coming in.'

I open the bathroom door slowly, just in case she's right behind it. Dad removed the lock last year after Mum slipped over getting out of the shower and hit her head on the towel rail.

She's standing by the loo, a clump of toilet paper in her right hand, the other hand clutching the folds of her skirt. The incontinence pants she now wears instead of normal knickers are crumpled around her ankles. Both the hot and cold taps are running, steam rising from the sink.

'Are you OK?' I repeat, turning them off.

She looks at me, her forehead creasing as she gropes for my name. I realize I'm holding my breath.

'Joe,' she says finally.

I breathe out.

One specialist described Mum's brain as being full of tiny bonfires that the Alzheimer's is extinguishing one by one. Some of the bonfires (her ability to set an alarm clock or poach an egg, her home address, how to send a text message) went out long ago; others (the memory of her wedding day, the lyrics to almost every Beatles song in existence, the name of her youngest son) are still burning. They won't burn forever though. I try not to fixate on it, but sometimes, when I'm lying in bed at night mostly, all I can do is visualize Mum's brain a few years from now – full of nothing but smoke and ash and lost memories.

'What do I do with this?' she asks, holding out the toilet paper.

'You wipe yourself then put it in the loo, Mum,' I say. 'Then flush the chain, remember?'

'Wait, what? Say all that again.'

I begin to repeat my instructions.

'Not so fast!' she snaps.

That's another thing that's changed. Pre-Alzheimer's Mum hardly ever snapped. Dad was the one with a bit of a temper – Mum always on hand to calm him down with soothing tones and a cup of tea and a biscuit. Now it's the other way around. Before Mum got her diagnosis, I thought dementia was just an extreme form of forgetfulness – old people losing their glasses and wandering off in the supermarket. I didn't have a bloody clue.

I take a deep breath and repeat my instructions as slowly and clearly as I can. It's no good though; I may as well be speaking a foreign language. And as I help her pull up her pants, I can't help but picture yet another bonfire being doused with water.

Back downstairs, I suggest we watch some telly for a bit. I install Mum in her armchair and stick on an old episode of *Dinnerladies*. It used to make her laugh like a drain without fail, but today she just frowns at the screen, like she's in pain almost.

'Who's she?' she asks.

'Which one, Mum?'

All five dinner ladies are in the scene.

'That one. The one with the thingamajig on her head.'

'You mean hat.'

'What?'

'The things they're wearing on their heads, they're called hats.'

She stares at me like I've just grown an extra head.

I glance up at the clock in the shape of a sunburst that hangs over the fireplace. It's not even 10 a.m.

Immediately, I feel guilty. Since packing in his job at Champion Biscuits last year, this is what Dad does every single day. He plasters on a smile, but I know it's killing him seeing her like this, not to mention the fact money is tighter than ever without his salary coming in. He point-blank refuses to take any of my student loan for food or board. He reckons it's not fair when I sacrificed my first-choice uni so I could stay living at home to help him out with Mum. I stick the odd twenty in his wallet or coat pocket every once in a while to try and make up for it. It's not enough though. But then nothing I do feels enough at the moment.

My concentration is shot to pieces. I like my uni course, and despite not being in halls, I've made some decent mates. But when I'm there, I'm worrying about home; and when I'm at home, I'm worrying about what I might be missing out on at uni. I still want to work in telly, but it's no longer the thing that burns most brightly in my brain. It's been shoved aside by all the stuff with Mum, and tiredness from commuting back and forth to Manchester every day, and the sneaking suspicion that maybe people like me don't get to be hotshot TV producers after all.

Dad's out with the carers' support group he belongs to. A day trip to Chatsworth House. He won't be back until late, so Craig's wife, Faye, is taking over from me at six o'clock so I can head out to meet Sasha, Dawson, Kaitlyn, Velvet and Hugo. I feel bad for skipping off early (Faye is seven months pregnant and absolutely massive). Not bad enough to cancel though – I've been looking forward to tonight for weeks. Ever since Carly dumped me, and Ivy moved to Canterbury for uni, this lot have been more of a lifeline than ever. Plus, I need their help figuring out what I'm going to tell Catrina tomorrow.

'These people,' Mum says, gesturing angrily at the screen. 'I don't like them.'

'But you love *Dinnerladies*,' I say. 'It's one of your favourite programmes.'

She throws me a look of disgust.

'Do you want to try something else instead? *Vicar of Dibley*? *Ab Fab*?'

She stares at me blankly, the names of her favourite television shows barely registering. I put on series one of *Absolutely Fabulous* anyway, hoping the familiar theme music will perk her up a bit.

'I'm going to the loo,' I say. 'Back in a minute.'

I don't actually need to go. I just want a break. Cue another stab of guilt. I bet Dad doesn't do this – hide in the loo every time he gets frustrated with her. I grip on to the sink and look at my reflection in the mirror. I remember when I had to stand on a stool to reach the taps. Now I'm the tallest person in our entire family – taller than Craig even, who, until only recently, always felt like such a giant to me. The other day I was walking down the high street, and some little kid on a scooter swerved in front of me, and his mum said, 'Mind out for that man.'

Man.

Not a boy. A man.

I'd always assumed that I'd love being an adult; that it would suit me in a way that being a kid and then a teenager never really did. But I was wrong. I may look like an adult, but I've never felt more useless in my entire life than I have done this year, mucking about at uni making stupid short films I doubt anyone will ever see, while Dad watches the woman he's loved since he was fifteen slowly fade away, knowing there's nothing he can do apart from hold her hand and pretend it's all OK.

I count to five and head back downstairs.

Mum's armchair is empty, and the patio doors to the garden are open.

She's in the middle of the lawn with her back to me.

'Mum, come inside,' I call. 'You're going to get your socks wet.'

It's been drizzling since dawn.

Slowly she turns around, her eyes flickering with confusion before coming to rest on me.

'Has my mum come to get me?' she asks.

I hesitate. Mum's mum has been dead for eight years now. We used to tell her the truth, but it would break her heart every time. So we stopped. The specialist says it's OK to play along. Validation therapy, they call it.

'Well, has she?' Mum demands.

Her socks must be soaked.

'Not yet,' I say. 'She's on her way. Why don't you come in and wait?'

She hesitates for a few seconds before making her way across the lawn towards me. I sit her down in her chair and peel off her wet socks and find her a new pair.

'How long will she be, do you think?' she asks as I roll them up her ankles.

'I'm not sure,' I say. 'It could be a while. Hey, why don't we do some colouring in while we wait, just to make the time go a bit faster?'

'Colouring in?' she asks uncertainly.

'Yeah. You really liked it when you did it with Dad that time, remember?'

About a month ago, I came home from uni to find the two of them sitting at the kitchen table colouring in pictures of flowers and birds.

'I was only going to do it with her for a bit,' Dad confided. 'But then I got right into it. Proper therapeutic, like.'

'Do you know where Dad keeps the colouring books and crayons and things?' I ask.

Mum just shakes her head and looks worried.

I rummage under the coffee table and in the junk drawer in the kitchen with no success.

'I'm just going to look upstairs,' I say, pocketing the patio door key and sprinting up the stairs.

I go into Mum and Dad's room. Before Mum got poorly, it used to be spotless, the bed always neatly made, complete with hospital corners, the bedside tables empty apart from a paperback on Mum's side and an alarm clock on Dad's. Today, the curtains are still drawn and the sheets rumpled. Dad's bedside table is cluttered with Mum's pill boxes and empty mugs and glasses of stale water and books with titles like *Learning to Speak Alzheimer's* and *Keeping Mum: Caring for Someone with Dementia*, dozens of Post-it notes sticking out from the pages.

I kneel down and pull out the drawer under Dad's side of the bed. The colouring books and a jumbo pack of pencil crayons are right on top. I'm lifting them out when I notice what they're on top of. Bills. Dozens of unopened bills. Swallowing, I set aside the colouring books and pick up an envelope at random. It's from the water board and has 'Final Warning' printed on it in big red letters. I pick up another. It looks like it's from the bank. Before I can talk myself out of it, I slice it open with my fingernail. It's dated three months ago. I turn it over, scanning the transactions until I reach the final balance. We're nearly a grand overdrawn.

I don't get it. My parents have never been in debt. They've always prided themselves on it. Then it dawns on me. It was always Mum who took care of the accounts, who paid the bills and balanced the cheque book and budgeted for Christmas and birthdays and holidays. All Mum. Plus now, we don't have Dad's salary coming in. He gets a carer's allowance, but it's only about sixty quid a week, and he won't start collecting his pension until next year.

My hands trembling, I open the rest of the envelopes, sorting them into piles. By the time I'm finished, I've worked out we're £1,500 overdrawn, owe £650 in unpaid bills, and another £7,000 on credit cards I didn't even know existed. I knew we were struggling, but I didn't think we were in actual trouble. The realization Dad has been dealing with all of this on top of looking after Mum makes my stomach turn somersaults.

Some adult I am. I didn't even notice.

I gather up the paperwork and take it to my room, then go downstairs and set Mum up at the kitchen table with some colouring in. She's reluctant at first, but after a while she settles into it, working on a picture of a tropical fish.

I go into the hallway, shut the door behind me, and sit down on the bottom step.

There's no point in waiting. Sasha and the others will only try to talk me out of it. An hour ago, they might have succeeded, but now I know I have no choice. It's time to step up, to stop daydreaming and be the adult Mum and Dad actually need me to be.

Catrina answers the phone after one ring.

I clear my throat.

'Hi, Catrina. It's Joe Lindsay here.'

'Joe! I didn't expect to hear from you until tomorrow.'

'I guess I made my mind up quicker than I thought.'

There's a pause. I close my eyes.

'And?'

I keep them closed.

'And I'd like to accept.'

'Oh, that's brilliant news,' Catrina says. 'As I said earlier, you're one of the strongest management trainee candidates we've had in a while.'

'Thanks,' I say faintly.

We talk for a bit longer, at least Catrina does, about start dates and contracts.

'I'd better let you go,' Catrina says eventually. 'I expect you'll be wanting to celebrate.'

'Something like that.'

She laughs. 'Well, whatever you get up to, have a brilliant night. Oh, and welcome to Champion Biscuits, Joe. We're lucky to have you.'

KAITLYN

All he has to do is pick up. All he *sodding* has to *bloody fucking* do is pick up.

And he doesn't. He doesn't pick up.

'Everything OK?' Avani asks pointedly. Pointed because I'm not paying her the attention she's owed. Pointed because I'm meant to be hanging out with my supposed best friend, and I've just been making pointless calls the whole time. Pointed because . . . Oh shit, her girlfriend just arrived at the pub, and I hadn't even noticed.

'Hi!' I say, flooded with guilt, leaping up and knocking my knee into the table leg. 'OK – ow. Sorry. Hi.'

'No worries,' the girlfriend says cheerfully.

Amber – I remember just in time. She has a half-shaved pixie cut and a line of piercings up one ear, just like Avani had described.

'You looked pretty intense about that call.'

I attempt a relaxed shrug. 'I'm waiting to hear about a job, so yeah.' She doesn't need to know I'm just another girl waiting for her boyfriend to call. *Prick*. 'I had an interview this morning.'

'Did you?' Avani asks, surprised.

Which is fair enough, considering I came to meet her straight after and didn't even mention it. I'm already regretting bringing it up; it went terribly, as usual, and I know I haven't got the job.

But I don't want to tell her that, to watch her face go all sympathetic, so I cross my fingers at her with exaggerated hope rather than reply, and she smiles.

I turn deliberately to Amber. 'Nice to meet you.'

'You too, Kait,' Amber says. She has a big, cheerful smile on her face. 'Vani's told me so much about you.' She drops suddenly to her knees. 'And *you!*' she coos, her whole voice instantly bubbly. 'Hello, Remy. Hello, Remy-dog.'

I look at Avani, and she beams at me. Remy, my guide dog, shifts against my feet.

'Um,' I say. 'He's kind of a working dog, so . . .' *So don't talk to him like he's a baby.* 'Do you mind, like . . . pretending he's not there?'

'Of course, sorry,' she says. To her credit, she stands immediately before sliding on to the stool next to Avani. 'I just really love dogs. And guide dogs are so amazing. It's like, if you looked at all the people in the world, a single guide dog would be better than all of them, you know?'

I reach my hand under the table and touch the top of Remy's sweet, soft head. Just doing that calms me, just a little. 'Yeah,' I say, even though what she said doesn't make a whole lot of sense. 'He definitely beats everyone I've ever met.'

'Even me?' Avani asks, lifting her J2o and taking a sip. She's been teetotal since last August, when she got so drunk she vomited down her then-girlfriend's cleavage and got herself royally dumped. I wonder if she's told Amber that story. Probably, knowing her.

'Hmmm,' I say, pretending to think about it, and she laughs. Which is lucky, because it means I don't actually have to answer.

'How long have you had him now?' Amber asks. 'Vani was saying that you were, like, training with him for a while?'

'We're still officially training together,' I say. 'It's a bit of learning curve. For me, I mean. He's great, obviously.'

'But he lives with you and stuff?'

I nod. 'Oh yeah. We're a team. He's my bud.' Understatement of the century. Remy is the solid point of golden light in the crappy year I've had. In my whole crappy life. I didn't think I liked dogs once.

Actually, a lot of things I used to think turned out to be wrong. Like that if something good happened, it would last.

'How's the FemSoc stuff going?' I ask, and they both light up.

The Feminist Society at their university is where they met, so I know I'm on safe ground. They talk happily for a while, telling me about a protest they helped organize against the opening of a Hooters in the city centre, and I nod and smile as if I care.

It's not like I don't want to care. I really *do*. I want to care about this life Avani's living, and the things *she* cares about. But I just feel . . . blank. Some friend I am. No wonder we don't really have anything to say to each other any more.

'Our friend Cammi had this Ann Summers party, and it was *so* heteronormative . . .'

Do all friendships just fade out this way? It feels like we've been drifting apart since . . . well, since Dawson, maybe? Since the lift? Or earlier, since my diagnosis, when it was so painfully clear that our lives were going to be different in a way that was once unimaginable?

'. . . And then Amber put a rainbow-coloured dildo on her head to make a unicorn horn and it got *stuck* . . .'

The thing is, I didn't even mind that much before, because I had Dawson. Not even as a boyfriend, but as my friend. My best mate. And then there was kissing, and then sex, and then love – all of it like the slow climb up a mountain for the best view ever. And what's the natural end to that analogy? Everything going downhill, far too fast. Falling in love with Dawson was like

283

this brilliant bonus on top of him being my friend, but if the relationship bit doesn't work out, do I lose both?

'Why aren't you laughing, Kait? The dildo got *stuck* on her *forehead*.'

Maybe I'm worrying too much. All relationships have ebbs and flows, right? Maybe this is just a really long, really shitty ebb. And – wait, what? Why have they stopped talking?

'Huh?'

I can tell by Avani's voice that she's sullen and disappointed – a bad mix. 'You're not listening, are you?'

'I am!' I say. Shit, what were they talking about? Take a punt, Kait. 'That's hilarious!' I try to laugh, which is a mistake, because it makes me sound like a hungover Santa Claus. *Ho, ho, ho*.

'Listen,' Avani says, and that's when my phone bursts into life.

I leap for it, far more energetically than I should, given that I should be apologizing right now, and I hear her let out one of those you've-just-confirmed-what-I-thought-of-you sighs. The leap is a waste of energy anyway, because I know almost instantly that it isn't Dawson ringing. I have a different ringtone keyed in for everyone who matters, and his is that old Stevie Wonder song 'Signed, Sealed, Delivered'. This ringtone is the anonymous drone of an unknown number. Great.

I make a big show of rejecting the call. 'Sorry,' I say, a bit too loudly. 'I'm not picking it up, OK?'

'You might as well,' Avani says, still in that same flat voice. 'Unless you're actually going to give us your attention, why bother?'

'Oh, Van,' I say, expecting her to interrupt me. But she doesn't, and the silence hangs between all three of us. I have no idea how to follow up those two words. Because she's right, isn't she? 'Look, I'm sorry. This is just . . . God, it's just not a great time.'

'What, because you're so *busy*?' she shoots back, then gives this little gasp that I hear even from across the table. Because it's *mean*, and Avani isn't mean.

Of course I'm not busy. I haven't been busy for months, not since my brilliant, lovely boss, who'd made such grand plans to take me on full time in her florist's when my apprenticeship ended, got cancer. Goddamn fucking cancer. And now there's no shop. No job. Goodbye and good luck.

You'd think the perk of being unemployed would be freedom, but that's not how it is at all. I feel more trapped than I ever did. No employment means no money, and that means no shopping, no spontaneous trips to Thorpe Park, not even the train fare to visit my boyfriend in London. And the one time I did manage to scrape it together, it was a disaster.

I'm trying my hardest to get another job, but it's just not working. I've applied for floristry and non-floristry jobs, and *no one wants me*. I could blame my visual impairment and discriminatory employers, but to be honest I actually think it's mostly about me. What if this is my lot from now on? What if no one ever wants me again?

Dawson. Dawson wants me. *Dawson. Just call me back, for God's sake.*

I never wanted to be the kind of person whose happiness depended on a boy. But when that boy is pretty much the only spark of happy left, am I a bad person for wanting it even more? I want *more* than a spark, that's the truth. I want flames again. I want the kind of passion that lights fires.

It's been a long time since we had fire. I know that. I do.

'No need to be a bitch,' I say. At my feet, Remy shifts his weight so he's leaning a little against my shins. Sometimes I think Remy knows my actual heart. 'Do you want me to play the unemployed-blind-girl card? Because I will.'

'I thought we weren't allowed to use the word "blind",' she says.

'That's not the point, Van!' I snap. But what *is* the point? I can't help wondering. That she's at university, and I'm not? That she's in the joyous, giddy part of a relationship, and I'm not? That she's *happy*, and I'm not?

'I just mean it's impossible to keep up with you,' she says. 'Like, what's even going on with you and Dawson anyway? Why's it been so long since he visited?'

'He's working,' I say defensively. I don't even know which one of us I'm protecting. 'In London, remember? He can't just pop up here whenever he wants.'

'I always loved Dawson Sharman,' Amber pipes in at this point. I'm not sure whether she's ballsy or just clueless. 'And *Dedman High*. He was so great.'

People talk like this about Dawson; always the past tense. *Loved* Dawson Sharman. Like he doesn't exist in the present.

'Is it true you met in a lift?' Amber adds when I don't say anything. 'With, like, a dead guy?'

I take a gulp of the vodka and Coke I'd been ignoring. 'Yeah.' I have a sudden, vivid memory of myself on the floor of the lift, the scratch of the industrial carpet against my knees, Steven's slack face in front of me. Where was Dawson in that moment? Behind me? I try to remember.

'Kait was never the same after that,' Avani says, a little too brightly.

'I guess death changes you,' Amber says. She gives a sombre nod. 'Seeing it up close like that.'

'What time is it?' I ask.

'Almost four,' Avani says. 'Why?'

'Ah, I should probably go,' I say, grimacing as if I'm sad about this. As if it's not a total lie. 'I'm meeting Dawson and the others soon.' We're actually not meeting until seven, but I can't stay in this poky pub any longer. I drain my vodka and Coke and reach for the handle of Remy's harness, saying in a softer voice, 'Come on, mate.'

The goodbyes are awkward. Avani's disappointment has made her sulky, and Amber insists on hugging me, even though we hardly know each other and I've been pretty rude to her the whole time. I have a vague thought that I should message Avani later to apologize and suggest we try again soon; explain that I'm just unhappy right now; beg forgiveness. But it's just a vague thought, and I know I won't.

Remy and I meander around the pub tables until we make it to the door, which is being held open for us by a silver-haired man. 'Have a good day!' he says as we pass. I pretend I haven't heard.

The city is busy and loud, but I like it. It's just Remy and me that matter now. His soft, confident paws carving a path for the two of us through the crowd. When I first met Remy, just under a year ago now, he'd come bounding up to me, all energy and light, pressing his nose against my knees. Until that moment, I'd still been uncertain about even getting a guide dog. I'd never been a dog person, for one thing. And for another, I didn't want to need one.

But then there was Remy, my golden boy. Learning how to navigate the world together has been tough – tougher than even I'd thought it would be – but, God, is it worth it. Even if I really do lose Dawson, even if I can't get a job, I have Remy. That's more than a lot of people have.

We pause at a bench outside a Superdry, and I pull out my phone. I will call Dawson one last time; I'll give him one more chance to come through for me. I start the call and touch Remy's ears with my free hand.

The phone rings. It rings again.

DAWSON

The prelude to being with someone has always been my favourite part of a relationship. When you like them, and you're sure they like you too, but you haven't done anything about it yet. You catch them staring, and they don't look away, but hold your gaze for a beat too long. They stand really close – so close, you can feel their body heat through your clothes – and you're sure it's doing to them what it's doing to you. You replay everything they say, late at night, once you've finally stopped messaging each other. It's the sweetest kind of agony, knowing it's only a matter of time. It's pure, unlimited potential. The world is a little brighter when you're falling for someone. You're a little brighter, a little kinder.

Except to your actual girlfriend.

For the fifth time in an hour, my phone lights up with Kait's name. I know I need to answer it. I know she needs to know if I'm going to get a cab to hers before the dinner, or if I'm meeting her there. All I have to do is tell her I'll be there at seven, or not. That's it.

I turn my phone over, face down.

'Everything OK?' Jasper Montagu-Khan asks.

Don't look up, I tell myself. Do not look at him.

I look at him.

'Yeah.' It takes an inhuman amount of effort to tear my eyes from his dark ones, and look back at the script we're working on. I'm way too old for this. I'm way too in a relationship for this.

He leans back and raises his hands over his head, his T-shirt rising up. I follow its journey as it reveals a golden band of skin above his waistband, and I forget about the need to oxygenate my body. Every day with this guy is an agonizing game of fanfic cliché bingo, and every day I get a full house.

'Fancy a tea?' he says.

I fancy you.

'Sure.' Is what I actually say.

He leans over to pick up my cup, and I hold my breath, like the big fat Mary Sue I am. He hovers, looking down at what I'm working on, and I try to focus on something else. So naturally, I stare at his hand, resting way too close to mine. There's a callus on the inside of his middle finger, because he likes to work on pen and paper instead of on his Mac when he's drafting. If it was anyone else, I'd think they were pretentious. But because it's Jasper, I'm fine with it. In fact, I want to kiss it.

'I like that bit,' he says, and I hear the smile in his voice. 'The bit about the dog. That's funny.'

If I turn . . . If I just turned . . .

'Thanks.'

He waits another moment, and then pulls back, taking my cup with him.

And I can breathe again.

In the first script I ever worked on with him, back in September last year, there was a whole section where the main female character, a sixteen-year-old on the run from the government, talked about the smell of her future love interest. It was going to be a voice-over: her saying she felt comforted by his scent – *the woody, spicy scent of it*. I rewrote it because, honestly, what kind of sixteen-year-old describes someone as smelling spicy, or woody? I replaced it with her talking about how aware she is of him. That without looking around, her body knew where he was, how far from her, how many steps it would take to close the gap and be in his arms.

Because I know, without looking around, the exact moment when Jasper comes back into the room, carrying two cups of tea, a packet of Party Rings clutched in his beautiful teeth. I feel him walking up behind me. I know the exact moment when, if I reached back, my hand would skim his thigh. *I know.*

He puts my cup down, and his next to it, and my entire body feels like it's twisting into a pretzel as he drags his chair over, sitting close enough for his arm to brush mine. He rips open the packet of biscuits and places them between our cups, like a little barrier. And the minute I think that, my mood plummets.

I give myself a mental slap. I. Have. A. Girlfriend. I. Love. My. Girlfriend.

'So . . . where are you at?' He dips a biscuit in his tea, and I follow its journey to his mouth.

When I look back at the script, I've forgotten how to read.

When I first met him at the interview, I didn't fancy him. I was terrified because he was Jasper Montagu-Khan, and his TV series was pretty much a shoe-in for best drama/best script/ best newcomer at every awards show, and I was only there because his godfather had recommended me. I wanted badly to impress him. But I didn't fancy him. He's not obviously hot: shorter than me, kind of stocky, too-thick eyebrows, an unnerving habit of not blinking when he's looking at you. And I was – *am* – with Kait. Was – *am* – in love with Kait.

That's what I tell myself at night, when I'm in my single bed in my single room in Brockley, ignoring Kait's messages and replying to Jasper's. At least I didn't take the job and move here because I liked him. That was an accident.

In two hours, I'm supposed to get the train back to Manchester, pick up Kait, and have our annual dinner with the others. I should be excited. But I'm not. Because the last couple of weeks, I've got the feeling that me liking Jasper isn't a one-way thing. While it was just me having a crush, it was easy enough to ignore. But now it's not a one-way crush. Like I said earlier – potential. It changes things. The impossible becomes possible. The forbidden becomes inevitable. And I become a total bastard.

I sigh, and Jasper nudges me.

'Seriously, Dawson, what is it?'

'I dunno.' I pull my reading glasses off and rub my nose. 'Just . . . relationship stuff, I guess.'

He doesn't say anything, waiting for me to continue.

'Long distance is tough,' is the best I can do. And it is. That's not a lie. Things have definitely been different between me and Kait since I moved down here. I said I wouldn't resent going back to see her, but I do. I hate that it's always me who has to go back up there, me who has to sit for three hours on the train on a Saturday morning and back again on Sunday night, so we can spend one poxy night together.

She tried coming here once, but it was terrible: too noisy and busy; no one cared that she had a dog and a stick. She was in the way, and they made sure she knew it, tutting and huffing as they sped past us. We ended up back at my place ordering Chinese, eating it on my bed to a soundtrack of police sirens.

My housemates kicking off about the dog was the final nail in the coffin of that experiment.

'You're going back tonight, right?' he says. 'For the anniversary.'

I'd told him about the gang, and Steven, and how it had all

started. It's weird, because I'd never told anyone before. Not even Mum or Dad. I'd never said anything to them about how I first met Kait. But I'd told Jasper about a week after I started working with him. Like I'd told him about Josh. And the other guys I'd been with. And Kait's eyes, and working at Chunder Burger that awful summer, and Hugo in Ibiza. Everything, basically. He knows everything.

'Yeah.'

'And you don't want to?'

'No.' I look at him, and he holds my gaze, staring at me with dark, dark eyes.

'Would you rather stay here?' he asks.

There's something about the way he says it that makes my stomach drop. Here. He means literally *here*. Not just in London. But here, in his flat, with him.

And for a second I let myself forget I'm with Kait, and I imagine it. The two of us walking down to the pub and getting food, arguing about whether some line one of us wrote worked or not. Picking up a bottle of wine on the way back, planning to open it and work some more, but never getting around to it because—

I cut the fantasy there, imagining the old-school record scratch as the scene ends. Me and Kait haven't slept together in almost three months. That's all this is – I'm just missing the intimacy. It's only natural I'd project that on to someone else. Maybe that's it. Maybe it's OK as long as nothing happens. Mentally cheating isn't as bad as actually cheating, right?

Jasper looks at me, his eyes narrowed as though I've said something confusing, and for a split second I think maybe I've spoken aloud.

And then he leans in.

I pull back, holding up my hands. 'I can't.'

'Sorry. I'm sorry,' he says, shoving his chair away. 'That was out of line. Way out of line.'

I can't look at him. 'I don't want to hurt Kait.' It sounds lame.

It *is* lame. It's not me saying, '*I'm in love with my girlfriend, and I don't want you.*' It's me trying not to be the bad guy. It's pathetic.

As though he agrees, he nods and runs a hand through his hair. 'I know. I shouldn't have . . . It's not your fault.' He lets out a long breath. 'Just . . . Let's forget about it, yeah? I don't want to mess things up for you.'

'Jasper . . .' I don't know how to finish my sentence.

I don't know when I started to want him. I remember the exact moment I first realized I fancied Kait: there, in Bridlington, on the seafront. I remember realizing when I fancied Josh: in a shit pub, after too many shit drinks. But I don't know when I started to think of Jasper as more than a boss, or a friend. If I did, maybe I could have stopped it.

Yeah, right.

'Look, Dawson,' he says, and for the first time since I met him he seems unsure, not looking at me. 'I like you. I've been trying really hard not to, because . . . Well, because I'm your boss. And you're with someone. But . . . I like you. And I think you might like me. I guess I'm just making sure you know how I feel. I know us working together adds an extra dimension to this, but . . . there it is . . .'

Again he trails off, and I nod miserably.

But beneath the misery is a tiny spark of joy. Because he likes me enough to say so.

And I like him more than I like Kaitlyn. I want to be with him more than I want to be with Kaitlyn.

I really am a bastard.

There aren't any words left in me, so I drink my tea, and he drinks his. And then it's time for me to leave, and he walks me to the door.

We both pause, because it feels like a Big Moment. It doesn't happen often, knowing at the time that it's a Big Moment – but I know it then. How this ends, what we do now, will change what happens next.

'See you Monday?' he asks, and because it's a Moment, it's a bigger question than it seems. A loaded gun of a question.

Like that old saying about scriptwriting, 'Chekov's Gun'. If you put a gun on stage, at some point it *has* to go off. He's put the gun on the stage. I can see the gun. It's by my hand.

'I'll be back Sunday afternoon. If you're free.'

I pick up the gun, and I fire it.

I don't remember getting the Tube, or getting on the train at Euston. I don't remember anything until the conductor asks me for my ticket, and I can tell from the way the girls opposite are giggling that he's been asking for a while. I show him, and shove it back in my wallet, turning to the window, watching the countryside roll by.

If I break up with Kait – and that's suddenly where we are – then I'll be the guy who dumped his blind girlfriend. I'll be the guy who left his blind girlfriend for someone else. Not only that, but I'll have to come out again to a whole bunch of people who've only ever known me with a girlfriend.

I'll be breaking up the group. Not just me and Kait.

They'll have to pick sides; people always want to pick sides. And I'll be the bad guy. I'll lose my friends. Tonight's the first time we'll all be together, Hugo included, since his party way back when. It's supposed to be a new beginning. Not an end.

Though it sounded weak, I meant it when I said I don't want to hurt Kait. But one way or the other, I'm going to. All my options are shit: I can stay with her and continue being a shit boyfriend, lusting after Jasper until I eventually cheat on her; or I can act like such a bastard that she's forced to dump me; or . . . I leave her.

Can I really throw away almost a year and a half with my best friend?

As the train pulls into Manchester Piccadilly, I realize I'm out of time.

I stay on the train as it empties, pulling out my phone.

'Mum, it's me,' I say when she answers.

'Are you calling from prison? Is this your one phone call? What have I done to deserve such an honour?' she says.

It makes me want to cry.

'Dawson?' she asks when I don't speak.

'Sorry. Listen, is my bed made up?' I ask.

She pauses for a moment. 'Your bed is always made up, son.'

'Cool. I'll, erm . . . I'll be staying tonight, if that's all right.'

'This is your home; of course it's all right.' Her voice is fierce, and she doesn't ask questions.

'I'll see you later then.'

'I love you, Dawson.'

I can't say it back, because I will actually cry, and I don't want to get beaten up. But she knows. I end the call, and go to find a cab.

SASHA

I can't find my phone. I lose things all the time, but I never *ever* lose my phone. A drowning sailor doesn't lose her lifebelt.

Normally I charge it overnight, by my bed, but I'd been moving things round and knocked the switch off at the wall. All night plugged in, and still only nineteen per cent charge. Well done, Sash.

I took it into the kitchen, messaging the group, winding Hugo up about dough balls. I remember because Dad sent me a message from across the room.

Your breakfast is over here.

When I looked up, he was sitting at the table, gesturing to a bowl of cereal I hadn't asked for. I prefer toast.

'You could have just said.'

I plugged my phone into the charger above the worktop and went to sit down next to Dad.

'I did. You never hear me when you're on that thing.' Dad twitched his eyebrows like it was a joke. But it's only a joke if you don't mean it.

After that, I went up to get ready for work. Black leggings, black vest, hair tied back and 'minimal make-up', as per Klean Sweep policy. Fresh slipper socks in the bag along with my apron and company-mandated cleaning kit. Every house I go to, I have to lug a bottle of silver cleaner. Never used it.

Dad was gone by the time I emerged. He'd invested some of the money Nan left in a new car – one that was suitable for passengers as well as packages. The plan was to expand the business, break into private hire – he got the license and everything. One month after buying himself a taxi, Dad worked out how little he liked having people in it.

So now it's back to deliveries. Packages don't try to talk to you.

I retrace my steps. I'm in the kitchen. The charger's there, but the phone is not. I must have taken it back up with me when I went . . .

Contrary to what Dad thinks, I *can* live without it, but I never saw which Pizza Express Joe booked.

There's a lot more than one Pizza Express in Manchester.

I'm out of time. If I don't get the bus, I'll be late, and I can't afford that. Instead I grab the grungy little address book I keep in my desk and bolt for the bus.

My first job is seven floors up one of the fancy new-build apartment blocks. A pristine glass lift is waiting for me in the lobby.

I still take the stairs.

Mr Novey has left a note for me asking that I clean the balcony doors inside and out. One hour is all he pays for in total, but the doors will take me ages, and I'm not supposed to cover extra work without permission from my manager.

If I had my phone, I could take a picture of the note and send it over, asking what to do. Fortunately there's a Klean Sweap flyer edging out under a Domino's mailer on the fridge. I grab the landline and dial.

'Hey, Bernice – it's me, Sasha.'

'Why's your number not come up?'

'My phone got stolen.' Play for sympathy. 'I'm calling using Mr Novey's home phone.'

'*Sasha* . . .' I can hear the warning in Bernice's voice. But she likes me, and – like everyone – she does not like tight, slovenly Mr Novey. 'Hang up now. Leave a note for Mr Novey explaining why you called us. I'll deal with the fallout.'

I hang up, then I try Joe's number from Mr Novey's phone. I feel so guilty about it that I'm almost relieved when there's no answer.

Two more jobs, and I'm finally home. Not mine, but the Jordans'. I love it here. Rose and Pete are the kind of people who feel so unutterably guilty about paying for a cleaner that they overcompensate by religiously tidying the house and leaving apologetic notes if they haven't had a chance to put the laundry away.

That's not why I like it though.

Rose is sitting in the kitchen when I get there, laptop out and papers all over the place.

'Sasha!'

She looks so pleased to see me. When I first started, both of us would do our best to pretend I wasn't the one cleaning her toilet, but then she started offering me tea whenever she made one for herself, and after a few weeks, I started accepting.

Before I've even got my kit sorted, the kettle's on, and the mugs are out.

'Do you mind if I use your phone?' I ask, and she hands it over without question. Did I say how much I love coming here?

I go for Velvet first, but there's no ring before it goes to voicemail, and I hang up. It's not like I can ask her to call me back here, is it? Then I tap in Joe's number. No luck. Kaitlyn ditto. I don't feel like it's appropriate to try any more.

'So,' Rose says, taking the phone back before reaching up to re-tie her hair. It's long and auburn and gorgeous. She's gorgeous. One of the reasons it took me so long to accept a cup of tea was because I found it hard to look at Rose Jordan for too long. 'Have you thought about our offer?'

Of course I have. It's all I can think about.

'I haven't got any qualifications,' I say. Again. It's the one thing that makes me nervous.

'Neither have Pete or I.' Rose turns to pour the tea. 'And yet we make perfectly serviceable parents.'

Rose and her husband both work. They also have kids. Super-cute red-haired twins (Hazel and Lily) that I've met during the holidays. They've gone to stay with their grandparents this week, but there's three weeks in the middle of the summer, before the family goes away, that they haven't childcare for. They need my answer by next week.

I *want* my answer to be yes.

People pay more for someone to take care of their kids than to take care of their house. If I take this job, I'll lose out at the agency, but the Jordans have also said that if I take the summer job, they'll keep me on after. They need someone to pick the girls up from school three days a week, take them to their clubs, and feed them tea. It might mean missing a lecture or two, but the money's good, and I'd save on meals by eating with Hazel and Lily.

I've done the budgeting. With this job plus five hours of cleaning, I could do it. I could move out of the flat I share with dad and into one I could share with friends.

All the way home, I think about it. This time last year, I never thought I'd be here. I was supposed to have left the cleaning agency and got myself a regular job. One that paid more and cost less. Cleaning takes it out of you. But then Nan died, which was awful, but she also left us some money, which wasn't awful, but also was, because it made me feel guilty. It wasn't a fortune, but it was enough to make our mortgage payments more manageable, enough for Dad to buy the car. We even had a holiday. A week in Lisbon is hardly the same as Dawson and Kaitlyn's secret summer of love in Ibiza, or Hugo's gap year in India, but it was the first time I'd been anywhere hot. Anywhere that needed a passport.

It was the last night of the holiday that Dad said it. That he'd managed to find the one thing that we could buy with Nan's money that wouldn't make me feel guilty.

'How about it then, Sash – you want to go to uni?'

I never thought I'd be able to, so when he offered, even with all the caveats about going somewhere local and living at home to cut down accommodation costs, I'd jumped at the chance.

French Studies at Manchester Met.

A year on, and I've learned that dreams can come true and still be nightmares.

It was such a mistake to live at home for my first year. I've missed out on so much. Everything that happens is in halls – nights out get organized last minute, and I've a twenty-five-minute train ride from wherever it's happening. Plus every time I try and go anywhere, there's Dad to answer to.

You treat this place like a hotel.

Out again?

Don't you have any work to do for this course that's costing me so much money?

Good job you don't live in halls, or you'd have no money left for all these parties.

Makes me want to scream. Hotels are places where someone else cleans your sheets, and all the work I have gets done in the library because I don't want to haul all the books back here. If I lived in halls, then I wouldn't always be going out –

sometimes the party would come to me.

But hell will freeze over before anyone from uni sets foot in our flat. I can't stand the thought of how they'd look at me, knowing that this is how I live.

University was supposed to be about freedom, but all it's done is draw more attention to how trapped I really am. University friendships are forged in halls, not lectures. I might be getting the education, but I'm not getting the experience. It's taken me three terms to make any proper friends, and even those I spend more time messaging than seeing.

Which is why I need my phone. Which I have lost.

Back home, I do the sensible thing and get ready first. After an hour of hunting for my phone, I give up when I find myself looking for it in the bathroom cabinet. Maybe I'm going loopy. For real. Looking in the bathroom cabinet for your phone sounds like exactly the sort of thing Joe's mum would do.

We don't have a phone in the flat, so I knock for Mrs Ageyman next door. She definitely has one. I hear it ringing all the time.

She doesn't like me using it though, lurks in the doorway as I dial through all my friends' numbers. Velvet's goes straight to voicemail again, no answer from Joe, no answer from Kaitlyn, no answer from Dawson. It's like they're ignoring me.

Are they ignoring me? But then I catch sight of Mrs Ageyman peering round the doorframe and remind myself that they don't know I'm the one who's ringing.

I'm so desperate that I try Hugo. Maybe I try him last just so he's the one I feel angriest with. There's something comforting in being cross with Hugo.

'Those had better not be mobile numbers you're dialling, young lady.'

I want to shout at her that of course they are, but instead I thank her for letting me use her phone.

There's no more time. I'll miss my train if I don't head off, and I'd rather walk round every single Pizza Express in the whole of Manchester city centre than spend another night with my dad pretending I'm going to live at home next year as well.

I've decided: I'm taking the Jordans up on their offer.

It's only once I'm on the train, gazing longingly at a girl over the aisle who's tapping a message out on her screen, that it occurs to me maybe I wasn't lying to Bernice when I told her my phone was stolen.

Funny how the last time I saw my phone was in the same place I last saw my dad.

VELVET

You know in books when they do that really obvious exposition thing, like, 'I caught a glimpse of myself in the mirror, and . . .' followed by a long description of the heroine's big brown eyes and long blonde hair, and how she's much prettier than she realizes . . . ?

Well, every time I look in the mirror now, that's how I feel. Like I'm looking at someone else. I haven't got used to it yet. Whenever I put a T-shirt on, I automatically go to swipe my long hair from the collar, and it's not there.

But though I say I *look* like someone else, I've actually never felt more like myself. Having my hair cut off might sound like a trivial thing, but it feels like finally getting rid of all the stuff I used to think was important but isn't. I'm not hiding behind my long straggly hair any more, and that's given me the confidence to stop hiding altogether. No more thick layers of make-up and fake tan. No more outfits that make me feel silly and incapable.

I'm probably less 'pretty' than I have ever been in my life, and yet somehow I feel absolutely fucking awesome. No matter what anyone says.

'Are you ill?' Mum asks, looking at me through narrowed eyes. 'You look like you've drowned.'

To be fair, this shouldn't exactly be news to her; this has been happening gradually for quite some time. It's just that I don't

303

see much of her these days. I should probably be offended that she's so appalled by my face in its natural state, but I've been learning not to take these things too personally.

'Well, surprisingly enough, Mum, no – I have not recently drowned.'

'It's that Scarlet's influence, I suppose,' Mum goes on, unable to contain a slight tut. 'Chelsea says you're inseparable these days. Said she's a lesbian.'

Chelsea coughs and ostentatiously busies herself with getting mugs out of a cupboard, not looking me in the eye. 'Did you say you wanted tea or coffee, Jacqui? What about you, Vee?'

'Yes, Mum,' I say, oh-so politely. 'It's not really relevant, but that is all correct information. And I'll have a cup of tea, thanks, Chels. Bit of milk, no sugar.'

I keep my voice even and clear, looking Chelsea in the eye. It seems funny to think that we were once so close – cousins and best friends. When we were little, people used to mistake us for twins.

'Yeah, I do remember how you have your tea, Vee.' She bristles. 'Surprised you're not having some sort of decaf-green-tea-matcha-latte something or other these days.'

'Don't worry – only after six o'clock . . .'

I can see she doesn't quite know if I'm joking or not. I only said I'd come round and see her new flat today because I couldn't keep putting it off forever. I've been too busy, but Mum started suggesting that I didn't want to because 'it must be hard not to be jealous'. So I said I'd come round with her today – thankfully, I have the excuse that I only have time for a quick cuppa before I have to go and get the train to Manchester.

'This is a lovely little kitchen, Chels,' Mum's saying, gesturing around the dark, narrow room that is a bit like walking into a smoker's lung. 'Everything you need here.'

They both automatically look over at me, sort of apologetically. They feel so sorry for me, it's insulting. To be honest, they would be surprised how very, very easy I am finding it *not* to be jealous of Chelsea. I genuinely hope she's happy, and I guess she is, living in a flat above Shoe Zone with Jamie King. In the same way that I guess I was happy for a little while, working in the hotel and living with Griff. That seems like another life now.

'Well, we're going to get an old sofa off Jamie's stepmum at the weekend, and the landlady said she was going to replace that lino in the bathroom, and . . .'

I don't mean to tune out, but it's really hard not to. I don't really care about lino, just like I don't expect them to care about my life. I don't mind that nobody ever asks me about being back at college, or how it's going. I know I'd only shrug and tell them it was fine anyway, so it's not like that would be a thrilling conversation for anyone involved.

They're not interested in how it was weird going back at first, but then it got better. They don't want to know about how I love *Wuthering Heights*, and that discussing books with Scarlet in Costa after our Thursday afternoon English Literature class is actually my new favourite part of the week.

I don't think they'd be even remotely impressed by my most exciting bit of news: that Mr Hicklin has suggested I should think about applying for university next year. I'm still working part time at the hotel and building up my savings, and it looks like it might not be impossible. Scarlet and I work harder than anyone on our course – people who have been given a second chance tend to do that, I think. The exam results for the end of the first year aren't out yet, but it looks like we'll both do well. We've even talked about maybe applying together and sharing a flat.

The two of us shouldn't even be friends really, so it's funny that she's ended up being the best friend I've ever had. 'The misfits', she calls us. I feel ashamed now that I never used to stick up for her at school when Chelsea and the others used to call her a weird goth. That sums up who I used to be at school – I wasn't the one giving it, but I never had the guts to stand up for anyone, which now I know is pretty much just as bad.

'Don't worry; I understand.' Scarlet had shrugged when I brought it up, just when we were starting to be friends. 'We all just did what we could to survive in that place. For you it was alcopops and snogging boys whose personality consisted of a haircut and a pair of skinny jeans. For me, it was reading Mary Shelley in the graveyard. Whatever gets you through the night, right?'

So, against the odds, the two misfits are doing OK. Whatever my mum or Chelsea think, I know Scarlet's been a great influence on me.

'Thanks for the tea, Chels,' I say, standing up while they are still mid-conversation about IKEA. 'I've got to get to the station, or I'll miss my train.'

I zip up my hoody and stop by the door to lace up my DMs ('lesbian shoes', my mum calls them). I give them both a quick hug and can see they're as relieved that I'm leaving as I am.

'See you later,' I call out over my shoulder.

When I get out into the fresh air, I actually feel good. The fact that my mum and Chelsea don't really get it is so trivial to me now. They're my family, and I love them, but I don't need their approval.

My phone rings in my pocket while I'm turning off the seafront and into town; I glance at it and quickly hit reject, seeing a number I don't recognize. That sort of thing instantly makes me nervous. An unknown number never means anything good.

Anyway, if I don't hurry, I'll miss my train. I'm cutting it fine already; I've got a long wait at Hull and will be getting into Manchester a bit late, as it was the cheapest fare. I'm trying to save every penny I can at the moment, but I don't want to have to skimp on the dough balls.

I walk through town wondering if all of this will one day soon be a distant memory. The beach, the chip shop, the bus stop, the all-you-can-eat Chinese we used to go to on birthdays, even the big Tesco . . . Maybe when I've gone, I'll miss it. I'm not sure.

When I get to the station and on to the train, I still feel the same thrill I always do just to be getting the hell out of here. I watch the scenery whizz by in a blur, my excitement mounting with every mile.

Finally getting off the train at Manchester Piccadilly, I can feel the energy of the big city fizzing in my brain, and I suddenly can't wait for my real life to start. To do all the things I'm supposed to do. I mean, I have no idea *what*, exactly. Something.

Walking through the streets, I'm feeling a heady mixture of being both powerful and totally anonymous. Like I'm part of something big, but still making my own way in the world. I can't wait to see everyone. It's going to be brilliant. I'm just in the mood to chat about everything while simultaneously stuffing my face with dough balls, maybe get a little bit tipsy on a couple of glasses of wine.

I'm even kind of looking forward to seeing Hugo after so long. I mean, I'm sure it'll be a bit weird and awkward, but I think I can handle it. He sounds like a different person now, and I know I certainly am. It's like we were kids back then. It feels like looking back on another person, another life.

When I get to the restaurant, I can see people silhouetted in the window, chatting and laughing, drinking glasses of wine and eating pizzas with names I don't quite know how to pronounce. This is the life I want for myself. Walking into the restaurant to meet my friends makes me feel cosmopolitan and glamorous. It beats the all-you-can-eat Chinese, hands down.

'Can I help you?' a waiter asks as I walk inside.

Even a year or two ago, I'd have felt self-conscious: like an imposter; like I didn't belong; not good enough.

'I think my friends are already here . . .' I say, looking him directly in the eye. 'Thanks very much.'

I'm fully expecting to be the last to arrive, as I walk through the restaurant, keeping my eye out for a big, jolly table of friendly faces.

'Velvet!'

The voice calling me doesn't sound that pleased about it. In fact, if I had to think up a word to describe how that person enunciated my name, I'd say *grim*.

I look up, and it's Dawson, waving at me, more of a grimace than a smile in greeting. Kaitlyn is sitting next to him, yet somehow managing to maintain a distance of a million miles between them. I have literally never seen them look so . . . unconnected. And I've only ever seen them together when they weren't officially 'together'. I thought at least Joe might look pleased to see me, but he looks like the world is weighing so heavily on his shoulders, he can't register my presence. He literally can't see me.

And then I see Hugo. It's a second before I look him in the eye because I'm so distracted by the beads around his neck. I can see instantly it's not just the beads that make the difference. Everything about him is different. Obviously that bone structure is pretty unarguable – let's face it, he's as good-looking as he ever was, the handsome bastard – but it doesn't make my heart beat faster or my breath catch in my throat any more.

I've been saying it was so long ago that I don't even care any more, but a little part of me was still worried about what seeing him after all this time might do to me. Unexpectedly, he looks so apprehensive, I almost want to give him a hug. We smile at each other tentatively.

And then I spot the empty chair. I'm late enough that I presumed I'd be last, making my apologies while everyone else was already stuck into the drinks and dough balls. But no Sasha.

My phone vibrates in my pocket, and I have a bad feeling. It's an unknown number again, but this time I answer instantly.

'Sasha, is that you – are you OK?'

When Sasha gets there, she's out of breath and dizzy with panic. The Pizza Express is exactly where Velvet said it would be – by the uni, opposite the bank. But there are university campuses all over Manchester – what if she's at the wrong one?

She lingers on the pavement, looking for them through the window, but all she can see is a group of women who've taken up one side of the restaurant for what looks like a hen party, judging by the L-plates and penis balloons. Sasha automatically reaches into her pocket for her phone so she can call Velvet, then remembers that she doesn't have it. Her frustration swiftly gives way to something sharper as she asks herself again if her father could really have taken her phone. The thought needles her as she sucks in a breath and heads inside.

As soon as she opens the door, she's confronted by a huddle of people waiting to be seated. She can't see past them, and when she tries, a man in a Blur T-shirt steps to the side, blocking her view. He gives her a look that says, *Don't even think about it*, but before she can explain that she's not pushing in, she hears Velvet – 'Excuse me' – and her face flushes with relief. The bloke makes no effort to move though, and a moment later, Velvet's hand is on the sleeve of Sasha's denim jacket. She tugs her out of the queue, then stops to look back at him over her shoulder with a sweet smile. 'Enjoy your Sloppy Giuseppe, mate.'

Sasha has no idea what a Sloppy Giuseppe is but he looks so pissed off that the pair of them dissolve into giggles as they walk away. If her father was there, he'd say that she was being childish, and perhaps she is. But it's so nice to laugh; it makes her feel soft and warm and loose, the muscles in her shoulders unclasping and opening up like flowers stretching towards the sun. So if that's childish, Sasha doesn't care, because only Velvet and the others make her feel like that: like whatever is happening to her – uni, work, her father – she can handle it.

It doesn't make much sense – she never sees them, and her only real contact with them is on WhatsApp – but in that moment, as she follows Velvet through the busy restaurant, she realizes that she'd follow her anywhere. Sasha trusts them. That's why they've kept in touch since that day in the lift – even Hugo – because this awful thing happened, and they survived, and she feels safe when she's with them.

Velvet looks back at her and smiles as if she knows what she's thinking, and with that, the stress of the day is forgotten. Sasha feels lighter, as though her feet aren't quite touching the ground as they walk through the restaurant, Velvet's hand fisted in the sleeve of Sasha's denim jacket. It's heaving, every table taken. Velvet's gushing about something, tossing a smile back at her every now and then when they stop to let a waiter pass, but Sasha can't hear what she's saying over the clatter of cutlery and chatter from the surrounding tables. The restaurant is a TARDIS, the modest entrance giving way to a vast space across two floors, which explains why she couldn't see them from the outside, and when Velvet stops at a table in the corner, they all look so different that Sasha asks herself if she would have recognized them even if she had seen them. The thought makes her so flustered, it takes her a second or two to respond to the chorus of *Hey!*s that greet her when Velvet thumbs at her and says, 'Look who I found!'

'Hey,' Sasha says finally, trying not to stare as she thinks back to the last time she saw them. It's been a year. No, actually, it's been two. Her nan's funeral doesn't count, does it? Hugo, Kaitlyn and Dawson were in Ibiza. Then she remembers that Hugo wasn't with them the year before when they surprised Velvet and showed up at the hotel, so it's been three years since they were together like this. *Three years.* Three years since she'd been in the same room with these people – these friends – she thought of so often. She doesn't know how that can be. There are people she sees every day who take up less space in her life, yet these guys have somehow become the centre of it.

They speak so often that Sasha hadn't noticed their physical absence, but as she looks around the table, she suddenly feels every minute of the time they've been apart. She's seen them, of course, in selfies and on FaceTime, but it's not the same as having them right there in front of her. They each look so different, so grown up. Joe fills his white shirt. It looks like his own, not like he's wearing one that he borrowed from his father, like he did that day in the lift. He sits up straight in his chair, his shoulders back and his chin up, any trace of the awkwardness that once made his fingers fidget and his knee bounce gone.

It's Dawson's knee that's bouncing this time, his usually cool demeanour has given way to something that is making him chew on his bottom lip. If his smile is tight when he waves and says hello, then Kaitlyn's is tighter. Actually, it's sharp – the sort of smile you'd cut your mouth on if you tried to kiss her. At the other end of the table is Hugo. As soon as their eyes meet, his hand goes to his neck, fingers fussing over the rosary beads he's wearing. Yes, rosary beads. As if tonight isn't enough of a head fuck as it is, Hugo Delaney is wearing rosary beads.

Finally, there's Velvet. She's the only one who looks younger, her eyes bright and her face pink with excitement. She's also the only one who looks remotely pleased to be there, the rest of them stealing glances at the door when they think no one is paying attention. Even Sasha, who hasn't sat down yet, can't help but look back the way she came as she feels the atmosphere weighing heavy on the table. Something's wrong. She feels another punch of panic as she asks herself if it's something she's done. Is it because she's late? Or because she's been calling them all day, bothering them about where to meet?

Joe gestures at the empty chair at the end of the table opposite Kaitlyn, then excuses himself, saying that he needs to call home and check in. Sasha watches him go, then sits, aware that Kaitlyn is watching her carefully, and she can't help but wonder if she looks as different to them as they do to her. She doesn't think she does, but she's suddenly desperate to ask them what they see when they look at her. Can they see that her eyeliner is wonky and her jeans are too tight? Can they smell the bleach she's been swilling around toilets all day? She can. It doesn't matter how often she showers, she can still smell it in her hair, that and the faint trace of rubber that lingers on her hands hours after she's taken her yellow gloves off.

Sasha shrugs off her jacket, and when she turns to hang it on the back of her chair, she sees the Labrador sitting quietly by Kaitlyn's side. She must be staring, because Kaitlyn puts her hand on the dog's blond head and says, 'This is Remy.' Sasha knows about Remy, knows why Kaitlyn needs Remy. They've all talked about it. All asked Dawson if she's OK, if there's anything they can do. But it's still a shock to see it first-hand. Sasha tries to hide it with a smile she's pretty sure borders on manic.

'Hey, sweet boy!' she gushes, reaching across the table to pat him on the head.

But Kaitlyn holds her hand up, stopping her before she can. 'He's working.'

Sasha's hand freezes in mid-air, and it makes the back of Kaitlyn's neck burn as she watches the others exchange wide-eyed looks around the table as though she's a drunk relative who's just said something horribly racist at Christmas dinner. The silence that follows is excruciating. She didn't mean to snap, especially at sweet Sasha who blushes and whips her hand away as though she's been scalded.

She's mad at Dawson, not her.

As if on cue, he nods at Remy. 'Don't fall for that face. He's just angling for a dough ball.'

And just like that, what Kaitlyn said is undone, and the tension evaporates. Sasha's face softens, and when she laughs, Kaitlyn feels a familiar heat pool at the corners of her eyes. She wants to tell him to stop, but he can't stop, can he? This is who Dawson is, what he does. He balances her out, and as she sits there, watching Sasha smile at him across the table, Kaitlyn can't help but ask herself what sort of person she'd be without him, if he is the only thing that makes her softer, more human.

Dawson pours Sasha a glass of wine, and when he asks her how her day's been, he shows her more affection in those few moments than he has shown Kaitlyn since he arrived at the restaurant. If Kaitlyn had asked him how he was doing – and she has, several times – he'd tell her that he was fine, that he was just tired. But he doesn't look tired now – the skin around his eyes crinkling, he's smiling so hard. Kaitlyn looks across at Sasha, and in that moment she hates her. 'That's mine!' she wants to shriek, as though Dawson only has a finite amount of attention and he's wasting it on Sasha. But as swiftly as the thought arrives, it's gone again, and she feels sick with guilt.

This isn't Sasha's fault. It's Dawson's.

'What do you fancy?' he asks Sasha before he can say anything else.

He sees the menu tremble as he hands it to her, and he wonders if she notices. If she does, she has the grace not to say anything. She had the grace not to say anything about Kaitlyn's swipe either. He loves that about her. She has such a big heart, and he envies her that; envies how quickly she forgives.

She tells him that she's probably going to have the lasagne, and when he feigns horror and tells her to try something more adventurous, they laugh, and it's so easy that he almost forgets about Kaitlyn. It used to be like this with her, and he misses the back and forth. Misses her. He doesn't know how you can miss someone who is sitting right next to you.

'Have what you want, Sasha. There's nothing wrong with lasagne,' Kaitlyn says suddenly, and Dawson and Sasha look at one another across the table like a couple of kids who've been told off for talking in church.

'OK,' Sasha says, and her voice sounds tiny. 'I'll have the lasagne.'

'Or not. Have whatever you want, that's the point.' Kaitlyn shrugs.

Dawson catches himself just before he rolls his eyes. He knows *that* shrug; he's been on the receiving end of it many, many times. It's her super-casual I-don't-care shrug, which actually means she's furious. Sasha obviously knows the shrug as well, because she has the sense not to say anything else as the three of them return to their menus, reading them with such scrutiny, you'd think they were trying to crack the Enigma code, not choose a pizza.

Then it's so quiet, Dawson can hear Velvet and Hugo chatting happily at the other end of the table. He's telling her about India, except he calls it 'IndYA', and Dawson feels the corners of his mouth twitch playfully, the awkwardness immediately forgotten as he starts to daydream about Jasper.

He'd probably think Hugo was a right knob.

His stomach turns to water at the thought of him, of his cola-coloured curls and the callus on the inside of his finger. And just like that, he's giddy. His head – and heart – spinning as he wishes he was back in Jasper's flat, drinking tea and talking about Barry

Jenkins. He indulges the feeling for a moment, diving in head first, wallowing in the warmth of it, the promise. He's suddenly aware of every hair on his body bristling as his eyes swim out of focus. If he could bottle this feeling, he would – get drunk on it and dance in the street under the midnight moon – because it never lasts. It's like a soap bubble that pops as soon as you touch it . . .

Kaitlyn reaches for the bottle of red wine to refill her glass, grazing him with her elbow as she does, and – *POP* – it's gone, and he's back in the busy, chilly restaurant with the menu in his hand. His eyes swim out of focus for another reason, the sudden rush of guilt making his stomach clench and his hands shiver. He's certain she can see it, see the shame pinching his cheeks so they're red raw.

I'm a prick, he thinks. I'm a prick. I'm a prick. I'm a prick. Why is he doing this to her? To them? Don't be such a fucking coward, he thinks, making himself turn his head to look at her. He gazes at the stubborn line of her jaw and the patch of skin behind her ear that he used to press his mouth to, whispering his secrets into her skin, and waits, waits to feel something – anything – but there's nothing.

There's nothing left.

Joe feels the tension shrouding the table from the other side of the restaurant and almost doesn't come back after calling home to check on his mother. Dawson and Kaitlyn are looking at everything but each other – their phones, their wine glasses, the white neon sign on the wall that says DOUGH – while Hugo and Velvet aren't looking at anything except each other, engrossed in a conversation so animated, it makes the silence between Dawson and Kaitlyn more obvious. It *should* bother him, how childish they're being. A year ago he would have wanted to bang Dawson and Kaitlyn's heads together and would have worried himself silly that Hugo was going to break Velvet's heart again. But he can't help but regard it fondly now – the fickleness of it all, the fighting and flirting and foolish decisions.

He misses it.

Sasha obviously doesn't. She's hiding behind her menu as though she isn't with them and looks relieved when he sits down next to her. He almost asks her what he's missed, but he doesn't want to know.

'Everything OK at home?' Dawson asks when Joe puts his phone down and picks up a menu. Dawson's smile is so fake – so 'Wow! Everything is fine!' like he's auditioning for a toothpaste advert – that it reminds Joe of when his parents used to argue, then pretend that everything was OK when he walked into the room.

He misses that as well.

'All good,' he says, playing along.

'Good.' Dawson nods, pouring him a glass of wine. 'Good. How's—?'

'Actually,' Joe interrupts before Dawson can ask what he's about to ask, 'I've got some good news.'

Dawson's eyes light up, clearly desperate for a distraction from whatever is going on with Kaitlyn.

'Did I hear someone say they had good news?' Velvet pipes up from the end of the table.

They each turn to look at him expectantly, and he immediately regrets saying it, because it isn't good news at all, is it? But he hasn't told anyone yet – not even his father – and he wants to know what they'll say.

Now it's his turn to plaster on a fake-toothpaste-advert smile.

'I've got a new job,' he says and waits.

Kaitlyn is the first to speak. 'Where?'

'Champion Biscuits.'

'Well done,' she says, then frowns as if to say, 'So?' clearly confused as to why he's making such a fuss about a part-time job at Champion Biscuits.

Dawson is the first to cotton on. 'Part time, yeah?'

'Full time.'

'Full time?' they all say at once.

'It's a management trainee position.'

'Management?' Sasha sounds genuinely panicked. 'How are you going to do that and go to uni?'

'He's not,' Kaitlyn says, arching an eyebrow at her in such a way that tells her to shut up.

There's an agonizing moment of silence as the others look around at each other. They eventually settle on Dawson, who's clearly been nominated as the one who will handle this with the most tact.

He hesitates then says, 'So you're dropping out of uni?'

'Why?' Velvet asks before Joe can respond. 'I thought you loved it.'

'Yeah,' Sasha adds, mirroring Dawson's frown. 'What about your film stuff?'

All Joe can do is shrug. 'It's a great opportunity.'

'A great opportunity?' Velvet shakes her head at him and throws her hands up. 'University is a great opportunity. Why the fuck would you drop out to go and work for Champion ruddy Biscuits?'

'Leave him alone,' Kaitlyn says suddenly, and it's enough to make each of them stop and look at her.

'We're not having a go at him,' Velvet says, glaring down the table at her. 'We're worried.'

'Worried?' Kaitlyn returns her glare. 'Do you have a fucking clue what he's going through?'

'Of course I do.'

'Well, why are you giving him a hard time?'

'I'm not giving him a hard time; I'm concerned.'

Joe holds his hands up. 'Guys—'

'Concerned?' Kaitlyn chuckles sourly, and Velvet's whole body stiffens.

'The fuck is that supposed to mean?'

'It means that no one drops out of uni unless they have to. Think about it.' Kaitlyn jabs her temple with her finger. 'His dad quit work to take care of his mum, so who's paying the bills?'

They all go deathly silent, and Joe is mortified, his cheeks stinging, and his chest hurting from the effort of keeping it all in. He tries to smile, but can't, and when Sasha reaches for his hand under the table and squeezes it, something in him finally buckles and it all spills out.

'Dad's in debt. A *lot* of debt.'

The silence that follows is even thicker – fuller – as each of them nod quietly. But there's no pity in their faces as they turn toward him. They don't smile and tell him that everything's going to be OK, that it's only temporary. And he's grateful, because things *aren't* going to be OK, and it isn't temporary: this is how it is.

How it always will be.

'How much?' Hugo says.

It's the first time he's spoken to anyone but Velvet since he arrived and exchanged pleasantries, so the shock of it makes each of them turn to stare at him.

'How much do you need?'

He looks down the table at Joe, his brow furrowed with such genuine concern that it knocks the air right out of him. Joe shakes his head, because it's all he can manage, and Hugo starts to say something, then stops and nods, and Joe's grateful, because he's just about holding it together and he can't cry, not in a Pizza

319

fucking Express. He supposes most people would take the money – after all, what's nine grand to someone like Hugo Delaney? But it isn't about money. Joe's parents worked their whole lives to make sure that he had a roof over his head and dinner on the table and money to go the cinema with Ivy. Now they can't, and he can, and it really is as simple as that. So no, it isn't about money; it's about family. The one we're born into, Joe thinks, looking around the table at the others, and the family we make for ourselves.

When the food arrives, and the chatter turns to why there's a hole in Dawson's pizza, Velvet nudges Hugo with her shoulder, and he looks up from the salad he's poking with a fork.

'That was sweet,' she tells him.

He pretends not to know what she's talking about, picking up a dough ball and inspecting it with a furious frown. 'What was?'

'You know what.'

He rolls his eyes. 'It's only money. I just blew ten grand on a trip to Goa.'

'Ten grand?' She gasps, her eyes wide.

'That's nothing.' He puts the dough ball back down. 'My mother's spent more on a handbag.'

'Jesus.'

'She still isn't happy.'

They sit quietly for a moment or two, picking at their food while they watch the others eat.

'Are you happy?' he asks suddenly.

The question catches her off guard.

She thinks about it for a second, then nods. 'Yeah, I guess. Are you?'

'I think so.'

'You *think* so?'

'It's been a while, you know?'

She knows.

She must be staring, because he looks up, and when their gaze meets she feels such a potent rush of affection, it makes her chest hurt. Not attraction, but affection – affection for this boy who's never eaten a dough ball and has just offered to help his friend for no reason other than because he could. It's like she's seeing him for the first time, really seeing him. Then she feels something else – pride, she realizes. She's proud of him and of herself for waiting. Waiting for him to become the person she knew he was all along.

Hugo has been waiting as well. So – as much as he wants to look away – he can't, because this is it, he realizes. This is the moment he's been waiting for since Velvet walked out of his mother's flat that night with her sandals in one hand and her phone in the other.

Sorry. He feels the word in his mouth, weighing heavy on his tongue, but it doesn't feel big enough – substantial enough – but it's all he's got.

'Listen, Velvet,' he says, but she shakes her head.

'Hugo, don't.'

His heart throws itself at his ribs so suddenly, he almost drops his fork. This is it, he thinks. She's going to annihilate me. He can feel the tips of his ears burning as he braces himself for it, but she just smiles.

'Let's just start again, OK? Right here. Right now.' She draws a line on the table with her finger. 'That was before.' She points above the line she just drew. 'And this is now.' She points under it.

'You sure?'

Velvet nods. She means it, he knows, and the relief is giddying. He can feel it burning off him, filling the space between them, filling the entire restaurant. But this time, it isn't blue; it's green. The

321

greenest of greens – the colour of his grandmother's lawn after it rains, of ripe avocados and sour limes and sweet frozen peas – and all he can hear is a voice in his head reminding him what he's known all along.

The past is the past is the past.

Hugo Delaney created group 'THEY'VE BROKEN UP!?'
Hugo Delaney added Velvet Brown
Hugo Delaney added Sasha Harris
Hugo Delaney added Joe Lindsay

Hugo:
Kaitlyn and Dawson!!!!!!

Joe:
I'm a bit heartbroken tbh

Sasha:
Same ☹☹☹

Velvet:
It's such a shame, but I'm kind of not surprised . . . I thought things seemed a bit weird between them. I'd just hoped I was wrong

Joe:
I KNEW something was up at Pizza Express

Sasha:
I didn't ☹
I thought it was just Kait being in a bad mood. I'm a terrible friend!

Joe:
Don't be mental. None of us were on great form

Hugo:
I'm taking this harder than my parents' divorce.
Seriously. I actually LIKE Kaitlyn and Dawson

Sasha:

Hey. Really sorry to hear about you and Dawson.
Hope you're OK. Here if you need me. We all are xxx

Kaitlyn:

Sasha:

Hey, Dawson! I know we don't talk much outside the group, but I wanted you to know I'm here if you want someone to chat to. Or not. I'll be here anyway xxx

Dawson:

Hey, Sash. Thank you xx

YEAR SIX

Please join Hugo Delaney at his
Black Tie Gala
To Raise Money For The British Heart Foundation

Saturday 12 June
7 p.m. to 11 p.m.

Westminster Pier, London
The boat will depart at 7.30 p.m. promptly

£200 per person
£2,000 table sponsorship for ten guests

River cruise, dinner, entertainment, silent and live auctions

Sasha:

OH MY GOD, YOU CHAMPION! (Sorry, poor choice of words . . .) Can't believe you're going to be working at the UKB!!! ☺☺☺

Joe:

I'll take champion!

Also, thank you ☺

Sasha:

Totally going to embarrass you in person when I see you at Hugo's

Joe:

I shall look forward to it ☺

I still can't believe I got on the scheme.

Do you know how many people apply? Literally hundreds!

Sasha:

SO?! None of those hundreds have your unique talents, Mr Lindsay. *I* can totally believe you got the place

Joe:

Sasha:

Although . . .

Um . . .

Joe:

Spit it out!

Sasha:

Don't take this the wrong way . . .

Joe:

Go on . . .

Are you still there???
Sitting on the edge of my seat here, Sash!

Sasha:

Sorrreeeeeeeeeee! I was trying to compose my question. It's delicate.

Joe:

Bloody hell, what is it?!!??!?

Sasha:

It's about your mum.

Joe:

OK . . .

Sasha:

When you decided, did you feel guilty? About leaving her I mean?
(I'm sorry. You can tell me to fuck right off if I'm being too nosy.)

Joe:

I felt well guilty at first. But then my dad (and you lot,
actually) reminded me to think about what Mum would say
if she knew I turned down the chance to work at the UKB.

She'd hate to know I was missing out on my life because
of her. It's the exact opposite of what she'd want.
So . . . yeah. I feel terrible.

Thanks for the reminder!

JOKE!

But I also know I'm doing the right thing.
And sometimes that feels like shit.

Why do you ask?

Sasha:

Dad stuff

(Thank you for being really lovely and not telling me to fuck off) ☺

Joe:

I could never tell you to fuck off, Sash.

Do you wanna talk about it?

The dad stuff, I mean?

Sasha:

Yes and no. Maybe when I see you? I'm kind of paranoid about my phone these days

Probs gonna have to delete this chat, tbh

Joe:

Seriously??

Sasha:

Well . . . since I'm deleting this . . . you know it was him who took my phone when we were meant to be eating at Pizza Express? Said he'd mistaken it for his. But he didn't

It's been getting worse, actually, these last few months. Dad's turned well clingy

As I said, I'll tell you in person

Joe:

I'm dead sorry, Sash. That's properly messed up.

Let's definitely find time to talk at the party.

Sasha:

I'd really like that xxx

Joe:

It's a date xxx

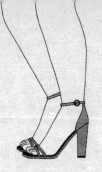

SASHA

A lift. One I shouldn't be in. Something is wrong, and I need to get out. Only I can't work out how. None of the buttons have anything on them, and I don't know which one to press.

So I dial. The number is long and complicated and made all the harder because I'm only guessing which button is what number, and I keep getting it wrong and starting again and getting it wrong and starting again and getting it wrong—

'You fucking idiot!'

I'm panicking now. My calls are getting through, but not to the right people, and I'm sobbing at the sound of their voices.

Joe and Velvet and Kaitlyn and Dawson and . . . Hugo? A tinny little voice, drawling and sarcastic echoing in this sealed metal box: '*Please come. I'll pay your train fare. Just get to the station . . .*'

If Hugo's on the other end of the line, then who's in here shouting at me? I don't know his voice. I don't know his face, but I know who he is.

I'm trapped in here with Steven Jeffords, and I'm never *ever* going to escape—

'SASHA!'

I'm woken by a screaming little cannonball to the ribs, instantly aware that I'm no longer alone as two small terrors bounce around the spare bed yelling my name and chanting for me to get up.

Rose doesn't appear until after I've given the girls breakfast, dressing gown on, a smudge of last night's eye-shadow across the bridge of her nose.

'Oh God . . .' she croaks, collapsing across the table. 'Hangovers in your thirties are the worst. Get all your drinking in now.'

'Good night?' I ask, pushing a coffee her way, hoping it's OK for me to go now she's up. I've a lot to do today.

'Definitely worth the babysitting money, put it that way.'

She straightens up a bit, although she's still hunched up and haggard. Still unnervingly crush-worthy. As with Joe, my slightly baffling feelings for Rose remain quiet and close and secret. Something delicate, and precious, like beautiful lingerie too precious to wear, it makes me happy enough to have it sitting in the drawers of my mind.

Ones I have to keep rammed shut when I'm actually near her.

Out in the hall, I pick up my overnight bag, and Rose hands me some cash and the plastic carrier that's slouched next to the kids' jumble of boots and shoes.

'I don't think that's mine . . .' I say.

'It is now.' Rose pushes it into my arms, managing to look like someone who is very pleased with themselves and who also might be sick. 'I got two sizes. Just in case. I've kept the receipt so I can return one of them, but absolutely under no circumstances will I return both. Understood?'

I'm too overwhelmed to actually say the thank you that's screaming through my brain.

I hadn't known it was a trick, yesterday in the shopping centre, the girls at soft play while I accompanied Rose round

John Lewis. We were looking for something for her date night, but she'd kept pulling things off the rack for me to try too because she said it was boring trying things on all by herself. I'd left her queuing for the cash desk while I fetched the girls before their soft-play session ended. I was standing, watching them wrangle their shoes on, when someone said my name.

I hadn't seen her in so long that when I turned to see who'd said it, I wasn't sure it was her.

'Michela! I like your hair,' I said. Always best to start with a compliment, even if it's a lie.

'Yeah?' Her hand drifted up to stroke the ends. They looked brittle and burned, like charcoal. 'Thanks. Did it myself. You look . . .'

'Thanks.' I pre-empted whatever backhanded compliment was coming. I know exactly how Michela sees me. 'How are things with you?'

'Same old. They've moved me to the front desk down at the hotel.'

'Really? That's awesome.'

'It's answering phone calls from guests who want extra towels. Any monkey could do it. But I'm hoping to get into sales. You sit in the back office and no one expects you to clean up vomit from the plant pots . . .' The pause that followed was a fraction too long for what followed to be anything other than a dig: 'Fucking students.'

I didn't say anything.

'How is it then, university?'

'Great, thanks.'

'You still living with your dad?'

'No. Course not. I've been sharing with some friends from uni.' No need to tell her that I'd not been able to persuade them to keep the flat over the summer.

'More mates? I'm surprised you can keep track of them all.'

I knew what she was driving at and didn't like the destination. So many of my conversations with her follow the same pattern as those I've been having with Dad.

'Speaking of,' I trilled, 'are you still in touch with Will?'

'That dickface? Why would you even ask? The second he fucked off to Plymouth, the twat dumped me by text.'

'That's really shitty.'

'Yeah? Well. At least he bothered to let me know.'

And so we finally arrive: Destination Guilt. A place I'm so familiar with, I may as well have a season ticket.

Michela went after that, passing Rose, who skipped round to avoid bumping her with all the carrier bags.

'Who was that?' she asked.

'No one,' I said, knowing with utter certainty that this is exactly what Michela would say too.

It's disappointing to think that I chose to spend so much time with someone who consistently made me feel like a terrible friend so that eventually I became one.

Exactly the way that I've become a terrible daughter.

The bus is slow, and I get a message from Dad saying lunch will be on the table in half an hour. I don't know what he expects me to do with this information, so I don't reply. It's been like that a lot lately. Me saying less and less to him because I can't work out how to say the one thing I really *have* to.

That next year, I won't just be living in another flat – I'll be living in another country.

One year in a French school. No coming home one weekend every fortnight – I'll be lucky if I make it home for Christmas.

The university set it up for me, but they're getting annoyed about it. I've been ignoring their emails, so they sent me a letter, only they sent it to the flat-share, and the landlord had to forward it on, so it only arrived two days ago.

There's documents and stuff they need. Confirmation of my start date. Applications for housing.

I can't do any of that until I've told my father.

Tomorrow. When I'm back from London, feeling brave and buoyed up the way I always do after I've seen the whole gang. Tomorrow, I will talk to my dad.

Today, I just want to pretend my life is perfect.

There's the smell of a roast coming from the kitchen. This last year, Dad's got into cooking. Every time I've walked into the lounge since I've been back home, there's been some chef on the telly throwing things in a pan like exuberance is all it takes.

But Dad's a plodder. He downloads recipes and spends time learning techniques. The food he makes is good. Really good.

Too good.

Like if I tell him I had a McDonald's earlier, then I'm scorning his culinary skills.

Like if I say I'm going out for dinner with my friends, he tells me I should invite them over so he can cook for us.

Like if I'm five minutes late, the whole thing's been ruined, because good food is a fine art, and timing is the brushstroke.

Sometimes, even when I'm bang on time, it feels like I'm late. Without being asked, I whip round the room, cutlery, drinks, sauces. My bags are just dumped in the door to my room, and I think longingly of the dress that I want to hang up to make sure any wrinkles fall out . . .

'Sash!'

I have to say how much I want to eat. The perfect balance between not so much that I'll feel bloated before tonight, enough that I'm being sufficiently appreciative.

'Thought you'd be home sooner,' Dad says over the table.

'Me too. The Jordans slept in.'

'Hope they paid you for it.'

They did not, but I don't say this. I'm not an idiot.

'Any plans for you to stay over again next weekend?'

'No.' *Don't say it, don't say it, don't say it . . .* 'Why?'

Dad grunts, watching me while he finishes his mouthful.

I'm flagging in the face of my meal. I only asked for one slice of lamb, and he's given me three.

'You spend so much time with that family that I'm starting to think you prefer it to your own.'

My reply is reflexive. 'Don't be daft.'

'Then why is it I never see you?'

'I *live* here.'

'For now.'

'What's that supposed to mean?'

But Dad says nothing, just looks down at my plate. 'Aren't you going to eat that?'

'I'm not hungry, sorry.' It really is delicious, but I can't force in any more. I try to find the right thing to say to make it better. 'It'll be great tomorrow night – bubble and squeak when I get back from London.'

I have two hours in which to get ready – Dad said he'd drive me to the station, which is a big help, and I feel a confusing pang of affection for him. I've been so resentful recently that I forget it's only because he loves me. That the low-level digs and passive-aggressive comments come from the same place as the hugs and the cooking and the lifts and all the things he pays for that I don't always remember come from him.

One hour fifty. I'm ahead of schedule – bag packed, dress and make-up on. I thought about doing all this on the train, but tonight's the swankiest night of my whole life, and I don't want to be trying to time my eyeliner application with the swing of the Pendolino, or scrabbling into my dress in the stinky train toilet. I have almost exactly twenty-four hours of being the Sasha I like best with the people I like most, and even the train journey, alone and in first class (because Hugo bought my ticket and he is *ridiculous*), is a part I intend to get maximum pleasure from.

When I pull my dress on, I feel like a movie star. The perfect shade of purple, swathes of sequins. It's the most expensive thing I've ever owned. One look at my reflection has me vowing to save more often to buy fewer, better clothes in future. My make-up is immaculate, my hair gorgeous and glossy, and I feel like it doesn't matter if no one in the world sees me the way I see Rose Jordan, or Joe Lindsay, or the really sexy bloke that I brought back to the other flat for a night of amazing sex without ever knowing his name.

Just for one night: I see *myself* that way.

And then I walk out of my room, and I see my dad.

It makes no sense. He's sitting on the front-door mat, back resting against the door, and there's a bottle of whisky on the floor, a glass in one hand, and an envelope in the other, and my father – my angry, stubborn, proud father – he's . . . crying.

HUGO

Two Hugos. Two different lives. And just the one fucking boat.

You know what? I'm not sure I've thought this through properly, come to think of it.

Everyone's arriving on time. There's nothing like the knowledge that the year's biggest party will sail off without you to make sure you rock up promptly. I'm stood at the end of the ramp, tux on, grin on. Mum's made me gel all my long hair back for the evening, and she probably has a point. I shake everyone's hand as they arrive.

'Joan! It's so lovely to see you. Thank you so much for coming.'

'Spenny! What is WITH that bowtie? You look like you should be sectioned.'

I'm looking over the head tops in the queue of people, trying to spot David and co., and then the Lift Lot and co. Under no circumstances whatsoever do I want those two sets of people to collide. I wish I hadn't had to invite David, but what can I do? This is a charity fundraiser, and funds need to be raised. The British Heart Foundation isn't going to benefit from me only inviting my poor, non-arsehole friends.

As if on cue, I spot David elbowing his way past all of the adults to get to me.

'HUGHIE! I CAN'T BELIEVE IT. YOU'VE NOT FORGOTTEN

HOW TO SCRUB UP THEN, HAVE YOU, YOU BRILLIANT CUN—'

'David!' I interrupt, just as Joan's eyebrows are about to skyrocket off her face. 'You made it.'

He envelops me into one of those macho, back-slapping squeezehugs, and I can smell the alcohol on his breath.

'What? Watching you? Helping charity? Wouldn't miss this for the WORLD.' He releases me from the hug, but stays close. 'I've got some charlie, by the way. Should get things going nicely.'

I wince because he can't see my face.

David pulls away, sniffs faux-loudly and then points to my chest, pushing me slightly. 'And I'll see YOU in a toilet cubicle some time very soon.' Then he spots Giles, Cat and all the others from school who are already on the deck. 'Yes! The old crew are back together again!'

He vanishes and leaves me with Joan and her eyebrows.

'Sorry about that, Joan. Old school friend. Thanks so much for coming. Here are your raffle tickets.'

I carry on welcoming everyone and saying *thank you so much for coming*, and soon the queue is dwindling.

I get a sudden stab of panic.

The Lift Lot aren't here yet. They are going to come, aren't they? I still worry sometimes that they're just tolerating me. That they secretly hate me, but are too kind to say so. Suki, my psychologist, says that it's due to my low self-esteem. When you have low self-worth, you can project it on to your interactions with people and read hidden messages that aren't actually there. Yes, apparently I, of all people, have low self-esteem. I'm still not sure I believe it either. But Suki has a PhD from Oxford, so I'm inclined to believe her.

A waiter swooshes past with a platter of filled champagne

glasses, offering me one with a nod of his head. My fingers twitch and my throat thumps with thirst, but I turn it down. I've got to do the speech later; I need to be on form. Plus, alcohol is poison, and all that. Must remember it's never helped me in the past.

Mum clops over in her heels, and I can tell by the way she clutches her glass that it isn't her first.

'Hugo, darling, it's actually going surprisingly well so far, isn't it?' She reaches out and pats my head ever so briefly. 'I have to say, the Smythes are most impressed. I think it's the first time they've not felt sorry for me for having you.'

Maybe it's not such a surprise I have low self-esteem after all.

'Cheers, Mum,' I say.

She looks me up and down. 'What is it? You're being all twitchy? Don't worry about your father and I. I've already gone and said hello to him and the slut. We're all being so very mature.'

I wince at her use of the word 'slut'. What can I say? I'm a changed man.

'I'm all right. I'm just . . .' I look at my watch. 'It's just the boat is setting off soon, and not everyone is here yet.'

'Worried that little gang of yours won't make it?' she asks. 'They'll be here. When else will they get the chance to do something like this?' She drains her glass and clops off across the deck towards a waiter, leaving me alone.

I check my watch again. Ten minutes until anchors up. I hear whoops from across the deck, and see David has lifted Poppy on to his shoulders for no discernible reason. They're all cackling and clinking their glasses of champagne, and I think about how I just described them to Joan.

Old school friends.

I realize that's all they're ever going to be, really. A group of people who represent a certain time and place in my life, a Hugo I once was. One I'm not particularly proud of. It's been five years since Steven Jeffords died in the lift. I don't know if that's what started the change in me, or if I'd have changed anyway. It's impossible to know. Life happens. Whatever was supposed to happen is what did happen, because there aren't alternative universes called 'What If' you can go and live in. Being in that lift that day changed me. You know what? It made me. Every good thing I've done can be traced back to that day, and that's why I'm holding this fundraiser tonight. To mark it. To mark Steven. But it's going to be downright ghastly if the others don't come.

They'll come.

I mean, we are friends now. It's fine. They've forgiven me.

And just when my heart is about to jump out through my designer suit, I spot them dashing towards the boat. Velvet can hardly walk in the ridiculous shoes she's trotting in, and Joe keeps putting his hand on her back to steady her as she wobbles along the jetty. Kaitlyn and Dawson are a bit behind, with Remy leading the way. A grin breaks across my face, relief flooding into my stomach.

I cup my hands around my mouth and call, 'They'll let any muck on to boat parties these days.'

They all walk up the gangplank, Kaitlyn needing a bit of extra help stepping on to the boat, though she bats Dawson off when he tries to take her shoulder and snaps, 'I'm good.' But they're all grinning at me in their variety of makeshift cocktail wear.

'You made it.' I'm hardly able to keep the relief out of my voice.

Joe gives me an awkward man hug. He looks good, in his skinny tie and tight trouser suit. And the fact he looks good doesn't mean I suddenly want to puff out my chest and be all alpha and make some quip so I can be in control. I'm just pleased my friend looks nice.

'And miss you, of all people, giving a speech about charity?' he says. 'I'm still not sure this boat is going to be able to sail through all the ice created by hell freezing over.'

'You're hilarious, Joe.'

I walk them through to the deck, steering them as far away from my school friends as I can. I've kind of made an allocated area for them, with a chair for Kaitlyn to sit on, and a water bowl for her dog. I have no idea if that's patronizing or not, but I know she'll bloody well tell me if it is.

A bell sounds, the boat lets out a giant honk, and we all cheer as the floor wobbles beneath us and we float out into the river. The sun is still blazing, making the edge of the London skyline glow like it's bordered in gold.

The plan is to get everyone a bit sozzled as we steer past all the big tourist places like the Houses of Parliament and Tower Bridge. Then I have to do my speech about Steven and hopefully encourage all the rich people on the boat to part with their inherited money. I'm completely bricking it – so many things could go wrong. I could mess up my words, or not get enough donations to break even, let alone earn any cash for charity . . . not forgetting my old life colliding with my new friends and all the horrors that could ensue if that happens. I'll just keep them separate. How hard can that be on a rather small boat that nobody is able to leave for the next two hours?

I look around at my friends, subconsciously checking they're still there. Everyone has been plied with a glass of champers and is starting to relax into it.

'It's so pretty,' Velvet says, pointing out Big Ben.

'Yeah, it is,' Joe replies, gazing over at her rather than the view.

A smile tugs at my lips. Old Hugo would've made a quip here – would've highlighted the bleeding obvious about Joe's feelings, and would have revelled in the awkwardness it caused before the guilt hit much later. But New Hugo just allows himself to smile and gives them the oxygen to just be and see how it turns out.

I look around fondly at them. Feeling this still-unfamiliar tug of affection. And that's when I realize . . .

'Hey, guys?' I say, jolting them out of their trance-like admiration. 'Where the hell is Sasha?'

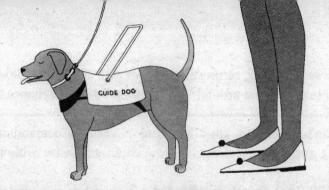

KAITLYN

There's a confused moment when we all look at each other, and then around, as if we expect Sasha to jump out from behind Joe and shout 'Aha!', which would be the least Sasha-esque thing ever.

'Oh no,' Joe says, looking suddenly like he wants to vomit with worry. 'Did we leave her behind? Oh no.'

'We obviously didn't leave her behind,' I say, and because I'm Kaitlyn Thomas, my worry comes out as an impatient snap. 'She never arrived. That's different.'

'Oh no,' Joe says again. 'We should've waited. We definitely should have waited.' He pulls out his phone and begins tapping anxiously at it. 'Oh God,' he mutters to himself. 'Three missed calls?!'

And suddenly everyone's talking at once. Velvet is insisting that we go right back to the dock to get her. Joe is tugging at his collar and demanding to know why none of us noticed earlier. Dawson, his voice dry and so painfully familiar, is telling them both to calm down. And Hugo just keeps saying, 'You can't turn the boat around; it's a fundraiser!'

I'm left standing there with Remy at my side, contributing nothing. I can't help thinking that Sasha's just bunked off this whole escapade, and quite frankly I'm admiring her foresight. That's what I would have done too, if I'd had any sense. What on earth was I thinking, getting on this boat with my ex? Maybe we *should* turn the boat around. At least then I'd have a chance to get off.

'Didn't you have a guest list, Hugo?' Velvet is demanding. 'Wasn't someone checking it? How could you leave without her?'

'*Me?!*' Hugo sounds so offended, his voice has gone up two octaves. 'I've planned this whole bloody fundraiser, Velvet. I had quite a lot of things to think about, you know.' He's changed in a lot of ways since we first met, but his voice, pompous and posh and bloody loud, is the same.

And then there's Velvet, hands on hips, shoulders back. Not at all pompous, not even slightly posh, but more than a match for him. When did she get so grown up? When did we *all* get so grown up?

'Sasha!' Joe bellows suddenly, and I assume at first that she's somehow appeared, but he's talking into his phone. 'Where are you? Oh no. God, of course not – don't worry. Listen, stay where you are. We'll pick you up.'

Hugo's eyebrows rise in alarm. 'Now, hang on—'

'We'll figure it out, don't worry,' Joe says, ignoring him. 'No, Sasha, don't say that. We all want you here. What? Of course we do! Don't go home. Please—'

He takes the phone from his ear and looks at it.

'She hung up,' he says quietly.

There's a silence.

'We can't just go back,' Hugo says eventually. 'It's a boat on the Thames; you can't turn it around like a bicycle.'

'It's *Sasha*,' Joe says. 'Find a way.'

'Listen, mate—' Hugo begins in that patronizing tone posh people use when they think they're being patient.

Joe interrupts. 'She ran from the train to get here in time to watch us sailing off, Hugo. She feels like we just abandoned her. Do you have any idea what that's like?'

I look over at Hugo, trying to read from the silence that follows these words what face he must be making. Because he does know, doesn't he? We all do. I look over at Dawson. He's looking at me.

'What do you think, Kait?' Joe asks, and I jolt in horror.

Oh God, why is he asking *me*? Why would my opinion matter? It's not like I'm in any position to commandeer the boat and go and rescue Sasha, even if I wanted to.

'Can you stop the boat?' I ask Hugo hesitantly. 'Maybe a couple of us could get off and run to get her?'

'It's a *boat*,' Hugo says. He's starting to sound very stressed. 'It doesn't make stops. And this is a *fundraiser*.' He looks around. 'Christ, I'm the host! I'm meant to be talking to people! I have to give a speech!'

'You're right,' Dawson says calmly. 'You're the host, and you've got other stuff to think about. But there's a captain, right? Why don't we speak to him? He'll know what to do. Because Joe's right too: Sasha's important.'

'Good idea,' Joe says, sounding relieved. 'Come on, Hugo. It'll only take a few minutes.'

Hugo tries to protest, flustered and increasingly high-pitched, but he's no match for a determined Joe. In less than a minute, Joe and Dawson are corralling Hugo back towards the bow of the boat, leaving Velvet, Remy and me standing on the deck, watching them go.

'Poor Sasha,' Velvet says.

'Yeah,' I say. 'She wouldn't really get on a train home, would she?'

Velvet doesn't reply, letting out a nervous 'mmmm' instead.

We sit on a long wooden bench, watching London drift slowly

by. Well, I assume Velvet's watching. I'm feeling the breeze on my face and thinking about Dawson . . . Dawson leaning in for a hug when we met at the station; Dawson murmuring to Remy, 'I missed you, handsome,' so quietly, I wasn't meant to hear.

There are stages after a big break-up. There's the immediate aftermath, where it's all tears and anger and regret. Then it's pain and wine and grief. And then things calm down a bit, like all the big emotions are out of your system, and what's left is more quiet, like a sadness that settles in for a while.

Usually that's the end of it for most people. They just wait the sadness out or distract themselves from it. But me? No. I had to see Dawson again, thanks to the Lift Lot. We don't get a chance to all meet up together much – this is the first time we've all been together for a year – but when someone tries to arrange something, I can never bring myself to say no. And so I have to hold myself upright and smile at Dawson and try not to make everyone else feel uncomfortable. Every time I see him, it's like I miss him even more. Which makes no sense.

'How are you doing?' Velvet asks me, and I don't know if the sympathy in her voice is about my sight or my ex.

'Better,' I say. It's true in its own way.

More and more, I'm realizing that what I miss is our closeness. I don't even mean the physical closeness – just the *us*-ness of us. Dawson and Kait. We used to be so close, he could make jokes about my sight. That seems impossible now. But I want to remember – I *need* to remember – because all of that came before kissing and sex and love and heartbreak. We were friends first, and I loved him then. I want that back. Could we ever have it back?

'How's the new job?' Velvet asks.

Someone comes past with a tray of champagne flutes, and she takes one for each of us with a joyful, 'Thanks!'

'Really great, actually,' I say, smiling. It feels good to have something positive to talk about. 'We just hit five hundred subscribers.'

'Oh, ace!' Velvet says. 'Cheers to that.'

She touches her flute to mine, and even the clink of the glasses sounds expensive. I take a sip, and the champagne is delicious, the best I've ever tasted. At the launch of Sendsation in January, we'd had sparkling wine instead of real champagne – one precious bottle shared between me, Jax and Penny to celebrate what had started as a conversation in a pub, and what had now become, somehow, a reality.

After Dawson, I'd wallowed until I could wallow no more, then picked myself up and forced myself out of my personal lovelorn exile. I did it by going along to a guide dog fun run with Remy, thinking – correctly, as it turned out – that what I needed was to do something completely new, with new people, in a new place. There, I met Jax and Penny (and Petey and Clover, their guide dogs) and we'd bonded. We'd bonded so much, we ended up starting a business together, because sometimes – *sometimes* – life throws you the kind of curveball that lights up the dark.

Sendsation is a subscription box designed specifically for people with sensory impairments. The whole idea came from me complaining to them both that people only cared about how flowers *look*, when so much of their beauty and general awesomeness comes from how they feel and smell. We'd joked about setting up a flower delivery service, which somehow turned into a perfume, soap *and* flower delivery service. And then Jax said, 'Why stop at scent?'

And so Sendsation was born.

We got a grant from the Prince's Trust, and everything. You never know, one day we might even turn a profit.

It's like the opposite way round of how stories like this are meant to go. The happiness bit is meant to come with falling in love, not falling out of it. But yet, this year *has* been happier. Losing Dawson felt at the time like losing the only happiness I had, and that was awful, but it also meant I had no choice but to get myself out there and find some more.

And you know what? I fucking did.

'I hope they hurry up,' Velvet says nervously. 'Hugo'll need to do his speech soon. It'd be nice if we could get Sasha in time.'

'Do you think they'll really stop the boat?' I ask.

'Well, I guess we're about to find out,' Velvet says, standing. 'Here they come.'

The boys – though I guess they're men now – are coming through the door out on to the deck. Joe reaches us first, triumphant.

'The captain's going to turn the boat around!' he says. 'That's all he could do, but at least it means we can go and get Sasha. She can be here for the later bit, but it does mean she'll miss Hugo's speech.'

'That's great,' Velvet says. 'Have you spoken to her?'

'I'm going to now,' Joe says, already holding his phone to his ear. He puts one finger up in the air and turns away from us, walking slightly away to make the call.

'I have to mingle,' Hugo says, sounding no less stressed than he was when they'd first gone to speak to the captain. 'I'm meant to be hosting this bloody thing.'

He disappears before anyone can protest.

Velvet stands there for a moment between me and Dawson, clears her throat as if to speak, and then turns and walks briskly after Hugo.

Great.

Just great.

'I hope Sasha's not already on a train, after all that,' Dawson says. 'The captain took a bit of convincing.'

'Convincing how?' I hope he means *talking* convincing, and not that he's paid him or something.

'It got sorted,' is all he says.

Well, fine. 'How's Jasper?' I ask. Subtlety is overrated.

There's a pause. 'Kait . . .' he says.

'Just asking.'

'He's good,' he says finally. 'Really good.'

'And the two of you?'

Another pause. 'Also good.'

'Good.' Ugh, this is painful. We used to tease and joke and touch.

'It's good to see you,' Dawson says.

How many times can two people say the word 'good' in one awkward conversation?

'Really, Kait. I miss you, you know?'

'I miss you too,' I say. I feel overwhelmed by how much I want us to be back where we used to be, so relaxed and easy. Is that the kind of thing you can wish into being? I reach my hand down and touch Remy's head. 'Hey, remember Hugo in Ibiza?'

'How could I forget?' Dawson lets out a small chuckle. 'Who would have thought that night would be the making of him?'

'I wonder if he'll mention it in his speech.'

'I doubt it. We might get a shout-out though.'

I smile. 'That would be nice.'

Maybe if we try, really try, we could find our closeness again. Maybe we could be Dawson and Kait, best mates, again. If we both want it, and we both try, why not? I'm not angry about the break-up any more (the occasional Jasper jibe permitted). I understand that he had to end it when he did, that there was no other option for him. So what's stopping us?

Joe is on his way back, and I see him pause when he realizes that it's just Dawson and me left.

'Did you speak to her?' I call so Joe knows it's fine to come over.

'Yeah,' he says, sitting down beside me on the bench. 'She—'

'Ladies and gentlemen!' a voice suddenly booms from the doorway to the cabin. 'Please make your way inside. Our host, Mr Hugo Delaney, is ready for his speech . . .'

VELVET

'What I'm trying to say is – that day in the lift, it changed me. Made me realize what's important in life. It was the beginning of a long journey, and that's what tonight is all about. Trying to give something back.

'So, I guess all that's left to say is thanks for listening, and thanks in advance for the shedloads of cash you're all going to pledge in the silent auction later. Most of all, thank you to my friends who've come a long way to be here tonight for a cause that's close to all of our hearts. You know who you are, and I appreciate it more than you realize.'

Hugo looks out into the audience until he finds us, our little group lurking to one side, towards the back. He makes eye contact with me for a split second and smiles. Silently, I take half a sideways step closer to Joe and lean fondly against his arm. I can sense all the others kind of doing some version of the same. Solidarity.

'Anyway, that's more than enough from me. Have a great night, everyone.'

My face feels weird. It's a second before I realize what's going on, as this is so unexpected. I mean, ridiculously unexpected.

I appear to be *crying*, FFS. I'm not weeping uncontrollably or anything like that, but a tear has rolled down my cheek with enough wet force to disturb my make-up slightly – enough that

I have to sniff and surreptitiously wipe a finger under my eye. Fortunately, none of the group of friends surrounding me seems to notice. They're all watching Hugo and clapping their hands off; admittedly, he slayed with his speech this evening, so this is not a surprise.

Who would have thought that Hugo Delaney was still capable of making me cry? Not only that, but in a *good* way. He told his story – *our* story, I suppose – in a way that was sincere and genuinely touching. When he talked about his charity work and organizing the fundraiser tonight, the passion was coming off him in waves. If I had any money, I'd probably want to donate it all right now. Watching him come off the stage, I can't believe he's the same person I met so long ago. We're both completely different people now.

Tonight, that's really obvious. Our little group members are all so different, but it works. That's why we really need Sasha here, to complete the circle.

Seeing the London sights from the deck of a boat that's bigger than my entire flat is a bit of a pinch-myself moment, I've got to admit. I've already killed my phone battery sending snaps to Scarlet, Amber and Tempest, laughing at the ones they've sent me back – mostly of them doing ironically faux-glamorous poses in our poky little student kitchen while they cook noodles and muck about. Tempest is casually wearing a sparkly jacket, which I considered but dismissed as being 'too much', over her pyjamas.

It's great being here, drinking champagne and eating tiny canapés and wearing my best dress – as well as hanging out with the friends I haven't seen for ages – but for once it's not an escape. I'm actually looking forward to going back to my real life. Hugo's crazy charity party is just a nice little oddity in my ordinary routine of studying, working in the cafe on Saturdays, and living in a room in a weird little flat that I've filled with fairy lights and books and vintage postcards of Paris. It makes tonight even nicer, not dreading going back. Feeling like I deserve to be here, and I can just enjoy this evening for what it is.

'Hugo,' I say, catching his arm as he heads towards us. 'Your speech was lovely.'

He looks at me, and then around the nodding group of us, with such pure gratitude and relief, it nearly sets me off blubbing all over again.

'Do you really think it was OK? I was shitting myself, couldn't you tell?'

'You were brilliant, mate,' Joe says with a wry smile. 'It's all that breeding; you're a natural.'

'Fuck off.' Hugo grins.

'I might even have shed a tear. Just a tiny one, mind. Minuscule.'

'Better watch those false eyelashes, Velvet,' Dawson says. 'Anyway, shouldn't you go and charm your public into getting their platinum cards out, Hugo? You've got them all on side; go for it.'

'Yeah, I guess so. It's what I'm here for tonight, after all. I'll feel a lot better when we get this whole Sasha situation sorted out though . . . I'm going to go and see what's happening with the captain.'

He raises a hand in a mock salute and quickly disappears through the crowd of sparkly dresses and pristine dinner jackets that smell of Tom Ford and twenty-pound notes. Until a sweaty guy with floppy hair and no chin grabs him and practically wrestles him to the ground right in front of us.

'Hey, hey! What's the hurry? I've barely seen you all evening, Hugo. Aren't you going to introduce me to your friends?'

He looks like the worst kind of posh cliché imaginable. Like an unflattering photograph of a minor young Royal on a 'My Drug Hell!' tabloid front page come to life. He's literally swigging champagne from the bottle while he staggers about with his bow tie undone and his shirt slightly gaping.

Hugo looks utterly mortified. A long time ago, I might have assumed it was us he was embarrassed about and taken offence. Now I know better. Everyone else looks pretty awkward about the whole situation though.

'Are you all something to do with the charity, or what? One of those Make-A-Wish things for underprivileged dying people?'

'Are you for real?' Kaitlyn shoots back. 'I mean, seriously?'

OK, this guy is probably truly awful, but I don't like to be judged on first appearances – it's happened to me enough times – so perhaps I owe him an attempt at the same courtesy. Plus, more importantly, somebody's got to do *something*. There's a weird tension in the air, and this could all get out of hand quickly.

'Hi,' I say, stepping forward and extending a hand. 'My name's Velvet. I'm a friend of Hugo's.'

'Velvet!' He roars with laughter like I've said something really funny. 'Now that's an interesting name. Very interesting. Hold up, now why does that name sound so familiar? Have we met before? I'm sure I'd remember a face as pretty as yours . . .'

'David, why don't we go and find the others – get you another drink?' Hugo suggests desperately, trying to hustle his friend out of my path.

Unlike David, it comes to me in a flash, and I know exactly where I remember his name from. Just for a second, I feel a hot, familiar prickle of shame come over me like a wave of nausea. David is leering at me, and I'm just waiting for the inevitable. The insinuating comment. The casual judgement. The slut shaming, basically.

Just for a second, I'm right back there. Shivering in the middle of Hugo's mum's vast and unfriendly bed, running out of the flat with my shoes in my hands, the taste of blood in my mouth—

Then something inside me snaps, and I just decide: No. This isn't his narrative. It's *mine*. *I* get to choose.

'No, it's OK, Hugo,' I say, my voice coming out so calmly, I surprise myself. 'David, right? We haven't actually met, but I think I've figured it out. You see, a long time ago, Hugo and I slept together. Immediately afterwards, I accidentally found a message on his phone asking whether he'd won the bet and "pulled the peasant" yet, or fucked the commoner, or whatever – I forget the exact wording. Maybe you remember? The message was from you. It was really unpleasant, and I found it quite upsetting at the time. That's probably why my name rings a bell. It's quite an unusual name, I know. Anyway, that was a long time ago. So I hope you know better now.'

I smile serenely while David blusters, tying himself in knots right in front of me.

'It . . . it was clearly just a joke. Right, Hugo?'

'That's what I used to tell myself,' Hugo says. 'But it wasn't that funny, really.'

'Well, it took a while, but Hugo's actually a pretty decent human being these days. I mean, it took Joe punching him, and Kaitlyn shouting at him *a lot*, but he's all right. He's one of us. We've got to go and get our mate Sasha now, but have a great night, David. Nice to put a face to the name after all these years. Enjoy your champagne.'

I wait until David has staggered off, shaking his head in confusion, and then I can't control my giggles for a moment longer. I laugh so hard, my eyeliner really does run this time. All over my face, and I don't care.

I'm not laughing because it's particularly funny, or laughing at putting David on the spot like that, even though he really did deserve it. I'm laughing because . . . well, who knew it was so easy? To stand up for myself; to not be silenced; to tell my own story how I want to tell it. It's about power. Hugo realized he needed to start using his for good. I'm only just realizing that I actually have some.

About time too.

'Velvet,' Hugo says with a huge grin, 'you are bloody magnificent.'

'Yeah, I know. Now, let's get this crazy boat turned around and find Sasha.'

JOE

Hugo leads the way, ignoring his posh mates as we troop through the crowd.

I fall into step with Velvet. She looks almost regal – head held high, an expression of tranquil determination on her face.

'You were incredible just then,' I say. 'Truly.'

She really was – strong and self-assured, and serenely badass.

'Cheers, Joe,' she says, reaching across and giving my hand a squeeze. 'That means a lot, especially coming from you.'

There was a time when a hand squeeze from Velvet would have sent me over the edge, and even though it still feels lovely to have her hand in mine, I'm mostly just really happy that she's my friend and that she's in such a good place.

The fact is, I'll probably always be a little bit in love with Velvet Brown. And that's OK, I think. Once upon a time, loving her was physically painful, but it's since been replaced by a different version of love – uncomplicated and pure. Occasionally I picture the two of us finally getting together when we're sixty or something, and this lot rolling their eyes and saying 'about time' as if it had been inevitable from the very beginning. I admitted this particular fantasy to Sasha a few months ago, and she hugged me and said, 'Oh, Joe, you soppy lug.'

God, I wish she was here. On the surface, she may not be the most prominent member of our group, but I honestly think she's the glue that holds the six of us together. Without her, we're just a bit . . . lopsided. Sasha is the one who remembers everyone's birthdays and reminds the rest of us; the one who always seems to be awake when I'm upset about Mum and bombarding our WhatsApp group with messages at 3 a.m.; the one who listens and quietly puts our dramas into perspective. She was amazing during the Dawson/Kaitlyn break-up – calm and practical, and never taking sides (at least not publicly). Basically, she's always there for us. And how do we repay her? By leaving her behind. Whether or not she made it in the first place is irrelevant – we should have checked she was with us before boarding the boat. *I* should have checked.

I try ringing her back, but it goes straight through to voicemail.

'Any luck?' Velvet asks as I hang up.

There's a tiny black smudge under her left eye where her mascara has run.

'No. I'll keep trying though.'

With the more-than-a-little-grumpy captain confirming we have at least another ten minutes until we dock, we all (minus Dawson) help ourselves to another glass of champagne and head for the deck below, where it's a bit quieter.

It's a proper stunner of a summer's evening, the sun glinting off the Thames and making it sparkle. I can't believe that in less than two months' time, this big bewildering city is going to be my home.

'All ready for the big move, Joe?' Kaitlyn asks, reading my mind the way she so often does with all of us.

She and Dawson are sitting next to each other, a Remy-sized gap between them.

'Not really,' I admit. 'I mean, a lot of the practical stuff is sorted, mostly thanks to Hugo.'

Hugo salutes. He's arranged for me to rent a room in his great-aunt's massive townhouse for next to nothing.

'Don't mention it, mate. Old Camilla's well excited about having a "strapping young man" about the place.'

Velvet giggles and reaches across to give my bicep a playful squeeze. I manage to tense it just in time.

'What about the non-practical stuff?' Kaitlyn asks.

I screw up my face. 'I have no idea. Dad keeps trying to reassure me that he's going to manage fine on his own, but I don't think that's going to make it any easier to leave.'

Sitting here now, it's mad to think that this time last year, I thought I'd be a junior supervisor at Champion Biscuits by now. I assumed Dad was going to be pleased when I told him I'd been accepted on to the training scheme. I was wrong. He went bonkers, getting all red in the face as he banged on about how I needed to 'stuff responsibility' and go after my dreams. When I refused, he nicked my phone and rang up Sasha, and before I knew it, I was blasted with phone calls and messages from all five of them, listing all the reasons I shouldn't go to work at Champion.

It was Dawson who told me about the apprenticeship scheme at the UKB studios in London and helped me fill in the epic application form, taking my clumsy sentences and turning each one into a mini masterpiece. We'd never really spent much time together before, just the two of us, and I was surprised at just how much I liked hanging out with him one-on-one, the last traces of intimidation dating back to our early meetings when he was still etched on my mind as 'Dawson Sharman: TV Star' finally falling away.

A couple of weeks ago, during one of Mum's rare lucid moments, I managed to tell her all about it. She was *so* chuffed for me, her face lighting up like a Christmas tree as I told her about all the UKB shows I'd be working on. And even though it didn't last long, and a few minutes later she was back to asking what time her mum was coming to pick her up, I felt like her response was the blessing I needed.

I'm still terrified at the prospect of being so many miles away from my family, but I've finally realized there's a massive difference between the thing you *think* is the right thing, and the actual right thing.

I try Sasha again. This time she picks up.

I frantically shush the others and put her on speakerphone.

'Sash?' I say. 'Where are you now?'

The five of us lean in to listen, our heads almost touching. I can hear a tannoy announcement in the background.

'On the train home,' she replies.

We all respond with a variety of gasps and groans.

'The train? Are you still on your way to London?'

'No, back to Manchester.'

'*Back* to Manchester? Why?' I cry.

'But we're docking in five minutes so you can get on,' Hugo adds.

Velvet swears under her breath. Dawson's head is in his hands.

'Look, don't worry about me,' Sasha continues. 'It was my fault I was late.'

Her voice doesn't match her words though. I know Sasha. We all do. And no matter what she says, she is not OK right now.

'But there must be something we can do.' I say. 'Sash? Sash, are you there?'

The line has gone dead.

'Ring her back, Joe!' Kaitlyn yelps.

I lunge for the phone, sending it skidding off the edge of the table and startling poor Remy in the process. By the time Dawson has retrieved it for me, Velvet is leaving a message on Sasha's voicemail.

She hangs up, holding her phone to her chest.

'Now what?' Dawson asks.

The boat is beginning to curve towards the embankment.

'I don't know,' I admit. 'I'm worried though. Something's up.'

'Joe's right,' Kaitlyn says. 'She sounded a mess just then.'

'Then there's only one thing we can do,' Velvet says.

We all turn to look at her.

'Go get her, of course.'

There's a beat before everyone jumps up and starts talking at once.

'We can go in my car,' Dawson offers. 'We won't beat the train, but if we bomb it, we might only be an hour or so behind her. If I move some stuff off the back seat, I reckon there should be plenty of room for the four of us plus Remy.'

'Hang on a second,' Hugo says. 'What do you mean, the four of us?'

'This is *your* party, mate,' Dawson says. 'You can't exactly abandon it after an hour. There's over two hundred people here, and every single one of them is probably wondering where the fuck you are right now.'

As if on cue, the noise from the party above suddenly seems to go up a notch.

'I doubt it,' Hugo says. 'They're all so hammered, I could probably strip naked and hurl myself off the side of the boat and they wouldn't notice. Besides which, this is a charity do. And what do they say about charity?'

We shake our heads.

'That it begins at home. And Sasha is fucking family.'

He says this so fiercely that if it wasn't for the fact we were all worried sick about Sasha, we'd probably piss ourselves laughing for a solid five minutes at least.

'Translation,' Hugo continues, puffing out his chest (I half expect him to put his hand on his heart like he's about to bellow out the national anthem). 'I'm coming to Manchester.'

'I think we got that,' Kaitlyn says quietly, biting her lip to stop herself from smiling.

'In that case,' Dawson says, 'prepare to get cosy, everyone.'

'Cosy?' Hugo asks, frowning.

'I drive a Fiesta,' Dawson explains. 'Oh, and Remy here –' he stoops to stroke Remy's ears – 'Remy quite likes to spread out.'

DAWSON

While everyone gathers their stuff, I slip away to call Jas. The South Bank is buzzing on my left, the faint hum of conversation and laughter audible over the dull roar of the boat's engines. The river reflects the lights from the National Theatre as we cruise upstream, back to Westminster Pier. London: my home now. I love it here.

Two girls wave at the boat, and I wave back as I hit 'call'.

Jasper answers on the first ring. 'What happened? Is this Plan B? I can be at Embankment in twenty minutes. I'll meet you in the Princess of Wales.'

I smile, despite everything. I love him too. 'We don't need to do Plan B. I'm fine . . .'

He pauses, reading between the lines. 'But Kaitlyn isn't?'

'No, it's not Kait. It's Sasha, actually. She missed the boat and got the train home. Back to Manchester. But it's more than that . . .'

I think of her messages lately. No gifs. No emojis. No Sasha-ness. Sasha-lite, as though she can't or won't say what's on her mind.

'We're worried about her, Jas. She's not right.'

She hasn't sounded right for a while, I realize. I should have read between those lines before now.

'You're going to go and get her,' Jasper says flatly.

'Yes. We're just waiting for the boat to dock, then we're heading up. How did you know?'

He sighs. 'Because of *course* you are. What else would you do?'

On paper, you'd be forgiven for thinking this was a positive comment. But Jasper's tone makes it very clear it isn't.

'Just . . . answer me this. What time did the boat leave?' he asks.

'Seven.' I get a sinking feeling in my stomach. Suddenly I know where this is leading.

'And it's quarter to eight now. Was it supposed to be an hour-long cruise?'

I don't reply.

'How much did it cost you? Because you can't just turn a boat around mid-cruise on the Thames, unless it's an emergency, and I'm pretty sure the captain wouldn't have seen Sasha missing the boat as a crisis.'

I still don't reply.

'How much, Dawson?'

'Five hundred.' It was the only way, I tell myself. He wouldn't have turned around otherwise.

He's quiet for a moment. 'I take it you're driving to Manchester?'

'It's the fastest way. Seriously, Jas, what's with the interrogation? Do you not want me to go?'

'You have a hero complex.'

'What?' I stare at my phone in disbelief, as though he could see me.

'You have a hero complex,' he repeats, as I lift the phone back to my ear. 'You're always trying to save people.'

'I'm not always trying to save people.'

'No? How about when you drove everyone across the North

to see Velvet when she was pregnant?'

'Hang on – we didn't go because she was pregnant. We didn't know there was drama until way after . . .'

'All right, fine . . . but what about Hugo, in Ibiza? You told me he was nothing but a shit to you, to you all, and you still scooped him up off the beach and took him back to your dad and Trish's.'

'Jasper, he could have fucking died. I couldn't just leave him stoned off his box on Sunset Strip. What was I supposed to do?'

'And then there's Joe,' he continues. 'When you gave up three nights – nights we were already on deadline for – to help him with his application? When you spent another two days emailing everyone you could think of on his behalf, days we were supposed to be on our first holiday together . . .'

I don't say anything because I know what – who – is coming next, and if he says it, then I'll . . . I don't know what I'll do.

'And now you're planning to speed off to Manchester to save Sasha. Never mind that we've got a meeting tomorrow.'

I breathe a sigh of relief that he didn't go where I thought he was heading, then instantly feel guilty for doubting him. 'I'll be back for it,' I promise.

'That's not my point . . . Dawson, what have they done for you? Where were they when we first got together and they stopped replying to your messages? Where have they been for the last year, while you've been here?'

'Sasha replied to me,' I say. 'Every time. And you know why things have been strained. Why are we fighting?'

'We're not,' he says. Then again, softer. 'We're not. I'm being overprotective, and kind of a dick. I'm sorry . . .'

He pauses, and I can picture him running a hand through his hair.

'Look, you do what you need to, Dawson. I'll see you at The Hospital Club tomorrow. Try to get some sleep before you drive back. I hate the idea of you driving on no sleep.'

'Bright side is I'll still be wearing my tux. So I'll look smart at least.'

Jasper groans. 'Thanks for the reminder that I'm going to miss you coming home in a tux. I had plans, Dawson.'

I grin. 'There's a two-hour dry cleaner on Berwick Street. Bring me some spare clothes, I'll put the tux in while we're at lunch, and then I can wear it home.'

'Deal,' I hear the smile in his voice. 'Drive safe.'

'Always.'

I hang up, and find the others are right there, just a few feet away, their faces carefully blank. And I wonder how much of that they heard.

We get the Tube to East Finchley, and I leave the others at the station while I jog up the road to collect the car from the car park. Kait and Remy end up in the front, the passenger seat pushed all the way back, with Hugo, Velvet and Joe in the back.

We're barely out of Greater London before Kait has fallen asleep, and it makes my stomach twist with familiarity. She never could stay awake on the move. Trains, planes, cars, she's out like a light. Never mind it's only half eight.

I turn the music down and hold a finger to my lips, meeting Hugo's eyes in the rear-view mirror. He nudges the others to let them know, and we all keep our voices down as we talk.

'What's the plan then?' Hugo asks softly.

'She's still not picking up,' Velvet says.

'Do we know her dad's address?' Joe says.

I nod. 'Yeah, I've got it.'

I expected everyone to take Kait's side after we broke up, and they did. I know I deserved it – that's the fate of the dumper; you're the bad guy by default – but it still hurt. I got off relatively lightly: they didn't exactly freeze me out, but for the first few months there was a definite cold front. Less quick to reply to my messages. Less keen to meet up when I went home to visit Mum. On a scale of One-to-Hugo, I was definitely at a low Hugo for a while. But not with Sasha.

Sasha messaged me pretty much every day to see how I was doing. I wanted to send her some flowers to thank her, but she wouldn't give me her address.

Luckily, it's the twenty-first century, so it was easy enough to find it through her dad's old company records.

She never thanked me for the flowers, I realize then. I figured she was just annoyed I'd found her address anyway.

'So . . . I guess we head there?' Joe leans between the seats.

'I guess so.'

And do what though?

By half eleven, we're well past Birmingham, and everyone is asleep. Hugo is slumped against the window, mouth open, and Velvet is leaning on Joe. I think about reaching back to wake him, because I'm sure he'd want to experience this, but I don't. Actually, I'm a bit miffed none of them have stayed awake to chat to me, and I can't help but think about what Jasper said, about them not loving me as much as I love them.

You did volunteer to drive, I remind myself. *No one asked you to.*

But it leaves a sickly feeling in my stomach.

I try to think of something else, focusing on the music. It takes a few bars before I realize the song my phone is piping softly into the car is 'Signed, Sealed, Delivered'. Stevie Wonder. I flash Kaitlyn a guilty glance and reach out to skip it.

'Don't.'

My skin heats. I didn't know she was awake.

371

She opens her eyes fully. 'I'm surprised you still have it on there,' she says, twisting to face me. At her feet, Remy lifts his head, waiting for an instruction, but when one doesn't come, he lies back down.

'It's a good song. I thought you were asleep.'

'No,' she says honestly. 'It was too weird, being back here, in your car, with you. I needed some space to deal with it.'

I nod.

'What was all that about earlier? On the phone?'

My knuckles tighten on the wheel, but I keep my voice light as I reply. 'Oh, yeah, that. Jasper was just reminding me we have a meeting tomorrow, and I need to be there for it.'

'Right. And what was all the stuff about Velvet . . . and Ibiza?'

Shit. 'Nothing.'

'Don't lie, Dawson. Not to me.'

'How did you even hear that over the engine and the water?'

'Super-enhanced hearing thanks to my terrible eyes,' she says, and I snort. 'I heard it because you were yelling over the engine and the water.'

'Oh.'

'Everyone heard. We talked about it when you went to get the car. It was about us, wasn't it? Jasper thinks we're using you, or something.'

'A bit.'

'Do you agree?'

'I'm thinking,' I say automatically.

It's a hangover from when we were together. Because Kait couldn't see me, I started to tell her *I'm thinking* when I fell silent, so she knew I was still there. I push the words around in my head until I think they make sense. Then I start talking.

'This past year has been the best of my life, so far,' I say, my stomach cramping when she flinches, but I press on. 'I feel like

I'm finally doing what I'm supposed to be doing. I'm where I'm supposed to be.'

'With who you're supposed to be with?' she says, the words only a little bitter.

'With who I'm supposed to be with right now,' I say, as kindly as I can. I don't want to hurt her, of all the people on the planet, but I can't betray Jasper by playing down our relationship. 'But it's also been kind of the worst. Worse than not getting into drama school. Worse than my agent dropping me, or having to work in Chunder Burger, or a surprise sexuality plot twist.'

'Why?' She sounds suspicious, a bright edge to her voice.

'Because of us. Because of them.' I jerk my head towards the back seat. 'I know how much I hurt you. Breaking up with you was the hardest thing I've ever done, and I was grieving too. But I wasn't allowed to. I wasn't allowed to be sad, or to say I missed you. No one wanted to hear it. And I know it's nothing compared to what I put you through, but I was losing stuff too. I lost my best friend – I thought I was losing all of my friends—'

'You weren't,' Kait interrupts. 'No one slagged you off. No one suggested cutting you out. And if they had, I would have stopped them . . .' She pauses. 'Eventually.'

My lips tug with the ghost of a smile.

'Thanks. But that's the point I'm trying to make. Jasper wanted to know what you've all done for me. While I'm being a "hero", as he called it, what have you done for me? And the answer is, be my friends. That's what you've done for me. Because it's not about the big gestures. It's about little, everyday ones. The ones that look like nothing. They're the ones that really count. Being a friend, every day. The last year has been awkward, for me, and I know that's my fault, but you all stuck around. It was different, but I know if anything terrible had happened, you would have had my back. So what you've done for me is be my friends. I've never had friends before.'

Kaitlyn makes a scoffing noise. 'Oh please, you know loads of people. Everyone loves you.'

'When I started *Dedman*, my mum had to take me out of school because I was bullied for it,' I say, eyes fixed on the road ahead. 'And then I spent the next three years on the *Dedman* set. No one stayed in touch after that ended. Three years of my life, practically living with each other, and as soon as the show was cancelled, that was it. I had no one. Then I met you lot, and I don't even know how we ended up friends, but we did. And it stuck. A bunch of total misfits, the only thing we have in common is we watched a guy die . . . and here we are. Six kids from completely different worlds, still hanging out, five years later. Still in the same dorky chat group. Nothing to keep us together except wanting to . . .'

I pause, checking my mirrors.

'We've all changed loads, you know. Everything's changed loads. Maybe I do have a hero complex. Maybe that's my job, in our crew: the hero. And Velvet's our conscience. Sash is our heart. Joe is our rock. You're our bruiser. And Hugo is . . . Well, Hugo is Hugo.' I smile. 'And together, we're us. That's enough. That's more than enough.'

'Ugh, did Hugo's hippiness rub off on you?' Kait looks simultaneously disgusted and delighted, and I grin.

A hand lands on my shoulder, making me jump, and I look in the mirror to see Joe, Velvet and Hugo are all wide awake, listening. It's Joe's hand on my shoulder, beside him Hugo's eyes are glistening. Velvet is smiling, a big beautiful smile.

'Pass me your phone,' she says, and I do.

In the silent moment between tracks, Hugo murmurs, 'I'm not a hippy,' then the speakers vibrate with the sound of swirling synthesized guitar.

When David Bowie starts to sing, we all join in.

I wish Jasper was here. I wish he could see this. He'd get it.

As the song finishes, we're all smiling. Joe and Velvet are holding hands, and Kait's face is soft, her hand on Remy's head, which rests on her knee. It feels like we're silently connected.

So of course Hugo speaks.

'Dawson,' he says. 'No offence, but—'

Everyone groans.

'I mean it!' Hugo says earnestly. 'I have a legitimate question.'

'Go ahead, Hugo,' I say, smiling as Kait rolls her eyes.

'It's just . . . Why do you only listen to old-people music? Don't get me wrong, "Heroes" is a classic. But do you listen to anything from this century?'

'Maybe you should send me some stuff.' I spot our exit coming up and switch lanes. 'But, more importantly, we're going to be at Sasha's house in about twenty minutes, so we need to come up with a plan. Is she answering her phone yet?'

'No,' Joe says. 'I think it's dead. Last time it rang was an hour ago, and then it just cut off. It hasn't connected since.'

'She must have gone home. We could throw stones at her window?' Velvet says.

'How do we know which one her window is?' Kait asks.

'True.'

We slide off the motorway, and the sodium glow of orange lights as we drive into suburbia makes the world feel post-nuclear, as though we're the last people on earth. No one says anything as we drive down the high street, past a solitary kebab shop, and turn into Sasha's road. I pull into the car park near Sasha's block of flats, startling a fox that was rummaging in an old carrier bag. As the headlights die, I see it running into a bush with what looks like an old nappy in its jaws.

'Time to go be heroes,' I say, unclipping my seat belt.

Time never lies. That's one of the few things Sasha remembers from Mr Murray's maths class. Time never lies. A minute is always sixty seconds. It doesn't matter what is happening. If bombs are falling from the sky, or the ground is splitting beneath your feet, a minute is still sixty seconds. Not fifty-nine or sixty-one. Sixty. With everything else there is room for persuasion, but time never changes. It cannot be bribed or seduced or distracted. When a minute passes, sixty seconds later, another will pass, then another, and another, and another, until . . . Well, there is no until when it comes to time.

It's the only thing you can truly rely on.

Still, as comforting as that is, a minute doesn't always *feel* like a minute. Time often slows down, and not always in a nice, anticipatory way either – like excitedly waiting for Christmas morning, or for Joe to text her back – but sometimes in that horrible, sticky kind of way, when it seems to stop altogether. Like Sasha's experiencing now, as she's waiting in the rain for the bus, and three minutes is feeling a lot more like *forever* . . .

Time hasn't stopped, of course – she knows that. She knows the bus will come, and she will get on it, and everything will speed up again until she's on the train, hoping that her new dress doesn't crease and her curls don't fall, while she looks out the window, willing it to go faster. Then the minutes until she's in London will feel impassably far apart again. It's so cruel, because when she wants time to slow down, it never does, it just goes faster – so fast that she can't catch her breath. Like when she's with the others, and it feels like she's only just said hello, and then it's time to leave again.

Time is fickle like that.

So are boats, apparently. Even party ones. They don't care that there were signalling faults at Stockport, or that she can't run in heels, or that she really, really needs to see the others.

When you're late, you're late.

And boats, much like time, go on without you.

All Sasha can do is watch the boat chug away, churning up the water as it does. She looks around, half-expecting to hear the clatter of Velvet's heels on the cobblestones as she runs towards her, asking where she's been. But there's no-one, the dock deserted except for a couple taking a selfie under a streetlight.

So she heads back to the tube, worried that one of them is waiting for her there but she missed them in her rush to get to the boat. As she approaches the station, she thinks she sees Joe and starts running, her overnight bag bumping against her hip as she does, but then the guy turns and when Sasha realises it isn't him, the disappointment is enough to knock the air right out of her. Still, she checks inside, getting on her tiptoes to see over the heads of the fierce flow of commuters in and out of the station. She can't see anyone and goes back outside, looking at the people assembled on the pavement, each of them waiting for someone, but not her, and a familiar heaviness settles into her bones.

They went without me.

It's the same way she felt the morning her mother left as she stood at her bedroom window watching her battered red car disappear down their street towards the main road, like everything she wants has just left without her because she wasn't enough to stay.

Sasha is grateful for the signalling faults at Stockport on the way back, willing the train to slow this time because she doesn't know what she's going to say to her father. Her stomach lurches so suddenly, she feels light-headed. The mere thought of it — of walking back into her flat to find him still sitting there on the bottom step with a bottle of whisky and the letter from the school in France . . .

She ran away. She literally ran away and left him there. She took her overnight bag and ran. Chose them — the others, her friends, her future, her only way out — and they weren't even waiting when she got there and now she has nowhere else to go but home.

She could have stayed. Now she's on the train, she doesn't know why she didn't. She could have waited at the dock for the boat to come back or checked into the hotel and waited there, pretended not to care that they went without her when they finally rolled back, tipsy and giggling. She could have listened to Hugo and Dawson sparring as she helped Velvet take off her strappy sandals and it would have been better than this, surely? Better than sitting by herself on a train, sick at the thought of going home and seeing her father. But it hadn't even occurred to her; she just joined the stream of commuters and let them lead her away.

It's her own fault. She should have called them. Why didn't she call Velvet and tell her about the signalling faults? If she hadn't put her phone in her overnight bag in an effort to avoid her father, she might have thought about it. But she thought she had time. When she got to Euston, she had half an hour to get to Westminster. It's only six stops, but between the escalators and the tourists with their Tube maps and wheely suitcases, it took ages to get down to the platform. Then she had to change at Embankment and do it all again, so when she finally emerged at Westminster, she didn't even bother to check the time, she just ran. If she had, she would have known that it was too late, but she thought she had time.

Actually, she thought they'd wait. That's the truth of it – what hurts the most: she thought they'd wait. Not all of them. Hugo couldn't, of course, but she thought that Velvet would have at least. Or Joe. So much for him calling it a date; so much for the bubble of excitement and hope she always felt ahead of seeing her friends; of seeing Joe. Sasha would wait for Joe. Like she always has been.

She read somewhere once that true disappointment lies in the gulf between what you would do for someone and what they will do for you and that's what she's thinking about as she sits on the train back to Manchester. She can hear her phone ringing in her overnight bag and doesn't want to answer it, unsure if it's them or her father. Curiosity gets the better of her eventually and she unzips it and reaches into the pocket. When she pulls out her phone she sees that it's Joe and she curses herself for the fizz of excitement she feels in her chest at seeing his name. She considers not answering, but it's him so she does.

'Sash, where are you now?' he asks before she can even say hello. He sounds out of breath and the fizz in her chest becomes a full blown firework as she asks herself if he's worried.

She has to suck in a breath before she can respond. 'On the train.'

'The train? Are you still on your way to London?'

'No, back to Manchester.'

'*Back* to Manchester? Why?'

He sounds genuinely confused and Sasha can't help but soften.

'Look, don't worry about me,' Sasha says. 'It was my fault I was late.'

But before she can explain what happened, her phone beeps and he's gone. The train hasn't gone through a tunnel so she checks to see if she has signal only to find that the screen is black. She presses Home with her thumb, but nothing happens. She tries again, but when the screen remains black, she closes her eyes and lets go of a tender sigh as she realises that the battery's dead.

The tears come then – big, fat, meaty tears that burn lines down her cheeks. Mercifully, the first-class carriage is empty, aside from a middle-aged man in a suit at the other end, who was drinking gin and tonic from a can and reading the FT when she got on. So, sure that no one can hear her, Sasha lets it out, heaving and sobbing, her hands balled into fists in her hair. She hasn't cried like this since she was kid, proper uncontainable, ugly crying, the way you cry when you fall over in the park and wait for your mother to come and pick you up.

Except no one's coming to pick her up, are they?

By the time the train pulls into Manchester Piccadilly, she's managed to pull herself together, at least enough to fix her make-up in the tiny bathroom and tie her hair back with the band she always wears around her wrist.

She keeps her head down as she makes her way out of the station. She's relieved to find that the rain has lightened to a drizzle, so she decides to avoid the inevitable for as long as possible and walk home. It'll take her an hour – maybe an hour and a half in heels – so if she's lucky, her father will have passed out in front of the telly by the time she gets in, and she can go straight to bed.

It's a bad idea though. She's not even halfway home before she has to stop at a bus shelter, her feet blistered and bleeding from her new shoes. She must look a right state, but she's so past caring that she doesn't even look up when a car beeps and the blokes inside cheer.

As the bus pulls up, it's all she can do to put one foot in front of the other.

*

Sasha opens the front door carefully. She's done this enough times to know not to use too much force, but just the right amount, so that the hinges don't squeak when it opens.

The first thing she hears is the telly. *Match of the Day*, it sounds like, which is good, because her father hates football, so he's probably asleep. She should be relieved, but something in her sags, and she wants to cry again at the thought of going inside, of spending another night in her narrow single bed and facing her father in the morning . . . and she realizes then what a terrible thing it is to want to go home and realize that you're already there.

But where else can she go? When she left for London, she had a group of friends she couldn't wait to see, and in the space of a few short hours all of that had unravelled, and she was back home with her father. The realization brings tears to her eyes as she admits defeat and heads down the hall to her bedroom.

She must have left the door open and light on, which isn't like her, but she was in such a rush to leave that she doesn't think anything of it until she walks into the room and stops, her heart suddenly in her throat. The room is a mess, the doors to her wardrobe flung open, and her shoes in a pile on the floor. Everything on top of her chest of drawers has been knocked over, and the drawers are open, clothes spilling out of them like they're trying to escape a sinking ship. For a second, she thinks they've been burgled, and when she sees that one of her bras is on the floor, the horror of it makes her shudder. Someone touched it. What else have they touched? she thinks as she looks around the room . . . And that's when she sees her father sitting on the floor, his back to the radiator.

'Dad?' Her voice sounds tiny, like it's coming from across the street.

He doesn't look up, and when she shrugs the strap of her overnight bag off her shoulder and steps closer, she can see her

381

laptop open on the floor in front of him, the light from the screen making his face look almost ghostly. He's smoking a cigarette, transfixed by whatever he's reading as he reaches up to flick the ash into the pint of water on her bedside table.

'Dad?' she says again, a little louder this time.

If he can hear her, he's ignoring her, so she takes another step towards him, and that's when she sees that the drawer to her bedside table is open too, the contents on the floor. It's nothing, just a few tampons, some loose change and receipts, but the thought of her father going through it makes the back of her neck burn.

'Dad,' she says through her teeth. 'What are you doing?'

He doesn't flinch. 'Looking at flights.' He takes a drag on his cigarette. 'I was thinking, the Eurostar might be better, because it stops in the centre of Paris, but you'll have to get to London, which will be a pain in the arse with luggage. But if you fly from Manchester, you won't have to worry about that.'

Sasha feels lighter for a moment and the corners of her mouth twitch up into a smile as she wonders if she's read it all wrong. Is he looking into ways he can visit her in France?

Then he chucks something on to the bed between them.

'Expensive though. This won't cover it,' he says without looking at her and her heart starts to beat very, very slowly. It's her My Little Pony lunchbox that she hides at the bottom of her wardrobe. That's where she keeps her money, everything she's saved. It isn't much – £48.50, last time she checked – but it's hers. Every spare pound she has, every time Rose gave her a fiver, it all went in there.

She looks at the lunchbox, then at him.

'I was going to tell you.' She stops to suck in a breath. 'Tomorrow. I was going to tell you.'

He shrugs, and it hurts. It actually, physically hurts, because he should be shouting. He should be shouting and screaming and breaking things. This is worse. So much worse.

'Dad, please.' She tries to keep her voice steady. 'Can we just talk about this?'

'About what?' He takes one more drag from the cigarette, then drops it into the pint glass.

'You know what.'

'There's nothing to talk about, is there? You've already decided.'

'Yeah. But –' She stops to suck in a breath. 'There's still stuff to talk about.'

'Like what?'

She suddenly can't think of a single thing.

'Like when you're going?' he says when she doesn't say anything.

She looks down at the overnight bag at her feet.

'Why wait, Sash?' he says, tossing her laptop on the floor and standing up. 'Go now.'

She watches in horror as he strides over to her wardrobe and pulls her suitcase from the top, throwing it on to the bed. He unzips it and begins tossing her clothes in, hangers and all.

'Go! Be with your friends!' He reaches for one of her boots and chucks it in. 'They going with you?'

When she doesn't answer, he looks at her for the first time. 'Where are they, by the way?' he asks with a sharp smile. 'Your precious new friends? Thought you were staying in London tonight?'

She turns her face away so he doesn't see her crying, and he chuckles bitterly.

'Well, there you go.'

She feels it like a punch in the stomach.

'Just like your mother.' He says it under his breath, but still manages to imbue it with such disdain – such contempt – that it turns Sasha's stomach inside out. 'Ungrateful,' he hisses. 'Never happy. No matter what I did, it was never good enough. She was never happy. Always dreaming. Always wanting more.'

She can't watch and turns her face away. She looks out the rain-speckled window at the rooftops and the glow of the city in the distance, and something inside tells her that it doesn't matter that she has nowhere to go, just run, run, and keep running.

But that's what her mother did, didn't she? She ran and she never looked back. And now here is Sasha, putting up with what her mother couldn't. Twenty-one years and she's still there, still trying to make up for a decision she didn't even make. She didn't break her father's heart, her mother did and she knows then that it doesn't matter how good she is, how good and quiet and obedient, she'll never be able to fix that. Even if she stayed, if she didn't go to France and spent another twenty-one years eating breakfast with her father every morning and eating dinner with him every night and turning the television off when he falls asleep on the sofa, it wouldn't be enough because she isn't the one that he needs to forgive.

Maybe disappointment does lie in the gulf between what you would do for someone and what they will do for you, but she knows then, in that moment, as she's looking out of the rain-speckled window at the black, black sky, that she needs to stop focusing on what she's willing to do for other people and start focusing on what she's willing to do for herself.

'Dad, I love you,' she says with such certainty, he finally stops. When he looks at her across the bedroom, his fingers curling into a fist around the T-shirt he's holding, she pushes her shoulders back and lifts her chin to look him in the eye for the first time since she got home. 'Dad, I love you,' she says again, more softly this time, 'but I have to do this.'

He stares at her for a moment, then throws the T-shirt into the suitcase and turns back to the wardrobe. He closes the doors and strides past her out of the bedroom without looking at her. Then she's alone – really truly alone – and she doesn't know if it's fear or doubt or sheer, giddy relief at finally saying it out loud, but suddenly everything is so blurry that she has to step over to window and reach for the windowsill to steady herself.

Is this it? she wonders as she looks down at the carpark. Should she go now? She has to go now, doesn't she? She can't stay, can she? She asks herself where she's going to go as she waits for the rows of cars to come back into focus. When they eventually do, she sees a car pull up. It looks like Dawson's Fiesta, but she immediately dismisses it, sure that she's seeing things because she wishes he was there. But then the door opens, and when she sees Velvet tumble out, she presses her palms to the cold glass, her lips parted . . . It's her. It's definitely her. Then Joe jumps out, and Hugo, and Dawson, and finally Remy leaps out, and when Kait emerges, the five of them start running towards the entrance to her building.

Sasha doesn't think, just runs as well, slamming the buzzer to let them in on her way out the front door. She's down the corridor in a few steps and when she gets to the lift, she jabs on the button so hard, she's surprised she doesn't break her finger. When the doors open, she dives in, her chest heaving as the lift makes its descent . . .

Sixth.

Fifth.

Fourth.

Third.

Second.

First.

Ground.

The doors open, and there they all are: the entrepreneur, the philanthropist, the future TV producer, the activist and the scriptwriter, rushing towards her and pulling her out of the lift.

'We've got you, Sash,' she hears Velvet say.

And they have.

ABOUT THE AUTHORS

Sara Barnard is the author of *Beautiful Broken Things*, *A Quiet Kind of the Thunder*, *Goodbye, Perfect* and the forthcoming *Fierce Fragile Hearts*.

Holly Bourne is the author of *Soulmates*, *The Manifesto on How to Be Interesting*, The Spinster Club series, *It Only Happens in the Movies* and *Are We All Lemmings and Snowflakes?*

Tanya Byrne is the author of *Heart-Shaped Bruise*, *Follow Me Down* and *For Holly*.

Non Pratt is the author of *Trouble*, *Remix*, *Unboxed*, *Truth Or Dare*, *My Second Best Friend* and the forthcoming *Giant Days*.

Melinda Salisbury is the author of The Sin Eater's Daughter series, and *State of Sorrow*.

Lisa Williamson is the author of *The Art of Being Normal*, *All About Mia* and the forthcoming *Paper Avalanche*.

Eleanor Wood is the author of *Becoming Betty* and *My Secret Rockstar Boyfriend*. She is also co-founder of the lo-fi 90s-style fanzine I *Am Not Ashamed*.

ACKNOWLEDGEMENTS

Sara Barnard
Thank you firstly and foremostly to my fellow collaborators and friends: WE DID IT?! What a joy it has been to share this creative journey with you all. I'm so proud to have my name on a cover with each of yours. Thanks also to Rachel Petty, George Lester and the team at Macmillan, who made it all happen with their usual brilliance, enthusiasm and unwavering support. And thanks, as ever, to my agent Claire Wilson, for being Claire Wilson.

Tanya Byrne
First of all, I want to thank Ellie, Holly, Lisa, Melinda, Non and Sara. It was a pleasure being stuck in a lift with you. I wish I could write all my books with you guys. Thanks also to Laura Callaghan for the beautiful cover and to Rachel, Sarah, George, Kat, Bea and the rest of the Macmillan team for working so hard to ensure that this book is in your hands right now. Finally, much love and thanks to my agent, Claire Wilson, for putting up with me and my ALLCAPS emails. It has been an honour to work with you all.

Non Pratt
With greatest thanks to Rachel Petty whose publishing nous continues to impress the hell out of me. Thanks, in fact to all the Macmillan bods – the sunshine in human form that is George

Lester, super cheerleaders Kat McKenna and Beatrice Cross and Rachel Vale and Laura Callaghan for quite the fabulous cover, also Sarah Hughes, for putting this to bed. And (as always) thanks to those nameless and tireless editorial, production, sales and marketing types who turn stories into books that people can actually read. Thanks to amazing agent Jane Finigan for being her usual badass self and for my family for feeding my face with food and my soul with reassurance. Thank you to everyone who donated to the Authors for Grenfell auction in return for a namecheck. I hope you like the characters you've become . . . ?! People always say books are a team effort, but never more than in this case. What a joy to have six of the most kickass writers in UKYA to work with on this – THANK YOU Ellie, Holly, Lisa, Mel, Sara and Tanya for the WhatsApp lolz, the best writing meetings and most uplifting email chains known to humankind. Can we write another one?

Melinda Salisbury
I would like to thank my agent, Claire Wilson, always and for everything; my amazing co-authors Sara, Holly, Tanya, Non, Lisa, and Ellie for being the best team ever; Bea Cross and Kat McKenna for all their excitement, enthusiasm and ideas; Sarah Hughes for stepping in to guide the book home; George Lester for making everything run like clockwork; and Katie Webber for keeping the secret. Most of all I'd like to thank Rachel Petty, for taking a chance on a fantasy author and letting me have a go at something new. It means the world.

Lisa Williamson
I would like to thank my agent, Catherine Clarke for being continually wise and wondrous; the entire team at David Fickling Books for their on-going support; Dylan Bray for just